THE BLESSED CHILD

THE BLESSED CHILD

by

Rosie Goodwin

Magna Large Print Books
Gargrave, North Yorkshire,
BD23 3SE, England.

British Library Cataloguing in Publication Data.

A catalogue record of this book is
available from the British Library

ISBN   978-0-7505-4761-1

First published in Great Britain in 2018 by Zaffre Publishing

Cover illustration © Gordon Crabb

Published in Large Print 2019 by arrangement with
Bonnier Zaffre Ltd.

Magna Large Print is an imprint of Library Magna Books Ltd.

Printed and bound in Great Britain by
T.J. (International) Ltd., Cornwall, PL28 8RW

In Loving Memory of
Matthew Robert Harding
October 1999 – January 2018

A very special little man who touched the lives
and the hearts of everyone who knew him in his
all too short life. I know the angels will love
him just as much as we on earth did.
R. I. P sweetheart, you will never be
more than a thought away xxxxxxxx

Also love and special thoughts
for Beryl, Nigel, Rachael and Ian xxxx

Wednesday's child is full of woe

The Open Door

*Do not cry nor weep for me now that my life on
  earth is done
I have gone on to a better place with the setting
  of the sun
I passed through a heavenly doorway but the door
  is left ajar
And although you cannot see me I have really
  not gone far
My earthly life is over, I am free from hurt and pain
And now I wait in perfect peace until you
  join me once again
Loved ones are truly never divided, some simply
  go on before
And there with sweet anticipation they eye
  the open door.*

Rosie Goodwin

Prologue

Nuneaton, March 1863

Nancy Carson loaded the last of the clean washing into a small wooden cart and laid a white sheet neatly across it. A fine drizzle had started to fall and the last thing she needed after all the effort she had put into washing and ironing was for it to be ruined. It had been a long, hard day and there was nothing she would have liked more than to put her feet up at the side of the fire, but needs must. At least now that she was taking washing in and Reuben, her seventeen-year-old son, had started work, they were managing to make ends meet a little. Wednesday, her daughter – affectionately known as Nessie – who was two years younger than Reuben, had recently started work too at the local corner shop so at last the future was beginning to look a little brighter. Not before time, she thought ruefully as she wrapped a shawl tightly about her slim shoulders. The last six months had wrought so many changes in their lives that sometimes Nancy felt dizzy just thinking about it.

Much of this had been caused by the birth of little Joseph, who was fast asleep beside the fireplace in a wooden cradle that Reuben had carved for him. Her husband had not been at all pleased to know that there was to be an addition to the family and had walked out on the lot of them shortly before the child had been born. They had not seen hide nor hair of him since and Nancy still missed him at times. Admittedly he had been no saint but he was her husband so his leaving had cut deep.

Nevertheless, Nancy was a survivor and when, soon after Joseph's birth, it became clear that they could no longer afford to live in their smart little cottage in Bedworth, she had moved them all, lock, stock and barrel, to a cheaper cottage in Stockingford in the neighbouring market town of Nuneaton.

Turning to Marcie, her youngest daughter, she told her, 'You'll have to watch Joseph for me until Nessie gets home. I'm delivering this clean laundry to Biddy Spooner. Goodness knows we need the money this week.' Biddy Spooner ran a lodging house in nearby Haunchwood Road and was well known for being somewhat eccentric and putting on airs and graces, but she was a good payer and one of Nancy's regular customers.

Marcie pouted. She hated their new home and constantly blamed her mother for bringing them there. She also resented the new baby and had as little to do with him as she could. Babies were dirty, smelly little creatures as far as she was concerned.

'It's no use pulling that face, my girl!' Nancy scolded as she dragged the cart towards the door. 'I'll not be gone long, so it won't hurt you to make yourself useful for a time. Nessie should be back soon.' With that she hauled the cart over the step and set off into the bitterly cold late afternoon.

16

No one would think we were into March already, Nancy thought, as she began to shiver. The weather had hardly improved since Christmas and soon her teeth were chattering and her threadbare shawl clung damply to her shoulders as the cart bumped across the rough ground behind her. Already it was dark and she had to pick her way carefully to avoid the bumps and hollows in the field. Still, she thought, at least coming this way would take a good ten minutes off her journey and then she could hurry back to the warmth of her fireside.

She was passing a small copse when she had the strangest feeling that someone was behind her. She wheeled about to peer into the darkness.

'I-Is anyone there?' Only the howling of the wind in the leafless trees answered her, so after a moment she grabbed the handle of the cart and set off again, but she had taken no more than a few steps when suddenly something hit her hard between the shoulder blades and she sprawled on to the muddy ground, winded. Somehow, she managed to turn on to her side and as she gazed up, a face slowly swam into focus.

'*You bitch!*'

Her eyes stretched wide with shock. 'But ... what are *you* doing here? What do you want?' she rasped as she struggled to catch her breath. And then she saw the cudgel of wood hurtling towards her again and felt a searing pain in her shoulder as she tried to raise her hand to defend herself.

'*S-stop!*' she pleaded, but her attacker was beyond reasoning, his face twisted with hatred. Again and again the blows rained down on her as she struggled to rise from the muddy ground.

'Please ... *no more!*' But her pleas fell on deaf ears and if anything, the attack became more frenzied as the man grunted with exertion. Soon, realising that her pleas were useless she curled herself into a ball until at last a comforting darkness rushed towards her and she knew no more.

Once he saw her take her final breath, the man stopped, staring down at the woman's inert form until his breathing returned to some sort of normality, then, with not an ounce of remorse, he slipped away into the night, leaving her lifeless body exposed to the cruel winter air.

Chapter One

September 1864

'Mr Grimshaw is at Ma Baker's, Nessie. Shall we hide under the table and pretend we're not in?' fifteen-year-old Marcie asked fearfully.

'No we will *not!*' her sister Nessie replied proudly. 'I've never hidden from the rent man yet and I'm not about to start now. Just sit down at the table and leave him to me.' Seeing the frightened look on her younger sister's face, her expression softened. 'It'll be all right, love,' she assured her. 'I've got some of the rent for him, he'll wait for the rest.'

Despite her brave words, Nessie's stomach was in knots. It was a well-known fact that their landlord was not a man to be messed with, but what alternative did she have? Before her horrific death some eighteen months before, her mother had always insisted that all of her offspring were out of the way when the landlord called and somehow she had always paid him. But now, with only Reuben's wage coming in, things were going from bad to worse and some days Nessie, as the oldest girl, struggled to even feed them all, let alone pay the rent.

She felt a moment's resentment as she thought of her father who had abandoned them all two years before when he had run off with the land-lady of the local inn close to where they had lived. They'd not seen him since and in some ways it had been a blessing. At least now they didn't have to live in fear of him rolling in drunk and aggressive from the pub. Compared to where they used to live, the rent on this cottage was much cheaper but it was reflected in their living conditions, which were sparse to say the least. 'But needs must,' their mother had told her brood cheerfully, and somehow, she had managed to hold the family together, bless her.

Blinking back tears as she thought of her mother and the unthinkable way in which her life had come to an end, Nessie smiled at her sister. 'Take Joseph out into the back yard for a few minutes, Marcie. The fresh air will do him good.'

Joseph was now almost twenty months old with light brown hair and hazel eyes. He was small for his age and had never been a robust child, but unlike Marcie, she and her brother, Reuben, adored him and spoiled him shamelessly. Nessie

19

watched as her sister swept him up into her arms and hurried away with a resentful look on her face. Then taking a deep breath, she squared her slight shoulders and waited for the knock on the door.

It came soon enough and with what she could muster of the rent money gripped tight in her hand, she went to answer it.

'Mr Grimshaw.' Her voice was icily polite and he grinned at her, his eyes sweeping over her lasciviously.

There was no doubt about it, this little filly was turning into a head-turner. Admittedly she wasn't beautiful in the classical sense. Her hair, which was unfashionably straight, hung almost to her waist like a shimmering copper cloak streaked with gold and her nose was a little too upturned to be deemed pretty. Her cheeks were deeply dimpled when she smiled and her mouth was just a fraction too wide. Even so, her lips were full and red and her skin like peaches and cream. But it was her eyes, easily her best feature, that fascinated him. They were fringed with dark, gold-tipped lashes and were a deep, tawny colour that could change to darkest brown if she was upset. They were quite unlike anything he'd seen before. At sixteen years old, her slim figure was filling out nicely and Seth Grimshaw desperately wanted to own her.

'So, me beauty, got me rent ready fer me, have you?' he asked as he licked his fat lips lecherously.

'Some of it, I'll make sure to have the rest ready for you the next time you call.' Nessie opened her hand and as he stared at the collection of ha'pennies and coppers he sneered, his nostrils widening repugnantly.

'That's no good to me, lass. The rent is three and sixpence per week, as you well know. There's just short of two bob there.'

'I'm quite aware of that,' Nessie answered coolly. Her face was outwardly calm but inside her stomach was churning. 'But Reuben sprained his ankle last week and had to have three days off work until he could put his weight on it again and it's made us short.'

She had expected him to turn nasty, he was known for it hereabouts, but instead he surprised her when he leaned in and told her in a low voice, 'Well, just see as you have it next time, pet ... otherwise we'll have to think of another way you can pay me, eh?' His putrid breath enveloped her as, reaching his hand forward, he suddenly tweaked her breast.

Cheeks flaming, she sprang away from him as if she had been burned. He had left her in no doubt of what he wanted and Nessie felt sick to her stomach as she stared at the disgusting creature. Seth Grimshaw was fat and forty if he was a day and even now he was at arm's length, the ripe smell of him assaulted her. He had a large moustache and the sight of the food caught in it made her want to gag. He was grossly overweight and his fat stomach strained against the buttons on his grubby, brightly coloured waistcoat. His hair was grey and plastered to his head with Macassar oil and Nessie found him totally repulsive.

'It will be here for you,' Nessie muttered primly

as she thrust the money into his podgy fingers.

He grinned as he dropped the coins into the bag about his waist. 'See that it is,' he said, then he walked away without another word.

Nessie hastily slammed the door and leaned heavily against it, shaking like a leaf in the wind. At that moment, Marcie's head popped around the back door and her eyes swiftly swept the room. 'Has he gone then?'

'Yes, he's gone.' Nessie sank onto the nearest chair, suddenly feeling weary. She was so tired of having to rob Peter to pay Paul and make ends meet, but what choice did she have? She had promised her mother, before she had been so cruelly taken away from them, that should anything ever happen to her she would keep the family together, and up until now she had, although she was well aware that she couldn't have managed it without the support of Reuben. He worked laying the train tracks that were springing up all over the country. Sometimes this meant that he had to work away from home but every Friday he turned up, as regular as clockwork, to tip his wages onto the table for her and Nessie wondered how they would ever manage without him. He was her rock and she depended on him.

Marcie, on the other hand, was a different matter altogether. Since leaving school, she'd worked in three different jobs but none of them had held her interest for long, much to Nessie's annoyance. Marcie wanted to be a lady and considered herself too good for manual work, so recently Nessie had suggested that they should change roles. She would go out to work to bring a little extra in while Marcie stayed at home to care for Joseph and keep the house running. But Marcie had been horrified at the idea. She was no fool and realised that staying at home would probably be harder than going out to work. 'No,' she had told her, 'I'm going to wait until a rich man comes along and sweeps me off my feet, then I shall be waited on and spoiled.'

Nessie knew that the girl was living in cloud cuckoo land. That sort of thing didn't happen to the likes of them. And yet, despite Marcie's selfishness, Nessie loved her and tried to turn a blind eye to her behaviour. Usually she managed to keep her patience, but just the day before they'd had a terrible row after Nessie had sent Marcie to the market for some food. Admittedly, Marcie had shopped wisely and got everything on the list, but then finding she had a few precious pennies spare she had bought a length of red ribbon for her hair. Nessie had cried tears of rage and frustration. Marcie didn't seem to realise that those miserly few pence might mean the difference between them eating or not towards the end of the following week, and worse still, she didn't seem to much care. But that was Marcie; she would always put herself first.

But all that faded into the background now as Nessie relived in her mind her confrontation with Seth Grimshaw. She shuddered. He'd made it more than obvious what he wanted from her and the thought of him laying his horrible fat hands on her made her tremble with fear. No matter what, somehow, she must find a way to pay him the rent next week.

That night when Reuben arrived home he found Nessie in a subdued mood, and as he washed the worst of the dust from his face, hands and arms in the deep, stone sink and dried himself on the piece of huckaback his sister had laid ready for him, he eyed her curiously.

'Is everything all right?' he questioned. Nessie didn't seem to be her usual cheery self at all.

'I suppose so,' she answered dully as she carried a pan of stew to the table before lifting Joseph onto a chair. He rewarded her with a smile that melted her heart and she quickly dropped a kiss on his springy curls. Marcie had been out for the last hour, as she was most nights, visiting her friends.

Reuben crossed to the table, slouching slightly to avoid banging his head on the low-beamed ceiling and Nessie realised with a little shock how tall he had become. 'Come on, out with it.' He lifted his spoon as she filled his dish and gave her an encouraging smile.

'Well, Seth Grimshaw called for the rent today and when I wasn't able to give him the whole amount he was quite...' She struggled to find the right way to explain his behaviour. 'Suggestive, I suppose,' she finished lamely, keeping her eyes downcast.

'I see.' Reuben frowned as he spooned stew into his mouth. Working out in the fresh air all day always gave him a hearty appetite. 'Then I'll work some extra shifts to make sure we can pay him properly next week.'

'You most certainly *will not!*' Nessie objected.

24

'You work far too many hours as it is. Why, if it wasn't for you, we'd all have ended up in the workhouse long since.' Her thoughts flew unbidden, as they often did, to the terrible night her mother had been found murdered. She would never forget that night for as long as she lived and still had nightmares about it as she imagined how her poor mother must have suffered. There was also always the niggling fear that whoever had murdered her was still out there somewhere and she found herself constantly looking over her shoulder and worrying about Marcie every time she went out, especially after dark.

Reuben shrugged and as her thoughts returned to the present Nessie was again struck by the difference between her brother and sister. Reuben had a heart as big as a bucket and would have done anything for any of them, whereas Marcie thought only of herself; although looking back, Nessie realised that she hadn't always been that way. Marcie had been a placid, good-natured child, and their father's favourite, until she hit her teenage years and then it was as if someone had suddenly waved a magic wand and she had changed dramatically.

'Happen it's time we gave our Marcie a good kick up the backside and got her out to work again,' he said, as if he had been able to read Nessie's mind.

'Hmm, you can try,' she answered with a wry grin, but Reuben wasn't smiling.

'I'll speak to her tonight,' he promised. 'And I'm going to tell her that she either gets out there and finds herself another job or she'll have to leave.'

Nessie was shocked. He sounded like he meant it, so she didn't argue. Glancing across at him she smiled. Reuben and Marcie were very much alike in looks if not in nature. They both had deep-brown eyes and dark brunette hair which had a tendency to curl, unlike her own, which her mother had always teased her was as straight as pump water! Little Joseph tended to take more after herself with slightly lighter hair and eyes. Now Nessie focused her attention on the youngest member of the family who was swirling the vegetables around his dish rather than eating them. It was nothing new. Joseph had always been a sickly child with little appetite and she constantly worried about him.

'Come on, sweetheart, you won't get to be a big, strong boy like your brother if you don't eat your dinner up,' she encouraged.

Holding his arms out to her for a cuddle he gurgled gleefully and she couldn't help but smile, but eventually she managed to coax a few spoonfuls into him.

Reuben meanwhile dropped heavily into the fireside chair and gingerly inched his boot off. His foot was still very painful from the injury he had sustained the week before at work. Nessie was only too aware that he had returned far too soon – the instant he could get his boot back on, in fact – but that was her brother all over and the difference between him and Marcie struck home once again. Planting Joseph gently on the floor, where he listlessly went back to playing with some wooden bricks Reuben had carved for him, Nessie leaned over and stared at the swelling worriedly.

'You shouldn't even be walking on that yet, let alone working,' she fretted as she stared at his ankle, which looked no better, but Reuben just smiled.

'It'll be fine. The swelling will have gone down again by morning.'

Nessie didn't bother to argue with him. She knew of old that there would be no point. Reuben could be as stubborn as a mule when he had a mind to be. Instead she began to carry the dirty pots to the sink and soon she was up to her elbows in water as she scoured them.

While she was washing up she couldn't resist peeking at her brother. Since their father had left them, Reuben had become the man of the house and she worried about what would happen to them all if he should meet someone he wanted to wed. After all, he was a good-looking lad – well, man almost now – and Nessie knew that more than the odd girl from the cottages thereabouts had set her cap at him. His arms and shoulders were heavily muscled from the many hours of strenuous manual work he did and his smile could light up a room. Sooner or later one of the girls was bound to catch his eye and then... She stopped her thoughts from going any further. There was no point in looking for trouble when as yet there was none, and she felt selfish for thinking that way. Reuben was entitled to a life, after all. She shouldn't expect him to spend the rest of his life supporting them.

Once she had finished washing up, Nessie lifted Joseph into the sink and tenderly washed him from head to toe while Reuben sat reading the local newspaper, which Mr Clarke from further along the row always supplied him with when he himself had read them. He's so small for his age, she thought worriedly. Despite all her best efforts to tempt him to eat, he hardly ate enough to keep a bird alive and she was concerned that as yet he had made no attempt to walk but she hoped that as he grew he would become stronger.

Eventually, when Joseph had been changed into a clean nightshirt and tucked into Nessie's bed in the room she shared with Marcie, she made her way back downstairs and lit the candles. It was late September and the nights were drawing in rapidly, which meant they needed extra candles – adding to their expenses. Taking up one of Reuben's socks that needed darning she sighed. It had had so many repairs there was hardly anything of the original sock left, but new ones were out of the question for now. She was still busily sewing when the back door opened, letting in a blast of cold air, and Marcie appeared. She kicked off her boots and pouted, saying, 'These boots are killing me, they pinch my toes. When can I have a new pair?'

'When you get off your lazy backside and go out to earn the money to buy some,' Reuben told her sharply.

Nessie held her breath as she felt a row brewing.

'And what am I supposed to do?' Marcie sniffed. 'It's all right for you. The railroad supply you with decent boots, at least.'

Reuben glared at her. 'Aye, they do. I need 'em working out in all weathers,' he ground out. 'I'm

28

throwing heavy railway sleepers and train tracks about all day long whereas you never step out o' the house unless it's for pleasure. I'm tellin' you now it has to change so first thing tomorrow I want you up and out looking for a new job otherwise you'll answer to me when I get home tomorrow evenin'.'

Seeing that her brother meant it, Marcie threw herself on to the wooden settle and crossed her arms across her chest with a sullen look on her face. Life was so unfair!

Chapter Two

Marcie did get up and leave the house early the next morning, although Nessie suspected she wasn't looking for work. The town was flooded with navvies who had come from Ireland to work on the railways with Reuben, and Ma Clarke, who lived along the row of cottages, had confided to Nessie that she had seen Marcie strolling out with one of them one evening. Nessie hoped that she was mistaken, but knowing what a flirt Marcie could be she didn't put it past her. Although she was a year younger than Nessie, Marcie had the shapely figure of a woman and used it to her advantage. Often, she came home with small presents from the numerous men who wanted to take her out and that always enraged Reuben even more.

Nessie made a number of fresh loaves with the

small amount of flour she had left then cleaned the cottage from top to bottom while Joseph had a nap. It had rained during the night and the sky was leaden and overcast and, as always, she worried about Reuben and hoped that he wouldn't get soaked to the skin if the rain started again. She emptied the buckets she had stood beneath the leaks in the roof in the two upstairs rooms then hurriedly replaced them, just in case. The roof had leaked ever since they had moved in but she had given up complaining about it to Seth Grimshaw. He was not a good landlord and considered that things like that should be attended to by the tenants of the properties he let rather than himself.

Thinking of him now, Nessie shuddered and lifted the tin box she kept on the mantelpiece to check how much was inside it. There was still only exactly the same amount as there had been the day before and she smiled ruefully as she wondered why there should magically be any more. There would certainly not be enough to get completely out of Grimshaw's debt even if she cut the food shopping down to the bone and she dreaded to think how he would react to the fact. But that was still some days away yet so she tried to push him to the back of her mind as she hurried to fetch Joseph who had just woken from his sleep. He gurgled at her as she lifted him from his cot, and the smile on his face melted Nessie's heart. Soon after, she carried a basket of washing out to the line which was strung across the yard they shared with their neighbours, the Hewitts.

Mrs Hewitt was hanging her load out too, although she commented through a mouthful of wooden pegs, 'Don't reckon we'll get much dry today, pet. Looks like rain to me.'

Mrs Hewitt was a great Amazon of a woman with hands like hams and a tongue as sharp as a knife; woe betide anyone who upset her. Yet she had a kind heart and had been good to the Carson family ever since the day they moved in, particularly after they lost their mother.

'I think you could be right, Mrs Hewitt.' Nessie stared up at the dark sky and sighed.

The older woman frowned. 'Is everything all right, Nessie? Only I couldn't help overhearing Old Grimshaw havin' a go at you t'other day. If it's money you're short of I could happen lend you a few bob.'

'Oh no, it's all right, really,' Nessie said hastily. She was a proud little thing. 'Although I do appreciate the offer.'

'Hmm, well just bear it in mind. That Grimshaw ain't to be trusted, 'specially wi' a pretty little thing like you. He's chatted our Zillah up when she's come visitin' more than once and she ain't that much older than you. Did I mention that my sister, Zillah, is a maid to a lady?' Her chest swelled with pride and Nessie grinned. She and Zillah had got on well during the few occasions she had visited and Nessie was happy for her to have acquired such a good position. Mrs Hewitt was so proud of her younger sister and had told Nessie at least two dozen times that she was a lady's maid to a woman who was married to a lord. In fact, she told anybody that would listen.

Smiling to herself, Nessie pegged the rest of the washing to the line where it hung limply in the

31

damp air. Mrs Hewitt had disappeared off back into her own cottage again by the time she'd finished and Nessie couldn't help but marvel at the woman. She had given birth to thirteen children over the years. Five of them had not survived their fifth birthdays but she and her husband had somehow managed to raise the eight surviving ones in the tiny cottage that was no bigger than Nessie's.

She hurried back inside out of the chill air then, to find that Joseph had fallen into a doze on the rug in front of the fire, which was burning low. After removing the old brass fire guard she threw a few chunks of coal onto the flames. She'd noticed with concern that the wood supply piled up outside the back door was dwindling. Reuben usually went off most evenings with the little cart he'd fashioned out of old bits of wood to collect fallen branches from the surrounding copses, but because of his injury he hadn't been able to go for some days.

Never mind, I'll go myself when he and Marcie get in this evening, she told herself. *And happen I'll pay a visit to the slag heap an' all.*

The slag heap was situated outside the gates of the local pit. It was where the poorer quality coal was dumped and locals were always scavenging there. After all, even poor-quality coal burned and it was essential that they kept the fire lit, for it was their only source of heat. It was also the only way for them to heat water and to cook in the little oven at the side of the fire. Even now the kettle was dangling above the dying flames, hissing softly, and just for a moment Nessie was tempted to make herself a pot of tea. But then she thought better of it. The tea leaves in the tea caddy were almost gone and she was determined that she would cut back on food this week so that she could pay the landlord what was owed. So instead, she gently drew a blanket over Joseph's slight body, careful not to wake him, then set about scrubbing the floor to keep herself warm. As she worked she began to feel a little more optimistic. If she could just catch up with the rent and Marcie managed to get a job they would be fine again. Perhaps Marcie would breeze in at any moment to tell her that she'd succeeded in securing a post. On that happy thought she began to hum quietly.

Her happy mood vanished mid-afternoon when the back door suddenly opened and Reuben appeared, his face ashen, leaning heavily on one of his workmate's arms.

'I 'ad to bring 'im 'ome, love,' the man apologised, dragging off his cap respectfully. 'His ankle 'as swelled so bad he can 'ardly put 'is weight on it. Wouldn't surprise me if it weren't broken. Per'aps yer should get the doctor to call an' take a look at it? He can't work like this, that's a fact, so I've 'elped 'im to get 'ome.'

Nessie ushered the men towards the fireside chair and Reuben dropped into it, wincing with pain.

'Thank you for bringing him back.' She flashed the man a radiant smile. 'I've been telling him he went back to work too soon but would he listen?'

'Right, well if yer can manage now I'd best get back ter work.' Slightly dazzled by her smile, the man backed towards the door telling Reuben, 'Hope all goes well fer yer, squire.'

Once he'd gone, Nessie stared worriedly at her brother as she dropped to her knees beside him.

'Right, we'd better get this boot off and have a look at it.' As she undid the laces, Reuben lolled back in the chair, his face contorted with agony as she gently manoeuvred the boot over his swollen ankle. It was at least twice the size it should have been and Nessie's small white teeth nipped at her lower lip in concern.

'Your friend was right,' she muttered. 'And you really *should* let the doctor see it.'

Reuben shook his head. 'And where are we goin' to magic the money for a doctor's visit from, eh?' He was all too aware how much they needed money at the moment, and he blamed himself for the fact that they had fallen behind with the rent.

'I dare say we'll manage,' Nessie assured him with a confidence she was far from feeling. 'Meantime, I'm going to make you a nice hot drink and then I'll strap it up for you and see if that's relieves the pain a bit. But I warn you, if it's no better tomorrow I shall send for the doctor whether you like it or not.'

She bustled away to make some tea then, after leaving it to mash, she took one of her mother's old pillowcases and tore it into strips and began to bind his ankle as tightly as she could. Reuben's face was almost grey with pain but he bit down hard on his lip and didn't complain. Anything was better than having to pay for a visit from the doctor.

'It'll probably be better by tomorrow,' he remarked hopefully when she was done but they both knew that he was lying. Looking at the state of it, it could be days, weeks even, before he would be able to walk on it again and now Nessie began to really worry. What would they do with no money at all coming in? There was the rent to find and how were they to eat? After propping Reuben's foot up on a low wooden stool, she began to prepare the vegetables for the evening meal at the sink. There was no meat to go in the stew but at least she had plenty of freshly baked bread so they wouldn't go hungry, for now at least. The vegetables were cooking in a pot over the fire when Reuben commented, 'The wood pile is lookin' low, I notice.'

Nessie gave him a bright smile. 'I already saw that but don't worry, once Marcie comes in to watch Joseph I'm going to take the cart along to the slag heaps.'

Reuben flushed. 'But you shouldn't have to do jobs like that, you do enough as it is.'

'Oh, so who will do it then?' Nessie asked firmly. 'You certainly can't, can you? And it won't hurt me just for once. I'll try and collect enough wood and coal to keep us going for a few days. At least we can have hot water and be warm then.'

Reuben crossed his arms and stared into the low-burning fire, deeply ashamed that his sister was having to do what he considered his job.

Two hours later, Marcie breezed in as if she hadn't a care in the world and instantly Nessie asked her, 'Any luck? In finding a job, I mean.'

Marcie pouted as she flung her shawl over the back of a chair. 'Nothing,' she answered sullenly.

'And did you even *try* to get one?' Reuben asked sarcastically and her head snapped towards him.

'Just what is *that* supposed to mean?' she retorted. *'Of course,* I tried but there's nothing going.'

'Oh aye, an' exactly *where* did you try? I didn't realise jobs were suddenly so hard to come by.'

Flustered now, Marcie pretended to brush the creases from her skirt as she avoided his eyes. 'Well er ... I tried a few places. Shops an' that...'

Reuben didn't believe a word of it. 'Hmm, well when me mate brought me home you weren't tryin' very hard. I saw you walkin' arm in arm through the marketplace with a bloke! He looked a right dandy!'

His eyes were like hard pebbles and knowing that she had been well and truly caught out, Marcie hung her head. But only for a moment because the next instant she lifted her gaze to him and asked insolently, 'So what were *you* doin' coming home anyway? You're supposed to be at work, aren't you?'

Sensing the tense atmosphere, Joseph began to whimper and Nessie hastily scooped him up from the rag rug where he was playing and sat him on her hip. She hated it when her brother and sister argued, even though Reuben had good cause to scold Marcie.

'Now then, you two arguing isn't going to improve the situation, is it?' she butted in. Then to Marcie, 'Reuben's ankle is too swollen for him to walk on so we'll have to manage as best we can for the next few weeks. Meantime I've got to go and get some wood and coal for us when we've had our meal so take your bonnet off and come to the table. Then you can watch Joseph and wash the pots up while I visit the slag heap.'

'*What?*' Marcie looked horrified as she stared at the small child on Nessie's hip. 'But I were plannin' on goin' out tonight!' she objected, much to her brother's disgust. 'And I suppose this means I shall have to wait even longer for some new boots now,' she ended peevishly.

'Here!' Nessie quickly dropped Joseph onto Reuben's lap. He looked in danger of exploding, but the sight of Joseph softened him slightly, although he gasped as the slight weight of the child made him move his ankle and Nessie hurriedly ran to fetch the stew to the table, placing the sooty-bottomed pan on a large brass trivet.

Marcie meanwhile took a seat and glared at her brother defiantly as Nessie began to fill their dishes and slice wedges from one of the loaves she'd baked that morning.

'Now can we *please* just eat our meal with no arguments!'

Hearing the note of despair in her voice, Reuben clamped his mouth shut as she carried a tray over to him and lifted Joseph back up. He knew how hard she worked to keep the house running and look after Joseph and the last thing he wanted to do was upset her more than she already was, although at that moment he could quite happily have throttled his younger sister, the selfish little madam. Sometimes he wondered how his mother had managed to give birth to two such different girls.

Soon, Joseph was settled at Nessie's side, dipping his bread into the stew with his sister's help and sucking it noisily. Every now and again, Marcie stared at him in disgust before suddenly saying, 'Shouldn't he be feeding himself by now? And what's this supposed to be anyway? I haven't found a single piece of meat in it so far!' As she spoke she was swilling the food around the dish with a look of distaste on her face and once again, Reuben's temper flared.

'Per'aps if we were both bringin' in a bob or two we could afford a bit more meat,' he snapped.

'There's plenty of bread to fill up with,' Nessie chipped in cheerily before Marcie could reply, once again hoping to avoid an argument, but Marcie merely slammed away from the table leaving her food untouched and stamped upstairs. Joseph began to gently cry.

Suddenly, Nessie's appetite was gone too. Very soon now Mr Grimshaw would be calling for his rent and once again she wouldn't be able to pay him. The thought of how he would react and what he would want from her made her feel sick to the stomach.

Chapter Three

When Nessie arrived at the slag heap later that evening she found the local women swarming across it like flies. A cold wind had blown up and a fine rain had begun to fall, soaking her to the

38

skin in seconds. Yet it was almost a relief to be away from the tense atmosphere between Marcie and Reuben back at home. She had left a begrudging Marcie to care for Joseph and now, pulling her thin shawl over her hair, she bent and began to search among the pile of cobbles. Very slowly the cart began to fill and after a back-breaking hour she straightened and rubbed her grimy hand across her eyes to wipe the rain from them. Her hands and feet were so cold that she could barely feel them and her fingernails were caked with dirt, as was the hem of her skirt.

But her work wasn't done yet. Now she would visit the copse at the back of the cottages and collect whatever fallen branches she could find. Wearily she grasped the handle of the cart and began to drag it across the rough ground, glancing fearfully over her shoulder all the time. After a while, the cottages came into sight and she sighed with relief. Smoke curled lazily from the chimneys and the curtains were drawn against the cold night. Only now did she realise just how hard Reuben worked to keep them all supplied with fuel for the fire, yet never once had he complained.

When she reached the fringes of the trees, she left the cart and tentatively stepped beneath the dark branches, her heart pounding. It looked totally different at night. In the daytime, when she could spare the time, she would sometimes bring Joseph here to play, and with the sun dappling through the trees, especially in the spring when the floor was a vast sea of bluebells, it was a magical place. But now it felt sinister and the swaying shadows made her jump and look nervously from side to side. Eventually her eyes adjusted to the light and she began to feel around the ground for any small branches that had fallen. When she was lucky enough to find any, she would carry them back to the cart, breathing heavily, before venturing back into the woods again. A dog fox suddenly barked loudly making her plaster herself against the trunk of a tree but when she realised what it was she sighed with relief and stood there for a time as her heart steadied to a gentler rhythm.

That's it, I've had enough for one night, she thought as she picked her way across the uneven ground to where she had left the cart. It was quite heavy and by the time she had hauled it to the back door of the cottage, she was puffing with exertion. But still she hadn't finished. Now she must load it all into the small wooden structure that Reuben had built to shelter their fuel in the back yard. She would chop the branches into fireside sizes tomorrow, she decided. When eventually she staggered into the kitchen she was almost dropping with exhaustion. Reuben glanced up from his fireside seat. Guilt stabbed at him sharp as a knife as he saw the state of her. Her hands were bleeding, her face was scratched and her clothes, which clung to her wetly, were filthy.

'Eeh, love, I'm so sorry you've had to do this.' He shook his head in frustration. 'Coal pickin' ain't no job fer a woman. Especially in this weather.'

Nessie managed a smile as she hurried to the fire and held her frozen hands out towards it. 'You wouldn't say that if you saw how many women there were at the slag heap tonight,' she answered.

'Happen they're all trying to stock up before the really bad weather comes, though I have to say it's so cold tonight you would think it was November instead of late September. I wonder if this is a sign we're going to have a really bad winter.' She looked about the room.

'Marcie's gone to bed,' he told her as if he were able to read her thoughts. 'I reckon she knows I'm sick of her behaviour so went up to get out o' me way.'

'She doesn't mean anything,' Nessie said in her sister's defence. 'She's just young, that's all.'

'Aye, and so are you,' he pointed out. 'But you're not on the want all the time. Fact is, I can't remember when you last had sommat new.'

'I don't need anything.' Nessie crossed to the teapot and felt it. The tea would be stewed by now no doubt but at least it would be wet and warm so she poured them both a cup. 'I'm afraid there's no milk left till I fetch some in the morning,' she told her brother but Reuben shrugged and took it uncomplainingly as Nessie peeled her wet shawl from her shoulders.

'I shall have to wear my Sunday best tomorrow,' she muttered as she looked down at the state she was in. 'This lot will have to be washed before I can wear them again.' She filled the kettle from the pail of water she kept full on the wooden draining board and set it on the fire to boil so that she could wash, before asking Reuben, 'Do you need me to help you out to the privy before you go to bed?'

He flushed and nodded. Truth was he had been dying to go for the past hour but hadn't been

41

sure how he was going to manage it alone.

'Better still, why don't I fetch the chamber pot down for you from under the bed?' she suggested then. 'Better that than have to venture out in the rain, eh?'

Deeply embarrassed, he nodded as Nessie hurried away to fetch it. She discreetly left the room while he used it then began to help him upstairs to his bed. She soon discovered it would be no easy task as Reuben couldn't put any weight on his foot at all without crying out with pain. Eventually he sat down on the stairs and shuffled up on his bottom while Nessie supported his injured foot, and at last she helped him onto his bed.

Once she knew he was as comfortable as she could make him she quietly closed the bedroom door and crossed the landing, peeping into her own bedroom on the way. Joseph was curled up into a little ball in her own bed but a glance at Marcie's showed her that it was empty and Nessie's heart did a little flip. Reuben had said that Marcie had gone to bed some time ago so perhaps she had just gone downstairs for a drink? Yet the kitchen was deserted and Nessie scowled as she realised that the girl must have slipped out while she was settling Reuben. Now she would have to wait up until her sister decided to put in an appearance. There was no way she would be able to sleep until she knew she was back safe and sound. After placing her dirty clothes to soak in a bucket overnight she curled up under a thin blanket in what had been her mother's favourite chair at the side of the fire, and before she knew it she fell into an exhausted sleep.

The wind howling around the cottage like a wounded child woke her in the early hours of the morning and she blinked blearily. The fire was almost out and she felt cold and shivery. Glancing towards the tin clock on the mantelpiece she saw that it was almost one o'clock in the morning. She groaned softly, every bone in her body ached and she was sick with worry about Marcie but she felt too ill to wait up for her sister any longer. At least she could lie in comfort in bed and wait for her. A thought occurred to her then. Perhaps Marcie had returned and crept upstairs while she was asleep? It was the sort of thoughtless thing she would do. Hastily, she threw just enough coal on the fire to keep it burning then wearily climbed the stairs. Marcie's bed was still empty and for a while she lay awake with Joseph's warm little body pressed against her; the wind rattled the window panes as she listened out for the sound of Marcie coming home, but finally exhaustion claimed her and she slept.

When next she woke, it was morning and Joseph was still fast asleep. A glance at Marcie's bed told her that it hadn't been slept in. Gently, so as not to disturb the sleeping child, she crept out of bed and after pulling an old shawl about her shoulders she went down to the kitchen and threw some wood onto the dying fire. She then raked the ashes and once a weak flame appeared she filled the kettle and placed it on to boil. She was shivering, hot one minute and cold the next and she guessed that she must have caught a chill the night before, but perhaps she would feel better with a hot drink inside her. But how was she going to explain Marcie's absence to Reuben?

Unbidden tears sprang to her eyes as her mind slipped back in time. Just a couple of years ago she'd had a mother and father and they'd all lived in a very comfortable little house in Bedworth. But then her father had disappeared and just weeks after moving to this cottage, Joseph had been born, adding to their financial burden. Yet even then they had managed to keep their heads above water, thanks to her mother who would take in washing and ironing or do any job she could find to supplement their income. It was only when her mother had been killed that the real hardships had begun.

She wondered where her father was now. They'd seen nothing of him since he left them and despite the numerous times he had rolled in drunk and aggressive, Nessie sometimes missed him. He hadn't been all bad. In fact, when he was sober he could be very kind and loving. She remembered the sleigh he had made for her and Reuben one winter and the way he had dragged them along on it in the snow; the way he would sometimes come into their bedroom at night to plant gentle kisses on their brows and tuck the blankets under their chins. The stories he would tell them. Giving herself a mental shake she brought her thoughts back to the present. Her father was gone so now they would have to manage alone ... somehow. It was a daunting thought.

Soon after, she carried a cup of tea up to Reuben. They decided that it might be sensible if he stayed in bed all day to completely rest his ankle. Hopefully he needn't ever know that Marcie had stayed out all night, it would only cause yet more arguments if he did. By the time Marcie breezed in around mid-morning, Nessie was worried sick.

'Where the hell have you been?' Nessie hissed, deliberately keeping her voice low so that Reuben wouldn't hear her.

Marcie flashed her a brilliant smile. 'Well, if you must know, I've been securin' a post for meself,' she answered smugly.

'You've got a job!' Nessie's mouth dropped open. 'Doing what? *Where?'*

'Hmm, I thought that would shock you.' Marcie crossed her arms and stared back at her sister. 'I'm to start at Haunchwood House next Monday, so what do you think about that?'

'Haunchwood House? Doing what?'

'Well, I shall be a kitchen maid for a start off but I intend to get to be the parlour maid afore too long, you just watch me.'

Nessie straightened from the poss-tub and wiped her wet hands down the coarse huckaback apron that enveloped her small frame from the waist down. 'And how did this happen?'

Marcie sniffed as she adjusted her bonnet and studied her fingernails. 'I just happened to be in the right place at the right time. I was in the post office when the housekeeper from the house came in all of a fluster to place an ad for a new kitchen maid in the window. The other one had cleared off unexpectedly, apparently, so when I heard her telling the postmistress about it I piped in an' told her that I was lookin' for a post. She eyed me up an' down an' asked if I'd be able to start within a week an' when I told her I could she nodded an' told me the job was mine, though I'll be on trial for the first three months o' course. But it don't really matter how it came about, does it? All you need to know is I'll be working ... and I'll be living in an' all so that will be one less for you to worry about, won't it?'

'But what about Reuben ... and Joseph?' Already she was realising that if Marcie had a live-in post it was highly unlikely she would be willing to contribute any of her wages towards the family's keep.

Avoiding her sister's eyes, Marcie stared down the long, narrow garden that stretched beyond each cottage to the privy that was shared by all four cottages.

'I shall only be paid quarterly and I'll get one Sunday in every four off, so I shan't have any wages for some time.'

Nessie sighed as she grappled with a mixture of emotions. She was pleased that Marcie would have a job. The Dorseys who lived in Haunchwood House were well known in the area and Mr Dorsey owned many of the local pits and brickworks thereabouts, as well as many smaller shops in the town. Nessie often saw them being driven about in their fine carriage and sighed with envy at the sight of Mrs Dorsey's and her daughter's fine gowns. They also had two sons who had both attended university. It was rumoured that the younger one was being trained to take over his father's businesses when he chose to retire. He was certainly rich enough to, if what she heard was true. The oldest son, Oliver, had been to medical school and word was out that he was soon to take a post in town as Dr Peek's assistant. She wasn't surprised at that; Dr Peek was knocking on in age and she supposed he'd want to retire before too much longer. And now here was her sister telling her that she was going to go and work for them and, furthermore, live in their house. She was thrilled for her and yet she also felt sad. Marcie could be a little minx, yet Nessie knew that she would miss her.

'Well, I don't mind saying you've right taken the wind out of me sails,' she admitted. 'And you've done well for yourself.'

Marcie perked up then and grinned. 'I know. I shall be supplied with a uniform *and* new boots,' she added pointedly. 'So you won't have to worry about layin' out any more money for me.'

'We'd best go and tell Reuben the good news then,' Nessie said after a moment, pushing her concerns to the back of her mind. 'He's having a day in bed to try and get his ankle right but if it's still as bad tomorrow I shall be getting the doctor to call, whether he likes it or not. Don't tell him you didn't come home last night though. He doesn't need any more stress at the minute.'

Reuben's ankle wasn't any better the next morning so after leaving a reluctant Marcie to keep an eye on Joseph, Nessie set off for the doctor's house to ask him to pay them a call. They could ill afford the penny it would cost, which would eat yet further into the rent money, but, Nessie asked herself, what choice did they have? The longer

Reuben was off work the deeper in debt they would get so it was imperative that his injured ankle was treated.

The doctor was out on a call when Nessie arrived at his house but after leaving their address with his wife, Nessie set off for home again. It was the first day of October and already the leaves were turning to reds and golds and beginning to flutter from the trees like confetti. Normally, Nessie would have found joy in the sight but she was so concerned about how they were to manage financially that today she barely noticed and hurried along in the biting wind with her head bent.

It was late afternoon when Dr Peek arrived, looking cold and weary, but his smile was warm when Nessie answered the door to him. He had developed a soft spot for the girl, for there weren't many who would have cared for their family as she did, especially following the horrific way her mother had died. Most girls of her age would have cracked under the strain and many of them were already walking out with chaps, or had even wed and had babies, but Nessie seemed to be totally devoted to her siblings. She was completely different to that younger sister of hers from what he could make of it; there was a little flibbertigibbet, if ever he'd seen one.

'So, what's the problem, pet?' he asked and when she told him about Reuben's accident, he sighed. This family had already had more than their share of bad fortune and he knew that Reuben was the only one bringing any money into the house, and if he couldn't work, how were they to eat or pay the rent?

'Let's have a look at him then,' he said brightly, hoping that the injury might prove to be just a bad sprain, as Nessie had suggested.

He crossed to Reuben, who had insisted on coming downstairs, and was sitting with his face downcast and his foot propped up on a stool, and smiled, asking, 'So what have you been up to then, me laddo?' Kneeling, he gingerly began to feel around his ankle making the colour in the young man's face leak away like water down a drain.

'I'm afraid it's not good news,' he said after a time, sitting back on his heels.

Nessie, who was standing close by, began to wring her hands nervously as she stared at him.

'It's broken, all right,' Dr Peek told them. 'And God alone knows how you've managed to hobble about on it. You must have been in agony. So, now I've got to get the bone back into position and strap it as tightly as I can and I have to warn you it's going to be very painful.' He began to rummage in his black bag and removed a small bottle with a cork stopper and a roll of bandages.

'But how long will it be before I can go back to work?' Reuben asked worriedly.

The doctor sighed. 'To be honest, I think your days of hard manual work are going to be over, lad. I can set your ankle as best I can but it's always going to be weak after this. There'll be no more throwing railway sleepers about and walking miles a day for you, I'm afraid.'

Reuben looked horrified as he sat up in the seat which made him wince again. 'But then how am I supposed to earn a living? I'm not trained to do anything but manual work.' A vision of them all incarcerated in the workhouse flashed in front of his eyes, and he visibly shuddered. He could picture the tall, forbidding gates and the dreary exterior, the long, grimy, sash-cord windows, and knew that somehow he must ensure that none of his family ever ended up there.

'I'm a great believer that as one door shuts another one opens,' the doctor said calmly as he coated a piece of rag with the evil-smelling contents of the bottle. 'But now just breathe this in for me, there's a good chap; it will soften the pain. And you, Nessie, I'll need you to help me.'

Reuben opened his mouth to object but then the cloth came across his nose and suddenly darkness was rushing towards him and thankfully he knew no more until the bone in his ankle had been eased back into place and his foot tightly strapped.

By the time it was done, Nessie looked almost as pale as he did but she thanked the doctor and hurried to fetch his fee from the tin on the mantelpiece.

The kindly doctor waved it aside. 'It's all right, my dear,' he told her. 'I was coming past here anyway so I didn't have to come out of my way. There's no charge for this time.'

'B-but...'

He held his hand up. 'Really. Now, give him a few drops of this in water whenever the pain gets too bad and whatever you do make sure that he doesn't try to walk on it for at least a couple of weeks.' He handed a small bottle of laudanum to her and she took it with shaking hands, wondering if things could possibly get any worse.

Chapter Four

Nessie's stomach had been in knots all day waiting for Mr Grimshaw's knock on the door but thankfully, when it eventually came, Reuben was dozing in the chair at the side of the fire. Drawing her shawl about her slim shoulders against the biting cold she stepped outside and faced her landlord calmly, showing no sign of the turmoil inside.

As soon as he saw her, he leered, his greedy eyes raking up and down her body, from the promising curve of her breasts to the tips of her toes.

Her eyes were drawn to his thick, grey eyebrows and she stared at them like someone in a trance. They rose up and down as if they had a life of their own and Nessie shuddered.

'So, you've got all the rent money for me this week, I assume?' It was more of a statement than a question and Nessie silently held her hand out displaying the coins on her palm.

He grimaced. 'Huh! That ain't even *half* of what you owe, so what we goin' to do about it, eh?' His thick, wet tongue was sliding from one end of his slobbery lips to the other, but just as she was about to answer, Ruby West from the end cottage suddenly sashayed up to him. Ruby had been widowed some years before and Nessie had often wondered how she managed to make ends meet, for she didn't appear to go out to work, she always seemed to be too busy entertaining the numerous gentlemen that called. Nessie had heard rumours that she sold her favours and she had no doubt that Ruby could have, for although she was now in her early forties she was still a fairly attractive woman, small and voluptuously plump with only the merest hint of grey in her hair.

'Now, Seth, you ain't hasslin' this poor little lass, are you?' she said flirtatiously.

At the sight of her, he ran his finger around the inside of his shirt collar and squirmed uncomfortably.

'Let her alone, can't you, or is she to carry on where her mother left off?'

Nessie frowned. What did Ruby mean? But then Mrs Hewitt appeared too with a laden shopping basket on her arm and, looking towards them, she said icily, 'So what you up to, Seth? Take what the poor lass is offerin' an' be patient, can't yer? Her brother is laid up wi' a broken ankle but she'll catch up on her arrears soon as she can, yer should know that be now.'

Looking decidedly uncomfortable again, Mr Grimshaw snatched the money from Nessie's hand and without another word followed Ruby to her cottage, disappearing through the door with her.

Mrs Hewitt tutted. 'Well, happen we won't see him fer another good hour or so an' we can guess how she's payin' her rent, can't we?'

'What do you mean, Mrs Hewitt?' Nessie asked innocently. 'And what did she mean when she asked him if I was to carry on where my mother had left off?'

Colour burned into Mrs Hewitt's cheeks as she stared at a spot above Nessie's head. And then suddenly Nessie realised what she had been intimating and she gasped as her hand flew to her throat.

'*Surely* she wasn't saying that my mother paid our rent by ... by *lying* with him?' Her voice was wobbly and tears had sprung to her eyes.

'Don't you go judgin' yer ma,' Mrs Hewitt scolded, annoyed, as she wagged a plump finger at her. 'She was a good woman an' she just did what she had to do to keep a roof over yer heads. She'd have done owt fer you kids. She ain't the only one hereabouts, neither. There's more than one poor woman pays Seth Grimshaw in kind, make no mistake about it. He's a lecherous old sod.'

Nessie could only stare back at her as she reeled in shock. The thought of her mother suffering Seth Grimshaw's hands on her made her feel physically sick and yet never once had her mother given any indication of what was going on, nor once had she complained. Seeing the horror on the girl's face, Mrs Hewitt softened and closing the gap between them she reached out and gently brushed Nessie's copper-gold hair from her face.

'Don't you get worryin' now,' she soothed. 'Here look, I did a bit o' shoppin' fer yer. An' no, don't get arguin' an' cuttin' yer nose off to spite yer face. There's more than enough there to keep yer goin' fer a few days an' I won't even miss it now that most o' my lot are workin'.' She pushed the basket into the girl's arms, and as Nessie began to protest, she ended gently, 'An' think on what they say, everythin' happens for a reason. Somethin' will turn up, pet, you'll see. Meanwhile, my Cecil is out lookin' fer a nice sturdy branch that Reuben can carve into a crutch. He's a knack wi' carvin' wood, ain't he? An' happen that'll enable him to get about a bit better. Away in now out o' the cold an' I'll see yer later. If Seth Grimshaw should show up again just send him round to me an' I'll sort the bugger out!'

Nessie couldn't help but grin through her tears as she watched Mrs Hewitt waddle away into her cottage.

'What's this then?' Reuben had just woken up and looked at the basket curiously as she entered the room.

'Mrs Hewitt got some food in for us, bless her,' Nessie answered as she began to unpack it, avoiding his eyes. Luckily it appeared that he had heard none of the conversation outside and she would never repeat it. Reuben had always put their mother on a pedestal, let it remain that way.

'Why would she do that?' he scowled. 'We're not quite charity cases yet!'

As Nessie thought of the weeks ahead, she began to panic; they very soon could be and the prospect of the workhouse loomed larger. How were they going to survive if Reuben couldn't go back to his job?

As the contents of the basket were piled onto the table, Nessie smiled. There was a twist of tea, flour, a large cabbage, onions and carrots as well as some liver and kidneys and other useful food items. She had even thought to buy them some cheap, tallow candles, which Nessie was more than grateful for. They had run out of oil for the lamps some days ago and now they wouldn't have to sit in darkness. Mrs Hewitt had done them proud and she immediately began to wash the liver and chop some onions. At least they would eat well this evening.

'Ugh, what's this?' Marcie grimaced when her meal was placed before her later that day. 'You *know* I don't like liver!'

'So don't eat it then,' Reuben answered shortly. 'You can't be that hungry if you can leave good food.'

Marcie glared at him as she flounced away from the table. 'I shall be glad when Monday comes and I can live somewhere civilised,' she retorted as she stamped upstairs to fetch her bonnet and her shawl.

'Oh, Reuben, she'll be gone in a few short days. I know she can be trying but can't you at least *pretend* to get on for the short time she's going to be here now? For *me?*' Nessie implored. 'I don't want her to leave with bad feeling between us.'

Reuben sighed and looked shamefaced. 'Sorry,' he muttered.

Nessie patted his hand and forced a smile as she passed him Marcie's dinner. It was better than seeing it go to waste.

Monday morning seemed to dawn in the blink of an eye and in no time at all, Marcie was ready to leave for her new life in Haunchwood House. The few clothes she had were packed into one of her mother's old linen pillowcases, not that she

55

thought she would need them for long. She would wear a uniform during the days she was working and once she was paid she intended to treat herself to some new clothes. She couldn't even remember the last time she'd had anything new and she was sick of going without.

'So, you're all ready to go then,' Nessie said tearfully as she stood on the front doorstep with her. Marcie had already said goodbye to Reuben and Joseph and could hardly wait to be gone.

'Yes, and if I don't get a shufty on I'll be late for my first day, which won't make a very good impression, will it?'

'No, I don't suppose it will.' Nessie pulled her sister into her arms tearfully. She felt like a mother hen seeing one of her chicks leave the nest. 'Off you go then and I'll look forward to seeing you on your first Sunday off in four weeks' time,' she said, trying to sound bright.

Marcie nodded as she turned about and set off down the path and not once did she look back as Nessie stood there with tears streaming from her eyes.

'Come away in, pet,' Reuben said kindly. Over the last few days he had fashioned a sturdy crutch out of the fallen branch Mr Hewitt had found for him and now he was managing to hobble about a bit, although he still couldn't put any weight on his injured ankle. She turned to see him standing behind her and with a sniff she nodded and went back inside, closing the door softly behind her.

'Well, that's one less we have to worry about,' Reuben said stoically, then seeing his sister's expression he hurried on, 'What I meant was, at least we know Marcie will be well fed and cared for. So now we just have to decide what we're going to do.'

'I've been thinking about that,' Nessie admitted. 'And I was thinking that, for now at least, I could perhaps go out and find a job to tide us over ... just till you're able to work again that is, and if you feel able to cope with Joseph.'

When his expression darkened, she rushed on, 'I'm sick of sitting here worrying about how we're going to manage, so it's time to do something about it. I know I couldn't earn as much as you but surely *anything* is better than nothing for the time being?'

His shoulders suddenly sagged as he lowered himself onto a chair. Reuben supposed she had a point but it went sorely against the grain to think that his sister had to go out to work to feed him when she did so much already.

'I've also been giving some thought about what sort of job you might be able to do if you are left with a weak ankle once the break has mended and I came up with an idea. One that I think you'd like, as it happens.'

'Go on then,' he muttered sullenly. The work on the railways had been hard and back-breaking at times, but for all that he'd enjoyed it and couldn't envisage himself in any other job.

'Carpentry!' Nessie smiled at him as he stared at her in amazement.

'But I've got no qualifications,' he objected.

'I know that but you certainly have a flair for it so I'm sure there's a cabinetmaker somewhere who would give you proper training.' She spread her hands to encompass the furniture in the room, as if to prove her point. He had carved the high-backed wooden bench that stood beside the fireplace, the shelves that held the pots and pans, he had even carved some cupboards from old wooden packing cases that they'd found at the local tip, and they'd raised many a comment because they were so beautifully finished.

His face brightened at the prospect for a second but then he frowned again. 'An' how would we live while I'm doing this training? An apprentice don't get paid much, I know, an' we have to eat an' pay the rent.'

'Ah well, I've thought about that too.' Nessie grinned. 'I was thinking we could perhaps ask Mrs Hewitt if she could watch Joseph during the day so that I could work as well. We'd pay her of course and it would only be until you were qualified then I probably wouldn't have to. What do you think?'

Reuben stroked his chin as he stared ahead thoughtfully. 'I suppose it *might* work,' he admitted eventually.

'In that case I shall go into town this very day and start to make a few enquiries,' she said jubilantly. Anything was better than just sitting there and fretting, as far as she was concerned. And so after a lunch of bread and cheese, she left Joseph in Reuben's care and set off for the town with a spring in her step for the first time in weeks.

Chapter Five

After leaving home, Marcie strode out purpose-fully until she turned into the tall, metal gates surrounding Haunchwood House where her steps slowed and for the first time she felt nervous. The drive leading to the house was bordered on either side by tall trees: ash, elm and cedar, but she could just glimpse the house through them and it looked very grand and imposing. A whole world apart from the hovel they'd been forced to live in, she thought, and her courage returned. What did she have to lose, after all? She would try the post and if she didn't like it she could always go home. Nessie was so soft she would never see her out on the streets, she was sure.

Taking a deep breath, she moved on again. She had been told to report to the kitchen at the back of the house and when the drive ended she saw there was a path curving away to the side. She figured this must lead to the kitchen. Before she followed it, though, she paused to admire the place. The house was huge and surrounded by sweeping lawns and flower beds that were tended by a small army of gardeners. Beautiful marble steps led up to a stout oak door, on either side of which were long, sash-cord windows hung with heavy velvet curtains. She guessed that the rooms would be light and airy, unlike the poky, dark rooms with their tiny leaded lights that she was used to.

She moved on and once she had rounded the end of the house, saw that she was going in the right direction. A stable block was ahead of her and a number of outbuildings, and a young, red-faced woman was hanging washing on a line that stretched from the back of the house to a thick post in the centre of a huge cobbled yard. She glanced up and Marcie asked, 'Could you tell me which door leads to the kitchen?'

The girl swiped her nose along the sleeve of her coarse, cotton blouse and pointed. ''Tis that one there. Is you the girl what's come to 'elp the cook?'

'I am,' Marcie answered imperiously, as if she was visiting royalty rather than a kitchen maid come to take up her new post. The girl looked a little simple to her, which was why she supposed she was only the laundry maid. She was short and dumpy, her mousy hair was dragged back from her face and tied with string and Marcie noticed that her hands were almost red raw.

Ignoring the girl now, who she noted was watching her with her mouth hanging slackly open, she headed for the door and, after tentatively knocking on it, stepped into a kitchen that almost took her breath away. She was sure it must be as big as the whole of the cottage she had lived in put together. A massive scrubbed, pine table littered with dirty pots stood in the centre of the room and on one of the walls was the most enormous dresser she had ever seen stacked with fine bone china plates, cups and saucers. On another wall was a large range, again covered in dirty pans, and under the window overlooking the yard was a huge stone sink and a large wooden draining board. She was so busy looking about that when someone spoke she almost jumped out of her skin.

'Ah, so you've decided to put in an appearance, 'ave you?'

Marcie's eyes flew towards the voice and she saw a plump woman with a large mob cap perched on her head sitting in a chair at the side of an inglenook fireplace, above which gleaming copper pans of all shapes and sizes were suspended. Her feet were bare and resting on a footstool and a cup and saucer were balancing on her ample bosom. This, she supposed, must be the cook.

'I was told to report here for eight o'clock and I'm sure I'm not late,' Marcie answered defensively, clutching her bundle to her. The woman looked quite intimidating.

'Hmm!' The woman narrowed her eyes and peered at her closely and Marcie had the feeling she could see right into her very soul. 'Well, whether yer late or not, breakfast is over so there's plenty fer you to do.' The woman swung her legs off the stool and slipped her swollen feet into a worn pair of house shoes. 'I'll call Mrs Bainbridge, she's the 'ousekeeper. She can sort you out wi' yer uniform an' show you yer room, then you can get crackin' on this 'ere pile o' dirty pots afore yer start preparin' the vegetables for lunch.'

Marcie stared about in dismay at the mountains of dirty crockery but wisely didn't argue. She had an idea she wasn't going to get away with much with this woman. Meanwhile the woman headed for a green baize door at the end of the room and disappeared through it only to appear again seconds later with another woman in tow. It was the woman she had met in the post office the week before. She was tall and thin and she held herself erect and Marcie thought she looked quite regal. The woman was dressed in a pale-grey dress with a high collar and long sleeves, its only adornment being a slight ruffle of lace at the collar and cuffs. The dress was fitted in tight to the waist, around which hung a chatelaine with a number of keys jangling from it, and it then fell into a full, flared skirt that rustled as she walked. Her dark hair, kissed with grey above the ears, was pulled into a tight bun that balanced precariously on the top of her head and her blue-grey eyes were cold.

'Ah, Marcie, you're here then,' she said rather unnecessarily. 'I'm Mrs Bainbridge, the housekeeper, as cook has told you, no doubt. We didn't really have a proper introduction when we met in town, did we?'

When Marcie shook her head, the woman frowned. 'When addressing me in future you will say, "Yes, *miss*." Is that understood?'

'Yes, miss.' Marcie was growing more nervous by the minute and was beginning to wonder what she had let herself in for.

'Good. Then come along ... but remember, after today you never go through this door unless invited.'

Marcie followed her through the green baize door into another world, and it was all she could do to stop herself from gasping. As they walked along a wide hallway she stared down at the wooden parquet tiles on the floor and marvelled at how shiny they were. She could almost see her face in them. Gilded mirrors and oil paintings, mainly of landscapes, hung on the walls. Here and there fine Turkish rugs covered the floor and everything smelled of beeswax and lavender polish. There was a fine hall table beneath one of the mirrors on which stood an enormous bunch of hothouse flowers that smelled divine as she passed them, and Marcie wondered if this was what heaven must be like. They had gone no more than a few yards when the woman halted and, taking one of the keys from the bunch that hung about her waist, opened a door and ushered Marcie through it. It was a long, narrow room with shelves on either side of it and after approaching one the woman turned to look at Marcie closely.

'Hmm.' She pulled two dresses from one of the shelves and after shaking one out she held it against Marcie. 'I think these should be about your size,' she muttered more to herself than Marcie. 'Should they need altering you will have to do it yourself of an evening when you've finished your chores.' She then selected two large, white aprons and after passing them to Marcie asked, 'What size shoe are you?'

Marcie flushed. Having never had a brand-new pair of shoes in her entire life she wasn't sure. She usually just tried on the second-hand ones at the rag stall in the market and took the pair that fit her best.

'Try these,' the woman said flatly.

She held out a pair of flat, black leather shoes with laces. They had obviously been worn before but even so they were far superior to any that Marcie had ever owned.

'They're a bit big,' Marcie told her after a moment, so the woman began to rummage along the shelf again and held out another pair.

This time Marcie sighed with pleasure as her foot slid into one and she nodded. 'This one is fine...' A glare from the woman made her add quickly, 'Miss.'

'Good, now you'll need a couple of nightgowns and some petticoats.'

Mrs Bainbridge continued to pile things into her arms until Marcie could barely see above them. Satisfied, eventually, that Marcie had all she needed, Mrs Bainbridge asked, 'Now, is there anything you would like to ask me?'

'Er, yes, miss, there is... What will me wages be?'

'I'm so sorry,' Mrs Bainbridge actually began to smile. 'How remiss of me. I should have told you ... *would* have told you had you come for an interview. You will earn seven pounds a year and you will be paid quarterly.' Her face became sterner, and folding her hands neatly at her waist she went on, 'The manner I employed you, on the spot, as it were, was quite ... should I say unorthodox? Normally I would interview anyone that came forward and ask for references but because I know Cook desperately needed the help I decided to give you a chance. You won't let me down, will you, Marcie?'

When Marcie solemnly shook her head, she smiled again. 'Good, then I shall give you the rules you are to live by while you are in employment in this house. Should a member of the family enter the kitchen, you will lower your head and not speak unless you are spoken to. In the unlikely event that you are called into the main house, should a member of the family encounter you, you will stand to one side and not attempt to address them, nor will you speak to another servant while any member of the family is present. Your hours will be from six in the morning until seven o'clock at night, unless the family are having a dinner party and then you will stay to see to the dishes after the guests have gone.'

'Yes, miss.'

'Good, then I think that's it for now.' Mrs Bainbridge ushered her towards the door. 'I'll get the house maid to show you where you're to sleep. You'll be sharing a room with her, but I'm afraid you'll have to put your things away this evening. Cook needs you in the kitchen but I'll give you time to get changed into your uniform before you start.' She stepped back into the hallway with Marcie close behind her and seconds later the person she was obviously looking for appeared from a door on her left.

'Ah, Eliza.' Mrs Bainbridge beckoned to her. 'This is Marcie Carson. She'll be sharing your room with you. Would you show her where it is?'

'Yes, miss.' The girl bobbed her knee and glanced at Marcie curiously. She was quite small, barely up to Marcie's shoulder, but even wearing her rough uniform and an enormous mob cap Marcie saw that she was quite pretty, with flaming red hair and violet-blue eyes. She had a merry face that dimpled when she smiled and as Mrs Bainbridge headed towards the magnificent staircase, Eliza led her back towards the kitchen.

'Our room is up in the servants' quarters,' she informed Marcie cheerfully before opening a door in the kitchen that led to a steep, wooden staircase. 'And I should warn you, it's hot as hell up here in the summer and cold as clouts in the winter. It's not so bad once you get used to it, though.'

Marcie was huffing and puffing as she jiggled her bundle and the clothes she'd been issued with up the narrow stairs but at last they arrived at the top of it.

'This is my ... well, our room now,' Eliza told her, throwing a door wide and Marcie stepped into what was to become her new home. It was already quite nippy up there and she could imagine how cold it would be in deep winter, but for all that it wasn't so bad. There were two iron-framed beds, one on either side of the room, and next to each one was a chest of drawers. A small window was set quite high up in the wall between them and the floor was bare floorboards, although there was a rag rug between the beds to step out onto.

'There's an indoor toilet and a washroom further along the landing, third door on your right, and you can pump hot water up into the bath straight from a copper in the kitchen,' Eliza informed her.

Marcie's eyes stretched open wide. Imagine that, hot water without having to cart it all the way upstairs in jugs. Perhaps it wasn't going to be so bad working here after all. A smile lifted at the corners of her lips as she thought of the real reason she had taken the job, but then she realised that Eliza was speaking again and dragged her mind back to the present.

'I'll leave you to get changed into your uniform then,' Eliza said good-naturedly. 'But if you take my advice, you won't be too long about it. Cook can be a demon if you keep 'er waitin'. See you later.' And with that she was gone, closing the door softly behind her as Marcie dropped her belongings onto the bed that was to be hers.

As quickly as she could she stripped off her Sunday best clothes and slid into the petticoats and one of the dresses that Mrs Bainbridge had issued her with. It was a thick linen material in a mid-grey colour with a high neck, long sleeves and buttons running from the waist up to the neckline. She slid her feet into the soft leather shoes and did a little twirl. The dress was plain but apart from being slightly long, it fit her well and was easily the nicest dress she'd ever worn. There wasn't a single patch on it and she loved the feel of the woollen petticoats against her skin. Aware that time was moving on, she quickly gathered her hair and pushed it beneath a white linen mob cap and hurried downstairs, tying her apron as she went.

Cook was still sitting in the chair when she reached the kitchen and she nodded towards the mountain of dirty pots that seemed to cover every available surface.

'You'd best get cracking on that lot. And be quick about it, it'll be time to start the lunch soon. An' mind yer don't break anythin' an' all. If yer do I'll make sure it's deducted from yer wages.' And with that she shook her newspaper, perched her spectacles on the end of her nose and carried on reading, as if Marcie wasn't even there.

Miserable old cow, Marcie thought, as she rolled her sleeves up and approached the sink, but she was wise enough not to say anything.

It took her well over an hour to scrub the pots and dry them and once they were piled onto the end of the table she asked the cook, 'Where should I put these?'

The woman glanced up from the pastry she was rolling and nodded towards the cupboard beneath the dresser. 'Gilt-edged ones, they're the family's, on the top o' the dresser an' the rest in them cupboards below. Then make a start on the potatoes. Peel me a good panful.'

No please or thank you, but then Marcie supposed she shouldn't expect it. She was only the kitchen maid ... for now.

By the time she was excused from her duties that evening, Marcie was so weary she was sure she'd never manage the stairs to her room. Every single bone in her body ached and her hands were red raw from the soda and the rough sand she had scrubbed the bottoms of the pans with. After the family had eaten she had sat down to her own meal with some of the other staff but already she had forgotten their names and was so tired she was sure she could have slept for a month straight off. She wasn't complaining about the meals though. Mrs Roe, the cook, had prepared a fillet of beef with all the trimmings for the family, which was so tender it almost fell off the bone, while the staff had dined on steak and kidney pie. The pastry was so soft that it melted in her mouth and it was served with creamy mashed potatoes. Her stomach was full for the first time in weeks and briefly she wondered what her family would be eating tonight, but then she quickly pushed the thought away.

When she finally made it to her room she found Eliza already in bed with just a single candle burning on the chest of drawers beside her. 'I left it burnin' for you so's you'd see your way about,' she mumbled sleepily. Marcie was glad the girl was tired. She was herself but the night hadn't begun yet for her so she slipped into bed fully clothed and snuffed the candle out, waiting impatiently until Eliza's soft snores echoed around the room.

When she was quite sure that Eliza was fast asleep, she sneaked out of the bed and left the room, quiet as a mouse. It was time to meet someone very special and then the fun could begin. Her first day at the house had been much harder than she had expected it to be, but then, she told herself, it was only for the time being. George had overheard the housekeeper telling his mother that she would be going into town the next morning to place an ad for a new maid in the shop window and he had told Marcie to be there to ensure that she was the first to apply for the job. Everything had gone to plan and now she had her foot in the door. Admittedly she was only a maid as yet but hopefully, given time, she would be joining the family and then the servants would be bowing and scraping to her! The thought made her tingle with excitement.

Chapter Six

'So how did you get on?' Reuben asked eagerly when Nessie returned late that afternoon.

'Well ... nothing as yet,' she admitted, trying her best not to sound downhearted, although she felt it. She was sure she must have approached every cabinetmaker in the town but none of them had been interested in taking on an apprentice. She hadn't done any better in securing a job for herself either, although she had tried numerous shops and factories. Many of the Irish navvies who were working on the railways had brought their families with them and now that their wives were also seeking work, the number of jobs available to local women were severely depleted.

Seeing Reuben's crestfallen face she emptied her purse onto the table and he gawped at the coins.

'At least I came back with enough to catch up with the rent and buy food for the coming week.'

'Oh aye, an' how did you manage that?'

'I, er, took a few things to the pawnbrokers,' she admitted and seeing the look of horror on his face she rushed on, 'It's only until we get back on our feet. I'll buy everything back then. And I only took things that we don't really need.'

'Oh yes, an' where's yer Sunday best bonnet then? I'm sure you were wearin' it when yer left?' Reuben asked suspiciously. 'An' the clock's gone from the mantelpiece. Is that in the pawnbrokers an' all?'

Nessie nodded guiltily as Reuben shook his head. He felt sick that things had come to this. He'd seen queues of people standing waiting for the pawnbrokers to open every week on his way to work and had always been proud that their family had never had to pawn their possessions to live before. He knew how much Nessie had loved that bonnet. He could clearly remember the day their mother had bought it from the rag stall for her and the many hours she and Nessie had spent trimming it with ribbons and flowers they had fashioned from scraps of silk. Since their mother had been so brutally killed, Nessie had treasured it even more and had kept it strictly for Sunday best and he knew what it must have cost her to part with it. But then he couldn't be mad at his sister for long. He knew deep down that she was only doing what she had to do to help them survive and the thought made him shudder with guilt. It was all his bloody fault! If only he hadn't hurt his ankle; he'd make sure he got that bonnet back for her, if it was the last thing he ever did.

Nessie, meanwhile, had turned her attention to Joseph who was sitting placidly on the rug in front of the fire staring at the low flames. His chubby cheeks were rosy pink and he reached out with his little hands, trying to catch the amber flecks.

'How's he been?' she asked, and Reuben shrugged.

'Same as always, no trouble at all.' That was the

71

problem, he thought worriedly. At his age, the child should have been toddling about getting into all sorts of mischief but half the time he seemed to be locked away in a world of his own. He wasn't even trying to crawl as yet. He knew that Nessie was worried too but they had never openly discussed it. It was as if by pretending that Joseph was fine they could ignore that there was a problem.

Soon as I'm fit and earning again I'm going to get him to a doctor, he vowed to himself, for now that the child was growing it was becoming increasingly obvious that something was seriously amiss. He couldn't speak a single word as yet and although he could manage a wobbly walk if someone held his hands and coaxed him, he never attempted it if left to his own devices. Sometimes he would sit for a time playing half-heartedly with the bricks that Reuben had lovingly carved for him but for most of the time he seemed content to just sit staring into space with a vacant expression on his lovely little face.

'Right, I'll get us some dinner then,' Nessie said, forcing a smile. 'And don't get worrying. I shall be out again tomorrow and at least we can pay the rent now, so perhaps things are looking up for us, eh?'

She began to peel some potatoes, but her heart was aching. Marcie had been a pest and a selfish little madam for the most part but she was still one of their family and now Nessie felt that yet another member of it was gone. Even so she kept up a cheerful chatter until she finally retired to bed and then the tears came thick and fast as she thought back to happier times.

Oblivious to her distress, Joseph slept peacefully beside her. She missed her mother, she missed Marcie and she was desperately worried about Reuben who was clearly frustrated and anxious about what the future held for him. Everything seemed to have started to go wrong a couple of years ago when their father had discovered that Joseph was on the way. There had been such a huge gap since Marcie was born that he'd thought he'd done with babies and she could clearly remember her parents bitterly arguing about it.

'It's there now and there's nothing to be done about it!' her mother had told him, hands on hips,' and eventually they had all thought that he had accepted it. Until the night he stormed off to the inn and never returned. Things seemed to go quickly downhill from then on. They could no longer afford to pay the rent on the house in Bedworth so had moved to the one they now lived in. There was further heartache ahead when Joseph was born, for from the start their mother suspected that something about him wasn't quite right. He didn't cry as other babies did and if someone didn't offer to feed him he would just lie there, making no complaint. As he'd grown older it became more and more apparent that something wasn't as it should be. Her mother had always intended to get him to see a doctor who would know about such things, but somehow they never seemed to find the money it would cost and now she was gone too. Following her tragic death, Nessie had immediately taken on her role. What else could she do? she asked herself. Marcie would certainly never step up to the mark. And now Reuben's accident. How much more was life going to throw at them? she wondered.

Normally Nessie just got on with things, but tonight everything seemed to have caught up with her, especially as she thought of the slim gold wedding band that had belonged to her mother that she had pawned along with her best bonnet and the clock. Nessie had been wearing it on a string about her neck ever since her mother had been murdered. It had been the only piece of jewellery her mother had ever owned and she had treasured it. Wearing it about her neck had made Nessie feel close to her somehow but now she'd been forced to part with it. She knew her mother would have said she'd done the right thing but even so, when she finally slipped into an uneasy sleep it was full of nightmares.

Her mother was there pointing to something and when Nessie followed her pointing finger she found herself gazing at a coffin.

'*No, no, no more deaths*,' she sobbed in her sleep as she tossed and turned until the sheets were in a sweaty tangle about her. She began to chase her mother, imploring her to come back, but it seemed that every time she almost managed to reach her, her mother drifted away towards a light shining brightly behind her.

'Come back ... *please* come back, we miss you,' Nessie choked as she held her arms out towards her. Suddenly she felt a pressure on her arm. Someone was shaking her and she sprang awake, her eyes wild.

'It's all right, pet. You're just havin' a bad dream.'

She found herself staring up into her brother's kind face. He was standing beside the bed in his nightshirt holding a candle and, realising that it had only been a dream, she sobbed harder.

'Oh, Reuben ... our mam was here,' she sobbed. 'She was trying to show me something but I can't remember what it was now!'

He tentatively sat on the side of the bed with his injured ankle sticking out straight and drew her into his arms. 'It's all right,' he soothed as he stroked the damp hair from her brow and rocked her back and forwards. Joseph was awake as well by now but he merely lay placidly, his big brown eyes watching them intently. 'Try an' get some rest.'

Nessie shook her head. She knew that she wouldn't sleep again that night. She was too afraid that the dream might return.

'I ... I'll just settle Joseph back down then I think I'll go an' make meself a cup of tea.'

He nodded, then rising cautiously he limped his way back to his room as Nessie fumbled in the darkness for the box of vestas she kept beside the candlestick. Eventually she managed to light the candle and settled Joseph back to sleep before going downstairs, where she sat staring for some time into the flickering fire. I shall have to go out coal-picking again tomorrow, she thought, as she stared at the dwindling supply. It was strange that the dream about her mother had been so vivid yet now she couldn't for the life of her think what it was her mother had been trying to tell her.

After a time, she filled the kettle and swung it across the fire to make a hot drink. Her mother

75

had always believed that a good cup of tea was a cure for anything. Perhaps it was time to put it to the test? The birds were just beginning to sing in the trees when she finally nodded off in the fireside chair and it was Reuben standing at the stove stirring a dish of porridge that woke her the next morning.

'Sorry, I was trying not to wake you.' He looked worried as he leaned heavily on his crutch and looked across at the dark shadows beneath her eyes. 'I thought I'd get something hot for you to wake up to. Joseph is still asleep so if you put the dishes on the table we'll have ours now, shall we?'

Nodding wearily, she rose and fetched two dishes from the dresser and soon they were sitting side by side eating their breakfast. The porridge was quite lumpy, but Nessie didn't complain. Their mother had always teased Reuben that he could have burned water – he would certainly never make a chef – but he'd tried and that was the main thing, as far as Nessie was concerned.

'I thought I'd try some of the big houses on the outskirts of town today to see if any of them need any help,' she told him.

'But don't the big houses usually have their staff live in like Marcie?'

'Don't worry, I'm not about to desert you.' She patted his hand reassuringly and Reuben heaved a sigh of relief.

By ten o'clock that morning, Nessie was ready to leave and she set off towards town again, only to spend another fruitless day searching for work – any work.

She was deeply depressed as she headed back

home in the fading light. Her stomach was grumbling ominously and she hoped Reuben had remembered to push the stew she'd prepared over the fire to cook. She'd eaten nothing since breakfast and her heels were blistered and raw from the tight boots she had worn all day. As she approached the cottages she saw the kindly doctor coming out of Mrs Hewitt's – her husband had come down with a nasty cough – and he stopped to have a word with her.

'Hello, my dear. I just popped in to have a look at your brother's ankle while I was here and he told me you'd gone to look for a job. Any luck?'

Nessie shook her head miserably.

'Ah well, there's always tomorrow,' he said optimistically as he patted her shoulder. 'I'm sure something will turn up.' He hoped so, for Mrs Hewitt had told him what dire straits the family was in, and his heart was sore for them. Nessie raised a smile and went on her way as the doctor turned and set off for home.

Reuben looked at her expectantly when she entered the cottage and when she shook her head his face fell.

All too soon it was rent day again and the dreaded knock came upon the door.

Nessie took the money she'd left ready on the table and once more went outside to face Mr Grimshaw, who was grinning from ear to ear, certain that she wouldn't have been able to raise sufficient funds to pay him.

'There's this week's rent and here's the back money we owe you. I think you'll find we're all straight again now.' She carefully counted the coins into his hand and he stared down at them incredulously, wondering how the hell she'd managed it with her brother off work. 'And now if you'll excuse me, I have things to do!' And without another word she turned and walked back into the cottage with her nose in the air. He could have no idea that the only way she had managed to raise the money was by parting with some of her most treasured possessions. But already she was worrying about how she was going to pay him the next time. Anything of any value had already been pawned.

'Stuck-up little mare,' Grimshaw grunted to no one in particular. 'But my time will come. She'll be glad to pay me the rent any way she can afore much longer if what I'm hearin' is true!' Turning about, he flounced down the lane, muttering to himself.

It was mid-morning the following day when there came a knock to the cottage door and Nessie, who was in the process of rolling pastry for a pie, hurried to open it.

'Doctor!' Her voice expressed her surprise and embarrassment at seeing him standing there again. He'd been so kind to them already and there was no way they could pay him. 'Reuben is fine, really. I mean .. it's very kind of you to–'

'May I come in?' The doctor removed his hat and, feeling that she had no choice, she held the door wider so he could step into the room. 'Actually,' he began, 'I'm here because I've heard something that just might be to the advantage of

78

both of you.' He nodded to Reuben, who was sitting beside the fire.

When Nessie raised her eyebrow, he rushed on, 'Mrs Hewitt was saying that Reuben here is very good at woodwork and that you've been trying to get him an apprenticeship with a cabinetmaker.'

'Yes, I have but I haven't had any luck,' she admitted, wondering where this was leading.

'I see. Well, as it happens, I know someone who just might be glad of his help. Yours as well, if it comes to that.'

'Really?' Nessie's eyes lit up with hope as her heart began to race faster.

'Mmm.' Dr Peek smiled at her kindly then nodding towards a chair, he asked, 'May I?'

'Oh yes, yes of course, I'm *so* sorry, I was forgetting my manners.' She hastily pulled a chair out for him and waited impatiently for him to continue.

'Now, I must warn you that I haven't spoken to the person about either of you as yet. Indeed, the idea only occurred to me this morning and you might not like the sound of the job anyway.'

'But we *would*,' Nessie assured him. 'We're prepared to work anywhere doing anything, aren't we, Reuben?'

'Aye, we are,' he answered solemnly, never once taking his eyes off the doctor.

'The person I have in mind is...' He coughed. 'Is Mr Chevalier, the undertaker in town.'

'*Undertaker!*' Nessie's hand flew to her chin leaving a floury beard there.

'Yes, you see I've heard that Ted Miller, who works with him and makes the coffins, is moving away with his wife. They've been left a house in Bath by an elderly aunt so they're going to go and live there, by all accounts.'

'But I ... I don't understand.' Nessie frowned in confusion. 'Even if Reuben could take over the making of the coffins why would he want *me?*'

'Because,' the doctor explained patiently, 'he has no one to keep house for him or work in the funeral parlour. Ted and his wife lived in with Mr Chevalier and Ted's wife spent most of the day in the funeral parlour dealing with the bereaved and the rest of her time keeping house for him. Now I've heard that he's having to do everything and is running himself into the ground. So, would you like me to have a word with him on your behalf?'

Reuben and Nessie glanced at each other, each having the same thoughts. The prospect of working at an undertaker's was not very appealing at all, but then a job was a job at the end of the day, they supposed.

'Please do, doctor, we'd be very grateful.' It was Reuben who answered.

The doctor nodded and rose, placing his hat back on his head. 'Very well. Leave it with me and rest assured I shall get back to you just as soon as I possibly can. Good day to you both.'

'So, what did you make of that then?' Reuben whistled through his teeth when the doctor had gone and Nessie giggled for the first time in days.

'It's not exactly what I'd have chosen,' she admitted. 'Working with the dead, I mean. But then I suppose we're in no position to be choosy, are we?'

'No, we're not, so fingers crossed Mr Chevalier is prepared to give us a chance. From the bit I've heard of him he's quite a reclusive sort of bloke and the business hasn't done that well since he bought it from old Mr Barrow when he came over from France some years ago.'

'He does speak English, doesn't he?' Nessie suddenly asked. She couldn't imagine working for a Frenchman. Having never set foot out of her home town, France sounded like the other side of the world to her.

'Of course he does, you daft goose.' Reuben grinned, making him look more like his old self. 'How would he deal with the families of the deceased if he couldn't speak the language?'

'I hadn't thought of that.' Nessie blushed, then with a shrug she went on with what she had been doing. It was in the lap of the gods now and all they could do was keep their fingers crossed, but if only the French gentleman would give them a chance it would be the answer to all their prayers; for the food cupboard was empty now and there was no way she would be able to pay the rent the following week.

Chapter Seven

'So, how is the new kitchen maid doing, Mrs Bainbridge?'

Mrs Bainbridge smiled at her mistress. 'Fine, I believe, although Cook has said that she can be a

81

bit mouthy at times.' She shook her head. 'But then, I suppose that could be said for most young people nowadays.'

'And don't I know it!' Constance Dorsey sighed. 'Two of my own included. And I lay the blame for that squarely on their father's shoulders. He would insist on all this fancy schooling and private tutors for them and now our George thinks he's a cut above everybody else.'

No one would have realised, could they have heard the two women, that they were mistress and servant, for Constance Dorsey, or Connie as she was known, had not forgotten her roots and could well remember when she was first married. She and her husband had counted themselves lucky to find a room to rent in the poorer part of town for they barely had two ha'pennies to rub together between them. Not that they'd been there for long. Oh no, her Johnny had had ambitions and somehow he had clawed his way up from nothing to being one of the wealthiest men in the town.

He'd started off selling fruit and veg from a small barrow in the marketplace until eventually he had managed to buy a run-down shop. Once that was refurbished and making a profit he'd saved every penny he could and bought another one and so on and so on until now he had his fingers into almost every business in the area. He even had part shares in the local pit and brickworks. Connie was proud of him, of course she was, but she was also painfully aware of what it had cost him. He had worked himself almost to death and now looked much older than his forty-six years. He was finally in a position to slow down and start enjoying life, to spend a little more time with his family. But would he? she asked herself. Would he, hell! She'd been forced to admit long ago that Johnny needed to work in the way some people needed to drink and had accepted that nothing was going to change him now. He was too set in his ways. Sometimes she would look about the vast house they owned and the servants they employed and have to pinch herself to believe that it was all real.

Connie's feet were still set firmly on the ground, however, whereas Johnny enjoyed being looked up to and expected the best from his workers. She just wished at times that he could be the same with his children, for he spoiled them shamelessly and was insistent that they would never have to know what it was like to go hungry or almost work themselves to death as he had. They had had the best of everything since the second they each drew breath. The best food, the best clothes and the best education that money could buy. It had paid off with Oliver, their eldest, who was now about to take up a post as a junior doctor in the town, having recently completed his medical training. She was proud of him and his chosen profession, but the same couldn't be said for Johnny, for when Oliver had told him what he wished to do his temper had been awful to behold.

'But I've worked meself nearly to a *standstill* so that you and George can take over the businesses when I'm too old or gone,' he'd screeched. 'I thought you'd join me in helpin' to keep every-thin' goin'.'

'I'm sure George will do that,' Oliver had answered calmly, refusing to be swayed.

'Huh!' Johnny had thumped the table making the cut-glass goblets dance. 'You've got far more of a business head on yer shoulders than your brother has. It takes him all of his time to roll out o' bed in the mornin' let alone roll into work.'

It was then that Connie had stepped in, her eyes flashing. 'Why, *shame* on you, Johnny Dorsey,' she'd scolded, waggling a finger in his face. 'Most parents would be proud that their offspring were clever enough to become a part o' the medical profession, so think on, man!'

Johnny had bowed his head and said no more. He knew better than to go against Connie, who was a strong woman. He supposed she'd had to be to put up with him all these years and he still adored her as much as he had on the day they had wed. Instead, he'd stormed from the room as Connie patted her son's hand encouragingly.

'Take no heed o' him, luv,' she'd said, a smile crinkling the corners of her eyes. 'Yer know what yer dad's like, he'll come round to your idea, given time.'

And Johnny had; although he still wasn't happy, he accepted that Oliver had a mind of his own, unlike his younger son who was mixing with a bad crowd at the moment. Still, Johnny had high hopes that George would settle down in time. He was still a young man, just nineteen, and he was entitled to be carefree for a while and sow his wild oats after all the years he had spent away at private school. Only for a time, mind, Johnny thought, and then he'd clamp down on him good and proper and he'd have to get his arse into gear and learn the ropes about the various businesses. Johnny had worked too long and hard to see everything go to the wall now, by God he had!

Now, Connie and Mrs Bainbridge sat down side by side to go over the next week's menus and they had almost finished when the drawing room door opened and Connie's youngest, her daughter, Leonora, entered in a swish of fine velvet skirts. At eighteen, Leonora had vivid blue eyes like her mother's and fair hair that had a tendency to curl. She was stunningly pretty and, unfortunately, she knew it. Being the youngest and the only girl, Johnny had spoiled her even more than her brothers and Connie sometimes despaired, for she could play her father like a fiddle. Today she was dressed in a fine dark-green velvet riding habit with a little matching hat perched at a jaunty angle on her fair curls and she was slapping a small leather whip against her palm.

'I'm going for a ride on Bracken,' she informed her mother with a frown.

Connie raised an eyebrow. 'So why are you looking so miserable then?' Unlike Johnny, she tried her hardest to keep her daughter's feet on the ground and not let her get ideas above her station.

'Because it's *raining!*' Leonora sulked and Connie laughed aloud.

'Well, even you can't command the weather, miss. If it bothers you that much don't go out in it.'

'But I'm *bored!*' Leonora pouted.

'Poor you!' Connie's expression hardened.

'Perhaps I should find you something useful to do then? How about you help young Eliza with her chores? Or you could perhaps go and give a hand in the laundry or the kitchen.'

Leonora looked horrified and turned and flounced out of the room. Connie shook her head apologetically as she glanced at Mrs Bainbridge. 'I'm sorry about that. I'm afraid that little madam is getting a bit too big for her boots. I blame her father. George is no better.' She sighed but then, remembering what they were supposed to be doing, she turned her attention back to the task in hand.

Leonora meanwhile was stamping through the kitchen and seeing Marcie she paused to stare at her. 'You're new, aren't you?' she asked imperiously as if she was addressing a peasant and Marcie flushed as she placed the clean pile of plates she'd just washed onto the table.

'Yes, I am.'

'Yes, I am, *miss*, when you address me!'

Marcie clamped her teeth together to stop herself from saying something she shouldn't, but then as Leonora continued to stare at her she answered reluctantly, 'Yes, I am ... *miss*.'

'Hmm, then let's just hope you don't decide to run away with the junior groom as your predecessor did,' Leonora barked nastily and walked on with her nose in the air.

'Don't take no notice of her,' the cook said when the girl was out of earshot and crossing the yard towards the stable block. 'She's always been a bit of a madam, has Miss Leonora, but you'll be fine so long as you give her a wide berth.'

'Don't worry, I will,' Marcie said huffily. 'Just who does she think she is anyway?'

'She's the daughter of the man who pays your wages and you'd do well to remember it,' the cook advised shortly. Inside, Marcie was simmering. The stuck-up little minx, talking to her like that! But then she smiled slyly. Very soon now, when George informed the family of his intention to marry her, the girl's smile would be on the other side of her face and Marcie could hardly wait.

Late that night when Eliza was finally asleep, Marcie crept cautiously down the stairs, feeling her way in the dark and praying that she wouldn't fall. It was too risky to bring a candle so she went down carefully. At last she reached the kitchen door and after quietly unlocking it she sneaked across the yard and into the stable block. The smell of horses and fresh hay greeted her and she stood for a moment letting her eyes adjust to the darkness.

'Psst, Marcie I'm here ... over by the ladder to the hayloft.'

Marcie's face broke into a wide smile as she picked her way through the darkness towards the voice, then suddenly she was in his arms and he was kissing her face, her brow or any part of her that he could.

'Wait until we're up in the loft,' she told him breathlessly, and without another word she turned to the ladder, gathered her skirts into a bunch in one hand and began to climb. She could hear him right behind her, his breath coming in short, excited gasps and her heart beat faster. Once they had reached the top he pushed her impatiently and as she toppled into the soft hay she began to giggle as he clawed at her clothes.

'I was beginning to think you weren't going to come,' he breathed as his hand found its way to the soft skin above her stocking top.

'I had to wait until Eliza fell asleep,' she answered as she lowered her hand to the bulge in his trousers and began to tease him.

'Ah, Marcie.' He groaned like a man in pain as he began to fumble with the buttons on her work dress. 'You're enough to drive a chap wild!'

She grinned in the darkness, enjoying the power she could wield over him, but then her breasts were bared and her passion rose to match his.

Much later, she struggled from beneath him and fumbled in the darkness for her clothes, which had been hastily discarded in his need for her.

'I ought to go,' she muttered, her euphoric mood gone. 'It's all right for *you* but I have to be up early in the morning. You didn't tell me what hard work this was going to be when you suggested I apply for the job here.'

He traced a finger lazily down her bare back as she yanked her stockings on. The hay had made her naked skin itchy, her face was sore from the slight stubble on his chin and her mouth was bruised from his kisses. 'My hands are red raw,' she grumbled. 'And Cook never lets up – it's do this, do that, all day long!'

He chuckled. 'It won't be for ever,' he soothed. He tried to pull her back towards him but this time she pushed his hands away as tears trembled on her lashes.

'It had better not be,' she answered in a wobbly voice. 'Because I don't know how long I'll be able to keep this up. I'm worn out already.'

'Look,' he placated her. 'I'll start to go in to work with Father soon and when he sees that I'm trying then we can make it known that we have feelings for each other.'

'When is soon?' she turned her face towards him. 'And do you really think there's any chance for us. Your father obviously has high hopes of all his children making a good marriage. I can't see him being pleased when he finds out you've taken up with a kitchen maid!'

'You forget that both my parents are from common working stock,' George reminded her. 'Just leave it to me. Mother will support us, I know she will.' She could hear the annoyance in his voice and decided she had pushed him far enough for now. But she wasn't done with him yet, not by a long chalk!

He stood up and she heard him foraging for his clothes in the hay. As soon as they were both dressed, they clambered down the ladder. At the door to the stables, as the moonlight played on his fair hair and his handsome face, her annoyance faded. But she knew it was unwise to dawdle. It wouldn't do if they were seen together until the time was right so she kissed him quickly and took her leave.

As she crept up the stairs to the servants' quarters, the grandfather clock in the hall struck midnight and she started. Her heart was in her mouth in case anyone should hear her. When she reached the door to the room that she shared with Eliza she stood for a moment, straining her ears into the darkness but all was silent so she gingerly stepped inside.

'Where the 'ell 'ave you been?' Eliza's quiet voice almost made her jump out of her skin. 'If you've been out wi' some bloke or another an' Mrs Bainbridge finds out she'll 'ave yer guts fer garters.'

'I know,' Marcie said humbly. 'But I wasn't with a bloke. I … I just needed some fresh air. I think I must be feelin' a bit homesick. I ain't never been away from me family before.'

'Oh, you poor thing.' Eliza was sympathetic now. 'Never mind, it'll get easier.'

It had better, Marcie thought grimly. She'd never known hard work before, for she'd always managed to twist her mother around her little finger and then Nessie had taken on the lion's share of running their home when their mother died. Reuben hadn't been so easy to con though. But that was in the past now. George was her future and sometime very soon she intended to marry him. She would soon be sixteen – quite old enough to wed. She smiled as she discarded her dress, imagining what it would be like to be waited on and pampered. To ride in the family carriage and wear jewels and fine clothes. Just for an instant she was tempted to confide in Eliza but then thought better of it. She buried herself beneath the scratchy blankets and curled into a tight little ball, trying to get warm. Soon she would be lying on silken sheets with a stone hot-water bottle tucked at her feet and a fire roaring up her bedroom chimney. On that happy thought, she fell asleep.

Chapter Eight

Over the next few days Nessie made frequent trips into town. The money she'd acquired from the pawnbroker was gone now and the food cupboard was almost bare. She had no idea how they were going to manage. There was no chance of paying the rent and she shuddered each time she thought of Seth Grimshaw's slobbery lips. There had been no sign of the doctor either so now she was losing hope of being offered the position at the undertaker. Surely, he would have been back to tell them if Mr Chevalier had been interested in employing them?

Thankfully, Reuben was slowly making progress and managing to hobble about quite well on his crutch, although he still daren't put any weight on his injured ankle and was as prickly as a hedgehog with frustration. He seemed to spend his time hovering between being optimistic that it would fully recover to being in the depths of depression in case it didn't, and there wasn't a thing she could do about it. Sometimes it was a relief just to get out of the cottage, even if she hadn't had any luck whatsoever in securing a job for herself yet. It certainly wasn't for the lack of trying. She'd tried every inn, every large house that she passed and every factory that she could think of. Now she was concentrating on the shops, even the ones on the fringes of the town. After all, anything was better than nothing, she reasoned.

As she walked along she found herself glancing from left to right, even though it was broad daylight, as once again she thought of her mother. It was still so hard to accept that she had gone out one evening to deliver some ironing and never returned. Or at least not alive. Her battered, lifeless body had been carried back to the cottage the following morning by two miners who had found her in Rapper's Hole on their way to the local pit, and even now Nessie couldn't think of it without tears springing to her eyes. It had only been during the past few months that she had dared to set foot out of the door again, but she was still anxious because despite a massive police hunt, as yet no one had been brought to justice for the murder.

They had given their mother as good a funeral as they could manage, which had left them dreadfully short of money and they seemed to have stayed that way ever since. The worst of it was, her mother wasn't the only victim. Over the next few months, two other local women had been found dead, each of them beaten until their poor faces were almost unrecognisable. The first had been a prostitute from the whorehouse in town, but the other woman was as respectable as her mother had been and so the police could find no link that might help trace the killer.

Knowing that the murderer was still out there somewhere was a constant worry, and that was why Reuben had got so irate when Marcie had stayed out late, or even, now and again, not come home at all. Nessie knew the scars of their mother's death would never leave them and every day was a struggle, but Nessie had inherited her mother's courage and so she went on doing her best to block out the horror of what had happened.

She had almost reached the top of the Cock and Bear hill when the sound of horse's hooves reached her and glancing over her shoulder, she saw the doctor in his trap heading towards her. He had a young man at his side and as he drew level he reined the horse to a halt.

'Ah, Nessie.' He smiled a greeting. 'I was going to call in to see you this afternoon. I just might be the bearer of good news. You see, Mr Chevalier has agreed to meet you. If you're going into town you could perhaps pop in and see him and have a word?'

Nessie's heart jumped with joy in her chest. Oh, if only they could secure this job their troubles might be over!

'I'd give you a lift,' the elderly doctor went on kindly. 'But I've got young Dr Dorsey here with me. He's going to be working with me from now on and when I retire he'll hopefully take over. If he can stand the pace,' he ended jokingly as he grinned at the young man. Then remembering his manners, he said, 'Oliver, this is Miss Nessie Carson. Her family are patients of mine.'

The young man removed his hat and inclined his head revealing a thatch of thick, blond, wavy hair and she noticed that his eyes were a lovely shade of blue. Then, realising that this must be one of the sons from Haunchwood House, she blushed and bobbed her knee as her heart began to beat faster.

'It's nice to meet you, sir,' she said politely as he bestowed a broad smile on her.

'It's very nice to meet you too, Miss Carson.'

Flustered, Nessie turned her attention back to Dr Peek and he went on, 'As I was saying, Mr Chevalier isn't promising anything, he can be a stubborn devil, but at least he's willing to meet you so it might be in your interest if you called in.'

'I shall go there straight away,' Nessie promised.

'Good, then I shall keep everything crossed for you,' the doctor told her good-naturedly. 'His premises are in Abbey Street, you shouldn't have any problems finding him.' And with that both gentleman doffed their hats and went on their way.

Nessie stood for a moment, wondering why the young doctor had made her feel so flustered. He's certainly the most handsome man I've ever seen, she thought, then, shaking her head, she set off with a spring in her step and soon she came to the funeral parlour, which she thought looked very shabby and uncared for from the outside. The window was grimy, as was the thick velvet curtain hanging inside it. A marble angel statue stood in solitary splendour in the window and the sign hanging above the door read, *Chevalier's Funeral Parlour;* even that was in need of a lick of paint. The thought of working, let alone living, in such a gloomy place filled her with dread, but then she wasn't in a position to be choosy so after taking a deep breath and drawing herself up to her full height, she pushed thoughts of the young doctor aside, opened the door, setting a bell jangling, and stepped inside.

It was even gloomier inside than out and it took some seconds for her eyes to adjust. When they did she wasn't at all impressed with what she saw. She was in a large square room with three doors leading off it and against the far wall was a long, wooden counter which was so thick with dust she could have written her name in it. No wonder he doesn't do much trade, she thought, noticing how the dust motes danced in the light that was struggling through the dirty glass. The door behind the counter opened and a tall, thin man dressed all in black appeared. He was younger than Nessie had expected him to be, somewhere in his mid- to late thirties, she supposed, with curly dark hair and solemn grey eyes, and he didn't look at all well.

'Good morning, may I help you?'

She was further surprised to find that he spoke beautiful English with only the slightest hint of a French accent, which was quite attractive.

'I'm Wednesday Carson, but I'm known as Nessie. Dr Peek told me that you may possibly have work for myself and my brother.'

'Ah yes, of course.' He shook her hand and when he smiled his face was transformed. 'Perhaps you would like to come through to the back where we can talk in private?'

Nessie inclined her head and followed him into the room he had just emerged from, stifling a sigh of dismay as she saw the state of the place. This was clearly his living room but it was very neglected. A dead aspidistra on a pot stand drooped dolefully in one corner of the room and a sofa covered in dirty cushions was placed before an empty fireplace that was choked with dead ashes. There were dirty pots and reams of paper everywhere she looked.

Seeing her look of dismay he spread his hand apologetically. 'I am afraid I am not the best at keeping house, as you can see. The good doctor probably told you that my employees recently left, yes? Since then I 'ave been trying to do everything for myself and not making too good a job of it. But, forgive me, you 'ave not come to speak of my housekeeping skills. Now tell me about your brother. He is good at carpentry, yes?'

'He's *very* good,' Nessie assured him. 'And I am very good at keeping house. I have had to be since my mother was ... since she died.'

'Ah yes, the good doctor told me of what happened to your *maman*. It was most tragic.'

His eyes were sympathetic and Nessie felt herself warming to him. For a moment they stood in awkward silence, until he said, 'Perhaps I should tell you what would be involved with the job should we feel we would be suited to each other, yes?'

She nodded and he told her of his requirements before showing her around. The only place he didn't show her was what he called the cold room where he prepared the bodies for burial.

'It can be a little upsetting until you become used to it,' he explained.

She nodded in agreement before asking, 'How

did you come to be in such a profession?' They were back in the living room by then and she noticed that some of the furniture looked to be quite fine pieces beneath the thick layers of dust and grime. She could already imagine what the place might look like when it was all clean and sparkling.

'My papa was an undertaker in France. He trained me to take over his business some day and so when I came to England it seemed natural for me to continue with work I knew. Unfortunately, trade isn't too good so I would not be able to pay you or your brother a high salary. Your board and keep and perhaps a few shillings each a week? I'm afraid that is all I could afford, that is if we think we will be compatible?'

'That would be quite acceptable,' Nessie answered. 'But there is one other thing. I have a young ... er ... brother, Joseph, you see. He's not yet two years old and I would have to bring him too.'

'A child?' He frowned. He'd had little to do with children and wasn't sure how he felt about that. 'Is he a quiet child?'

'Oh *yes*,' Nessie assured him quickly. 'You never hear a peep out of him, he's as good as gold.'

'Hmm.' Mr Chevalier tapped his lip, looking uncertain, but then he sighed as he stared around at the chaos he was living in. The girl in front of him was shabbily dressed but spotlessly clean and she sounded intelligent and honest, the sort of person he needed to deal with his customers.

'Before I make a decision, perhaps I could see a sample of your brother's work, yes? Something he has carved?'

Nessie's mind was whirling as she wondered what she could show him. Most of the furniture Reuben had made was far too heavy for her to carry into town and until Reuben's ankle had healed he certainly couldn't. And then it occurred to her.

'Why don't you come to our home and then you can see a number of pieces he's carved?' she suggested hopefully. 'You could meet Reuben too, which is important if you might be working together.'

He nodded. 'I could do that but it would have to be later this evening after I 'ave closed the shop, you understand? I may be called upon to fetch a body should someone pass away.'

'Of course.' Nessie smiled at him, then taking the piece of paper and pencil he handed to her she hastily wrote down their address and gave him directions. It seemed that there was nothing more to be said so she shook his hand and followed him back into the shop where he courteously held the door open for her.

'Until this evening, *mademoiselle.*'

She nodded and set off for home, her stomach churning with excitement, bursting to tell Reuben their good news.

He was watching from the window for her as she neared the cottage and when she ran in with a smile on her face he raised an eyebrow. 'I take it you managed to find yourself a job then?'

'*Better* than that. I think I might have found us both one and *somewhere* for us all to live rent-free.' She hurried on to tell him about her meeting with

98

the doctor and going to introduce herself to Mr Chevalier and he listened in amazement.

'Crikey,' he said when she halted to draw breath. 'You have had a busy morning but what's this Chevalier chap like?'

She screwed her nose up as she tried to think how best to describe him. 'Well ... he's very tall and painfully thin, in fact I didn't think he looked very well,' she began. 'He's got dark hair and grey eyes and he's much younger than I thought he'd be. I expected an old man with a big waxed moustache but I should think he's in his thirties and quite good-looking. He's nice too and after a while I felt at ease with him. But you'll see for yourself when he calls this evening so now you can help me tidy up. I don't want him to think we live like pigs.'

Reuben grinned ruefully. The whole place was spotless, just as it had been when their mother was alive, because Nessie was forever cleaning. All the same he limped across to the sink on his crutch to wash up the few pots that were there.

It was almost seven o'clock that evening when the sound of a horse neighing had Nessie rushing across to the window. She twitched the curtain aside just in time to see Mr Chevalier tie a jet-black stallion's reins to the picket fence that surrounded the garden and set off up the path.

'*He's here!*' she hissed urgently, her eyes scanning the room to ensure that everything was clean and tidy. When the tap came at the door she opened it almost instantly and ushered him inside, wishing that they could have afforded some oil for the lamps in honour of their visitor. They looked so much better than the guttering candles but they would have to do.

Reuben rose from the settle and hobbled across to shake the visitor's hand. 'I'm Reuben Carson, sir. Nessie has told me all about you.'

'Andre Chevalier.' He accepted Reuben's hand and then his eyes went to Joseph who was sitting quietly on the settle chewing on a crust, not even aware that they had a visitor. 'And this must be Joseph?' He crossed to stroke the child's hair but when he got no response whatsoever Nessie saw a flicker of something in his eyes. Was it pity? Mr Chevalier had obviously realised that Joseph wasn't behaving as most almost two-year-olds should. Instantly she crossed to the child and gave his shoulder a little squeeze, which earned her a rare smile that melted her heart before she turned her attention back to their visitor.

'Do sit down,' she gushed, pulling out a chair from the kitchen table. 'Would you like a cup of tea? I was just about to make one, wasn't I, Reuben?' She knew that she was gabbling but she was so nervous she couldn't seem to help herself. While she hurried over to warm the teapot, Reuben joined Mr Chevalier at the table and soon the two were quietly chattering away as their visitor explained to Reuben what would be expected of him.

'So, I wouldn't have to actually *do* anything to the dead bodies then?'

Nessie could hear the relief in Reuben's voice.

'The only time you would be called on to touch a body is when we collect the deceased from their home. Then once you 'ave helped me get them into what I term "the cold room" I would proceed with the embalming. Once that is done and I 'ave prepared them for burial I may need help lifting them into the coffin but other than that, no. It is more the carving of the coffins that would be your job and helping to get them to the church service on the day of the funeral.'

He looked around the room then at the things Nessie pointed out to him that Reuben had carved and he was impressed.

'Carving the coffins should be easy compared to some of the things you 'ave made here.' He narrowed his eyes and stared at Reuben pointedly then asked bluntly, 'But are you sure you will be strong enough to do this job ... your ankle...'

Reuben flexed his muscles, almost making the buttons on his shirt pop. 'It's only my ankle that is weak,' he said. 'The rest of me is fit as a fiddle and I'm strong as an ox.'

'Then in that case, when would you wish to start? Shall we say in another week? That will give your ankle a little more time to heal.'

Nessie looked on in delight as Reuben nodded. 'Done!'

And so it was decided and she could hardly wait for their new life to begin.

Chapter Nine

'Oh, I've just had a thought,' Nessie said the next morning as she divided porridge into three dishes. They'd been practically living on the damn stuff for days to try and eke out the rest of their food. 'How are we going to get word to Marcie that we're moving? When she gets her first day off and comes home we shall be gone.'

As usual at the mention of his youngest sister, Reuben's face darkened. 'I dare say we'll just have to get Mrs Hewitt to look out for her and tell her where we've gone,' he answered. Despite his words he did care about Marcie deep down and Nessie knew it.

Nessie chewed on her fingernail as she stared towards the window, perplexed. 'But that seems a bit heartless, doesn't it? I could write her a letter, but maybe it's better if I go to the house and leave word for her at the kitchen door.'

Reuben shrugged. He was coming to terms with the fact that he would soon be living and working at an undertaker's but he still wasn't completely happy about it and knew he'd miss working outdoors on the railways with his mates. Still, he supposed he should be grateful that he had a job, any sort of job, at least.

'You could try I dare say.'

Nessie scowled at him as she helped Joseph to eat his porridge. If she left him to feed himself she knew that half of it would go down his shirt front. He ate the food complacently, opening his mouth like a little bird each time she offered him the spoon. 'Reuben, do you think Joseph's head looks a little too large for his body?' she asked suddenly and Reuben looked at the child closely.

'I suppose it does look a bit out of proportion,' he admitted after a while. 'But don't get reading anything in to it. No doubt it will level out as he grows.'

'What do you mean – *level out!'* Nessie snorted in disgust. Joseph didn't even smile as often as he had anymore and with every day that passed she became more and more concerned about him; he was so little and vulnerable. When we've got some money saved after we've started our new jobs I'm going to take him to see a good doctor, she silently vowed to herself, as she gave the child a loving smile and carefully wiped the dribbles from his chin. Joseph simply stared vacantly ahead.

Later that day Nessie set off for Haunchwood House, keen to share her good news with her sister. Much as Marcie had been, at her first glimpse of the place she was a little overawed at the size of it. Standing in thirty-six acres of ground it was a grand setting and her eyes were fixed on the house as she marched purposefully down the drive. She had almost reached it when a man on horseback came cantering towards her. As he drew closer Nessie saw that it was the young doctor she had met with Dr Peek. Her heart began to pound. Would he accuse her of trespassing? But she needn't have worried because as he drew closer his face broke into a smile and he reined his black stallion to a halt, looking down at her. The magnificent animal pawed at the ground, impatient to be off again.

'Why, it's Miss Carson, isn't it?' He could never forget those beautiful tawny eyes. 'What brings you here?'

Suddenly Nessie's lips were dry and she found that she couldn't take her eyes off him. 'Actually, my sister recently started work here,' Nessie explained awkwardly, her heart pounding. 'And as my brother and I secured the post at the undertaker's with Dr Peek's help I wanted to let her know that we would be moving. I hope that's all right, sir?'

'That's wonderful.' He looked truly happy for her. 'And of course, you must share the good news with her. Just follow the path around to the back of the house and you'll see the kitchen then I'm sure someone will find her for you. Good day, Miss Carson.'

He dug his heels into the sides of the horse and it was off like the wind. Nessie stood and watched them go for a second, impressed at how in tune man and beast seemed to be, then she went on her way with a funny little fluttery feeling in her stomach.

Fortunately, the kitchen door was opened by Marcie herself and her mouth gaped wide when she saw Nessie standing there.

'What are *you* doing here?' she greeted her and Nessie grinned.

That was so typical of Marcie. However, she had no time to answer before a voice behind

Marcie shouted, 'Who is it at the door?'

Marcie flushed as she shuffled from foot to foot, sure that she was going to be in trouble. 'Er ... it's me sister, Cook.'

'Then ask her in out o' the cold, girl,' the cook ordered. 'Ain't yer got any manners?'

Marcie reluctantly stood to one side as Nessie stepped past her and instantly addressed the woman she assumed was the cook, saying, 'I'm so sorry to disturb your work. But the family will be moving house shortly and I didn't want Marcie to come home on her first Sunday off and find us not there.'

'Going somewhere nice are yer?' the cook asked pleasantly as she paused from kneading the dough in front of her.

'My brother and I are going to work for Chevalier's Undertaker in the town.'

The cook frowned. 'Oh yes, he's French, ain't he? I've heard as he don't mix much. Happen that's why most o' the locals favour Smith's. But anyway, that's by the by. I wish yer well. An', Marcie, pour yer sister a cup o' tea. You can have a quick tea break with her if yer like.' She went on with what she had been doing as Marcie led Nessie to a chair at the side of the fire and hurried away to get them a drink.

'She seems nice,' Nessie whispered once she was holding a cup of hot, sweet tea. She had almost forgotten what sweetened tea tasted like so it was a treat.

'Huh! She's a bloody old slave-driver, I knows that much,' Marcie grumbled as she sipped at her own drink. 'Sometimes me feet hardly touch the

105

floor from the minute I get up till the second I tumble into bed of a night. An' look at me poor hands.' She held one out expecting sympathy. 'They're in an' out o' water all day long.'

Nessie grinned and wondered how long Marcie would stick it. She'd never been one for hard work. She hurriedly told her about the new job she and Reuben were going to then and when she'd finished, Marcie grimaced.

'Ugh, I reckon I'd rather do what I'm doin' than have dead bodies all round me.' She shuddered at the thought of it. 'Couldn't you have found something better than that?'

Nessie raised an eyebrow. 'You should know how hard it is to find a job,' she scolded gently. 'And we'll be fine. We actually have our own rooms to live in at the back of Mr Chevalier's and they're a lot nicer than the ones we live in now. At least they will be when I've given them a good clean and we've got our own things in them. Mr Chevalier has been really helpful. He's going to send a cart so that Reuben doesn't have to do too much heavy lifting till his ankle has healed a bit more. He's getting better by the day now and Joseph is fine too,' she ended, painfully aware that Marcie hadn't asked about either of them.

'Oh, er ... that's good.' Marcie had the good grace to look slightly embarrassed but then, as always, her thoughts turned to herself again. 'So will I still be able to come an' see you on me days off?'

'Of course you will,' Nessie assured her. Then quickly draining her cup she handed it back to Marcie. She didn't want to take advantage of the cook's good nature. 'I'd best be going then.' She thanked the cook for her hospitality as she passed her and Marcie saw her to the door.

'See you soon then, be good.' And with that she hurried back the way she had come, half hoping for another glimpse of the young Dr Dorsey. He wasn't at all what she had expected. He had spoken to her on a level and he was very good-looking. She blushed at the thought. She'd never looked at a young man in that way before and was confused why he should be any different. Don't be daft, she scolded herself. He's miles away from me in class and he'd never look at me even if I wanted him to, which I don't, of course!

Her thoughts were interrupted by the sound of horse's hooves again and she saw yet another horse pounding down the drive towards her. But to her disappointment it wasn't the young doctor. It was a young woman this time and Nessie rightly guessed that this must be the daughter of the house. The horse she was riding was quite magnificent, pure white with a long, flowing mane. But as it drew closer she saw that the poor thing was foaming at the bit and its rump was crossed with weals from the girl's riding whip.

The girl reined him to an abrupt halt and glaring at Nessie, her fine eyes flashing, she demanded, 'Who are *you*? Are you aware that this is private property and that you are trespassing?'

She was staring down at Nessie as if she was rubbish and Nessie instantly drew herself up to her full height and stuck her chin in the air.

'Actually, I have just been to visit my sister who is one of your employees,' she told her haughtily.

'Well, if you've seen her then I suggest you get off our land now,' the girl snapped and with that she brought the whip down on the horse's flank and disappeared in a cloud of dust. She wasn't used to be being spoken to by the working class in such a way and she'd speak to her mother about making sure the servants were not allowed to have visitors in the future!

Nessie was equally riled as she marched through the gates and onto the main road. That girl needs bringing down a peg or two, she thought. She was so angry that she didn't notice someone walking towards her until they were almost level.

'Well, well, if it isn't pretty little Miss Carson!'

Nessie started and when she raised her eyes to find herself face to face with Seth Grimshaw, her heart sank. That was all she needed after the confrontation she'd just had with the stuck-up little madam!

'Good day, Mr Grimshaw.' She forced herself to remain calm and polite although she wanted to lift her skirts and run away as fast as she was able to. She would have carried on but he had positioned himself in such a way that she couldn't unless she made a point of stepping past him.

'And what brings you into this neck of the woods then, little lady?'

He had that look on his face again, as if he could see right through her clothes, but she managed a weak smile. What could he do to her here in broad daylight after all? And she was going to have to give him notice sooner or later so she may as well get it over with.

'Actually, I've just been to see Marcie...' She

faltered for a moment. 'To tell her that we're leaving the cottage. I was going to give you notice when you came for the rent. The problem is, I don't have it, but I do have a new job so as soon as I'm paid I shall make sure you have anything we owe you immediately.'

The smile slid from his face. 'Leaving the cottage? To go where?'

Nessie didn't really think it was any of his business but she supposed he would find out where they had gone eventually. Word spread quickly in small communities.

'We're both ... that is Reuben and me, are going to work for Mr Chevalier in the town and it's a live-in position so we shall be moving within the next few days.'

'The *undertaker?*'

She nodded, expecting him to get angry but to her surprise he simpered. 'And you say you can't give me the rent before you leave?' When she shook her head, he let out a long, drawn-out sigh.

'Now that *isn't* good, is it? Most landlords would tell you to get out straight away if you can't pay your way. But I like to think I'm a fair man so...' He reached out to touch her cheek. Her skin looked as soft as satin and he could feel himself hardening. He was having sleepless nights thinking about this young lady. The way her hair glinted in the sun, those deep, tawny eyes, the pert breasts straining against the coarse material of her work blouse. She was turning into a very attractive young lady and he knew he wouldn't rest until he'd bedded her.

Nessie slapped his hand away and stepped back

from him, her eyes hard. It's funny, he thought, how they seemed to change colour depending on her mood. When she was smiling they reminded him of an amber brooch he had once seen in a jeweller's shop window, but now they were as dark as treacle.

'I've just told you we'll make sure you get your money and I always keep my word. But if it's a problem I'm sure Mrs Hewitt would let us stay with her until we take up our new posts.'

'No, no, my dear, I'm sure there'll be no need for that.' He licked his fat lips. She was like an untrained filly; she needed to be treated gently. 'I trust you. Just bring the money you owe to my house when you have it. You do know where I live?'

She nodded and to her surprise, he gave a courteous little bow and went on his way. She sighed. He was a strange one but at least she'd told him now and it was a weight off her shoulders. Feeling slightly better she moved on.

Mr Grimshaw, meanwhile, was feeling very pleased with himself. I handled that well, he thought. And when she does turn up with the money she owes I shall demand a little bonus!

Chapter Ten

One week later on a cold, drizzly day in late October the cart that Andre Chevalier had promised to send rolled up outside the cottage. For the next hour they were busy loading their possessions onto the back of it and then, after lifting little Joseph to sit beside Reuben, Nessie hurried away to say goodbye to Mrs Hewitt.

'Eeh, luv, I shall miss yer,' the kindly woman sniffed, wiping her eyes on the edge of her apron.

'We shall miss you too,' Nessie told her. 'I don't know what we'd have done without you since my mam...'

'Don't get thinkin' about sad things today,' the woman urged, catching her to her ample breasts in a fierce hug. 'Think o' this as a new beginnin' and make sure you come an' see us from time to time. An' you just be sure to look after those fellas an' all,' she added with a tearful smile for Reuben and Joseph.

'I will,' Nessie promised, then after planting a kiss on her cheek she skipped out to the cart and clambered onto the back with the furniture.

The driver smiled and urged the horses on and Nessie looked behind her just once to wave to Mrs Hewitt. She felt no sadness at leaving the place. It held a lot of unhappy memories for her and she hoped, as Mrs Hewitt had said, that this might indeed be a change in their fortunes.

When they reached the town, the driver urged the horse through the large gates at the side of the funeral parlour and into the yard beyond. The two coal-black horses that pulled the glass-sided hearse were stabled there and they stuck their heads over the tops of their stalls to see what was going on.

'This is it then, Joseph.' Nessie smiled at her little brother as she lifted him down. 'Your new home and I hope we're all going to be really happy here.'

The child stared vacantly ahead, only a little sound escaping his lips, and once again Nessie felt a flutter of anxiety, but now wasn't the time to go worrying about Joseph again. They had things to do.

The rear door opened and Mr Chevalier stepped outside.

'Ah, you're here. You will be wanting to get settled in to your rooms. I, er ... got you a few provisions in case you hadn't had time to shop. I hope they will be acceptable. I am afraid I am not too good at such things so I merely got the basics. I do hope you will not be offended?'

Offended? Nessie thought. Why, that was wonderful; they hadn't had a decent meal in days so anything was going to be gratefully received.

'That's very kind of you,' she told him as she followed him into their new home. There was a living room-cum-kitchen with a sink, and an oven at the side of a small inglenook fireplace where she could cook. Above that room were two bedrooms, one quite a decent size and one that was smaller, which would suit Reuben. She saw that he had also taken the trouble to light the fire, which made the grubby room look quite cosy, even on such a dull day and she was more grateful than she could express. There were tears glistening on her lashes as she glanced around, deciding where their furniture would go.

'It is no trouble at all,' he assured her. 'So now I will leave you to get yourselves organised. Perhaps tomorrow I can show Reuben the workshop where he will make the coffins and you could perhaps start work in the shop and tidy my rooms, yes?'

'Oh yes,' she assured him.

With a little bow he took his leave and Nessie crossed to look at what was in the bags he had left on the draining board. There was a twist of tea and sugar along with a jug of fresh milk. Fresh fish from the fishmonger, a selection of fresh vegetables and some nice pork chops from the butcher as well as some apples and oranges. Nessie's mouth watered at the sight of such a feast. She couldn't remember the last time she had tasted an orange and thought how they would do Joseph the world of good.

Reuben's ankle was greatly improved, although he was still unable to put his full weight on it and had to keep it tightly strapped, but all the same he and the man who had fetched them eventually had all the furniture stacked into the room. Nessie wished she could have given the man a tip, he had been so helpful, but she didn't have so much as a ha'penny in her purse, so instead she thanked him profusely and he went on his way.

'Right!' Her eyes sparkled as she flung her shawl over the chair and rolled her sleeves up. 'Let's make this place into a home!'

After fetching water from the pump in the yard outside she began to scrub the windows and the floors while Reuben heaved the beds upstairs. It took him twice as long as it normally would but he managed it eventually. Nessie, meanwhile, dragged the horsehair sofa in front of the fire and settled Joseph down on it for a nap. She hung the curtains her mother had so lovingly stitched then began to place their mismatched china onto the dresser, and slowly, very slowly it began to look homely. When she was happy with downstairs she carried the bucket upstairs and did the same up there, and at last, as the afternoon darkened, everything was put away and the place gleamed from top to bottom.

'It ain't very big, is it,' Reuben commented dismally when they finally stopped for a well-earned cup of tea. A pan of vegetables was bubbling above the fire and in the oven the fish was slowly poaching in milk.

'No, I don't suppose it is, but at least we won't have to worry about paying rent and we'll be earning,' she pointed out. 'Beggars can't be choosers, Reuben, so let's just make the best of it, eh?' Hearing the note of annoyance in her voice, he shrugged. He supposed she was right but he still felt hard done by. It seemed they'd had nothing but bad luck for the last couple of years and he wondered when it was going to end.

When Nessie came to dish the dinner up he noticed that she was laying out four plates and he raised an eyebrow.

'I'm doing some for Mr Chevalier,' she informed him in a voice that brooked no argument. 'It's the least I can do seeing it was him who supplied the food. Looking at how thin he is, I doubt he ever bothers to cook for himself.'

'Suit yerself,' he mumbled, slinking lower down in the armchair and glaring into the fire.

Nessie suddenly felt sorry for him. His work on the railway had been arduous but she knew that he'd loved being out in the fresh air. She wondered if she'd perhaps been a little hard on him and said gently, 'Things will work out, you'll see. Remember what Mam used to say, "Things always look better in the morning."'

When she knocked on Mr Chevalier's door some minutes later, he glanced down at the steaming plate of food in her hand in surprise. Over his shoulder on the table in his kitchen she could see a loaf of bread and a block of cheese and she guessed that this was probably what he had been about to have for his dinner.

'Why I, er ... please, come in. You really didn't need to go to so much trouble.' He held the door wide and Nessie quickly crossed to the table and put the plate down.

'It's no trouble at all to cook for an extra one when I'm cooking for us anyway,' she assured him. 'I hope you enjoy it.' She left him quickly, smiling as she glanced back through the door to see him hurrying to fetch a knife and fork. Poor chap, she thought, I bet he doesn't bother with a hot meal very often.

Despite being in a new home, Nessie slept well that night and the next morning she got up in an optimistic frame of mind. Marcie had a job, one she could do well in if she tried, and now she and Reuben were set up too. They might even be able to afford a doctor to look at Joseph soon, but not until she'd paid Seth Grimshaw what they owed him. Nessie always kept her word and that would be her priority.

After breakfast, she reported to her new boss who was going over some figures in a large ledger in the reception room of the funeral parlour. It was the first place people saw when they came to book his services and she thought how dismal it was.

'Reuben said to tell you he'll go through to the workshop with you whenever you're ready,' she informed him brightly. 'And while you're showing him what you want him to do, I thought perhaps I could start cleaning in here and fetch you if anyone comes needing your services... I will have to bring Joseph through with me, though, but he'll sit quietly on the chair,' she ended almost apologetically.

He raised a questioning eyebrow. He'd had very little experience of young children but he'd never seen a little one who could sit still for more than two minutes at a time. The ones he had seen were all over the place and into everything.

'But will he not get bored?'

'Oh no.' She twisted her hands nervously. 'Joseph is ... a quiet child.'

'I see, then if you are sure you can manage I shall go and instruct Reuben.'

Minutes later, Nessie had assembled everything she would need to give the place a thorough spring clean and Joseph was sitting as still as a statue, just as she'd said he would. She began with the floors, getting down on her hands and knees and scrubbing into all the nooks and crannies. Occasionally she disturbed a spider and almost leapt into the air when it scurried away. Again and again she carried the filthy water out to the yard and replaced it with clean but at last, after her third attempt, she could see the pattern on the floor tiles, and very nice they were too, she thought. Next, she unhooked the heavy velvet curtain from the window, sneezing as a shower of dust got up her nose. That would need a good wash too and she dreaded to think how long it would take to dry. It would be no use hanging it in the yard. The weather was damp and miserable and getting colder by the day. She would have to rig up a line in their kitchen and let it dry in the heat from the fire. It was a deep purple colour and despite the filth she couldn't stop herself from stroking the lush fabric, imagining how beautiful it would look when it was clean and fresh. She tackled the windows next and when Mr Chevalier returned just as she was finishing she glimpsed the surprise on his face as he looked around.

'*Mon dieu!*' he exclaimed, slipping easily back into his native language. Then remembering himself, he hurried on, 'Excuse me, please, I meant to say goodness me! What a difference you have made to the place in such a short time.'

It didn't feel like a short time to Nessie. Her dress was soiled from where the water on the filthy floor had soaked through her apron and there was a smudge of dirt on her nose.

Even so she grinned. 'It's surprising what a bit of elbow grease will do. I've just got the desk and the furniture to polish now and then I'll start on your living quarters. But before I do ... may I suggest something?'

He nodded so she hurried on, 'I was thinking that it might be nice to keep a vase of fresh flowers on that table over there by the window. It's traditional for people to bring flowers to a funeral so it might be nice for the people who require your services to see some in here. It needn't cost that much if we bought them from the flower stall on the market. And perhaps a nice mirror on the wall over there? It would brighten the place up.'

She watched him looking about, his face solemn and held her breath. Oh dear, I shouldn't have interfered, she reflected.

'I, er ... I'm so sorry,' she stammered. 'I wasn't trying to interfe–'

'What sort of a mirror?'

She gulped and wiped her grubby hands down the sides of her skirt. 'Well, perhaps a nice big one to reflect the light in a mahogany frame to match the desk?'

He tapped his chin with his forefinger as he stared at the wall, trying to picture it in his mind, then nodded. 'Yes, I think perhaps you are right,' he agreed, much to her relief. 'And perhaps when you have a little spare time you could go and choose some flowers and a vase?'

'I'd be happy to.' She started to rub beeswax polish into his desk as if her life depended on it and when next she glanced up he had disappeared into his living quarters.

When the furniture was gleaming in the light that streamed through the freshly washed window, she took the curtain outside and put it to soak in the tin bath they had brought with them from their old home. It was far too big to fit into a bucket and she was horrified to see the way the water changed colour to a sludgy brown when she immersed it. It was almost lunchtime, and she wondered where the time had gone as she hurried back inside to collect Joseph and returned to her own kitchen to prepare something light for lunch.

Reuben came in when she was halfway through carving a loaf of bread and she looked at him questioningly. 'So, how's it going then?'

He sniffed. 'All right, I suppose. Although I have to admit I never realised there was such a choice of woods for coffins. It seems pine is the most used here because that's the cheapest. Then there's all the handles: rope for the cheapest ones right up to solid brass and bronze. You can get lead-lined coffins an' all, but they're custom-made in London and the boss said he don't get much call for them. It's only the toffs as can afford 'em.'

'I can quite believe it, but I'm sure he'd get more trade if he spruced the place up a bit and made the shop look a little more salubrious. I've already made a few suggestions.'

'Bein' French wouldn't help him either,' Reuben agreed. 'The folks round here take a while to get used to somebody from foreign parts.'

Nessie giggled. 'I don't think it's that; he's been here for some years already,' she pointed out. 'But do you think you'll manage?'

'It's quite easy.' Reuben laughed. 'But how are you gettin' on. You look like you've done a shift down the pit!'

Glancing down at her dirty apron and skirt, she shrugged. 'Well, the whole place is so dirty I'm just having to scrub everything. Wait till you see the shop area, it looks different already and when I get the curtain back up and put some fresh

119

flowers in there it'll look better still.' She placed a plate full of sandwiches in front of Reuben then began to break little pieces off another slice to feed to Joseph. He opened and shut his mouth but made no attempt to feed himself and Nessie sighed with concern.

'Is it all right if I start the cleaning in your living quarters now?' she asked Mr Chevalier after lunch, but before he had time to reply the door opened and a middle-aged woman appeared, her eyes red-rimmed from crying. Nessie discreetly stood to one side as Mr Chevalier rose to greet her.

'Good afternoon, madam, may I help you?'

The woman sniffed and taking a grubby handkerchief from her pocket she mopped at her eyes, which were streaming tears again.

'It's me husband... He's died an' I need to arrange his funeral.'

'Very well,' Mr Chevalier said matter-of-factly. 'What sort of funeral did you have in mind?'

'Well ... it all depends how much it's gonna cost,' she spluttered. 'I ain't got much money, see? An' there'll be nowt comin' in now he's gone.'

Mr Chevalier placed a large brochure on the counter with the various styles of coffins and headstones available and when she looked at the prices she gasped with dismay.

'But I can't afford these,' she choked. 'Not even the cheapest one.'

Nessie had the urge to take the poor soul in her arms and offer words of comfort to her but not wishing to interfere she forced herself to remain silent. Then taking up her bucket and her rags she hurried into Mr Chevalier's living room and closed the door firmly behind her. She wasn't at all impressed with the way he had handled a prospective client and thought it was no wonder that people chose to go to the other undertaker, but she couldn't say that, of course. Minutes later she heard the shop door close again and guessed, rightly, that the woman had left. She was down on her hands and knees scrubbing the floor when Mr Chevalier came to join her looking crestfallen.

'That's another customer lost,' he commented with a frown. 'But surely they can't expect me to offer my services for free?'

Nessie sat back on her heels and looked up at him. She had come up with an idea that just might work but wasn't sure if she should suggest it. Would he think she was interfering?

'Do you lose a lot of customers because of cost?' she asked.

He nodded. 'Oh yes, most of the people who come here have barely got two ha'pennies to put together. I do make exceptions for children, though. If one dies I take them and put them into the coffin of the next paying customer and just charge their parents a penny.'

Nessie was horrified. 'So the parents never know where their child's final resting place is?' she asked in disbelief.

'I'm afraid not but at least they get the comfort of knowing they will be buried in hallowed ground.' He shrugged. 'I think that's better than having to have them put in a pauper's grave,

121

don't you?'

Nessie went back to what she was doing, too appalled to answer. From what she could see, a lot of changes needed to be made here but she felt it was too soon to suggest them.

Chapter Eleven

Her first Sunday off had finally arrived and as Marcie stretched and yawned in bed that morning, she smiled. It was so lovely not having to get up in the dark and set about lighting the fire in the kitchen. It was her most hated job, though, if truth be told, she didn't like any of the chores she had to do. Still, she told herself, today was hers to do as she wished with and she intended to enjoy every minute. Eliza, she noted, was already up and about, no doubt in the washroom getting herself ready to go to see her family.

Marcie, too, was meant to be going home. Nessie was expecting her and had promised to have a nice dinner ready for her, but Marcie had made other arrangements. The fact that Nessie would worry when she didn't turn up hardly entered her head. Marcie, as usual, was thinking only of herself.

Today George was taking her out for the whole day! And on the train too; she had never been on a train before and could hardly wait. He was taking her to Coventry where, he'd said, there was less chance of them being seen together, and although that had rankled, she had agreed. They were going to visit the cathedral and then he had told her he would take her somewhere really swanky for lunch.

She frowned as she wondered what she should wear. Even her Sunday best outfit was terribly outdated and shabby but she supposed it would have to do for now... Unless Eliza had something she could borrow. The thought made her spring out of bed and when Eliza returned from the washroom with her hair damp and a towel over her arm she found Marcie waiting for her and smiling sweetly.

'I don't suppose you have something pretty I might borrow just for today, do you?' she asked. 'Only I want to look my best seeing as I haven't seen my family since I started here and I can't buy myself anything until I get paid.' She felt no remorse whatsoever for lying.

'I dare say I could find you something.' Eliza crossed to her chest of drawers and began to rummage through it until eventually she held up a rather pretty white blouse. It was high-necked with ruffles down the front and at the cuffs.

'This might fit you if you have a skirt to go with it,' she suggested. 'I don't think my skirts would fit you.'

Marcie eyed the blouse. It was a huge improvement on her own, though not what she would have chosen, if truth be known. It would mean she would have to wear her own skirt which was darned and well past its best, but then she supposed it was better than nothing.

'Thanks, and I don't suppose you've got a nice

123

shawl I could borrow as well, have you?'

Eliza looked uncertain as she held up her Sunday best shawl. She'd been intending to wear it herself today but reasoned she could wear her old woollen one. She was only going to visit her family after all. Of course, Marcie was too, hadn't she just told her so? But then she probably wanted to make a good impression when visiting their new home for the first time in case she bumped into her family's employer.

'Here, take this.' When she held the shawl out, Marcie's eyes lit up. It was made of a thick woollen material that had a slight shimmer to it. It was a lovely pale green colour that reminded Marcie of the leaves on the trees when they were first beginning to unfurl in the spring, and it was edged all around with a deep fringe.

'Thanks.' Marcie snatched the shawl greedily in case Eliza should have a change of heart and then she too hurried off to the washroom, impatient for this special day to begin.

By the time she came back to their room, Eliza was just leaving and once the girl had gone, Marcie began to pin her hair up and get ready herself. The blouse actually looked much better on than it did off and with the pretty shawl about her shoulders she preened in the cracked mirror above her chest of drawers.

'Hmm, not bad, even if I do say so myself,' she told her reflection as she pinched her cheeks to add a little colour to them. Then, snatching up her bag, she set off for the railway station. This was another thing that she and George had argued about. He would be driven there in his father's carriage and it seemed silly for her to have to walk but George had again pointed out that it was still too soon for anyone to guess what they meant to each other. Far better that they meet on the platform, he had insisted, and having little choice Marcie had reluctantly agreed.

It was a good walk into town and by the time the train station came into view, Marcie's teeth were chattering with cold. But she forgot about her discomfort as she hurried to the platform and headed for the waiting room; George shouldn't be long now. Meanwhile she warmed her hands at the little fire that was blazing in there and hummed merrily to herself. When the clock on the platform struck the hour, the first flickers of unease sprang to life in her stomach. George was cutting it very fine. But then, as she knew of old, he was almost always late.

At five past ten the train roared into the station like some great monster belching smoke and steam into the sky. Marcie had never been so close to one before and felt quite nervous about getting aboard. Mind you, if George didn't hurry, she wouldn't be getting on at all. She began to count the minutes and then the seconds until suddenly the monster shuddered and roared into life again and pulled away from the platform. Tears of frustration sprang to her eyes. Where was George and what should she do now? She began to pace up and down the close confines of the waiting room and eventually decided that there was bound to be another train. If George was merely late they could catch that one, but she'd give him what for when he did show his face, she promised herself.

At half past ten she ventured back out onto the road outside to see if there was any sign of him. She was so frustrated that she felt she might explode. This was the one day a month she had to herself, the *only* day, and here was George making her waste it hanging about for him. When the cold once more began to bite into her she returned to the waiting room and as she passed the ticket office the man there smiled at her sympathetically.

'Been stood up have yer, luvvie?'

Marcie bristled, drew herself up to her full height and stuck her chin out proudly. 'Not at all,' she answered. 'My friend has probably just been delayed, that's all.'

He nodded and she went back to the waiting room where she continued to pace. As the minutes passed, Marcie was fairly sure that he wasn't going to come. With what pride she could muster, she once more left the waiting room and sailed past the ticket office into the street outside. Only then did she allow her chin to sink to her chest as she tried to swallow back her tears. She had been looking forward to this day for weeks. The question now was, what was she to do with the rest of her day? She baulked at the thought of returning to the house. Those of the staff that were there were bound to ask questions and in the mood she was in Marcie was afraid she might give them more than they'd bargained for. It was too cold to just walk the streets, so that left her with only one alternative. She would have to go and visit Nessie and the rest of the family, as she'd promised.

Her steps dragged as she walked away from the station, her eyes still trained on the road ahead as she prayed for a sight of the fine Dorsey carriage, but the streets were almost deserted.

She had no trouble at all in finding Chevalier's Undertaker and she paused outside to stare at the exterior. It looked much nicer than the last time she'd passed it, she thought. Down to Nessie, no doubt. She stepped inside and almost immediately a door behind the long, highly polished counter opened and a gentleman appeared. This must be Mr Chevalier, she thought. He was much younger than she'd expected and quite good-looking too, so she instantly batted her long, dark eyelashes at him and dimpled into a sweet smile.

'I'm here to see Nessie, she's my sister,' she explained and he gave her a welcoming smile.

'But of course, she did tell me that she was expecting you today. Go through that door there, their living quarters are out the back.'

Marcie gave a little bob of her knee and sashayed towards the door he had pointed to. As she pushed it open the heat wrapped around her like a warm blanket.

'Marcie!' Nessie had been in the process of basting the pork joint in the oven but now she rammed it back in and with a cry of joy she raced across the room to welcome her sister. Reuben was sitting in the chair by the fire but he barely glanced up from the newspaper he was reading. He and Marcie hadn't got on well for a long time now and he found he couldn't pretend to be pleased to see her when he wasn't. As for Joseph,

Marcie barely glanced at him as she submitted to Nessie's embrace but that was nothing new.

'So, how are you? You look well. Do you like your job? Are they treating you all right?'

Marcie, who was still stinging about George letting her down, held up her hand to stop her sister's flow of words.

'I'm fine and it looks like you are too. You've dropped on your feet here, haven't you? I haven't seen a fire like that for some time, and real coal an' all. An' that Frenchman is quite handsome, ain't he?' As she spoke, she took off Eliza's shawl and flung it carelessly across the back of a chair.

'I think we have actually.' Nessie looked around at their little home and beamed with pride. Everything gleamed, from the floorboards she had painstakingly waxed and polished to the old copper pans suspended above the fireplace. 'Mr Chevalier is more than generous,' she gushed as she reached for the big stone teapot. 'We can help ourselves to as much coal as we need from the coal shed in the yard and he's more than kind when it comes to food. I cook him a meal each day but he insists on giving me enough money to feed us all. We've already almost saved up enough to pay off Mr Grimshaw. Then we're going to start saving for a doctor to look at Joseph.' Her smile vanished as she glanced at the child who was sitting on the rug staring at the brightly coloured bricks in front of him. He didn't even play with them anymore.

'I think you'll just have to accept that he's a simpleton,' Marcie said flatly, helping herself to sugar from the heavy glass bowl in the middle of the table.

'Marcie, how could you say such a horrible thing!' Nessie was clearly distressed but Marcie merely shrugged.

'I'm only voicing what you don't care to admit.' She stirred her tea, ignoring the tears in her sister's eyes and her brother's angry glare. *Why can't they see it?* she asked herself, as she forced herself to look at Joseph. He was like a little cabbage sitting there yet they both clearly doted on him. Still, at least she was well out of it and soon she would shock them when George made her his wife. She imagined herself rolling up outside in the Dorsey carriage to see them and her smile returned. Even though he had let her down badly she was sure he must have had good cause to.

The next few hours went by in the blink of an eye and soon the afternoon was darkening. Marcie didn't have to be back till seven o'clock but she was eager to seek George out and was bored with listening to Nessie go on about how kind her new employer was.

'Right, well I'd best set off,' she said, lifting Eliza's shawl and wrapping it tightly about her head and shoulders. An icy wind had blown up and she could hear it howling around the courtyard outside.

Nessie immediately looked concerned. 'Do you have to go so soon?' She knew that she would have to wait another whole month before she saw her sister again and she was worried about her walking home alone. The madman that had killed their mother and the other two women was still out there somewhere.

'I'll walk you back, if you like? You shouldn't be out on these streets alone.' Reuben offered but Marcie shook her head.

'I shall be fine.' She gave Nessie a perfunctory kiss on the cheek then without another word she left, leaving her sister worriedly gnawing on her lip.

'Do you think she'll be all right?' she asked Reuben anxiously.

He gave a snort of laughter, but beneath it he felt the same fears. 'Well, put it this way, I don't think much o' the chances of anyone who tried to set on our Marcie. She's got more spirit than a bottle o' raw gin. I guarantee they'd come off the worse.'

And with that Nessie had to be satisfied.

It seemed to take forever for Eliza to fall asleep that night and Marcie waited impatiently, staring at the moonlight struggling through the window, but at last Eliza began to snore gently and, still fully clothed, Marcie crept out of bed. She reached the stables in no time. She knew every stair that creaked in the servants' quarters now and had perfected her escape each night.

'George,' she hissed as she let herself into the stables. The horses snickered but other than that all was silent. The Dorseys were entertaining some close friends of the family, according to Eliza, so she knew she would have to be extra vigilant this evening when she returned to the house. Some of the other maids were still rushing about serving drinks and the last thing she wanted was to bump into any of them. Quietly she climbed the ladder to the hay loft then she sat impatiently, rubbing her hands together to try to keep them warm. After what seemed like an eternity her patience was rewarded when she heard the barn door open and footsteps crunching across the hay. And then hands on hips she waited for George to appear. He could see at a glance how angry she was and began to fawn over her.

'Oh, Marcie, I'm *so* sorry I had to let you down.' He held his hands out to her in supplication but she slapped them away. 'Father informed me first thing this morning that we had company coming for the whole day and ordered me to be there. They're close friends of my family that we've known for years and he puts a lot of business my father's way, so I could hardly refuse. I did try to find you to tell you but you must have already left for the station. I'm so very sorry. Try to imagine the position I was in.'

Slightly mollified, Marcie sniffed. She supposed he had been put in rather an awkward position and the last thing they wanted was to upset his father right now.

'Just so long as you don't do it again,' she muttered and before she knew it she was in his arms and he was fumbling with the buttons on Eliza's best blouse. From the second she stared into his deep-blue eyes and ran her fingers through his thick, blond hair she began to soften. Her blouse was open now and as he gently fondled her breast, her nipple stood erect and she sighed with pleasure as he lowered his head and gently began to tease it with his tongue. Then suddenly she was on her back in the hay and his hand was stroking her most private parts and she was putty in his hands. The fact that he had let her down flew right out of her head as she gave herself up to the pure pleasure of their lovemaking.

Chapter Twelve

'I've got enough money now to pay Mr Grimshaw what we owe for the back rent,' Nessie informed Reuben as they sat at breakfast one morning the following week in early November. She had already redeemed her mother's precious wedding ring, which she again wore on a piece of ribbon about her neck, although she hadn't bothered to redeem her best bonnet. She considered that to be a luxury and was more interested in paying back their former landlord.

'Huh! I shouldn't bother,' Reuben growled through a mouthful of bacon. 'The state that cottage of his was in he should have paid us to live there!'

'Even so, we owe him. You know how religious our mother was about paying her debts.' A lump rose in her throat as a picture of her mother's poor battered face on the night they had brought her back to the cottage flashed in front of her eyes. She still had nightmares about it but she kept her tears for when she was tucked up to Joseph's warm little body in bed at night where no one could see them.

'Then I'll take it to him,' Reuben said grudgingly and she couldn't help but breathe a sigh of relief. 'It'll have to be this evenin' though. I doubt you'll catch him at home durin' the day.'

When Nessie nodded he turned his attention back to the meal in front of him and she found herself smiling. It was so nice not to have to worry about where the next meal was coming from anymore. Mr Chevalier had begun to look a little better since she'd been making sure that he had a hot meal each day too. It was lovely to be warm as well, although Nessie was careful not to take advantage of her employer's generosity and, despite his urging her to take as much coal as she wanted, she only took what they needed to keep the place comfortable. It was the same when she shopped. She would scour the shops and the market to get the very best prices and she always returned any money left over to him immediately she got home.

As for Andre, his admiration for Nessie had grown. The whole place was spick and span, and Nessie had worked tirelessly since coming to live there. Every window gleamed, every carpet had been taken into the back yard and beaten to within an inch of its life and every floor shone. Reuben was proving to be a great help too, although Andre was concerned that he didn't appear to be as content as his sister. He had gone with him the day before to collect a body to prepare it for burial and it was obvious that he didn't feel comfortable being around the dead. Still, Andre hoped that this was something he would get used to in time. He did all the preparations and embalming himself when necessary so all Reuben had to do was help him collect the deceased and then settle them into the coffins once they had been prepared. His carpentry was second to none, but he just wished that the business was doing a little better. The people of the town still tended to use the rival parlour, despite the fact that he tried to keep his rates reasonable.

He commented as much to Nessie as she was polishing in the front office that morning and she paused to look at him. She had been in the office twice that week when grieving customers had come to see him and she was concerned about the reception he had given them. Needless to say, they had taken their custom elsewhere but now Nessie wondered if she should voice some suggestions. Would he think she was trying to interfere in the running of his business? Glancing up from the ledger he was working on, he noticed Nessie's tentative expression. 'Was there something you wanted to suggest, perhaps?'

Nessie wondered if he was a mind reader as she rose and came to stand in front of the small desk he was sitting at. 'Well...' she began carefully, 'I couldn't help but notice how distraught the parents of the child who had died were when they came to see you the other day.'

He raised an eyebrow. 'Surely that is to be expected? I offered them the chance to bury their child for a penny in the coffin of the next paying client I had but they refused it. What else could I do? They clearly couldn't afford any other sort of burial.'

'I understand that ... but perhaps there is a way

134

to get around it? Especially as so many children die in the winter, particularly in the courtyards.'

He frowned now and inclined his head for her to go on.

Nessie gulped. 'I was just thinking that perhaps you could offer a way for people to pay a certain amount each week or month after the funeral until the amount it would cost is paid off? The majority of these poor people are honourable and I'm sure they wouldn't let you down when they see that you are giving their children a proper burial place where they can go to pay their respects. Also, I was thinking... Well, when they first visit you, they are grieving and sometimes in shock. Perhaps you could show them sympathy and offer refreshments. Just tea and a little kindness...'

Her voice trailed away as she saw him tapping his lip. She was terrified she might have upset him and mumbled, 'I'm so sorry, Mr Chevalier. It wasn't my place to poke my nose in.'

'No, no, not at all.' He was nodding ardently now. 'I think this could be a *very* good idea. But please, no more Mr Chevalier, it is so formal. Call me Andre and with your permission I shall call you Wednesday, yes?'

She blushed and nodded as she plucked at her apron and he smiled. 'Forgive me for asking but your name is most curious, is it not?'

She smiled. 'Yes, I suppose it is. My mother told me she called me that because she was in labour with me all day on the Tuesday and then when I was finally born at one minute after midnight on Wednesday morning she decided I should be named after the day I was born on. But please, call me Nessie, like my family do.'

He nodded, then became serious again as he began to think about her suggestions. After a moment he said, 'I too have a suggestion to make to you now but I am not sure how you might feel about it.'

'Then go ahead and tell me what it is,' she urged. Somehow, she felt that they had crossed a line and she could speak more on an equal footing to him now.

'The thing is...' He spread his hands and sighed. 'I do not have what you might call the right manner with people. My father always told me so. Oh, I have knowledge on embalming but I find it difficult to speak to strangers, so I was thinking – and do say if you do not like this idea – but I was thinking that perhaps *you* could welcome the people who come to the funeral parlour.'

'*Me!*' Nessie looked shocked but he nodded vigorously.

'Yes, I have noticed that you have a very kind nature. I have seen how tender you are to Joseph and I'm sure that you could do a wonderful job with the families of the deceased.'

'But I don't know the first thing about the prices of funerals and coffins or anything,' she pointed out.

He waved her concerns aside. 'That is something that I can teach you but foremost I would like you to be the one to greet the bereaved when they arrive here. Show them sympathy and offer refreshments as you suggested, it is a splendid idea, then for the time being I can go over the financial side of things with them.'

Nessie stared at him doubtfully. Mr Chevalier looked every inch the undertaker in his smart black frock coat and sober grey waistcoat, whereas she ... she glanced down at her darned skirt and apron, she looked exactly what she was: the cleaner. Once again, he seemed to be able to read her thoughts and he smiled.

'Of course, we would need to get you a new gown,' he said softly. 'Something discreet, in perhaps black or grey or even mauve or purple.'

Now she shook her head as pride set in. 'I don't have enough wages saved up yet to be buying new gowns,' she told him with her chin in the air. She had actually never had a brand-new gown in the whole of her life but she wasn't going to tell him that of course.

'No, no, you misunderstand me. It would be my pleasure to buy whatever you need. After all, it is for my benefit, no?'

'Well ... I suppose so,' she said uncertainly. She still wasn't at all sure if this was the right thing to do. After all, she had only been employed to keep house for him. But then, as his face fell, she relented and said, 'Oh, I suppose we could give it a try.'

He nodded with a wide smile on his face. 'Good, then perhaps now you would be kind enough to tell me what you think we should charge monthly for the cost of a funeral. You will have more of an idea what the people hereabouts could afford than me.'

And so, for the next half an hour they sat side by side as he explained the costs to her. He was impressed to find that she seemed to have a good grasp of English and maths and once more she went up in his estimation.

'It will be so nice for the poor parents who have lost a child to know where their little ones are buried and for them to be able to say a proper goodbye to them in a church,' she said when they had finally settled on a sum that seemed reasonable.

'Quite, and tomorrow you must go and see the dressmaker and be measured for a new gown and...' he flushed slightly as he shifted from foot to foot uncomfortably. 'And, er ... buy whatever it is that ladies need ... petticoats etc. And of course, some suitable footwear and a warm cloak.'

'But all that will cost a fortune,' she remarked, deeply embarrassed.

He waved aside her objections. 'As you know, I am away from the shop each Saturday evening and so I have to close it,' he pointed out. 'But with you on the premises to deal with the bereaved and Reuben here to fetch the bodies I shall no longer have to lose custom. The new clothes will be an investment and will pay for themselves in no time at all, especially once it becomes known that we are willing to let people pay a little each month for the cost of funerals.'

'Well, if you put it like that...' Nessie nodded her agreement, and so it was decided.

'You'll never guess what,' she said to Reuben that evening as they sat down to their meal of juicy lamb chops and mashed potatoes with winter cabbage. She hurried on to tell him about her

138

conversation with their employer and he paused with his fork halfway to his mouth to listen to her. When she'd finished, he frowned.

'I'm surprised he didn't think yer were over-steppin' the mark,' he remarked.

'I thought that too but in fact he thought my ideas were excellent.' She glanced at Reuben and saw that he looked none too pleased at all.

'If you ask me I reckon he's got his eye on yer.'

She was so shocked that she almost dropped her knife as she gawked at him. 'Don't be so silly,' she scolded. 'Why, Mr Chevalier, Andre is years older than me!'

'Oh, *Andre* now, is it,' he said with an ironic grin. 'And what difference does your age make? Most men like a young wife.'

Annoyed, Nessie turned to Joseph who was sitting quietly beside her and spooned some mashed potato into his mouth. 'That's the most ridiculous thing I ever heard,' she said scathingly and the rest of the meal passed in silence.

Soon after they'd finished, Reuben set off to pay Seth Grimshaw what they owed him before visiting the local inn. He'd taken to doing this on a fairly regular basis now and it concerned Nessie a little. Reuben had never been a drinker, but she knew he was still struggling to adjust to his new job. Once Nessie had settled Joseph in bed she cleared away all the dirty pots into the sink and as she worked, her mind was buzzing with ideas. Perhaps she should also suggest that Andre made more of the tiny chapel of rest at the back of the shop. It was somewhere loved ones could say goodbye to the deceased before the coffin was

139

closed, but if the dust in there was anything to go by, it hadn't been used for some time. Humming softly, she lost herself in plans.

Chapter Thirteen

When Seth Grimshaw opened the door to his cottage to find Reuben on the doorstep he frowned and looked across his shoulder before barking, 'Whadda you want?'

Reuben glowered as he thrust some money towards him. 'I've brought what we owe yer so that's an end to it now an' I'll thank you to leave us alone in future.' Even though the money had been promised, Seth had called at the funeral parlour demanding payment twice since they had moved there, causing Nessie a great deal of embarrassment.

Reuben turned to leave but Seth wasn't done with him yet. 'Hold yer horses,' he snapped. 'I need to check it's all here. I should rightly fine yer fer leavin' as quickly as yer did wi'out givin' proper notice.'

Reuben snorted in disgust. 'You'll find it's all there, all right, down to the last penny,' he informed him coldly. 'Though how yer can charge what yer do fer such hovels is beyond me.'

Seth bristled but Reuben was already walking away so he slammed the door and seethed. He'd been hoping that Nessie would bring the money herself but still, he wasn't done with that little filly yet, not by a long shot. He licked his lips and rubbed the bulge in his trousers as he thought of her ripe young body. I'll have her one way or another, he promised himself, as he threw the drink down his throat. In the meantime, he'd perhaps pay a visit to the local whorehouse.

The next morning, once Nessie had done her jobs, Andre insisted that she pay a visit to the dressmaker's shop, so mildly excited at the thought of owning a brand-new outfit, she set off into town.

The woman was helpful when Nessie explained what sort of gown she needed and brought out bolts of material for her to choose from. She looked longingly at the rolls of fine satins and silks in all the colours of the rainbow but then turned her attention to the more sensible choices. Eventually, she chose a soft, mid-grey fine wool and the woman nodded her approval.

'It will look a treat when it's made up, and it will be very warm and practical for the winter,' she assured her. 'Perhaps I could trim it with black braid and buttons from the waist to the neckline?' She got busy with the tape measure then and when she was satisfied that she had all the measurements she needed they chose the material for a warm cloak in a slightly darker shade of grey. She had a number of petticoats already made and once she had suggested which ones she thought would be suitable for beneath the gown she wrapped them up for Nessie to take with her. The next stop was the bootmaker where Nessie ordered a pair of lace-up boots with a small heel in soft, black leather. The boot-maker assured her that he would have them ready within a week and she almost skipped home in her excitement as she tried to imagine how she would feel dressed in new clothes from head to toe. Her happy mood vanished, however, when she stepped back into their kitchen to find Reuben standing over Joseph who was lying on the stuffed horsehair sofa.

'He ain't well,' her brother told her and instantly she rushed to the child. Andre was there too, looking concerned.

'What's wrong with him?' She felt the child's forehead and was worried to find that he had a fever. His face was flushed and his eyes were bright and he was whimpering softly like a little wounded animal.

'I think we should send for the doctor,' Andre said, but Nessie shook her head. All the money they had managed to save from their wages had been paid to Seth Grimshaw the night before and there was nothing left for doctor's fees.

'I'll just keep my eye on him for today,' she responded, trying not to show how panicked she felt. 'He's probably just coming down with a little chill. I'm sure he'll be better by morning.'

Andre didn't look too sure about that but had no wish to interfere. 'As you wish,' he said politely and with a little bow he turned and left the room. Shortly after, Reuben left too. They had to collect a body, never one of his favourite jobs, and he wanted to get it over and done with. That was one side of the business that he was still struggling with.

For the rest of the day, Nessie hovered over

Joseph, forcing him to take sips of water and trying to encourage him to eat with little tempting treats she had made for him but he refused everything, his damp body clinging restlessly to Nessie for comfort.

'I think I'll stay down here with him tonight,' she told Reuben over dinner that evening. 'It's warmer.'

It was one of the longest nights Nessie had ever known. Joseph tossed and turned and although she repeatedly sponged him down with cool water his temperature refused to come down. Reuben found her exhausted the next morning when he came downstairs and told her, 'It's no good. We're going to have to call the doctor. He's not getting any better, is he? And he can't even tell us if he hurts anywhere.'

She nodded resignedly. Reuben was right, there was no other option left to them now. They would just have to promise the doctor that they would pay him as soon as they were paid.

Reuben slid his long arms into his coat and lifting his walking stick he went out into the yard. He hated using the damned thing, as he thought of it, but had found that his ankle pained him far more in the cold weather and the stick took some of the pressure off it. Andre was at the stable door when Reuben appeared. He often began his day by checking on the horses and he raised an eyebrow to see him out and about so early.

'You're an early bird,' he commented.

Reuben shrugged. 'Joseph is no better so I'm just off to ask the doctor to call to have a look at him.'

Andre frowned. 'Please, allow me to call for you. I have to go into town anyway.'

'Well ... if yer sure.'

It was mid-morning when there was a tap at the door and Nessie hurried to answer it, shocked to find the young Dr Dorsey standing there. For no reason that she could explain she became all of a fluster and blushed furiously as he removed his hat and gave a gallant little bow. He was so tall that she had to look up to him, and she found it hard to look away from his handsome face and his deep-blue eyes.

'Good morning, Miss Carson. Mr Chevalier called earlier to the practice to say that your young brother is unwell?'

She really didn't know why she was so surprised to see him. Dr Peek had informed her that Oliver Dorsey was joining the practice so it was natural that he would begin to do some of the older doctor's house calls.

'Th-that's right,' she stammered as she tried to regain her composure. She was suddenly aware of how awful she must look after the sleepless night she had just had and raised her hand to try and tame her mass of copper hair which hung loose about her shoulders. She motioned towards Joseph, 'He's over there.'

'Right.' He smiled at her reassuringly before approaching the sofa where Joseph was lying and dropped to his hunkers. 'So, young man, not feeling so good, are we?'

When Joseph continued to stare into space uncomprehendingly, the first flutter of unease started to life in the pit of his stomach. Without even examining the child he knew that this was something much more serious than a common cold or virus.

Nessie meanwhile went to fill the kettle at the sink and set it onto the range to boil as the doctor gently began to feel about the child's head and body.

'Is he normally an energetic child?' he questioned and Nessie slowly shook her head.

'Not really...'

'I see, and how is his speech coming on. He must be going on for two years old now so he should be saying quite a few little words.'

Nessie lowered her eyes and shook her head miserably. 'He doesn't say anything,' she admitted in a small voice.

'Ah, and does he run about and play?'

Her silence was his answer and he sighed as he again began to gently feel about the little boy's head. Joseph moaned softly until eventually the doctor rose and took a seat. Minutes later Nessie handed him a cup of tea and after thanking her he sipped it and cautiously peeped at her over the rim.

'I have no wish to alarm you,' he said eventually, replacing the cup gently in the saucer. 'But I thought I detected a swelling on Joseph's head. Has he tumbled recently or banged himself?'

Reuben had just entered the room and it was he who answered, 'He don't even move about. Just stays wherever you put him with a blank look in his eye.'

Dr Dorsey's concerns were growing by the minute. 'In that case, if you have no objections, I

145

would like my partner, Dr Peek, to take a look at him too before I voice what I think may be wrong with him.'

Panic flared in Nessie's lovely tawny eyes and the doctor's heart went out to her. She clearly loved the little boy and if his suspicions were confirmed he feared that there could be no happy outcome for the poor chap.

'I ... I don't think we can afford to let Dr Peek look at him yet awhile because...'

Oliver Dorsey raised his hand to stay her words. 'Please don't worry about that. Mr Chevalier has already settled the bill and told me that I must return as often as necessary at his expense.'

Nessie flushed again. She was proud and it went sorely against the grain to know that her employer was paying for Joseph's medical expenses, but then she vowed she would pay him back, every last penny, no matter how long it took. She nodded. 'Very well. Thank you.'

The doctor rose and passed her his empty cup and saucer, telling her, 'Hopefully Dr Peek will be able to accompany me back here later this afternoon. Would that suit you, Miss Carson?'

She nodded numbly. A terrible sense of foreboding had come over her. If Joseph had something seriously wrong with him, she would rather live in ignorance, but of course she couldn't do that for his sake. 'Very well, thank you, doctor.' She was strangely comforted by the young doctor's presence; he seemed such a caring man and Nessie was sure he would do his best for the child. Perhaps, with Dr Dorsey's help, she'd be able to face whatever was to come for her poor little brother.

When he had gone she sank down onto the nearest chair and stared at her older brother fearfully. 'What do you think might be wrong with him?' she asked in a wobbly voice.

Reuben sniffed and avoided her eyes. He had known for some long time that something was severely amiss with Joseph but knowing how much Nessie doted on him he had tried not to voice his concerns too much.

'I'm no doctor so I can't say, love,' he answered eventually. 'But if there is sommat wrong it's best we know, surely?'

She had already accepted deep down that he was right but still she dreaded the doctor return-ing and found herself watching the clock like a hawk. Even so when the tap on the door came late that afternoon, Nessie almost jumped out of her skin. She had washed and tidied herself as best she could, although there was nothing she could do about the dark circles beneath her eyes. Now, straightening her apron, she glanced at Joseph who was sleeping at last and went to answer it.

'Dr Peek, Dr Dorsey, thank you for coming.' She held the door wide and the two men stepped into the room, letting in a blast of cold air that made the fire crackle and spit. 'I, er ... I'll make us all a nice hot drink while you see Joseph, shall I?'

She was relieved when Dr Peek nodded. She needed to be doing something other than watch-ing them poke and prod the little boy. As she busied herself with the teapot she could hear the two doctors speaking quietly together as they leaned over the patient and she was relieved when the door opened and Reuben appeared. At least now, if they were going to give her bad news, she wouldn't have to hear it alone.

The examination seemed to take forever and every now and again she glanced anxiously over her shoulder at them but at last they both stood and Dr Peek told her kindly, 'We'll have that tea now, if you please, Nessie.'

Nessie nodded and brought the tea over to the table. She was so nervous that she sloshed some of it over the snow-white tablecloth.

Dr Peek sipped at his drink as he stared into the flames of the fire, wishing he were a million miles away. The Carson family had been through so much already in the time since he had known them, yet through it all they had battled to keep the family together with Nessie at the heart of it. Now he was about to add to their heartache and there was not a damn thing he could do about it.

Eventually, he laid his cup down on a small table and glancing at the brother and sister who stood side by side, as if drawing comfort from each other, he told them gravely, 'I'm afraid it's not good news.'

There was a sharp intake of breath from Nessie but she remained silent as she nervously twisted her apron into folds.

'For some time, on the rare occasions when I've seen Joseph, I have feared that something was not quite right with him.' He rubbed his brow wearily. 'I have suspected some sort of brain damage, which I fear there is. But worse, Dr Dorsey and I now believe that Joseph has a growth in his brain.

That would account for his head looking rather too large for his body.'

Nessie stood unblinking for a second, as if she had been turned to stone, but then her words came out all in a rush as she spurted, 'So what can be done for him?'

The two doctors glanced at each other and it was Oliver who replied, 'Unfortunately, we fear because of the position of the growth it is inoperable. Even if it wasn't, Joseph is so young and small I doubt he would survive such a huge operation. However, I do have a colleague in London who specialises in this sort of thing who might be able to give you a second opinion if you wish it?'

'I see.' Nessie knew that they could never afford to pay such a doctor and everything seemed hopeless.

Oliver Dorsey was impressed with the young woman's composure. Her eyes told of the devastation she was feeling but she kept her dignity as she asked, 'So ... will he die?'

His Adam's apple bobbed up and down as he slowly nodded. 'I'm afraid so.'

'How long has he got?'

Dr Peek shrugged before answering, 'It's hard to say. It all depends on how fast the tumour is growing. We can have no way of knowing that. It could be months, it could be years, but what I will say is that we can keep him relatively pain-free for whatever time he does have left. There are medicines we can prescribe that will keep the little chap happy and calm. I'm so sorry I can't give you better news.'

Nessie nodded as she struggled to hold back

149

the tears that were stinging her eyes. 'I see. Thank you.' But she didn't see, not at all, and inside she was screaming, *No, no no!* This can't be happening. They were still struggling to come to terms with the loss of their mother and now they must face losing Joseph. It seemed so unfair!

'We will leave you now but do let us know if you would like our London colleague to visit him,' Dr Dorsey said kindly, gently patting her arm.

Nessie was so deep in shock that she barely noticed the doctors leaving and Reuben had to see them out. How were they ever supposed to find enough money to have such a man visit Joseph all the way from London?

'We shall have to let Marcie know,' she told Reuben dully and he snorted.

'Huh! And do you *really* think she'll be interested? She's barely been able to bring herself to look at him since he drew breath!'

Nessie knew that he was right and lowering her head she finally allowed herself to weep at the injustice of life.

Chapter Fourteen

'Eeh, I'm all in, an' that's a fact,' Cook said as she lowered herself into the fireside chair and kicked her slippers off. Her feet felt as if they were on fire.

Marcie pouted bitterly as she carried yet another pile of dirty pots from the table to the sink.

She felt as if she was fighting a losing battle because as fast as she managed to wash them, the maids delivered another lot and she was beginning to think that she would be standing there all night!

The Dorseys were giving a party and by the sounds that were echoing along the hallway they were all having a whale of a time. The maids had been scurrying to and from the dining room all day, laying the table with the mistress's finest china and silverware. Mid-afternoon, Cook had allowed her to slip along to take a peep at the table and the sight of the glittering cut-glass goblets, the snow-white napkins and the vases full of fresh hothouse flowers had almost taken her breath away. It had also made her feel bitterly resentful. If only George would tell his family that he loved her then she would be in there with them instead of skivvying here in the kitchen while he enjoyed himself.

She winced as she angrily plunged her sore hands into yet another sinkful of hot water. The Dorseys had had some friends of the family staying with them for three days now and during that time George hadn't managed to slip away to see her once, which had further added to her bitterness. Even worse was the fact that one of the maids had confided to the kitchen staff that the friends had a rather pretty daughter who had been flirting shamelessly with George. Her name was Belinda, by all accounts, and George took her riding each morning. She knew that because the junior groom had told them so the night before during supper. Marcie had been so affected by

151

the news that she hadn't been able to swallow a single morsel and she felt if she didn't see him soon she would burst with rage. What did he think he was playing at anyway? It was *her* he loved so why was he going out riding with this damned Belinda?

'When you've finished those pots yer can put the kettle on an' make me a nice cup o' tea.' Cook's voice interrupted her angry thoughts and Marcie scowled. *Stick a brush up me arse an' I'll sweep the floor at the same time, why don't you?* she thought as she slammed yet another dinner plate into the water. Five courses they'd served at dinner and four at lunchtime and she felt as if she'd spent the last few days doing nothing but preparing vegetables and washing up. She'd be glad when the Lewises left and woe betide George when she did get to see him an' all! Riding out with that hussy every morning, indeed!

The sound of a sweet, girlish voice echoed down the hallway, further adding to Marcie's sense of injustice.

'Cor, that Miss Belinda 'as got the voice of an angel!' Eliza declared as she came into the kitchen bearing yet another tray full of dirty pots, which earned her a glare from Marcie. Just for the duration of the Lewises' stay, Eliza had been promoted to waiting on tables at mealtimes and she was making the most of it. She felt like the bee's knees in her pretty frilled apron and mop cap and her smart black dress.

'So what's up wi' your face, then?' Eliza asked Marcie as she caught the girl glaring at her but Marcie merely shrugged and turned her attention back to what she was doing. The kitchen had been as hot as a furnace all day with the many pots and pans Cook had had bubbling away on the range and now Marcie's dress was stuck to her with sweat and the hair that had escaped from her cap was straggling damply on her forehead and at the nape of her neck. She was ready to drop with exhaustion but she knew that she wouldn't be allowed to rest until the kitchen was cleaned to Cook's satisfaction. Just for a second she felt like throwing off her apron and walking away from it all. This was so much harder than she had ever expected it to be.

It was past ten o'clock by the time Marcie wearily climbed the stairs to her bed with no chance of seeing George again. Eliza was still downstairs serving drinks and snacks and by the time she retired Marcie knew that she would be fast asleep. Ah well, she thought, with a little tingle of satisfaction, it'll serve George right if he slips across to the stables and I'm not there. She was so tired that she didn't even bother to wash, she merely threw her clothes across the back of the chair, slipped into her nightgown and slid into bed and within seconds of her head hitting the pillow she was fast asleep.

'Take that bundle of drying cloths to the laundry room. The way we're usin' 'em we'll be runnin' short at this rate,' Cook instructed Marcie the next morning. 'Then come back and get stuck into the breakfast pots afore yer start preparing the vegetables for lunch.'

With a martyred sigh, Marcie collected the

153

cloths together. Once again, she had been up since five-thirty and already she was tired with another long day stretching ahead of her. Her hands were so dry that they had cracked during the night and now they were sore and bleeding. Eliza had told her to dip them in the chamber pot saying that urine was good for sore hands but Marcie had blanched at the thought. No, she decided, she'd wait until she next went into town where she would buy some ointment for them.

As she stepped out into the bitterly cold morning she heard laughter and gazing through the thick fog she was just able to distinguish Belinda Lewis standing next to one of the Dorseys' fine horses. She was dressed in a stunning maroon riding habit and a matching feathered hat and Marcie felt a stab of envy. Belinda was laughing at something someone had said and the next second Marcie's heart started to race as she saw that it was George. He too was dressed for riding and as she watched he lifted Belinda into the side saddle and smiled up at her. Marcie's hand flew to her mouth as the cloths she had been carrying fluttered to the floor, but she was oblivious to everything except the scene before her. Belinda and George looked for all the world like a couple in love and jealousy ripped through her. George mounted his horse, a magnificent coal-black stallion, and before Marcie could move they began to trot towards her. She stood rooted to the spot, staring at him; just once their eyes briefly met but he looked quickly away and then they had gone by her.

'Why are servants so stupid?' she heard Belinda

trill with a laugh. 'We could have mowed that silly girl down in this fog.'

George laughed and made some reply but Marcie couldn't hear what it was for the sound of the horses' hooves clattering on the cobbles. Blinking back tears she bent to retrieve the cloths before hurrying on to the laundry room.

'Eeh, somebody got out o' bed the wrong side this mornin' lookin' at the face on yer,' the laundry maid commented when Marcie dumped the cloths unceremoniously next to the sink. Marcie ignored her and turning about she strode back to the kitchen with her mind all over the place. George will have some explaining to do when I next speak to him, she fumed silently. She was so angry that she even forgot about her sore hands for a time.

It was Eliza who informed them all that the Lewises would be leaving the following day and Marcie felt a rush of relief. Just one more day to get through and then hopefully she and George could take up where they had left off – after he had explained himself that was!

Once more it was past ten o'clock before Marcie was able to stagger up to bed again. The whole day had passed in a blur of scurrying here and there, preparing vegetables, washing and drying pots and dancing to Cook's tune. But at least now she knew that the guests would be leaving the next day.

'They've just gone,' Molly the parlour maid informed the kitchen staff mid-morning the next day. It was a bitterly cold and foggy day. 'An'

155

while I was helping to load their luggage into the carriage I overheard Mrs Lewis invite the master and mistress to go and stay with 'em for Christmas. Eeh, wouldn't it be grand if the mistress decides to take 'em up on their offer. We left here could have a right easy time of it.'

'Did she just invite the master and mistress?' Marcie asked worriedly.

'From what I could gather the invite was for the whole family.' Molly helped herself to a scone fresh out of the oven and got a smack on the hand from Cook, who had just put them on a rack on the table to cool. 'They have a town house in London, apparently, and I heard the mistress say how nice it would be for Miss Leonora to be able to mix with young people her age there. I think they mentioned having a coming-out ball for her.'

Marcie relaxed a little. Surely George wouldn't want to go along to something like that? He would need to stay at home to help his father keep his businesses running, particularly if the mistress and Leonora were planning on being away for any length of time. She would find out that very night, she decided. George was sure to come and meet her now that the guests had left. She began to feel a little better.

'Oh, and you should have seen Mr George saying his goodbyes to Miss Belinda. He held on to her hand as if he never wanted to let it go.'

'Really?' Cook looked surprised.

'Well, from what I can gather the two families have known each other since the children were babies and I think they've always hoped that Miss Belinda and George would get married

156

when they were old enough. Stands to reason the master would be pleased about it, don't it? The Lewises are rollin' in money, by all accounts.'

The colour left Marcie's face like water down a drain and the next second the fine china dinner plate she had been in the process of drying slid through her fingers and smashed into a thousand pieces on the flagstones.

'Butter fingers!' Cook scolded sharply. 'That were from one o' the mistress's best dinner sets. Any more breakages, my girl, an' I'll see as you pay for 'em out o' yer wages. Now get it cleaned up and be more careful.'

Feeling sick at heart, Marcie scuttled away to fetch a broom. Surely what Molly had heard, or *thought* she had heard, must be wrong. George loved *her*, she was sure of it. Even so, she barely managed to drag herself through the rest of the day and couldn't wait for the night to come when hopefully she would finally get to see him again.

Thankfully she and Eliza were allowed to retire much earlier that evening and after the hard few days they'd had, Eliza was asleep and snoring softly within minutes. It was bitterly cold in their attic room and as Marcie crept out of bed her breath hung on the air like fine lace. Within no time she was speeding across the yard to the stables and once inside she stood quite still, listening. Other than the horses snickering softly in their stalls it was silent so she pulled her shawl more tightly about her and leaned against the wall to wait.

Within minutes her teeth were chattering with cold and she began to march up and down to try to keep warm, cursing George beneath her breath. Where the hell was he, blast him! He would know that she was there waiting for him and now that the guests were gone there was no excuse for him to keep away. The time ticked by until at last she had to reluctantly admit to herself that he wasn't coming. Eventually she wearily made her way back to her room and once in bed she cried herself to sleep.

The following afternoon, as she was standing at the kitchen sink, she glimpsed George heading for the stables and making the excuse to the cook that she needed to use the privy she shot off after him.

'George ... *George!*' she hissed and turning about he frowned as he saw her beckoning to him. After glancing about to ensure that no one was watching he marched across to her, slapping his riding whip irritably against his high riding boots. Instantly she yanked him into the quiet of the dairy room and demanded, 'What the *hell* is going on? I waited and waited for you last night in the stables but you didn't come!' Her eyes were flashing fire and she looked so angry that he took a step back from her.

'I wasn't aware that we'd arranged to meet,' he said coldly and her heart sank.

'B-but we always meet there when you've no visitors,' she stammered, suddenly feeling uncertain before growing angry again. 'Molly saw you kiss that girl as they were leaving,' she spat accusingly.

'What if I did?' He shrugged. 'Our parents are

lifelong friends and we've grown up together. Why shouldn't I kiss an old friend goodbye and wish her a safe journey? I'm surprised at such a petty show of jealousy. Don't you trust me?'

Marcie's temper ebbed away and she felt foolish. 'Of course I do and I'm sorry,' she muttered. 'Shall we meet tonight?'

He nodded, clearly impatient to be off, then turning on his heel he was gone without a second glance.

Throughout the rest of the day, Marcie's emotions were in turmoil. She was afraid that George was tiring of her but if he thought he was going to get away from her that easily he was mistaken. As she began to calm down she cold-heartedly began to hatch a plan. She had always used a sponge when they made love, which she had assured him was sure to prevent her getting pregnant. But what if she were to stop taking precautions?

That evening, he arrived at the stables as promised, but she instantly sensed a difference in him. Normally his hands were all over her the second they met but tonight he sat on the hay in the loft above the stables with his arms crossed across his chest.

'I think we ought to slow down a little,' he said after a while. 'I fear we've rushed into this relationship a little too hastily and we want to be sure, don't we?'

'Sure of *what?*' Her hand snaked up his leg and she began to unbutton his flies. 'We're good together, you know we are, and I love you.'

He was tense for a few moments but then she

heard his breathing deepen and seconds later he began to fiddle with the buttons on her blouse. 'Of course we are.'

Suddenly he was his normal, charming self again as he eased her back onto the hay. His breathing became even more erratic as she fondled him through the material of his trousers with one hand and slowly undid the buttons on her blouse with the other, exposing her naked breasts. And then he thrust her hand away, struggling with his flies as he forced her legs apart and fell on her.

'Say you love me,' she said as his hands probed between her legs. *'Say it!'*

He hesitated and then, 'Of course I do, you silly girl, now shut up and let me prove it.'

Marcie smiled to herself as she did just that, lying compliant beneath him.

Chapter Fifteen

As Nessie gazed into the mirror she hardly recognised herself. The day before she had picked up her new clothes from the dressmaker and her new shoes from the bootmaker and now she could hardly believe her eyes. The dress fitted snugly into her slim waist and the full skirt billowed around her over the petticoats she wore beneath it. She had twisted her hair onto the top of her head and she felt very grown up. She just hoped that Mr Chevalier would approve when she entered the shop.

'Blimey!' Reuben croaked when she entered the kitchen. 'You look a fair treat, girl.'

Nessie flushed becomingly, loving the feel of the soft leather shoes on her feet.

'Thank you.' She smoothed her skirt self-consciously. 'I just hope Andre thinks it was worth all the money he's spent.'

Reuben chortled with laughter. 'Oh, I think it's safe to say he will. I've told you, I reckon he's got a soft spot for you.'

'Rubbish!' Nessie said a little more harshly than she'd meant to. 'I have an idea he might already have a young lady. That's probably where he disappears to every Saturday evening.'

Reuben shrugged as he rose from the table. 'We'll see. Meantime I've got work to do. I've got that expensive coffin to make for the deceased that we picked up last night. This is going to be a very posh funeral, by all accounts, so I have to make sure that the casket is perfect. It's even going to be lined; Chevalier is goin' to show me how to line it once I've finished it. The family has money and they want the best. It's the last of the mahogany he has an' he said that he's going to have to go to London to get some more once this has gone. It's shipped in from abroad, so I'm told.'

'Really, and will you be going with him?' she asked curiously.

He shook his head. 'I shouldn't think so. Somebody has to be here to keep the shop open and collect the deceased if need be while he's away.'

Nessie nodded and lifting little Joseph she carried him through to the shop where she placed him gently on a chair.

161

Andre was there looking at some paperwork and when he glanced up his mouth fell open. 'My goodness.' She could hear the approval in his voice as he eyed her up and down. 'You look wonderful. I could take you for gentry in that outfit.'

'Gentry or not there's still cleaning to do,' she told him with a grin, shaking out an apron she had brought through with her. 'I shall go about my other duties and hastily take this off when anyone enters the shop.'

He smiled his approval before disappearing through into his living quarters. Nessie glanced around to see what needed to be done and smiled with satisfaction. The large vase of lilies on the end of the desk had filled the room with perfume and the place looked totally different compared to when she had first arrived. A large quantity of lavender and beeswax polish and an enormous amount of elbow grease had seen to that. The next part of her job would begin when a customer entered the parlour. Andre had schooled her on what to ask them regarding what kind of funeral they would like for their loved one and she knew the different prices of each one and what they entailed off by heart already.

At eleven o'clock she heard the bell above the door tinkle and for a moment she froze. This might well be her very first customer and suddenly she was nervous. Even so, she hastily removed her apron, smoothed her hair and after checking on Joseph who was dozing, she entered the parlour to find the handsome Dr Dorsey and a policeman standing there.

The doctor raised an eyebrow when he saw her.

He had thought the girl he had seen before was attractive but now, in her smart new clothes, she looked utterly beautiful.

'Ah, Miss Carson.' He stared at her admiringly for a moment, then remembering himself he hastily removed his hat and smiled. 'I believe we have need of the funeral parlour's services. Unfortunately, another woman was killed last night. A miner on his way to work came across her body in the woods near Caldecote this morning. The woman was a cleaner up at Caldecote Hall and when she didn't arrive home yesterday after her shift her husband reported her missing.'

'How dreadful!' The colour drained from Nessie's face as terrible memories of her mother's brutal murder came flooding back and she wondered if the same person was responsible.

Even so, she maintained her composure as Dr Dorsey went on, 'The family is not rich but I recommended Mr Chevalier to the husband. Her body was taken back to their cottage in Abbey Green and now that the police doctor has finished his examination I wondered if Mr Chevalier might be able to collect the body and bring it here? She was the mother of three young children and the husband feels it's too distressing for them to have the body of their dead mother there until the day of the funeral.'

'Of course.' Nessie efficiently reached for a pen and paper and after carefully taking down the deceased's name and address she asked, 'Will the woman's husband be able to call in and speak to me about what sort of funeral he would like for his wife? I'm sure we can help.'

The policeman nodded. 'Aye, he'll come all right. Poor chap, he's devastated. Such a nice family they were an' all. She were a lovely girl, I've known her an' her family since she were knee high to a grasshopper.'

'It's dreadful,' Nessie agreed. 'Will we have to delay the funeral because of the circumstances of her death?'

'I shouldn't think so.' He shook his head. 'The police doctor has all he needs. It appears she was bludgeoned to death, same as the other three women.' Then remembering that Nessie's mother had been one of them, he frowned. 'Sorry, miss, I weren't thinking. But I reckon it's the same chap as did it.'

Nessie swallowed the lump in her throat before turning her attention back to Dr Dorsey and saying politely, 'Thank you for thinking of us. I shall make sure that Mr Chevalier collects the deceased as soon as possible.'

He smiled as he replaced his hat and her heart did a little flip as she stared into his deep-blue eyes, they reminded her of the colour of bluebells. He really was very handsome. 'My pleasure, Miss Carson. And now if you'll excuse us?'

The two men made to depart but at the door Oliver stopped and said hesitantly, 'May I say how lovely you look today, Miss Carson.' He flushed and disappeared through the door before she had the chance to answer. Feeling ridiculously pleased Nessie went to find Andre.

He was in the workshop with Reuben and when she told him what had happened he asked Reuben, 'Would you go and get the horse and cart ready, please? I shall collect the body immedi-ately.' He sighed. 'But how terrible for this poor family.'

Reuben nodded bitterly. 'Aye, it is.' Like Nessie he was thinking of their mother and the night she had been murdered. 'I can't understand why they don't draft in more police to catch the murderer! How many more women have got to die before they do?' Grumbling beneath his breath, he went off to do as he was asked.

'I was thinking in a situation like this that it might be nice to have the chapel of rest in order,' she suggested tentatively. Andre raised his eye-brow. 'What I mean is,' she hurried on, 'I couldn't help but notice that it hasn't been used for some time. This poor woman's husband clearly can't keep his wife's body at home because of the im-pact it would have on the children, but if we could make the chapel inviting and peaceful he could come and spend some time here with her should he wish to and pay his last respects.'

'It seems you are full of good ideas,' Andre admitted eventually. 'But as you quite rightly say the chapel is rather dirty and that's being polite. In fact, I think it has stood empty ever since I took over the business so it will take some work to make it fit for what you are suggesting.'

'Oh, don't worry about that.' Nessie smiled at him. 'I could make a start on it this evening once Joseph is in bed, it only needs a good scrub out and some nice flowers like the ones we have in the shop. I came across a nice piece of purple vel-vet while I was cleaning the cupboards out in the parlour. We could drape that across the trestle and lay the coffin on it and just make the place look more appealing and bright.'

'Very well, I suppose we could try it if you are quite sure you don't mind the extra work. And of course, all these extra jobs you have taken on will mean an increase in your wages. I can't expect you to do all this for nothing. I have to admit you have made a tremendous difference to the place already and I am most grateful. Perhaps more people will put their business my way now. I fear that because I was a man alone it put a lot of them off. My rivals are a family-run firm and people tend to feel safer with people like that.'

'Perhaps you should get married and make it into a family business then,' she teased with an impish grin. They had come to the stage now where she felt easy in his company and they were able to talk to each other. Andre merely flushed and made no reply so she told him, 'Leave it with me.'

For the first time in a long while she felt safe and secure. It was nice to have a warm bed, a roof over her head and no financial concerns. If only they could catch her mother's killer and cure poor Joseph all would be well.

Two days later, Nessie led Andre into the chapel of rest and his eyes widened with delighted surprise. The small room was spotlessly clean and on either side of the velvet-covered trestle which would hold the coffins she had filled two vases with large bunches of holly. There was a small table behind the trestle on which she had stood a large, freshly polished brass crucifix and light now flooded through the small window set high in the wall. She had even whitewashed the walls and now the room felt calm and peaceful. A fitting place for the families of the deceased to come and pay their last respects in private.

'It's quite amazing.' Andre was clearly impressed as he smiled his approval. 'I shall inform Mr Haynes that his wife is ready to be seen should he wish to come.'

Later that morning, the murdered woman was carried through and placed gently in the chapel and that very afternoon her husband arrived to see her. Nessie offered him tea and sympathy and after showing him into the chapel, she discreetly took her leave and left him to grieve and say his goodbyes. When he eventually emerged back into the funeral parlour she could see that he had been crying but he looked more at ease than when he had arrived.

'She looks beautiful and at peace, thank you,' he breathed. Nessie gave him a sympathetic smile, thankful for his sake that his wife's face was unmarked. Andre had managed to cover the injuries on her body with a sheet.

'Would you like us to bring your wife home to lie there for the night or would you rather we take her straight to the church tomorrow for the service?' she probed gently. She had arranged the funeral for the following day at Chilvers Coton Church. This was yet another job she had offered to take on for, as she had told Andre, most relatives were too distressed to wish to bother with all the details and funeral arrangements.

'I think it might be easier for the children if we

all meet you at the church,' he muttered. 'And now I must pay you for all the trouble you've gone to.'

Nessie shook her head. 'No really, there's no need for you to worry about that right now. After the funeral we shall send you a bill. Everything we have done will be itemised and then you may call in and pay Mr Chevalier at your convenience.'

He seemed quite surprised. Most people wanted paying straight away for services rendered, and this young woman had been so kind. She had been like a little bright light at a very dark time in his life. He wouldn't forget it.

A couple of days later the bell over the funeral parlour door tinkled yet again and Nessie was faced with a distraught young woman from the courts in Abbey Street.

'Me babby's died,' she told Nessie as tears streamed down her pale cheeks. 'And me man is on short time so ... I was wonderin' if Mr Chevalier would do me a penny funeral. He did one fer me last year when another o' me little 'uns passed away.'

Nessie's heart went out to her as she gently led her towards a chair and pressed her into it. 'I think we can do much better than that. But first let me get you a nice hot cup of tea.' The young woman was as skinny as a rake and there were dark circles beneath her eyes. Her clothes were threadbare and thin, not at all suitable for the bitterly cold weather outside and she looked as if she hadn't had a decent meal in ages. Nessie decided she would bring through some of the scones she had baked that very morning too.

The woman drank the tea greedily and two of the buttered scones that Nessie offered on one of Andre's fine bone china plates disappeared in the blink of an eye.

'Sorry,' the woman apologised, spraying crumbs everywhere as she gulped the food down. 'I er … ain't had no breakfast today.'

Nessie thought it would be truer to say that she hadn't had a good square meal in days but discreetly didn't comment, instead she asked gently, 'How old was the child who has died?'

The woman's eyes instantly flooded with tears again as she gripped her shabby shawl about her skinny shoulders and answered, 'Seven months. His name is … was Stephen.' She gulped and tried to compose herself before going on, 'It were the influenza bug that everyone seems to be comin' down wi'. He were never a strong little chap an' he were just too weak to fight it. The same happened to one o' me girls this time last year, but I've still got three livin'.'

Nessie was shocked. The poor soul couldn't have been more than in her mid-twenties and yet years of hardship had etched lines on her face. The women in the courts tended to breed like rabbits and sadly many of their infants did not survive past their first birthdays.

'Well, hopefully we will be able to help you and there will be no need for you to send your baby into an unknown, unmarked grave,' Nessie assured her. As she explained about the scheme she had agreed with Andre the woman's face lit up.

'Eeh, yer don't know what that would mean to

169

me, miss.' She clung to Nessie's hand. 'To see me little 'un put away proper an' to be able to visit his grave. An' you've no need to worry about the money. If you're willin' to do this fer me I'll make sure I pay yer back every last penny, God bless yer!'

Within a week there were three more infant burials booked as news of Andre's pay-later scheme spread.

'I think you will be the making of this business,' he told Nessie proudly one day early in December. 'You have a way with people that puts them instantly at ease.'

She shrugged. 'It's just sad to see so many old people and infants dying.'

He nodded. 'Yes, it is, but as an undertaker you must accept that death is a part of life. None of us can escape it; it is part of a natural cycle. All we can do is ensure that the loved ones left behind get the best service possible. And now I have something to tell you and I pray that when I have you will not think I have interfered in your life.'

'Oh?' Nessie was intrigued.

'The thing is ... what Dr Dorsey told you about little Joseph's condition has been preying on my mind and so I took it upon myself to ask him to get his colleague in London to come and give a second opinion.'

'But that will cost a fortune!' Nessie stated in dismay. 'And I haven't–'

'Stop, please!' He held his hand up to stay her words. 'I shall pay for the consultation. It will be my pleasure. You have worked so tirelessly for me, *please* allow me to do this one thing for you and

Joseph in return.'

Put that way Nessie didn't feel like she had much choice and deep down she was relieved, although she still didn't feel quite right about Andre paying for it. She had no doubt that the consultant's fee would be high and dreaded to think what Reuben would have to say about it. He was fiercely proud. Still, she decided she would cross that bridge when she came to it.

'It's very kind of you. When do you expect him?'

'The end of next week,' Andre told her. 'The other alternative was to take you and Joseph to see him in London but I explained to Dr Dorsey that I thought such a long journey might not be good for him. I am right ... yes?'

'Yes, I think you are,' Nessie agreed as a little ray of hope lodged in her heart. Perhaps there would be something that could be done for Joseph after all? Each time a grieving mother came to arrange her child's funeral, Nessie would find herself thinking of Joseph. She adored him and couldn't bear to think of life without him. Suddenly the end of the following week seemed a very long way away.

Chapter Sixteen

On Sunday morning, Marcie arrived at the funeral parlour for her monthly day off looking disgruntled and out of sorts. Even so Nessie greeted her warmly and ushered her into the living room where a fire was glowing. The smell of the meal she was cooking filled the room and everywhere looked homely and cosy. Marcie barely glanced at Joseph, who was fast asleep on the sofa covered with a thick blanket, but flinging her shawl off she eyed Nessie's new gown jealously.

'Come into money, have you?' she asked sarcastically.

Nessie giggled. 'No, of course I haven't. Andre bought it for me because I help in the shop now dealing with the clients, so I have to look the part. I could hardly greet them in my old clothes, could I?' As she filled the kettle at the sink she hurriedly told Marcie of all that happened since she had last seen her.

'Seems to me that Mr Chevalier is eyeing you up as possible wife material,' she sneered. 'An' speakin' of him, where is he?'

Nessie shook her head. 'It's not like that at all. Andre and I are just on friendly terms. He's never been anything other than a gentleman towards me. And as for where he is – I have no idea. He goes off every Saturday evening and comes back on Sunday. While he's gone I'm able to deal with anything that crops up here so he doesn't have to close the funeral parlour. It's the sort of business that never really closes. People don't choose when they're going to pass away, do they?'

Marcie shrugged. 'I suppose not but if you play your cards right I still think you could become Mrs Chevalier. He's a lot older than you, admittedly, but he's quite handsome an' you'd be set up for life.'

'I have no intention of getting married to Andre, or anyone else for that matter, at the minute,' Nessie assured her as she warmed the teapot.

Marcie glanced around before asking, 'And where's Reuben?'

Nessie grinned. 'Ah well, I could be entirely wrong but I have a feeling he's met a young lady,' she confided. 'He's been going out of an evening quite a bit this last couple of weeks when he hasn't been needed here.'

'Huh!' Marcie snorted. 'He's so grumpy I'm surprised anyone would be interested in him, but I suppose stranger things have happened.'

Nessie could have replied that Reuben was usually only grumpy with her because she seemed to go out of her way to try and annoy him but she thought better of it. She got to see so little of her sister that she didn't want them to spend the time they did have at odds with each other. So instead she told Marcie about the doctor that Andre had arranged to come from London to see Joseph.

Marcie wasn't much interested, she had enough problems of her own, and when Nessie eventually placed her drink in front of her she sipped at it, staring thoughtfully into the flames flickering up the chimney. Things were hectic at Haunchwood House at present as the family prepared to leave for London where they would spend Christmas. She'd only got to see George twice that week, despite the fact that she had sat shivering in the hay loft every night waiting for him. Even when he had come she had sensed that he was distancing himself from her and now she was really worried. Somehow, she was determined that she would tie him to her but what would happen if her plan to snare him didn't work? George was still convinced that she was practising a method of birth control so was still quite willing to lie with her when it suited him. But she wanted to be a lady and this time the following year she had promised herself that she would be living the life of Riley if all went to plan.

'Penny for them?'

Nessie's voice brought her thoughts sharply back to the present and she looked around, thinking how different from their previous home it looked. Nessie had made these rooms into a comfortable home and she'd noticed how smart it was in the funeral parlour too. But then that was Nessie all over. She took after their mother for being a homemaker. Marcie, on the other hand, wasn't interested in that sort of thing at all and the only reason she had stuck her job for as long as she had was so that she could be close to George.

'So where exactly does the handsome Frenchman disappear off to each week then? Does he go to visit his family?' she asked.

'No, his family are still in France and during the time I've been here there's been no correspondence from them so I wonder if there's been a family rift.'

'Hmm, he must be going to see a woman then. Perhaps you're not in with a chance after all.'

Nessie laughed. 'I've told you, there is no chance of anything like that between us so can we change the subject now? You can tell me all about what you've been up to.'

So Marcie told her all about the family's proposed trip to London and during the conversation her sister couldn't help but notice that George, the family's younger son's name, popped up fairly often.

'You're not getting a crush on this young man, are you?' she asked worriedly. 'Because you must know that there could be no future together for you. We're working class and they have money. They'll want him to make a good marriage. That's how it works in their circles.'

Marcie's pretty face flushed. 'What you're forgetting is the family might have money now but his parents started with nothing.'

'Even so, their children have been brought up with private tutors and nannies.' Nessie was concerned that Marcie might get her heart broken but she soon realised that her warnings were falling on deaf ears. Marcie could be as stubborn as a mule when she wanted to be, so eventually she changed the subject and went about the finishing touches for their meal.

Both Reuben and Andre arrived back within minutes of each other shortly before lunchtime. Reuben seemed to be in fine spirits, fuelling his sister's suspicions that there might be a special young lady on the scene. Andre, however, entered by the front entrance looking waxen and distraught. During the times she'd been there she'd more than once noticed him discreetly taking a small white pill from the drawer of his desk, which he kept locked, but today he didn't seem to care if she saw him take it and quickly unlocking the drawer he took a pill from the bottle and swal-

175

lowed it back.

'Andre, are you all right?'

Hearing the concern in her voice he turned to see her standing by the door that led into her rooms and he nodded wearily. 'Yes … yes thank you... But I wonder, do you think you could cope without me for this evening too? I have to go out again but I will be back tomorrow for the funeral we have on Tuesday.'

'Are you quite sure you're well enough to go out again?' she asked worriedly. He really did look very ill indeed.

He nodded. 'I shall be fine but thank you for your concern. A very close … friend of mine is grievously ill so I need to be with them. I only came back to check that all is well.'

'We shall be fine and of course you must go. But will you have something to eat first? The meal is almost ready.'

'No, thank you.' He ran his hand distractedly through his thick thatch of hair as Marcie came to stand behind her sister, watching him curiously. Seconds later he had gone off to his own living quarters for a quick change of clothes and minutes after that he was off out of the door again without so much as a goodbye.

'What did you make o' that, then?' Marcie asked as they heard the parlour door close behind him. 'Anyone would 'ave thought his tail was on fire he was in an' out so quickly.'

'I have no idea what to make of it and it's his business, at the end of the day,' Nessie responded. 'But now I'm going to dish the dinner up. It'll be ruined if I leave it much longer.'

Soon they were all sitting down to a succulent roast beef meal and for a short time none of them gave a lot of thought to Andre Chevalier.

Marcie left early that afternoon. She hoped that she might catch a glimpse of George if she hovered about by the house for long enough, although she wasn't looking forward to standing about in the cold. Reuben had said that he wouldn't be surprised if they didn't have snow soon and for once Marcie agreed with him. It was certainly cold enough.

'Do try and get Christmas Day off so you can come and spend it with us,' Nessie urged as she hugged her sister at the door. Christmas would be hard for them all that year, as it had been every year since their mother died.

'There's every chance I will if the family all stay away,' Marcie told her.

'Why don't you let Reuben walk you back?' Nessie suggested worriedly. 'Another woman has been killed and I really don't like you being out and about on your own.' The light was fast fading from the afternoon already.

'I know, I read about it in the paper.' Marcie tied the ribbons of her bonnet beneath her chin. 'Cook reckons it's got to be someone local responsible, but I shall be fine.' And she set off for her lengthy walk back to the house without giving her sister a backward glance, leaving Nessie to worry and fret about her.

As luck would have it she saw George cantering towards her on his stallion the second she turned into the drive leading to the house. The trouble was, Leonora was beside him on her much

177

smaller horse so there was no opportunity to speak to him. As they drew closer she stepped to the side, keeping her eyes firmly fixed on his face but he hardly gave her a second glance as he rode past and she fumed inwardly.

'I think that little maid is smitten with you,' Leonora commented when they had gone past. 'Did you see the way she was watching you?'

'Can't say that I noticed,' George replied, and digging his heels into the stallion's sides he urged his horse into a gallop and was gone like the wind, leaving Marcie to stare after him with tears in her eyes.

Marcie found Cook in a rare good mood when she entered the kitchen and Eliza was quick to tell her why as she removed her bonnet and shawl.

'The mistress has just informed us that the whole family will be away for Christmas an' the New Year,' she chortled gleefully. 'Which means that we can all get to spend some time with us families. Ain't that great news?'

Marcie's heart sank. She thought it was anything but, but she managed a weak smile.

'They're goin' four days before Christmas Eve,' Eliza rambled on. 'So then we can more or less do as we please till they come back.'

'Exactly how long are they going for?' Marcie asked with a sick feeling in the pit of her stomach. She had allowed herself to believe that George would tell the family about how he felt about her at Christmas and now he wasn't even going to be here!

'I think Mr Dorsey and Master George are comin' back after a couple of weeks but the missus an' Miss Leonora could be gone fer a couple o' months.'

'Right, well I'm going to go up to my room for a bit of a rest now,' Marcie told her, turning away abruptly and setting off up the steep, narrow stairs that led to the servants' quarters.

Once in her room she flung her bonnet onto the bed and sobbed. How could George do this to her? And how much longer would he expect her to be a skivvy for the family? He'd better come and meet her tonight otherwise it might be time to have a little word in his mother's ear!

The hours passed intolerably slowly and things got worse when Eliza finally rolled into bed with her chatterbox head on. She was as excited as a child about Christmas, but at last she became silent and soon after began to snore. Only then was Marcie able to sneak down the stairs and make her way to the hay loft.

'I'm here.' A voice came from the darkness as she neared the top of the ladder.

Crossing to her George put his hands out towards her but she slapped them away. 'Just what the bloody hell do you think you're playin' at?' She was so angry that it was all she could do to stop herself from smacking him. 'I ain't some little floozy you can pick up an' drop at will, you know! An' now I find yer goin' to be away all over Christmas! I thought that was when you was goin' to tell your mam about us?'

'Calm down,' he soothed. 'Who says I wasn't going to? I thought it would be better to tell her while she was staying at the Lewises'. She's far less likely to kick up a fuss there, isn't she? And then by the time she comes back she'll have had time to get used to the idea. That's why I agreed to go, not because I wanted to leave you, you silly little goose.'

'Oh!' Marcie felt suddenly foolish for doubting him. 'Then in that case...'

'Come here.'

She went willingly into his arms and for the next hour she forgot about everything but being with him and all was forgiven ... for now.

Chapter Seventeen

It was Dr Dorsey who met his colleague off the train from London and brought him to see Joseph. It hadn't been the best of weeks. Andre had been absent for most of the time with his sick friend and Nessie was worried about him as, when she did see him, he looked ill himself. Now she welcomed the two doctors, thanked Dr Mellor profusely for coming and then stood back. She was surprised at how young the consultant was. Only about the same age as Oliver Dorsey, who told her that they had studied at medical college together.

She watched from the corner of her eye as the two doctors leaned over the child and gave him a very thorough examination, which involved taking measurements of his head and gently poking and probing. Dr Mellor also listened to his heart through his stethoscope, took his blood pressure and his temperature. Joseph sat motionless throughout, apart from once when he whimpered as the doctor pressed the back of his neck. She could hear the two men murmuring to each other although she couldn't quite catch what they said as she waited in an agony of suspense for the verdict.

At last they rose and sat on either side of Joseph and she hurried across to them.

Dr Mellor was quite a short chap with a bushy beard and a mass of mousy brown hair. He wore thick glasses but his eyes were kindly as he smiled at her and glanced at Oliver.

'I'm afraid it isn't good news, Miss Carson,' he said eventually. 'I have to agree with Dr Dorsey's diagnosis. I believe that Joseph does have an inoperable brain tumour.'

'I see.' Nessie's lip wobbled dangerously but she managed to maintain her composure. 'So ... is there nothing that can be done?'

He shook his head gravely. 'The medicine that Dr Dorsey has prescribed will keep him pain-free and I would just advise you to make every day as pleasant as you can for the little chap. I'm so sorry. I assure you that if there was anything at all I could do, I would do it.'

'I'm sure you would and I'm very grateful to you for coming all this way,' she answered graciously. She kept her hands clasped tightly at her waist so that they wouldn't see them trembling.

'I shall be here to help you through whatever lies ahead,' Oliver Dorsey told her sincerely. His kind words were almost her undoing and she was so choked that she could only nod, and shortly

181

after, Dr Dorsey escorted the other doctor back to the train station.

'It's tragic,' Dr Mellor said sadly as they strode along Abbey Street. 'I just wish there were something I could do. That sister of his is quite special though, isn't she? Most people would have gone to pieces but she managed to stay dignified.' He smiled when Oliver flushed slightly and asked, 'Ah, got a soft spot for her, have you, old chap?'

'I don't know her all that well,' Oliver answered. 'But she does seem like a remarkable young woman. She's got that business up and running since she's been there. It looks like a different place. And after all she's been through over the last couple of years as well. First her father left them and they had to move house. Then her mother gives birth to Joseph and gets murdered. And now here she is bringing the child up as her own. Most women would have cracked under all the strain.'

The man nodded in agreement. He wouldn't be a bit surprised to see a romance develop in that direction if the way Oliver had looked at Nessie was anything to go by. But then their talk turned to medical matters as they neared the station, although his friend's words stayed at the back of Oliver's mind.

Once the doctors had left, Nessie began to sob but then after a time she thrust her chin in the air, wiped her eyes and tried to get on with things. Weeping and wailing wasn't going to alter anything. She would make whatever time Joseph had left as comfortable as possible.

As soon as she had managed to pull herself together, she went up to Reuben's room to collect his washing and tidy his bed. But as she was straightening the blankets, she noticed something sticking out from under the mattress. Seconds later her mouth gaped open as she stared at a small pile of pound notes, which Reuben had obviously intended to hide. There was more money there than they could earn between them in a whole year, so where had it come from? Her first reaction was to take it downstairs to the workshop and wave it under his nose, demanding to know whose it was, but then common sense took over and she knew that this would only make things worse. Reuben was a grown man and he'd taken to going out quite a lot lately. She had assumed that he had met a young lady but what if he had started gambling? But he obviously hadn't wanted her to know about it so eventually she tucked it back where she had found it and left the room. She would bide her time and see if he mentioned it.

Shortly after, Reuben came in to find out what the doctor had had to say about Joseph and when she told him he shook his head and nodded. Like Nessie, he wasn't surprised. He hadn't really expected good news after seeing the way the child had deteriorated.

'Is Andre back yet?' he asked as she made him some tea and she shook her head.

'No but he promised he would be by this evening. We have Mr Jenkins's funeral in the morning. Is the coffin ready?'

'Almost.' He bit into one of the biscuits she had

made the day before. 'Then I've got to get crackin' on the two little ones for them babies.' He glanced at Joseph and a little shiver ran up his spine as he realised that in the not-too-distant future he might be making one for him. 'Actually, I could have done with measurin' them before I started but the door to the preparation room is locked as usual.'

The preparation room, or the cold room, was the term used for the place where Andre prepared the bodies for burial on cold marble slabs. 'Why do you think he keeps it locked all the time an' won't let either of us in there?' He mused then. 'He seems happy enough for you to clean the rest of the place. The only time I'm admitted is if he needs a hand liftin' a body into a coffin.'

Nessie shrugged. 'I dare say he has his reasons. It's probably because he knows you don't like going in there, and I certainly don't want to,' she commented, her thoughts still very much focused on the doctor's visit. He nodded and soon went back to work, leaving her with her thoughts.

Andre returned late that afternoon. Already a thick hoar frost had formed on the grass and on the cobblestones and his hands were blue with cold. His nose was glowing red too, standing out in stark contrast to his ashen skin.

'I'll get you a nice hot drink,' Nessie told him as she helped him off with his coat but he waved her away. 'No, I'm fine but I should tell you that I have decided to bring my friend here to stay. We can use the empty bedroom next to mine. Would you mind preparing it?'

'Of course I wouldn't mind. I'll make a start on it this evening,' she agreed. 'But we had two more clients in this afternoon. Both bodies will need to be collected as soon as possible. Are you well enough?'

He nodded. 'Tell Reuben to prepare the cart.' She thought he seemed preoccupied and then he said suddenly, 'I should warn you that my friend is very ill. Dying in fact.'

'Oh!' Nessie bit her lip, not sure how she should reply. She could only imagine that Andre must think a great deal of his friend to want them to spend their final days with him here.

'Do you mind me asking how she is going to get here? If she's so ill, I mean.' She had assumed that it was a woman that Andre went to see each weekend, and now that she knew how ill she was it explained why he hadn't liked her teasing him about getting married.

'My friend is a man,' Andre informed her shortly. 'And I shall be personally fetching him back here tomorrow after I have attended to the funeral we have booked.'

'Very well.' Nessie was mildly surprised but she made no comment as she hurried away to ask Reuben to prepare the cart.

'Sounds a bit strange to me,' Reuben said, frowning, when she told him about Andre's sick friend coming to stay that evening.

'Why does it? Men are allowed to have male friends you know.' Nessie paused in the act of stirring the large pan of stew she had cooking on the range.

'And why have you cooked that huge pan full of

185

stew? There's enough there to last us all for a week at least.'

'It's not all for us,' she admitted. 'I've cooked some extra to take round to the family whose little boy we buried yesterday. They live in the courts and they're having a really hard time of it at the minute. Her husband is on short time and when I called round there they didn't even have a fire in the grate. The children looked hungry so I thought I'd cook for them.'

Reuben frowned again but she hurried on, 'Don't worry. I bought enough for the extra out of my wages.'

'You're too soft by half,' he grunted as he turned his attention back to the newspaper and she thought again of the money hidden beneath his mattress. Hopefully he would tell her where it had come from soon.

It was pitch black when Nessie set off for the courtyards that evening and within minutes she was shivering despite the pot of hot stew she was clutching and the warm cloak that Andre had bought for her. She had left Reuben washing and shaving as he got ready to go out for the evening yet again, and Andre was in the preparation room with the two deceased they had fetched from their homes late that afternoon. She would need to be quick, for she didn't want Joseph to be left on his own for too long.

As she turned into the court the sound of a pig grunting echoed on the chill air and the smell that emanated from the sty and the privy made her feel nauseous. Each courtyard consisted of four

186

tiny two-up two-down cottages, two on either side. At the end of the courtyard was a sty. The pig that was housed there was fed on scraps by the four families that lived there throughout the year before it was slaughtered on Christmas Eve to provide them all with a Christmas dinner. In the New Year they would then buy a new piglet and the fattening-up process would begin all over again. Nessie couldn't help but feel sorry for the creature as it snuffled about in the dirty straw, although she knew that without it the poor families would have had very meagre Christmas fare.

Next to the sty was the outdoor privy. It was nothing more than a wooden hut which contained an ash toilet, nowhere near adequate enough for the four families that shared it. In the summer the smell was unbearable and the children, with nowhere else to go, often played in the raw sewage that escaped from it. It was no wonder that so many of them died, Nessie thought as she tapped on the door of the cottage of the recently bereaved young mother.

It was answered almost immediately and when the woman saw who it was she looked dismayed. 'Me husband don't get paid till Friday,' she told Nessie, thinking that she had come to collect money.

'Oh, goodness, I'm not here for that,' Nessie assured her with a friendly smile.

'Er ... you'd best come in then,' the woman said, holding the door a little wider. 'Though I can't promise that it's much warmer in 'ere.'

Nessie thought she had never seen such poverty as she entered the tiny kitchen. Three very thin children with huge eyes were huddled together under a thin blanket in one corner of the room, which was illuminated by a single tallow candle that cast dancing shadows on the walls. A rickety table surrounded by mismatched chairs stood in the centre but other than that there was no furniture that Nessie could see apart from a few wooden crates that were clearly being used for seating. The rest of the furniture had no doubt been taken to the pawnshop, along with anything else of value they might once have owned.

'Me 'usband 'as gone to the slag 'eap to see if he can pick us a bit o' coal,' the woman explained.

Nodding, Nessie placed the heavy pot on the table.

'I hope you don't mind but I got rather carried away when I was cooking the stew earlier on in the day.' As she lifted the lid, a delicious aroma wafted around the room and she saw the children's eyes widen with anticipation. 'So, I was wondering if you could use it up? It'll only get thrown away if you don't.'

She had been very careful how she worded it, for she knew that although many of the people thereabouts were desperately poor they could also be desperately proud.

The woman licked her lips and eyed the pot warily, but soon her hunger overcame her pride and she said airily, 'I dare say we could 'elp yer out if yer want rid of it. Ta, very much, miss.' The children had already emerged from the blanket and were warily approaching the table as Nessie hurriedly made for the door. The poor little things looked as if they were starving.

'You can drop the pot back into the parlour when you're done with it,' she said over her shoulder and as she quietly closed the door behind her she saw the children dive on the pot with spoons at the ready like a little pack of hungry wolves. Suddenly, Nessie felt privileged. Her own family had struggled from time to time but they had never had to live in the dire poverty that these families did. She just wished there was something she could do to help them.

As she was emerging from the courtyards into Abbey Street, she glimpsed two men talking on the other side of the road. Realising that one of them was Reuben, she paused and drew back into the shadows. Her heart sank as she saw that the other man was Snowy White, a well-known local villain. Why would her brother be talking to *him?* How did he even know him? The police had been trying to put the finger on Snowy for years, everyone knew that. They also knew that he was responsible for almost every robbery or burglary that took place within a twenty-mile radius. But Snowy was clever, he always made sure that he had an alibi and let his gang do the dirty work so that he could milk the profits. He owned a number of businesses in town, which ensured that he could always account for being so well off. But people knew some of these businesses were only fronts for all sorts of illegal doings.

It was common knowledge that he owned a whorehouse and it was whispered that his tobacconist shop was just a cover for an opium den. Now Nessie stood quietly trying her best to hear what the two men were saying but their heads were bent close together and they were too far away. Eventually she saw Snowy pass something to Reuben and then the two men parted and went their separate ways.

Nessie stood for a few moments chewing on her lip as her mind whirled. She knew that Reuben missed the outdoor work he had done on the railways but had hoped that in time he would settle to their new lifestyle. But if anything, he seemed to become ever more restless. And now to see him talking to Snowy... He was a bad man to mix with and what was it that she had seen him pass to Reuben? Her thoughts flew to the money tucked beneath his mattress and a feeling of foreboding came over her. Surely Reuben hadn't resorted to stealing? Not now when they finally had a safe house to live in and they were secure? She felt sick at the thought of it. From now on she determined she would watch Reuben very closely indeed.

Chapter Eighteen

'So, is his lordship's visitor here yet?' Reuben asked sarcastically when he came into the kitchen for his meal at lunchtime the following day.

Nessie nodded as she cut a large wedge of bread and cheese for him. 'Yes, but I didn't see him. Andre took him straight through to his own quarters and up to the room I prepared for him.

Dr Dorsey is up there with them now.'

The words had barely left her lips when the doctor himself appeared in the doorway and instantly, much to her confusion, she was all of a fluster.

'Hello, Miss Carson. I thought while I was here I might look in on Joseph and drop this off to you.'

Trying to hide her nerves, she nodded. Why does he have this effect on me? she wondered.

He held out a small glass bottle and at a glance she saw that it was laudanum. 'Just put a few drops into his drink if he appears to be in any discomfort. It will calm him.'

'I will ... thank you.' Nessie watched as the doctor crossed to Joseph who was lying motionless on the sofa. It was all he ever seemed able to do now. It was an effort for him to even sit at the table with them any longer and it broke her heart as she thought of what lay ahead. The doctor meanwhile was gently examining the child, listening to his heart and talking soothingly to him all the time, even though the little boy didn't appear to be aware that he was even there. When he had finished he gently patted Joseph's arm and snapped his black bag shut as he asked, 'How has he been?'

'No different.'

'I see. Just continue to keep him warm and don't be afraid to use that if the need arises.'

She nodded, then asked, 'And how is Mr Chevalier's friend?'

He lowered his eyes. Patient confidentiality ensured that he wasn't able to tell her much so he just answered, 'As well as can be expected.'

191

She wished then that she hadn't asked. He clearly wasn't comfortable speaking about the man and she surprised herself when she suddenly blurted out, 'Would you like a cup of tea? I've just made a fresh pot.'

After glancing at the gold hunter watch that was fastened by a thick gold chain to his waistcoat, he smiled. 'That would be very nice... Thank you.'

Nessie flushed as she whirled about and began to prepare two cups and saucers. *Why did I do that?* She silently questioned herself as she placed the cups on a small wooden tray, all fingers and thumbs. Minutes later he was helping himself to sugar from the pressed glass bowl in the middle of the table and adding milk.

'My sister was saying that your family are going to London for Christmas,' she said for want of something to say.

He nodded. 'Yes, they are, although I won't be going, of course. I can't leave old Dr Peek in the lurch. Between you and me my father isn't all that keen on going either. I'm afraid he hates leaving his work. But my mother and my sister are really looking forward to it. So is my younger brother. I wouldn't be surprised if George didn't become engaged to Belinda, the Lewises' daughter while they're there. The two families have known each other for years and it's always been expected that she and George would make a match.' He laughed then and confided, 'My father would certainly be happy about it. The Lewises are one of the richest families in Knightsbridge.'

Nessie smiled and began to relax. He was so easy to talk to that sometimes she forgot that they were miles apart in class. She'd almost forgotten that Reuben was still in the room until he passed them saying, 'I'd best get back to work then. It wouldn't do fer us all to sit about gossipin'.'

Hot colour flamed into Nessie's cheeks and she sloshed some tea into her saucer as she stammered, 'I'm s-so sorry about that. I'm afraid Reuben is finding this new way of life rather hard to adjust to. He likes working outside, you see.'

He nodded sympathetically and his eyes momentarily locked with hers. 'I can understand that, it must be hard for him.' Then quickly dragging his gaze away from hers and hoping to change the subject he hurried on, 'I called in to see Mrs Liggins earlier this morning. You know, Molly Liggins? The lady from the courts who recently lost her baby. She was telling me that you took a dish of stew round to the family. That was very kind of you.'

Nessie shook her head. 'Not really. It's nothing in the greater scheme of things, is it? And that would only have provided her family with one good meal. The poor things. I never knew such poverty existed until I moved into the town and I just wish there was more I could do for these people.'

'I know exactly what you mean.' He smiled ruefully. The more he got to see of this young woman the more he felt drawn to her. 'I'm afraid Dr Peek has told me off more than once for not charging a fee from some of these poor souls that I go to visit, but they hardly have two ha'pennies to rub together. I know that if I charge them they won't eat that day, so what am I to do?' He shook his head and went on, 'Mrs Liggins also told me that you gave her baby a proper burial, even though she couldn't pay for the cost of the funeral up front. What a marvellous idea. When word spreads I've no doubt you'll be kept busy once the really bad weather sets in. It's always the worst time of year for the very young and the very old.' He placed his cup and saucer on the table then and, rising from his seat, he smiled at her. 'Thanks for the tea and the chat but I really should be getting on now. Good day, Miss Carson.'

'Oh please ... call me Nessie,' she said, then flushed with embarrassment again.

'Very well, I'd like that but only if you agree to call me Oliver.' He held his hand out and as she placed her smaller one in his she felt the heat from his palm and butterflies fluttered to life in her stomach once again. He, meanwhile, was thinking what a truly lovely person she was. The light from the lamp in the centre of the table was turning her hair to burnished copper, and those eyes... They really were extraordinarily beautiful. As they said their goodbyes, their eyes again locked in mutual appreciation.

Over the next week Nessie was almost rushed off her feet, just as Dr Dorsey had predicted. Andre was spending most of his time upstairs nursing his sick friend so the running of the shop fell mainly to her; not that she was complaining. She was just grateful that she and the family had a roof over their heads, warm beds to retire to and a regular wage coming in. Andre's friend re-mained faceless, although Nessie made sure that

194

she supplied him with nourishing meals that Andre took up to him. And then, out of the blue one morning, Andre told her, 'My friend is much recovered so I will be accompanying him back to his own home this morning.'

'Oh!' Nessie looked a little worried. 'But we have a funeral booked at St Nicholas's Church for three this afternoon.'

Andre waved aside her concerns, assuring her that he would be back in time to ensure that everything was done. A short time later, a horse-drawn cab drew up outside and Andre ushered his friend into it.

Soon after Reuben came in for his morning break. 'Phew!' He looked harassed. 'I can't keep up wi' the amount o' coffins that need making. At this rate Chevalier is goin' to have to hire me someone to help. We're running low on wood an' all. He needs to get some ordered else we'll run out.'

'I'm sure he will now that he doesn't have to look after his friend,' she assured him. In truth, she had been finding it hard too, what with running the parlour, cleaning, washing, ironing and caring for Joseph, not to mention cooking for them all.

As promised, Andre was back in plenty of time for the service and when he and Reuben left with the glass-sided hearse, the horses looking elegant in their plumed headgear, she began to tackle the never-ending pile of paperwork.

It was dark by the time the men returned and while Reuben rubbed down the horses in the stable Andre came and handed her a substantial sum of money from the deceased's relatives. 'They insisted on paying for our services today,' he told her as he removed his shiny black top hat and frock coat. 'Could you put it in the safe for me, please?'

'Certainly.' Nessie hurried off to do as she was told. When she returned he eyed her for a moment before commenting, 'You look a little tired. Are you feeling unwell?'

'Not at all,' she assured him, although she was indeed very tired. Her days began very early in the morning and it was usually very late at night before she managed to tumble into bed, exhausted after she'd done all the jobs that needed doing.

'Hmm, well I've been thinking. Now that you've taken over the running of the parlour and now that the business is doing so much better we could afford to bring in someone to do the cleaning. What do you think of the idea?'

Nessie paused before answering. In truth it would make her life a lot easier if at least one job was taken off her shoulders, but she was afraid that he might think she couldn't cope.

'I am managing,' she answered hesitantly.

'Oh, I wasn't for a moment suggesting that you weren't.' Andre looked embarrassed. 'I was just trying to make all of our lives a little easier. Business is brisk now, thanks to you, so we could afford it. I thought I might employ someone to help Reuben too; he can hardly keep up with the sudden need for coffins.'

'Then if you're quite sure, I might know just the people who may be able to help you.' Nessie was smiling now. 'I was thinking of Mrs Liggins, the poor woman who lost her baby recently. I'm sure she would jump at the chance of earning some money and her husband has been laid off work so he might be able to help Reuben?'

She stared at him hopefully as he thought on her words then eventually he nodded. 'Very well, if you think they may be suitable. I will work out what I can afford to pay them and what hours I would wish them to work then perhaps you could put it to them? As you know, I am no good at this sort of thing. You are far better than me at dealing with the public.'

Nessie nodded enthusiastically as she thought of the cold, damp cottage the Liggins family were forced to live in. This would be a godsend to them, she was sure.

She told Reuben about Andre's idea that evening over dinner and he nodded his approval. 'Sounds good to me an' I've no doubt Mrs Liggins'll jump at the chance to earn a few bob. As fer her old man, I'm sure I can find him enough to do to keep him busy. I'm run off me feet at present.'

But not enough to keep you in at night, Nessie thought as she cut into the pork chop on her plate. Reuben was out most evenings now and since seeing him with Snowy White she was very worried about what he might be up to.

Sure enough, after finishing his meal, Reuben got washed and changed and went out into the freezing night as Nessie chewed on her lip with concern. Where could he be going? Nessie settled Joseph down then went through to Andre's living quarters to collect his dirty pots. She was dismayed to see that once again he had barely touched his meal and she asked worriedly, 'Are you feeling all right, Andre? You haven't eaten much again.' She'd noticed that he'd been taking his pills more often over the last couple of days when he thought she wasn't watching, and he certainly didn't look very grand. His face was the colour of candle wax and once more there was a bluish tinge to his lips.

'I am fine, thank you. But it is good of you to show concern.' Andre was always the perfect gentleman and she sighed. There was clearly something wrong with him but it appeared that he wasn't about to confide what it was yet. Until he did she wasn't sure how she could help him. Lifting the pots, she was about to leave the room when she suddenly remembered the envelope in her pocket. 'I'm so sorry. The postman delivered this for you earlier today. I was dealing with a customer at the time and stuffed it in my pocket then forgot all about it, but I noticed that the postmark is French.'

'Ah.' He took the letter. 'It will probably be from my *maman*. Thank you.' Then much to her disappointment he placed it down, clearly with no intention of reading it while she was still there.

'I'll bid you good evening then.' With curiosity eating away at her, Nessie lifted the tray again and headed back to her own quarters. It was the first time Andre had received a letter from France while she had been working there and she wondered why. She knew that it was absolutely none of her business of course but it didn't stop her feeling curious.

By the time she retired there was still no sign of her brother and she lay awake worrying until eventually she fell into a fitful sleep.

The sound of Reuben pottering about in the kitchen woke her the next morning. Beside her Joseph was still sleeping so she inched to the edge of the bed and thrust her feet into her boots. She hadn't been able to afford a pair of house slippers as yet but she hoped to be able to very soon now. Shivering in the chilly bedroom, she wrapped a shawl about her shoulders and hurried down-stairs to find the kettle singing on the hob and the fire blazing merrily up the chimney.

'You're an early bird,' she commented as she placed a slice of bread onto the toasting fork and held it out towards the flames. A slice of buttered toast would go down nicely with a cup of tea on such a cold morning.

Reuben shrugged. 'I was awake so I thought I may as well make meself useful.'

'Oh, I'm not complaining,' Nessie assured him. 'You're quite welcome to do this every morning if you've a mind to. It's nice to come down to a warm room and the kettle boiling.'

Minutes later they sat together buttering their toast at the table in a companionable silence until Nessie said, 'I'll be going to see the Ligginses this morning once Andre has told me what hours and what wages to offer them. If Mr Liggins agrees to the terms when would you like him to start?'

'Well, we've got a funeral this morning and another one tomorrow afternoon so as soon as he

199

likes. As well as helping me in the workshop, he can double as a pall-bearer an' all. That'll save Chevalier havin' to pay someone else to do it.'

She nodded, wondering how she might broach the subject of where he was disappearing off to each night but then, deciding that it would only cause an argument, she held her tongue and soon after they went their separate ways to get dressed and prepare for yet another busy day ahead.

Chapter Nineteen

The fog was thick as Nessie fumbled her way along Abbey Street and when she turned into the alley that led to the courtyards where the Liggins family lived it seemed to get even denser. Nessie had the curious feeling that she might be the only person left in the world as she inched her way along, nervously glancing from side to side, even though she could barely see her hand in front of her. What if the murderer was lurking?

Finally she emerged into the courtyard and breathed a sigh of relief. She stood for a minute, trying to get her bearings and as she did so something ran across her foot and she shrieked as she kicked out at it. It was a rat and she shuddered as she stared down just in time to see its fat tail disappear into a hole in the wall. The pig in the sty began to snuffle and even in the bitterly cold air, the overpowering smell from the privy made her retch. This must be what hell is like, she thought, as she gingerly picked her way across the cobbles in the general direction of the Ligginses' cottage. Once there she took a deep, steadying breath, then raising her hand she tapped gently. Within seconds the door was inched open and Molly Liggins's pale face peered out at her.

'Eeh, miss.' The woman instantly flew into a panic. 'If it's yer stew pot yer after I was goin' to bring it back today, honest I was!'

Nessie gave her a reassuring smile. 'No, it's not the pot I'm after and I'm sure you were, Mrs Liggins. As it happens I was hoping to have a word with you.'

'Come on in,' the young woman urged, holding the door wider. 'I'm forgettin' me manners.'

Nessie edged into the room and her eyes instantly settled on the children who were once more huddled together beneath a thin blanket trying to get warm. Once again, the fireplace was empty and the cold and damp seemed to creep into her bones. There was no comfort whatsoever in the room and yet she noticed that the floor was swept and what there was in there was as clean as Mrs Liggins could make it. Her husband was sitting in the only chair, his eyes dull and without hope and he barely acknowledged her, apart from a small nod of his head.

'The thing is,' Nessie said, turning her attention back to Molly Liggins, 'I have a bit of a proposition to put to you. You see, since I began at the funeral parlour, business has become brisker and we're all struggling to get everything done, so I wondered if you and your husband might be interested in coming to work there for Mr Chevalier?'

She then hurriedly relayed the wage that Andre had suggested and the hours they would be required to work as Mrs Liggins listened open-mouthed. When she was done, a silence settled on the room as the husband and wife stared at each other as if they could hardly believe their ears, then suddenly Molly sprang forward and hugged Nessie so hard that she almost knocked the breath out of her.

'Oh, miss, yer an angel, so you are,' she said gleefully. 'This means that we'll be able to give the childer the sort o' Christmas they deserve this year. What do yer think, Charlie?'

Her husband smiled, transforming his whole face. He was quite attractive when he smiled, Nessie noticed.

'I think yer right, pet. This young lady *is* an angel to give us an opportunity like this an' I'm all for it. I'll start as soon as yer want, miss. Today if yer like, I'm only sittin' about here mopin'.'

Nessie was delighted as she placed a wicker basket that she had brought with her on the table, saying, 'There's a few bits in here that you might be able to use. Nothing much just some bread and cheese and a few scones that I made yesterday.'

Instantly the children stood and began to inch towards the table, their hungry eyes fixed on the basket. Poor little mites, Nessie thought, as a lump formed in her throat, but she kept her voice light as she turned for the door, saying, 'Right, I'll tell my brother you'll be along shortly then, shall I, Mr Liggins? And you'll start in the morning, will you, Mrs Liggins? Shall we say nine in the morning till one each weekday?'

Molly's smile was her answer and Nessie stepped back out into the fog, closing the door softly behind her. The day had got off to a good start despite the harsh weather and could she have known it was about to get even better, for later that morning the door to the parlour opened and Mrs Hewitt appeared.

'Mrs Hewitt!' Nessie almost pounced on her she was so thrilled to see her. 'Oh, it's so lovely to see you. How are you and everyone back at home?' Then suddenly remembering that Andre was there and she was supposed to be working she flushed guiltily. But she needn't have worried.

He smiled and said, 'Ah, this is your friend, yes? Then you must take her through to your rooms and make her a nice hot drink. I am perfectly capable of managing out here on my own for a while. Take as long as you like.'

And so after thanking him Nessie and Mrs Hewitt went into her cosy sitting room. 'By, but you've got this comfy, pet,' Mrs Hewitt said approvingly. 'An' how is our young man?' She crossed to Joseph, who was dozing on the settee, and stroked his cheek gently.

While she put the kettle over the fire, Nessie told the kindly woman about the London doctor's visit and his diagnosis.

Mrs Hewitt sighed. 'Poor little lamb,' she said quietly. 'But yer have to think that when his time comes he'll be goin' to a better place. Happen he'll share a little bit o' heaven wi' yer mam, God rest her soul.'

She hurriedly changed the subject then as she

told Nessie of all the goings on back at home while the girl plied her with tea and scones. Then eventually she said, with a twinkle in her eye, 'I must say, that Frenchman is a bit of all right! A bit older than you, admittedly, but if yer play yer cards right, yer could be made fer life wi' him. He obviously thinks a lot of yer an' I've been hearin' of all the changes yer've made to the place.'

'There's nothing like that going on with me and Andre, we're just friends...'

'Hmm! *Andre* now, is it,' Mrs Hewitt teased as she took a noisy slurp of her third cup of tea.

Nessie giggled and shook her head. Why was everyone trying to marry her off? The mood became sombre again, though, as Mrs Hewitt went on, 'Did yer know there was another woman murdered last night? Everyone's talkin' about it on the market.'

Nessie shook her head. 'No, I didn't know. Whereabouts did this happen?'

'Up close to Haunchwood House be all accounts,' Mrs Hewitt informed her. 'The poor woman were bludgeoned to death just like the others, they reckon, poor bugger. That's five now.' Seeing Nessie blanch, she hastily changed the subject to happier things, silently cursing herself for being so thoughtless. 'An' how's young Marcie doin' up at the house? I must say I'm surprised she's stuck it this long. She must be turnin' over a new leaf.'

Half an hour later, she reluctantly got to her feet and fastened her hat back on to her head with two vicious-looking hat pins. 'Just in case the bugger who's on the prowl ever tries to get me. They'll get these jabbed up their arse,' she informed Nessie straight-faced.

Nessie almost choked with laughter. It would be woe betide anyone who ever tried to get the better of Mrs Hewitt. They wandered out into the parlour together. 'This bloody fog don't seem to be shiftin' at all,' she grumbled. Then planting a sloppy kiss on Nessie's cheek, she told her, 'You look after yerself an' that babby in there now, pet, an' I'll see yer again soon. Ta-ra fer now.' And with that she was off, waddling away down the street until the fog swallowed her up.

Later that day, when Reuben came in for his lunch, Nessie asked him how Charlie Liggins was getting on.

'He's enthusiastic I'll say that for him. I've got him sanding down, saves me time doin' it,' Reuben commented. Charlie had gone home to his family for a short break although Nessie doubted there would be much for him to eat apart from the bits she'd taken round to his home earlier that morning. But hopefully soon that would change.

She glanced over at Joseph, who was sleeping on the settee. He'd seemed more restless than usual that day and Nessie had resorted to putting a few drops of the laudanum that Oliver Dorsey had left for him in his milk. He was peaceful now but she kept a close eye on him all the same, constantly worrying that his condition might be deteriorating. It was heartbreaking to see him looking so small and vulnerable. She knew that it was inevitable but she dreaded losing him.

The following morning, Molly Liggins turned up for work spot on time. Her patched and darned clothes were as neat and clean as she could make them and she'd clearly gone to a lot of effort to look her best, but even so there was no disguising her down-at-heel boots and her threadbare shawl, which had been washed so many times the original colour was now indistinguishable. Nessie showed her where the cleaning things were kept and told her what needed doing and Molly set to with a will, leaving Nessie free to concentrate on the account books. She was as good as Andre himself at balancing them now, thanks to his tuition, but she had barely turned the first page when the bell above the door tinkled and a young boy appeared bearing an enormous box.

'Delivery fer Miss Nessie Carson,' he stated importantly.

'For me ... are you quite sure?' Nessie frowned.

The boy nodded. 'I am that, miss. Can yer sign 'ere fer me please?'

Nessie hastily scrawled her signature on the scrap of paper he held out to her and once the boy had gone whistling merrily on his way with a penny for his troubles burning a hole in his tattered trousers, Nessie tentatively opened the box, then gasped. Inside, neatly folded, was a lovely gown in a beautiful shade of pale lilac.

As she stared down at it completely bemused, Andre appeared and smiled. 'Ah, so it has arrived then!'

'I-I don't understand.'

'I took the liberty of ordering you another gown,' he informed her. 'I thought it would make

206

it a little easier for you to have one to change into. It is so hard to get clothes dry in this weather. The seamstress who made your other one had your measurements and suggested the style and the colour.' Looking a little embarrassed he waved his hand airily. 'I am no good at women's fashions so I hope it will be acceptable. If not, I am sure she would make alterations for you.'

'But, Andre, it's just *beautiful*,' Nessie breathed as she took it from the box and shook it out. It was of a very similar style to her other one but the colour was so much prettier and it was trimmed about the neck and the cuffs with purple ribbon. 'You really shouldn't have. You've done so much for me ... for all of us, already.'

'It is my pleasure.' He gave a gallant little bow. 'After all, I must have my staff looking suitably attired.'

'Then perhaps you will let me pay you back so much a week from my wages?' she suggested but he shook his head.

'I would be greatly offended if you did and so now let us say no more about it.' He frowned before going on, 'My friend, Jean-Paul, who stayed with us recently is not well again. I shall be staying in Coventry with him tonight, if you think that you can manage here? But of course, I shall be back first thing in the morning in plenty of time for the funeral we have.'

'I can manage,' she assured him.

With a nod he disappeared off into the court-yard and Nessie hurriedly carried her new gown through to her living quarters, checked on Joseph and went back to what she had been doing. *So, his friend's name is Jean-Paul,* she thought. He must be French too and she wondered if he had come to England with Andre? He was somewhat of a mystery, for during his stay she hadn't managed to get so much as a peek at him. Andre had ushered him in and up to the guest room then out again to the waiting cab on the day he left with the minimum of fuss, insisting on caring for him himself. They must be very good friends, Nessie thought, then, applying herself to the job in hand, she thought no more about it.

Within a few short days, Molly Liggins had proved her worth, as had her husband, and Nessie found herself better able to cope now that some of the chores had been delegated to Molly. One morning she presented Molly with a skirt and blouse that she would no longer need. They were far from being fashionable and were patched and darned in places but even so they were much better than the rags that Molly was wearing and she was touchingly grateful for them. Andre had advanced some of her first week's wages to her and for the first time in months she had been able to feed her family good nourishing food.

'I shall never be able to thank yer enough fer gettin' me this job,' she told Nessie sincerely. 'Me an' Charlie were only sayin' last night that once we've caught up wi' what we owe on our rent we might even be able to send the little 'uns to school a couple of days a week. We ain't been able to afford the penny a day each it costs before. An' I ain't worryin' about Christmas now neither. I might even be able to buy us a goose!'

Nessie smiled, glad to have been able to help and then with a little shock she realised that Christmas would be upon them in just a couple of days. She had been so busy learning how to run the business that she hadn't given it a thought. She viewed Christmas with mixed feelings now. When the family had been all together, it had always been such a joyous time. Her mother had ensured that each of them received a little gift and their cottage would be full of the enticing aromas of mince pies and Christmas puddings. But those days were gone now and once more Nessie felt the weight of responsibility on her shoulders. It was up to *her* now to make sure that the Christmas holidays were as good as she could make them and that's exactly what she intended to do. One thing she had learned since losing her mother – she could step up to a challenge when necessary.

Later that afternoon, as Nessie was arranging a vase of holly in the funeral parlour, the bell above the door tinkled and glancing up her blood turned to water as she saw Seth Grimshaw standing there. She'd hoped never to have to set eyes on the repulsive little man again but here he was, twice as nasty, with a suggestive grin on his face and holding a bunch of rather bedraggled flowers.

As she stared at him questioningly he swept off his hat and gave a little bow before trying to give the flowers to her. Nessie stood with her hands folded primly at her waist, making no effort to take them and he gave her an oily smile.

'Good day, m'dear. I thought I'd just call in an'

see how yer settlin' in.' His eyes swept up and down her and he licked his fat lips. Nessie Carson, for all she was young enough to be his daughter, had affected him as no other woman ever had. Seth had always been happy to take his pleasures where he could but there was something about this young lady that drew him like a bee to a honey pot. Now, in her smart dress and with her hair coiled high on top of her head, she looked every inch the lady and Seth Grimshaw was prepared to woo her if that's what it took. He was sick of living in a dirty cottage and coming home to an empty grate each night. He needed a wife and Nessie would fit the bill admirably.

'As you can see, I am settling in very well thank you, Mr Grimshaw. And now if that's all you've come to say, I will bid you good day. I have work to do.' Her voice and her eyes were as cold as the frost already forming outside but Seth wasn't prepared to be put off that easily.

'I was er ... wondering if you might like to accompany me out to an eating house for a meal one evenin'?' He waited expectantly for her reaction, but when it came it was not at all what he had hoped for.

'A meal ... *with you?*' She stared at him as if he had lost his senses. 'Why *ever* would I want to do that? If my memory serves me correctly it wasn't so very long ago that you were hounding me and my family for the rent we owed even though you knew we were struggling.' Her eyes were flashing dangerously now and colour had risen to her cheeks, which only made her all the more appealing to him. He liked a woman wi' a bit of spirit!

'As far as I'm concerned, we have paid what we owe to you so there is no need for us to see you ever again. Good day to you, Mr Grimshaw!' And with that she turned her back on him and continued to arrange the holly in the vase. Seth laid the flowers on the desk before quietly leaving the shop.

Nessie waited until she heard the door close behind him then turned and flung the flowers into the bin. Suddenly the day was spoiled.

Chapter Twenty

Marcie stood with tears coursing down her cheeks as she peeped around the side of the house to watch the family preparing to leave for Christmas in London. She should have been hard at work in the dairy but she had to have just one last look at George before he left. Miss Leonora was already standing by the second carriage overseeing the trunks and bossily telling the groom where she wanted them to go. They would travel in the first carriage to the train station, the second was purely for the mountain of luggage they were taking with them. In fact, there was so much of it, anyone would think they were leaving home. Though it wasn't surprising really, Marcie thought. Leonora had been feverishly shopping and visiting her dressmaker for weeks. She should know because she was the unfortunate one who had had to iron everything before it was packed.

The gowns had made her almost green with jealousy: morning gowns, day gowns, evening gowns in all the colours of the rainbow. Silks, satins and taffetas, most of them with brand-new bonnets to go with them. And then there had been the gloves and the shoes and the petticoats. Marcie dreaded to think how much they must all have cost, but one day, she promised herself, I shall have even more when George marries me! She thought of the stolen hour they had shared together in the hay loft the night before and her hand fell to the brooch he had given her as an early Christmas present. It was gold, in the shape of a bird with ruby eyes. Admittedly, she would rather it had been a ring but even so she absolutely loved it and was longing for some time off so that she could wear it. In the meantime, it was tucked deep in the pocket of her apron.

'Is it *real* gold and rubies?' she had asked him as she stared at it in the palm of her hand in awe.

George had looked affronted. 'Why, of course it is. Would I give my girl any less?'

She had clung to him and sobbed. He had promised that he and his father would be back early in the New Year but that seemed like a lifetime away. Suddenly the mistress appeared on the steps, closely followed by Mr Dorsey who opened the carriage door for her.

'Come along, Leonora, the groom is more than capable of doin' that without you standing over him,' Connie Dorsey scolded, then she turned to Mrs Bainbridge who was standing close behind her. 'Now, are you quite sure that you have everythin' you need, dear?'

The housekeeper nodded and smiled. That was at least the tenth time in as many minutes that her mistress had asked the same question and she was getting herself all in a fluster.

'Perfectly sure, ma'am. Now you just go off and enjoy yourself. Everything here will be fine.'

Oliver joined them now; only to see them off of course, for he was staying behind to help Dr Peek with his practice and had flatly refused to go, much to his mother's chagrin. Then there was George, looking so handsome in a cream satin waistcoat and dark suit that Marcie's heart did a little somersault in her chest. Just for a second he looked her way and their eyes momentarily locked but then he hastily averted his gaze and clambered into the carriage to squash up to his sister.

'Come on, we'll miss the bloody train at this rate with all this fartin' about,' Mr Dorsey exploded and Marcie heard the mistress scold him.

Seconds later they were off and Marcie, choking back her tears, felt wretched as she turned and wearily made her way back to the dairy.

For the next two days Mrs Bainbridge kept them all busy putting the house back to rights following the family's departure but then suddenly there was nowhere near as much to do and she became a little more lenient.

'If anyone would like a few hours off this afternoon to do your Christmas shopping you may go,' she graciously told them and Marcie's hand was in the air immediately. She would buy what bits and bobs she wanted from the market then visit Nessie. It wasn't a very exciting prospect but she supposed it was better than being locked away in the dairy.

Later that day, clad in her Sunday best with George's brooch pinned to her blouse, Marcie entered the kitchen. Cook, who was enjoying not having the family to cater for, was sitting in the fireside chair with her feet up enjoying a cup of tea and Eliza, who had agreed to walk into town with her, was waiting for her.

'Ooh, that's a pretty brooch,' Eliza said with a smile as she tied the ribbons of her bonnet beneath her chin. 'I was thinking of buying one very similar to that for myself on my last day off.'

Marcie preened. 'I doubt you would afford this one,' she said cockily. 'It was a gift and I imagine it would have been rather expensive.'

Eliza chuckled. 'Well, it's an exact copy of some of the ones they do on the market then.' Oblivious to the flush that had risen in Marcie's cheeks she told the cook, 'See you later, Mrs Roe, we shan't be late.'

'See as you ain't,' the cook answered. 'It's dark be four o'clock now an' it ain't safe fer young women to be out on their own wi' a murderer on the loose.'

Now in a thoroughly bad humour, Marcie followed Eliza out into the bitterly cold air and they set off for the town in silence as Marcie's brain whirled. Surely Eliza was mistaken. George had told her that the brooch was solid gold and he wouldn't lie to her ... would he? When they eventually reached the marketplace, even though it was still early afternoon, the best of the light had already faded from the day and it was so cold that Marcie lost some of the feeling in her fingers and feet. The first stop was the rag stall where, as usual, there was a crowd of women feverishly rummaging through the piles of clothes and shoes looking for a bargain.

Both girls had been paid a small bonus, and each was determined to find a bargain – Eliza was looking for a new skirt, while Marcie wanted to find some new boots. After a time, she spotted a pair of black leather button boots and she grabbed them. They weren't as pretty as she would have liked but they were ten times better than the ones she was wearing so she hastily tried them on and smiled with relief when she found that they were actually quite a good fit. They hadn't had much wear either, by the looks of them, which was a bonus.

'How much?' she asked the stallholder as she slipped her foot into her old boot.

'Hmm, well they come from a good house on the outskirts o' town, if I remember rightly. An' they're a nice soft leather an' all so they've got to be worth a shillin' of anybody's money.'

'A shilling!' Marcie was horrified. That wouldn't leave her with a great deal to spend on presents for the family. But then she considered her need was greater than theirs so she began to barter.

'How about sixpence?'

The woman snorted. 'Not on yer nelly. But I'll tell yer what I'll do, seein' as it's nearly Christmas. I'll take ninepence ha'penny an' not a penny less.'

'What about if I traded in the pair I'm wear-

215

ing?' Marcie pushed cheekily.

The woman stared down at the girl's feet and sighed. 'Yer drive a hard bargain, but I'll give yer tuppence fer 'em. They've seen better days an' they ain't worth more than that.'

Deciding not to push her luck any further, Marcie quickly slipped on the new boots then handed her old ones over along with sevenpence ha'penny. Soon after she bought a scarf for Nessie in a pretty blue colour and a pair of woollen gloves for Reuben. She couldn't see the point of buying anything for Joseph. The way she saw it he wasn't going to be around for much longer and she would rather save the money she had left for a present for George. She found it on the second-hand bookstall. It was a rather fine, leather-bound volume of maps of the world and although it was admittedly used she thought he would like it and happily paid the stallholder one shilling and sixpence for it. It was an awful lot of money but then, she reasoned, George was used to nice things and wouldn't appreciate anything cheap.

Eliza had also been busily shopping for her family but now they were both almost done so they decided to part and meet up later for the long walk home. They had almost reached the corner of Stratford Street when Eliza suddenly said, 'Oh look, there's the stall where I saw a brooch like yours. I'll bet it's doin' a roarin' trade today wi' Christmas comin' up. Ta-ra fer now. I'll see yer in a couple of hours.' With a cheery wave she was gone and Marcie curiously approached the stall. Half of her didn't want to look for fear that what Eliza had said was right. The other half couldn't resist a peep. Spread out on the stall was an array of cheap jewellery. There were necklaces, earrings and bracelets but it was the brooches that Marcie concentrated her attention on and sure enough her eyes lit on a brooch exactly the same as the one George had given her.

'How much?' She stabbed her finger at it and the portly stall-holder told her cheerily, 'Tuppence to you, me duck!'

Her heart sank. *Tuppence*. Was she really only worth so little to him? Turning away she blinked back tears as she felt the weight of the book she had bought for him beneath her arm. He had so much compared to her and yet he had only thought to spend a measly tuppence on her!

By the time she arrived at the funeral parlour she was in a very ill humour indeed. It got worse when she saw Oliver Dorsey there through the window chatting away to Nessie as if they were the best of friends.

'I was thinking if Reverend Lockett was willing to go and visit them it might help the grieving process,' Oliver suggested.

'I think it's a *wonderful* idea,' Nessie agreed, then as the bell tinkled she glanced up and saw Marcie entering.

'Why, what a lovely surprise. What are you doing here?' Nessie instantly rose and, hands outstretched in welcome, she advanced on her sister with a broad smile on her face. But Marcie didn't see the smile. She was too busy staring at the smart lilac gown her sister was wearing. Her eyes then travelled past Nessie to the doctor who was also rising and preparing to leave.

So that's how it is, is it? Marcie thought. Not only has she got the Frenchman slobbering over her but George's brother as well. Marcie's rosebud lips drew into a pout and colour crept into her cheeks. It wasn't fair, she thought jealously. She knew *she* was the pretty one so why was Nessie suddenly getting all the attention.

Oliver Dorsey smiled politely at her then turned back to Nessie. 'Right then, as you're in favour, I'll get the reverend to pop round to discuss it with you, if that's all right? Good day, Nessie.' Then he nodded to Marcie and headed for the door.

'Goodbye, Oliver.'

Once the door had closed behind him, Nessie turned back to her sister to find her sneering. 'Getting to be quite the little temptress, aren't you?' she said spitefully and the smile on Nessie's face instantly disappeared.

'Just what is *that* supposed to mean?' Nessie retaliated. 'As it happens, Oliv... Dr Dorsey popped in to check on Joseph.' She had to stop herself from adding, not that you give a hoot about the child. 'And while he was here I happened to mention that many of the poorer townspeople have a terrible fear of death. He suggested that if he could get the reverend to speak to them following a bereavement and help them to realise that their loved ones are going to a better place it might bring them some comfort.'

'Hmm, well, from where I was standing you looked to be very chummy! And isn't that another new gown you're wearing? Which of your admirers bought you that?'

'*Marcie!*' Nessie looked hurt. 'If you must know, Andre bought me the gown so that I would have one to wash and one to wear. I can hardly greet customers in the parlour in rags, can I?'

Marcie sniffed. Her sister suddenly looked every inch a lady and she was consumed with jealousy. Here was she being presented with a cheap brooch by the man who professed to love her while Nessie stood there in all her finery with two very attractive men fawning over her from what she could see of it.

'Look, don't let's argue.' Nessie's face softened. 'Come through to the back and I'll make you a nice hot drink. You look cold; I wouldn't be surprised if we didn't have some snow soon.'

Marcie followed her sister through to her living quarters and instantly her eyes spotted the warm cloak hanging on a nail on the back of the door. She pouted but didn't comment as Nessie hurried off to put the kettle on. Joseph's bright blue eyes followed Marcie across the room but she gave him no more than a cursory glance.

'There,' Nessie said brightly as Marcie settled in a chair. 'It shouldn't take long to boil so tell me what you're doing here on a week day.'

'The family have left to spend Christmas in London, as yer doctor friend probably told you,' she answered sarcastically. 'So being as we're all on top of the work, Cook gave us a bit o' time off to come into town an' do our Christmas shopping.'

'How lovely!' Nessie glanced at the bags and smiled, then becoming more serious she informed Marcie, 'Joseph has come down with a cold.

219

Andre has one too.'

Marcie shrugged, not that much interested as Nessie said cautiously, 'The doctor from London came a couple of weeks ago and he agreed with Dr Dorsey about what's wrong with Joseph. You did understand Joseph's diagnosis, didn't you?' She was shocked that Marcie hadn't seemed too interested in Joseph's condition, but then she supposed she shouldn't have been. She'd never shown much interest in the child since the day he'd been born.

'Yes, I understand, what I did forget to ask you is how long the doctors think he'll last.'

'There's no way of knowing, apparently. It depends how fast the tumour grows,' Nessie answered. 'He could have weeks, months or even a few years. Everyone is different.'

Marcie looked unconcerned. 'I dare say it's not a bad thing. We've always known there was something not right about him and he won't have much of a life as he is, will he?'

Thankfully the kettle began to sing then, preventing Nessie from making a stinging reply. Marcie really could be heartless at times.

They spent the next hour making small talk until it was time for Marcie to go and meet Eliza and once she was gone, Nessie felt almost relieved. She loved her sister but couldn't deny that there were times when she wanted to grab her by the shoulders and shake her till her teeth rattled!

Andre, Charlie and Reuben returned soon after following the funeral and while Reuben and Charlie went to stable the horses, Andre joined her in the parlour looking pale and unwell. He popped one of his pills into his mouth almost immediately and feeling that she knew him well enough to ask now, Nessie ventured cautiously, 'Do you have a medical condition, Andre? I notice that you keep those pills very close to hand.'

He eyed her for a moment as if he was deciding whether to confide in her or not and then answered, 'As it happens I have a bad heart. It was diagnosed when I was just a child and sadly as I grew up it worsened.'

'Oh!' Nessie looked so dismayed that he smiled at her.

'It's all right, as long as I keep taking the pills when they are needed and I don't overtax myself, I could go on for years.'

It suddenly hit her like a blow how much he had come to mean to her in a short time. He had shown her and her family nothing but kindness and the thought of anything happening to him was disturbing.

'Is there anything I could do that would make things easier for you?' she questioned.

His eyes softened. 'You already do. You almost run this part of the business now, which takes a great strain off me, I assure you. As I once admitted, I do not enjoy dealing with the public and Reuben has been a great help too. All in all, I think our little arrangement is working well, don't you?'

'Oh yes,' she answered hastily, and to herself she thought, and long may it continue.

Chapter Twenty-One

It began to snow on Christmas Eve and suddenly everywhere looked as if some giant unseen hand had painted everything white. The sooty chimneys in the town were covered in virgin snow and children played in the streets throwing snowballs and giggling, but Nessie was worried that Marcie wouldn't manage to get to them if it settled too deeply.

'She'll be here,' Reuben assured her as he mopped up the last of the juice from his bacon with a slice of bread. 'But I'd best get on now. We've another funeral the day after Boxing Day and me an' Charlie need to get the coffin finished. This one's a posh affair, solid mahogany, brass handles – the works – fer some toff who lived in one o' the big houses in Swan Lane.'

She nodded as she glanced towards Joseph who was sitting quietly on the chair beside her while she tried to tempt him to eat. He had hardly taken more than a few spoonfuls despite her best efforts, but then she supposed that his cold would have robbed him of his appetite. The smell of the Christmas puddings that were cooking in the range filled the kitchen and she smiled as she thought of how pleased Molly Liggins would be when she found out that one of them was for her. Nessie had also ordered a goose to be delivered to her cottage later that day and she felt a little ripple of satisfaction as she remembered Molly's hungry-eyed little offspring. She heard Molly enter the shop then to begin her morning work and thought what a godsend she had turned out to be. She was happy to do anything she was asked and she did it well, which had made a tremendous difference to Nessie's workload. Charlie was working hard too and he and Reuben appeared to be getting along famously, which was a bonus.

After tucking Joseph up on the sofa, she went through to Andre's quarters, armed with polish and a duster, as she still preferred to clean his rooms herself. Although this morning she wondered why she was bothering. He had told her the day before that he was going to spend Christmas with his friend, Jean-Paul, in Coventry and return late on Boxing Day. She found him poring over the letter that had arrived from France and before she could stop herself she asked carefully, 'From your parents is it, Andre?'

He glanced up. 'From my *maman* actually.' He sighed. 'My father and I are not ... how do you say? On good terms?'

'Oh, that's a shame. Especially at this time of year.' Nessie smiled at him sympathetically. 'Perhaps if you were to visit him you could mend the rift between you?'

He shook his head. 'No, I would not be welcome; he made that more than clear when I left. I am sure that he will be unaware that *maman* has written to me.'

Nessie frowned before going on, 'At least you still have your good friend, Jean-Paul. Did you

223

come to England together?'

'He came to England shortly after me and started his own business in Coventry, although he is too ill to work now.'

'He's no better then?'

Andre shook his head. 'No. Nor is he likely to be.' He jammed the letter from his mother into the pocket of his jacket and, clearly wishing to change the subject, said, 'Are you quite sure that you and Reuben are able to cope over Christmas?'

'We do every weekend, don't we?' she answered with a cheeky smile. 'So why should tonight and tomorrow be any different? You just go and enjoy your friend's company, we shall be fine.'

Humming, she set to polishing the fine old sideboard that took up almost the entire length of one wall.

Andre watched her and thanked the lord for sending her and Reuben to him. In just a short time they had turned his life around. His business was thriving for the first time and he didn't feel so alone now; in fact, he was feeling in a festive mood for the first time in years. If only Jean-Paul had been well it would have been perfect.

On Christmas Day, Marcie arrived mid-morning and Nessie greeted her with a warm hug. The fire was roaring up the chimney, the lamp in the middle of the table was giving off a cosy glow and everywhere looked warm and inviting. The goose that was cooking in the oven along with Nessie's home-made stuffing, a recipe that had been passed on to her by her mother, was making Reuben's stomach rumble with anticipation, although sadly, to Joseph, it was just another day.

'Merry Christmas,' Nessie greeted her as Marcie stamped the snow from her feet and glanced around at all the bowls of freshly cut holly that Nessie had placed about the room.

'Same to you,' Marcie muttered as she passed Nessie and Reuben their hastily wrapped presents, then hurried to the fireside to warm her hands and feet. Thankfully her boots didn't let in water like her old ones had but her toes were still icily cold.

Nessie was thrilled with the scarf she had bought for her and Reuben thanked her for his gloves, then Nessie passed her a large parcel and Marcie smiled expectantly.

'What is it?'

'Why, it's your Christmas present of course,' Nessie chuckled. 'You didn't think we wouldn't buy you anything, did you?'

Marcie quickly undid the string to reveal a thick cloak edged with fur in a warm russet colour and she gurgled with delight.

'Blimey, this'll be *so* much warmer than me old shawl,' she breathed, hardly able to believe her eyes.

'It isn't brand new,' Nessie admitted. 'And I stitched the fur around the edges to make it a little more fashionable but it's a lovely quality and it has a nice warm hood too.'

Marcie couldn't resist slipping it on and sashaying about the room. 'Cor, I feel like a proper lady in this,' she giggled. 'Eliza's goin' to be green with envy when she sees it.'

'Thanks, Nessie ... and Reuben,' she added as an afterthought.

Reuben grunted something and went back to the newspaper he was reading. Just for a second Nessie felt sad. She wished that Marcie and her brother could be a little closer. Even so, she was determined not to spoil this special day. It was already bittersweet as she thought of Christmases past when the family had all been together. Those days could never come again but she was grateful for the opportunity that Andre had offered them and for their warm, cosy home. More than ever, she realised just how lucky they were now that she had seen first-hand the poverty that existed in the surrounding courtyards.

'Right, I think it's time we gave Joseph his presents now,' she said brightly. She had bought him an abacus from the local toyshop with brightly coloured beads and Reuben had carved him a little toy train out of some of the offcuts of wood left over in the workshop. Thankfully he seemed much brighter today. His cold had gone and he was looking about with interest.

'Look, Joseph ... pretty.' She dropped to her knees beside him sliding the beads along the frame of the abacus and he suddenly gave her such a wonderful smile that her heart missed a beat. 'Perhaps the doctors were wrong,' she muttered hopefully. 'Perhaps it isn't a tumour and he's starting to get better.' She planted a gentle kiss on his pale cheek.

Reuben sighed as he looked across at her. He knew how much she adored Joseph but didn't want her to go raising her hopes. 'The doctors said that he'd have good days and bad days,' he pointed out gently and Marcie tossed her head.

'Of course he will, but I think we all know what the outcome will be,' she said heartlessly. 'And then you won't have to look after him and you can have a life of your own. I don't know why you took on the burden of caring for him when Mam... Well, all I'm saying is, he shouldn't be your responsibility. You should have let him go into the workhouse!'

'I can't believe you just said that,' Nessie retaliated. 'I've heard what happens to babies that end up in that awful place. One of the ladies from the courtyards works there sometimes and she said that the poor little mites in the nursery don't even cry after a time. They learn quickly that no one will come to them even if they do and more than half of them never even reach their first birthday. Could you really have expected me to condemn Joseph to that? He's still our family whether Mam is here or not.'

'Then go ahead and play Miss Goody Two Shoes,' Marcie replied furiously.

'Now then.' Reuben's voice sliced through the air, stopping what was fast developing into a row from going any further. 'Have you two forgotten what day it is?'

Both young women looked shamefaced then and glancing at Marcie, Nessie muttered, 'Sorry.'

'Me too.'

'That's better.' Reuben folded his paper and rose from the chair. 'Now, if you two think you can behave yourselves, I have to pop out for a while.'

'Pop out ... on Christmas morning?' Nessie was surprised and more than a little concerned.

'Yes, pop out,' he stated firmly. 'But I'll be back in plenty of time for dinner.' And with that he shrugged into his coat and disappeared out into the snow which had just started to fall again.

As he strode down Abbey Street wearing the warm gloves that Marcie had bought him he thought how pretty everywhere was. Even the dirty alleyways that led into the courtyards seemed as if they had been given a coat of gleaming white paint and looked brand new. The shop windows in the town had been decorated with holly and tinsel and there was a festive feeling in the air as the people who were out and about shouted greetings to each other. Today they could forget about work and the poverty most of them endured and enjoy the time with their families. Of course, he knew that it wouldn't last. Once the traffic started to stream along the road again the snow would turn to dirty slush and the gutters would overflow causing problems for the residents, but he didn't want to think about that for now.

His face creased into a frown as he fingered the wedge of money in his pocket and thought of the meeting ahead. He wasn't looking forward to it one little bit but felt that he had no alternative. Still, he tried to cheer himself, the sooner it's done the sooner I can go back to enjoying Christmas Day, and with that thought in mind he hurried on his way.

The town was almost deserted apart from the occasional family rushing to spend their day with

228

loved ones, the children's faces wreathed with smiles as they stepped along in their Sunday best, clinging to their parents' hands, and trying not to skid on the fast-falling snow. Soon he had left the marketplace in the town centre behind and made his way to the Pingle Fields. That too was deserted and he cut across the field towards Attleborough, leaving a trail of footprints in the undisturbed snow. He had almost reached it when a voice hissed, 'Psst ... Reuben... Over here!'

He turned to see a figure lurking among the bushes and after glancing quickly about to make sure that he wasn't being observed, he approached it.

'Have yer got me money?'

Reuben nodded, his lips set in a grim line. 'Aye, I have. But don't expect me to be doin' this again.' He fumbled in his pocket and as he extended the wad of money it was snatched from his hand and then the figure turned about and disappeared into the snow as if he had never been there. There had been no word of thanks, nothing, and with a shake of his head Reuben turned about and wearily retraced his steps.

Nessie looked at him with a question in her eyes when he returned but he merely hung his coat up and warmed himself at the fire with no explanation as to where he'd been, and she sensed it would be useless to ask. Reuben could close up like a clam when he wished to, as she knew to her cost.

The dinner she presented them with shortly after was delicious. The goose was cooked to perfection as were the crispy roast potatoes and the vegetables that she served with it. The Christmas pudding was a success too and Marcie crowed with delight when she found a shiny penny in her portion. 'I shall treat meself to some new ribbons on me next day off wi' this,' she informed them, sucking the coin clean and tucking it into her pocket and Nessie couldn't help but laugh at her.

As the afternoon began to darken, at Nessie's insistence, Reuben walked Marcie home, promising to be back as quickly as possible so he could watch Joseph while Nessie went to the Christmas Day service at Chilvers Coton Church.

The church was ablaze with candles when Nessie got there and as the choir sang much-loved carols and rejoiced in Christ's birth, she felt blessed. She was pleased, too, to see Dr Dorsey in the congregation and when the service was over she found him waiting for her at the lychgate looking so handsome in his smart suit and brightly patterned waistcoat that her heart gave a little lurch. He greeted her like an old friend and offered to give her a lift home in the family carriage and she flushed with confusion.

'Umm, I, er ... don't want you to go out of your way,' she stammered.

'It's hardly out of my way at all,' he insisted and the next minute he was handing her up onto the plush leather seat. Staring around at the luxurious upholstery, Nessie felt flustered. She had never been in a carriage like this before in the whole of her life, though she would have died rather than admit it to him.

'This is really kind of you,' she told him with a

smile that set his heart fluttering. 'But you really didn't have to. I was going to cut through the Pingle Fields and I'd have been home in no time at all.'

'Not such a good idea when there's still a murderer out there somewhere, is it? Better safe than sorry, eh?' His handsome face creased into a smile.

'The snow looks so pretty, doesn't it?' she remarked dreamily.

'I suppose it does but it isn't as pretty as you,' he said softly and now her heart began to hammer so loudly that she was afraid he must hear it. Oh, *why* couldn't we have been born of the same class? She knew that there could be no future for them. He was an educated doctor from an upper-class family while she was little more than a servant in a funeral parlour.

'Did you, er ... have a nice day?' she quickly asked, hoping to get the conversation onto safer ground.

He chuckled. 'As it happens, I did, although it wasn't much fun having Christmas dinner alone and it's very quiet back at the house with just the servants for company. Never mind, I'll bet the family are having a whale of a time in London.'

She nodded although, never having gone further than the neighbouring town of Bedworth, she had no idea what London was like apart from what she had read about in books.

'Have you ever visited the capital?' he asked, as if he had been able to read her mind, and she reluctantly shook her head.

'Hmm, well I read something the other day that

231

made me think of you.' When she raised an eye-brow he hurried on, 'Apparently, in some of the poorer parts of the city they are opening soup kitchens for the starving and the homeless. I thought if I could visit one and get an idea of how it's run I might open one in Nuneaton. What do you think of the idea? Do you think there's a need for one?'

'Oh yes, I do, I think it's a wonderful idea!' She leaned forward in her seat, her face animated and as the gas lamps in the street outside shone on her hair they turned it to bronzed gold. 'But I don't quite understand why this made you think of me?'

'Ah well, the thing is, I know how hard you are working to improve Andre's business and I thought if I could get him to sponsor the soup kitchen and it became common knowledge, it would endear him to the locals. And then of course I would need someone to help me run it, perhaps two or three times a week, do you think? That's if Andre was agreeable to the idea and he could spare you.'

'I'm sure he would be, he can be very generous,' she assured him, excited at the prospect. There were so many poor people in the courtyards and surrounding areas who often went for weeks with-out a proper meal. And then, as an idea occurred to her, she said excitedly, 'What if I could raise some more sponsors? Rich people from here-abouts. We could perhaps be able to supply the poor people with a meal *every* day then. I'm sure I could raise some interest in the project. Some of the women may even be willing to help run it.'

232

They were both leaning forward on their seats now, almost nose to nose in their excitement. Suddenly she frowned. 'But where would we serve these meals?'

'Leave that to me. There's a room behind Dr Peek's surgery that stands empty. It would be ideal and I'm sure he'd have no objection to me using it. We'd have to advertise what we're doing though, otherwise we could be left with an awful lot of soup on our hands.' There was a mischievous twinkle in his eye and suddenly aware of their closeness, Nessie sat back in her seat just as the carriage drew to a halt outside the funeral parlour.

'Let's talk some more about this when I pop in to see Joseph after the holiday,' he suggested and she nodded eagerly as he opened the door and helped her down onto the cobbles. The touch of his hand on hers sent shivers up her spine and when he bent and kissed her lightly on the cheek she felt as if it were on fire.

'Merry Christmas, sweet Nessie,' he muttered before getting back in the carriage.

She watched it pull away as the snow fell softly all around her.

Chapter Twenty-Two

'Oliver has had the most wonderful idea,' Nessie told Reuben when she hurried in out of the cold some minutes after Oliver had left.

'Oh yes, what's that then?' Reuben glanced up.

He was toasting his toes by the fire and had been enjoying a nap. Joseph was already tucked up in bed fast asleep.

Nessie hurriedly told him and Reuben frowned, not sure what to make of it. 'It all sounds well and good but do you think anyone would turn up?'

She nodded fervently. 'Oh yes, I'm sure they would.' Her face was glowing he noted and her eyes were sparkling with enthusiasm. 'Just think of it, Reuben. What a difference it would make to people who barely have enough food to survive. We could provide bread with the soup too, to make it more filling. And if we could get enough people willing to sponsor the soup kitchen we might even be able to provide proper cooked meals eventually.'

Reuben thought she was being rather optimistic but she was clearly so taken with the idea that he didn't want to spoil it for her. His sister had a heart as big as a bucket. Sometimes he wished that she wasn't quite so generous and thought of herself for once. He thought of little Joseph lying upstairs and sighed. Nessie loved him as if he were her own child but what would happen if she decided that she wanted to get wed one day? Would a man be willing to take on a child like Joseph – if he were still alive, that was? Still, that was something to worry about in the future. For now, he supposed they should count their blessings, although he still desperately missed the work he had once done on the railways before his accident.

His thoughts moved on to a certain young lady he had met the week before and without realising it colour crept into his cheeks. He had spoken to her outside the church following a service and she had shyly thanked him for the respect the funeral parlour had paid to her uncle, the deceased.

'He was such a kind man,' she'd told him with tears glistening on her long, dark lashes, and Reuben's heart had done a little lurch. He discovered that her father owned Harding's, the hardware shop in town, and she told him to pop in and see her if he ever happened to be passing. As yet he hadn't taken her up on the invite. The funeral parlour had been too busy for a start and what with Christmas and one thing and another he hadn't found the time. *But I will, as soon as things settle down a bit*, he promised himself, and while Nessie bustled away to check on Joseph, he sat by the fire and thought of seeing her again.

Andre did not return on Boxing Day evening, as he had promised. But he was back fairly early the following morning. When Nessie heard his key in the lock she hurried into the shop to greet him with a smile on her face but it died away instantly when she saw his expression. He looked truly ghastly and when he sank down onto the nearest chair and buried his face in his hands she rushed over to him. Something was very clearly amiss.

'Andre, has something happened?' Dropping to her knees beside him she put her arm across his shoulder.

For a moment, he remained in the same position then he raised his head and she saw the raw pain in his eyes.

'It's my friend ... Jean-Paul, he passed away last night.'

'Oh no, I'm so sorry.' It sounded so inadequate but what more could she say? She was used to dealing with people who had lost loved ones by now but knew all too well how different it was when one of those people was someone close to you.

'When we have attended to the funeral we have booked this afternoon, I am going to ask Charlie and Reuben to come with me to Coventry to bring him back here in the hearse.'

'Are the roads clear enough for the horses to get through?' she asked worriedly. Coventry was at least nine or ten miles away, which was far enough for the horses to go there and back even in good weather.

He nodded. 'Yes, I think we'll manage it. Most of the main roads aren't too bad from what I could see of it.'

'Will you be arranging his funeral?'

Another nod. 'Of course, and I must also write to his parents to inform them of his death,' he said woodenly.

'Do you think they'll come from France to attend the funeral?'

He shook his head, his eyes hardening. 'I think it is highly unlikely. They turned their backs on him as my parents, or at least my father, did on me.'

'But why?'

He stared at her for a moment. They were on easy terms now and could talk to each other on most subjects but he had always kept his past and his personal life very private.

'They all turned their backs on us because they

discovered that Jean-Paul and I were...' He struggled to find the right words. 'That Jean-Paul and I were ... more than friends.'

She stared at him uncomprehendingly for a moment and then as his words sank in and she realised the meaning of them she gasped.

'Y ... you mean that you and he ... *loved* each other?' her words came out as a whisper.

He nodded and lowered his head again as he struggled with his grief, and instantly sympathy overcame the shock and she held him tightly as she might have a child.

'Oh, Andre, I'm *so* sorry,' she muttered, rocking him gently. Andre and Jean-Paul had obviously been lovers, but who was she to judge them? Suddenly things began to fall into place like the pieces of a jigsaw puzzle. The reason he had disappeared off each week. His reluctance to speak of Jean-Paul. Should his secret ever get out it would be the end of his business, for no one would wish to use his services then. He was openly sobbing now.

'I ... I would be grateful if you could keep what I have just told you to yourself,' he said through his tears. 'Not all people are as understanding as you and it is hard enough...'

'It will be our secret,' she assured him, then, rising, she headed for his drawing room where he kept a cut-glass decanter full of brandy on a small polished table. Today she felt he was in need of something a little stronger than tea.

It was late that evening by the time the men arrived back home with Jean-Paul's body.

'Phew, that was some trek,' Reuben said tiredly

when he finally joined his sister in their cosy sitting room. She hurriedly sawed some generous slices from a fresh baked loaf and placed it beside a big dish of broth she had been keeping warm for him. There was some more for Andre too, although she doubted that he would eat it.

'Did you get to see Jean-Paul?' she enquired curiously.

Reuben shook his head. 'Not a glimpse. Andre had him thoroughly wrapped in a sheet before we were allowed to carry him out to the hearse. Why do you ask?'

She shrugged. 'Just curious, I suppose.' She retired to bed, thinking of Andre who was still locked away in the preparation room with his lover. She knew that the relationship the two men had shared would be frowned on as being unnatural as well as illegal but something her mother had once said popped into her head. *Love will strike where it will.* We can't always choose who we fall in love with. It just happens.

Why, she wondered, did that saying suddenly conjure up a picture of Oliver Dorsey's handsome face? It was the last thing she thought of as she fell into a deep and contented sleep.

The New Year came and went quietly and Nessie didn't feel it would be right to celebrate while Andre grieved for his friend. 'I have arranged Jean-Paul's funeral for the day after tomorrow,' he told her. 'It will be a quiet affair and following a short service he will be interred in Chilvers Coton churchyard.'

'Would you mind if I attended? I'm sure Molly

could manage everything here for a while,' she asked. She saw the gratitude in his eyes as he nodded. She couldn't bear to think of him being the only mourner. And so, the next day, Nessie attended Jean-Paul's funeral standing close to Andre's side in the pew. At one point, she discreetly held his hand and she could feel him shaking. In life they had been forced to hide the love they felt for each other and now in death Andre was having to do the same because people would never understand. She would stand by Andre come what may. He was far more than her employer now. He was her friend and he had shown her and her family nothing but trust and kindness and she would never forget that. But for now, she could only offer what comfort she could and help him through the dark days ahead.

Chapter Twenty-Three

January 1865

'Eeh, just 'ark at this,' Mrs Roe said. She was sitting in the fireside chair in the kitchen reading an old newspaper with a pair of steel-rimmed spectacles perched on the end of her nose. 'It says that they opened the Clifton Suspension Bridge linkin' Somerset an' Gloucestershire last month, twenty-eight years after startin' it. It's 254 feet above the River Avon! Huh! Yer wouldn't get me on it, I'm tellin' yer. How could it be safe danglin' so high up in the air?'

'Hmm, well I'm afraid that's what you call progress,' Mrs Bainbridge, who was sitting at the table sipping tea from a bone china cup, primly replied. Things had been very relaxed since the family's departure for London with only Master Oliver to cater to, but everything was due to change now, for Mrs Bainbridge had received a letter from Mr Dorsey that morning saying that he would be returning the day after next.

'Will any of the family be returning with him?' Marcie had asked innocently when the house-keeper informed them.

'He didn't say so,' the housekeeper said. 'Although I wouldn't be surprised if Master George didn't come back with him. I doubt his father will want him to be gone for too long.'

Marcie's heart had begun to thump with excitement at the thought of seeing George again. It felt like a lifetime since they had been together. Admittedly she was still miffed with him over the cheap gift he had given her for Christmas but everything would be different when he got home, she was sure. He had promised her that he would talk to his mother and tell her how he felt about her while he was away so things were bound to change, she thought excitedly. She doubted she would be allowed to live in the house till after their wedding but neither could she be allowed to continue as a servant, and so she had already planned to ask Nessie if she could stay with her and Reuben while she got her trousseau together and made plans for the wedding.

Now outside in the bitterly cold laundry room,

where she had been sent to work because the laundry maid was ill, she paused in the act of feeding the wet washing through the mangle and pictured herself drifting down the aisle towards George in a beautiful gown with a matching bonnet. She would have to ask Reuben to give her away. They'd not got along too well for the last couple of years admittedly, but in the absence of their father she had nobody else. She was still standing there locked in a daydream when Mrs Bainbridge barged in with a pile of dirty towels in her arm. She dumped them unceremoniously on the floor and barked, 'That washing won't wring itself, girl. Get your head out of the clouds and put your back into it. If you get it done early I just might let you have a few hours off this afternoon before the master returns. It'll be back to normal hours then. No more slacking from any of you.'

'Yes, Mrs Bainbridge,' Marcie answered meekly and as the woman turned to leave she poked her tongue out at her and grinned. By, she'd make sure she suffered when she was one of the mistresses of the house, she thought with satisfaction and humming merrily she got on with the job in hand.

That afternoon she walked into town to visit Nessie, who had just finished arranging yet another funeral. As predicted, the cold weather was creating havoc with both the old and the young alike and the parlour had never been so busy. Reuben was really struggling to keep up with the work, despite having Charlie Liggins to help him, and Nessie was spending more and more time on the paperwork side of the business as she attempted to keep the books up to date.

'No admirers today?' Marcie quipped as she entered the parlour and Nessie smiled as she glanced up, wondering why Marcie always tried to be so awkward. After what Andre had confided to her about his relationship with Jean-Paul he was certainly not able to be classed as an admirer, could Marcie have known it.

'And good afternoon to you too,' she answered a little sarcastically. Marcie had the good grace to look a little ashamed. 'So, what brings you here today?'

'It's the last chance of freedom before the master returns.' She leaned over and sniffed at a large vase of lilies appreciatively. The shop always smelled so nice and everywhere was gleaming. Her sister had certainly made a huge difference to the place, she had to grudgingly admit to herself. She always looked so smart as well but then the gowns she owned would be nothing compared to the ones Marcie intended to invest in once George had made his intentions clear to his family. She imagined drawing up outside in the family carriage, all clad in her satins and lace, and Nessie's face as the groom helped her down, and had to stifle a giggle. That would show her! Glancing round, she asked, 'Where's Mr Chevalier?'

'In his rooms. He's not feeling too well.' Nessie avoided her eyes. If truth be told, Andre had almost locked himself away to grieve for Jean-Paul, leaving the running of the place to her.

'Go through to the sitting room,' she told Marcie as the shop bell tinkled and a red-eyed woman entered. 'I'll be in as soon as I can.'

'Actually, I think I'll have a walk round the shops and come back later,' she told Nessie, feeling slightly disgruntled. She had just celebrated her birthday and had hoped that Nessie would have a present for her but if she had, it didn't look like she was going to get it today!

Marcie wandered through the town, glancing into the shops, and paused to stare enviously at the gowns in the dressmaker's window. She was still there when a salacious voice behind her said, 'Why, it's Marcie Carson, ain't it?'

She whipped about to find Seth Grimshaw standing there.

'How's that sister o' yours goin' on?' he asked, and despite the fact that Marcie found the man repulsive, jealousy ripped through her again. What was it about her sister that drew men to her like moths to a flame?

'Hmm, an' how are you gettin' along? Workin' up at the Dorseys' place now, ain't yer? The family 'ave done well fer themselves from what I can see of it. Yer sister seems very cosily settled in wi' the Frenchman.'

'As it happens, Nessie and Reuben have separate living quarters to Mr Chevalier,' Marcie informed him icily. Even though she and Nessie didn't always see eye to eye she wasn't going to let him stand there and slander her sister. She turned her back on him then and strode away, leaving him with a grin on his face as he stroked his hairy chin. Nessie might well be living with her brother at present but if he had his way she'd be living with him shortly. Perhaps it was time he started to woo her properly? With this in mind he headed for the flower stall. She'd given him short shrift the last time he visited her but perhaps now she might be a little more amenable to what he intended to say.

Soon after, armed with a bunch of roses that he considered he had paid an extortionate price for because they were out of season, he headed for the funeral parlour where Nessie was sitting at Andre's desk working out the details for the next funeral. When the bell tinkled, she glanced up and he saw a frown appear.

'These are fer you, m'dear.' He swept off his hat and gave a theatrical little bow before holding the roses out to her as if he was presenting her with the crown jewels.

'Why would you be bringing me flowers?' she asked, and Seth squirmed. This wasn't going nearly as well as he'd hoped it would.

'Because...' he faltered eventually. 'I've decided it's finally time I took meself a wife and you would do nicely. I have me own cottage and business, as you know, so you'd have no money worries. So what do you say?'

Nessie supposed that she should be angry but instead she felt amused. Seth seemed to think that she was going to jump at the chance but as he soon discovered he was about to be very disappointed.

'I thank you for the offer, Mr Grimshaw,' she answered primly. 'But actually I have no plans to marry you or anybody else for that matter for some time to come, so I'll wish you good day.'

Angry red colour rose in his cheeks as he stared back at her as if he could hardly believe his ears.

Not so very long ago he'd had the power to turn her and her family out on the streets. Now he was offering her the chance to have a home of her own and she was turning him down. Just who the *hell* did the ungrateful little bitch think she was?

'You just might live to regret this,' he growled viciously, trembling with rage. 'You might be shacked up comfortably here with the Frenchman for the time being but I'm offering to make you *my wife,* not my bit on the side!'

'I am no one's bit on the side, as you so crudely put it.' Nessie was angry now too. 'So please leave immediately.'

Hearing the raised voices, Andre suddenly appeared from his sitting room and looking from one to the other of them he asked, 'What is going on out here?'

'I've just asked this ... this gentleman to leave,' Nessie told him through gritted teeth.

'Then, sir, I suggest you do as the lady asks,' Andre said calmly.

'Don't worry, I'm goin'.' Grimshaw's lip curled in disgust as he stared at Nessie. This was the second time she had humiliated him but he would make sure she didn't get a third chance. 'Your name will be mud in this town by the time I've done wi' yer,' he threatened. 'When people know what a den o' vice yer run here they'll take their business elsewhere an' they'll all hear what a *slut* you are!'

Andre, his lips set in a straight grim line, advanced on him angrily but Grimshaw turned quickly and hurried towards the door. 'I'll see meself out,' he spat spitefully. 'You just stay 'ere

245

an' take care o' yer whore cos I wouldn't touch 'er wi' a bargepole now!' As the door slammed resoundingly behind him, Nessie slumped against the desk, the colour drained from her face.

'What a despicable man! And you told me he was once your landlord?'

When Nessie nodded, he shook his head. 'Then let us be grateful you got away from him. And don't worry, if he returns I shall personally throw him out of the door.'

'I ... I don't think he'll come back but I think he's more than capable of spreading rumours as he threatened,' Nessie said in a shaky voice.

'Pah, let him. While he is lying about us he'll be leaving some other poor person alone.' It was at that moment that Marcie returned and seeing her sister's pale face she asked, 'What's wrong? You're as pale as a piece o' putty.'

Nessie told her what had happened with Grimshaw but like Andre, Marcie wasn't overly concerned. 'Take no notice of him, he's a poisonous little weasel,' she advised, then taking her sister's elbow she led her towards the sitting room. It was time for her to make Nessie a cup of tea for a change, by the looks of it. She wanted to keep in her sister's good books so that she would get her birthday present. She hoped it would be something nice, she was sixteen now after all and that was a special birthday!

While Marcie pottered about busily filling the kettle and putting it on the range to boil Nessie sat at the table gazing into space as she relived the threats that Mr Grimshaw had made and she had the awful feeling that she had just made herself the most terrible enemy. She and Reuben had worked so hard to set Andre's business on the right track and now, just when it was beginning to thrive, this had to happen. Only time would tell whether he would carry his threats through and whether or not it would lose them custom.

Chapter Twenty-Four

Marcie was sitting in the kitchen having a tea break with the cook two days later when Eliza came bustling in excitedly saying, 'The coach is comin' down the drive. The master is back!'

'Is anyone else with him?' Marcie asked innocently.

Eliza giggled. 'Well 'ow should I know, I can't see through the walls o' the carriage, can I? But we'll see soon enough.'

Marcie longed to go to the front door to see for herself but she wasn't allowed to go beyond the green baize door into the main house and so she sat impatiently waiting for someone to come and tell them. Soon Mrs Bainbridge entered the room to inform Cook, 'There'll be just the master for dinner in the dining room tonight, Mrs Roe.'

'On his own then, is he?' the woman asked.

Mrs Bainbridge nodded. 'Yes. The rest of the family have stayed on in London.'

'I bet they're havin' a wonderful time what wi' goin' to all them balls an' parties,' Eliza com-

247

mented with a dreamy look in her eye. 'Especially Miss Leonora an' Master George.'

Marcie's lips tightened as she blinked back tears and stared hastily down into her cup. George had promised her he wouldn't be gone for more than a couple of weeks so where the hell was he?

'Did he say when the others might be coming back?' she asked the housekeeper in a small voice. The woman blinked, surprised that she should want to know.

'He did mention that Master George might be returning next week but he didn't say what day. Why do you ask?' she questioned suspiciously.

'Oh, just curious, I suppose,' Marcie answered, aware that Eliza was watching her closely but then the subject was changed and soon after Marcie returned to the laundry room.

As they were getting ready for bed that night in their room up in the servants' quarters, Eliza said casually, 'Yer seemed to be upset when yer learned that Master George hadn't come back. Why was that?'

'No, I wasn't,' Marcie snapped defensively but Eliza was like a dog with a bone.

'Now I come to think about it, I've noticed that you ain't been goin' out fer yer nightly walks since the young master's been gone. There weren't nothin' goin' on between yer, was there?'

Marcie longed to tell her that, yes, there was something going on between them but instead she answered, 'Of course there wasn't. Why would the master's son look at me?' Part of her longed to confide her feelings for George to Eliza, because they had grown close and Marcie was fond of her. In fact, Marcie counted her as a friend now but she didn't feel the time was right yet.

'Hmm. Why wouldn't he? It's a known fact that he's got an eye for a pretty face.' Eliza lifted her hairbrush and began to tug it through her tangles but thankfully she didn't say any more and shortly after they hopped into bed and Eliza blew out the candle. Marcie lay in the darkness, her heart thumping. Had Eliza guessed their secret? She sighed. Hopefully there was only one more week to go before he came home and then the need for all the secrecy would be over, once he'd told his parents about his intentions towards her. Turning on her side she closed her eyes and waited for sleep to claim her.

One week to the day later a carriage drew up outside and Mrs Dorsey and George alighted.

There had been no word to say when they might be arriving but Mrs Bainbridge was on hand to greet them.

'Good afternoon, sir, madam. We weren't expecting you back.'

Connie Dorsey grinned. 'I wasn't planning on coming back so soon to be honest, Harriet, but I couldn't stand the thought of attendin' one more ball or party!' She grinned. 'I'm afraid I'm too old fer all that fuss and palaver now, but Leonora is having the time of her life an' she's got a string of admirers a mile long hanging on her every word. But tell me, is everything all right here?'

'Everything is fine,' Mrs Bainbridge assured her as they walked up the steps together leaving the groom to unload the luggage, while George went inside to find his father.

'Good, then would you get the maid to have our bags taken up to our rooms, please, and I could kill for a cup of tea. It's been a long journey.' She entered the hall where the maid was hovering to take her hat and coat then headed for the drawing room to stand by the fire and get warm.

It was teatime when Marcie had finished her chores in the laundry and discovering that the family were back, she beamed from ear to ear. Oh, how she wished she could just rush through and see George straight away but she would have to be patient. He was sure to want to meet her that evening to tell her how his family had taken the news that he intended to marry her.

When she and Eliza finally retired to bed she lay in an agony of impatience waiting for Eliza to drop off to sleep. At last her breathing became even and she began to gently snore as Marcie sneaked out of bed and stealthily crept down the back staircase. She had made the journey so many times now that she knew every stair that creaked and was able to avoid them. Outside it was raining and a vicious wind tugged at her skirts but she was oblivious to the cold and wet as she skipped towards the stables.

At the bottom of the steep ladder she paused to whisper, 'George ... are you there?' There was no answer save for the whinnying of the horses and the sighing of the wind outside. Carefully she climbed the ladder and once she had reached the top she sat in a corner with her shawl wrapped tightly about her and her knees tucked under her chin to try to keep out the cold. The minutes ticked away and soon she was so cold that she had lost the feeling in her hands and feet but still she sat on, convinced that he would come. She had no idea at what time she slipped into an uneasy doze but when she blinked awake she was horrified to see that an eerie grey light was shining through the grubby window. It was dawn. The house would be awake soon and there would be hell to pay if Eliza reported her missing. She rose quickly and swayed. Her limbs were stiff from the awkward position she had sat in all night and she felt bilious and weak. Even so she forced herself to hurry back to her room, relieved to see that Eliza was only just beginning to stir.

'Crikey you're up bright an' early,' Eliza commented when she woke and stretched some minutes later. As Marcie had hoped, Eliza had assumed that she'd just got up and dressed. But then seeing the bits of hay in her hair she frowned, 'You ain't been to bed, have you?'

'Of course I have,' Marcie snapped a little too quickly.

'Then why have yer gots bits of hay in yer hair, then?'

Marcie's hand rose to her head and she flushed. 'I, er ... couldn't sleep so I got up early and went for a walk over to the stables to see the horses.'

'Hmm!' Eliza's raised eyebrows told Marcie that she didn't believe her but there was no time to discuss it now. If they didn't get a shufty on and get themselves down to the kitchen, Mrs Roe would have their guts for garters.

Throughout breakfast, Marcie sat miserably picking at her food and she was almost glad when it was over and she could escape to the laundry room, from which she had a view of the stables. George was sure to come out to see his horse soon and when he did he'd have some explaining to do! Despite the bitterly cold weather she kept the door open all morning so as not to restrict the view of anyone crossing the yard as she tackled the mountain of washing that had been dumped ready for her to attend to following the family's return. She knew every item of clothing that belonged to George and she was particularly vicious as she scrubbed at the neck of his shirts, as if she was taking her disappointment and her frustrations out on him. At last her patience was rewarded when she saw him striding towards the stable block wearing riding breeches and holding a riding crop. He looked so handsome that for a moment she could only admire him but then she was up and running like the wind in his wake.

'George!'

Her voice sliced through the air and he paused to look back at her with a frown on his face before quickly glancing around to make sure that no one else had heard her. As she reached him he grabbed her arm and yanked her roughly around the side of the stables where they couldn't be seen.

She pulled her arm from his grasp and, rubbing at the bruised flesh, stared at him accusingly. 'Why didn't you come last night? I fell asleep waiting for you and ended up in the hay loft all night!' Her voice was heavy with tears as he nervously swiped a thick lock of hair from his forehead.

'I meant to but I was so tired after the journey home that I fell asleep.'

Marcie tossed her head. 'Huh! *That* desperate to see me, were you?' she spat accusingly.

'Look, Marcie ... I do need to talk to you, as it happens, but we can't talk here. I'll meet you tonight ... I promise.'

'Just see as you do, because I need to talk to you too,' she said threateningly. 'There's something I need to tell you.'

He gave a curt nod and strode away without another word. He hadn't said that he'd missed her or given any indication of whether he'd spoken to his parents about her, but he would after tonight, she silently vowed as she made her way back to the laundry. By God he would!

'*George* ... are you here?' she hissed that night as she entered the stables. She was much later than she'd planned to be because Eliza had lain awake chatting.

'Yes, up here!'

Relief washed over her as she lifted her drab skirt and began to climb the ladder to the hay loft. He was waiting for her at the top but he made no move to take her in his arms as he normally would. His face was in shadow but she sensed that he was tense.

'Did you miss me?' she cooed suggestively as she held her arms out to him but he quickly stepped away from her and her face fell. 'What's wrong?'

He gave a deep sigh. 'Look, there's no easy way to tell you this so I may as well get it over with. I'm not going to be able to see you for a while... Not here at least.'

Marcie felt as if someone had slapped her in the face. 'Wh-what do you mean?' she faltered. 'We're promised to each other. You were going to tell your parents about us. You *have* told them, haven't you?'

Her eyes were adjusting to the darkness now and she saw how uncomfortable he looked. 'The thing is...' he began shakily. 'While I was away ... in London I, er ... became betrothed to ... Belinda Lewis.'

'*You what!*' Marcie swayed for a moment as her hand flew to her mouth.

'I'm so sorry,' he rushed on. 'But you must realise that in my position I have to do what the family expects of me. Me and Belinda have known each other all our lives and it's always been taken for granted that one day we would marry... But don't fret, that doesn't mean it has to be the end of us. We can still go on seeing each other. Belinda need never know.'

Marcie's lips peeled back from her teeth as she snarled, 'What you mean is you want me to be your bit on the side. You want me to carry on scrubbing your dirty washing while you and Belinda live the life of Riley! Huh! I don't *think* so!' She was trembling with rage as she leaned towards him and stabbed a finger viciously into his chest. 'You *promised* me that we'd be together. You took advantage of me and now you're going to have to pay for it and stand by your word.'

'Be reasonable, Marcie,' he implored. 'I know I said we could be together and we can. I'll rent you a little cottage somewhere, if you like, and come and see you when I'm able to.'

'I don't *think* so.'

'What do you mean?' He looked nervous now.

'What I *mean* is ... you're going to have to do the right thing by me. You see I'm carrying your *child!*' She watched with satisfaction as the colour drained from his face like water from a dam.

After a moment he gulped deep in his throat before saying, 'B-but you told me that you were taking precautions!'

She shrugged. 'I was but we must have slipped up.'

He made a huge effort to calm himself. 'In that case I certainly will have to find you somewhere nice to live.'

'Oh no, you won't! I want to live *here* not be some dirty little secret that you keep hidden away. And I'm sure your mother will want to know that I'm carrying her first grandchild.'

'Y-you won't tell her, will you?' he asked faintly.

Marcie grinned, she had the upper hand now. 'Only if you don't. And I hardly think your darling Belinda will want you when she knows you're going to be a father, do you?'

George buried his face in his hands as he suddenly saw the wonderful future he'd had planned slipping away from him.

'You've got *one* week to tell your parents about me and what's happening!' Marcie warned and as he stared helplessly back at her he knew that she meant it.

Chapter Twenty-Five

Nessie peeped beneath the mattress of Reuben's bed and frowned when she saw the money that had been there was gone. Half of her was relieved, the other half wondered what was going on. Reuben couldn't possibly have spent that amount and how had he come by it in the first place? On many occasions she had come close to questioning him about it, especially since she had seen him speaking to Snowy White. Thankfully, she hadn't and now she just hoped that this would be the end of it. Reuben seemed so happy at the minute and she had a suspicion that it was something to do with a certain Miss Maria Harding, whose father owned a shop in town. Twice this week he'd got all togged up in his Sunday best and disappeared out sporting a posy of flowers. Nessie had teased him about it and he'd got all defensive.

'Why shouldn't I have a lady friend?' he'd asked and Nessie had giggled.

'I'm actually really pleased for you, I haven't seen you looking so happy in ages,' she'd teased and his face had turned the colour of a boiled beetroot. 'So when are you going to bring her home to tea so that I can meet her?'

'Soon, I suppose,' Reuben had muttered and Nessie was looking forward to it. Molly had told her that the Hardings were a lovely family.

Now Nessie hurried away to get ready for

Oliver who was coming to pick her up to take her to see the room that might become the new soup kitchen.

She took especial pains over doing her hair and changed into her best lilac gown. Then she daringly applied a tiny amount of rouge to her cheeks and a small amount of lip salve to her lips.

'I shouldn't be too long, Molly,' she told her. 'And you do know that Joseph's dinner is all ready for him and—'

'Will you *please* stop fussing.' Molly giggled. 'I'm more than capable and take as long as you like.'

Nessie gave her a grateful smile, marvelling at how much Molly had changed in the time she had known her. She had gained a little weight and there was colour in her cheeks and a twinkle in her eye now. She was always spotlessly dressed, even if her clothes were still somewhat shabby and sometimes Nessie wondered how she had ever managed without her. They heard the rattle of wheels on the cobbles outside and seconds later a carriage drew up and Oliver hopped out and hurried in, his eyes alight with excitement.

'All fit then?'

Nessie could hear the enthusiasm in his voice and nodded.

'Then let's be on our way, shall we?' He smiled at Molly as Nessie headed for the door and soon they were on their way to Red Roofs, the surgery in Riversley Road.

'It's been shut up for some time, so Dr Peek informs me, so I don't know what state it will be in,' Oliver warned her as he fiddled with a bunch of keys. The door groaned as he pushed it open and the rusty hinges creaked alarmingly but Oliver didn't seem concerned. 'It just needs a bit of oil on it,' he said optimistically.

Nessie glanced about and had to stop herself from shuddering. The place was in a terrible state. There were empty boxes and pieces of out-of-date medical equipment scattered everywhere. The windows and floor were filthy and festoons of cobwebs hung from the ceiling.

'Blimey, how are we *ever* going to get this place clean enough to serve food in? I didn't realise it was going to be this bad,' Oliver said, not looking quite so sure about the idea.

'There's nothing wrong with it that a bit of hot soapy water and elbow grease won't put right! We can get Reuben, Charlie and Molly to come and help and between us we'll have it right as rain in no time.' She set off across the room, sending clouds of dust flying into the air. 'There's room for a nice long counter here where we can serve the food, look,' she said, trying to build his enthusiasm again. 'And there's space where people can sit to eat. Didn't Dr Peek say he had some old chairs we could have?'

'Well yes, he did, but I can't promise what state they'll be in,' Oliver answered.

'What if they are in a state? We can always paint them,' Nessie pointed out.

He grinned as he looked towards her, wondering if there was anything this young woman couldn't do and suddenly he felt optimistic again. Somehow he felt anything was possible with Nessie. 'So you think this room will eventually be suitable then?'

'Why ever not? It's right on the edge of town, easy for people to get to and not too far out and it's a very nice size room.'

'And when do you think we should make a start on it?'

'Just as soon as we can. If either Andre or Reuben will keep an eye on Joseph tonight I can come round and start clearing the rubbish out into the yard. We'll be able to see where we're going then and exactly what needs doing.' She began to walk around among the boxes and the rubbish. There was a big fireplace with a large bread oven in the wall, which led her to think that at one time this might have been part of a doctor's living quarters. 'I can cook the soup over the fire,' she said thoughtfully. 'Though the chimney will need a good sweep ... and there's a sink there with a pump, so that will be useful. Oh, and we'll need oil lamps to light the place, of course, we can't expect people to sit and eat in darkness, and pots and pans and cutlery, and some tables...The walls will probably need a coat of limewash too, once the place has been cleared and scrubbed.'

Oliver grinned, happy to leave this side of the planning to her; she clearly knew what she was doing.

'The only trouble is all this is going to cost,' she fretted. 'And I know I haven't anywhere near enough saved to pay for it all.'

'I shall be seeing to that side of it,' Oliver told her firmly. 'And I'll also be happy to help get the place ready. I'm not afraid of getting my hands dirty.'

When she smiled at him he found himself thinking how pretty she was and had to force himself to drag his eyes away from her. Then he gave a little cough and said, 'Perhaps I should be getting you back now?'

'What was it like then?' Molly asked the second she stepped through the door. Nessie had told her what they hoped to do and Molly thought it was an excellent idea. In fact, she had already started to spread the word among the people in the courtyards and they were all for it.

'The room was perfect for what we had in mind. At least it will be when it's had a huge tidy up,' Nessie told her. 'It's absolutely filthy at the moment but it's nothing a good scrub can't cure.'

'And I'm just the woman to help yer do it,' Molly declared. 'An' I reckon some o' the women from the courtyard's u'd muck in an' help, an' all, if I asked 'em.'

'Any help would be welcome,' Nessie admitted.

So that evening she and Molly set off through the marketplace armed with mops and buckets and a pile of rags. Nessie gawped in amazement to see a number of women waiting for them when they got to the surgery.

'What...?'

Molly tittered. 'Didn't I say I'd put the word out for volunteers? The people in the courtyards appreciate what yer tryin' to do so those as can have come to help.'

'Thank you all so much,' Nessie said, trying to swallow the large lump that had formed in her throat.

'Just let us in out o' the cold, dear, an' let us get crackin',' one of the women piped up, so Nessie hastily unlocked the door and somehow they all piled in.

'*Bleedin' 'ell!*' Molly didn't usually swear in front of Nessie but once she saw the state of the place she couldn't stop herself. 'Ugh! It's *filthy*.' She rolled her sleeves up, and ordered bossily, 'Come on, ladies, let's get all this old rubbish out inter the yard so as we can see what we're doin'.'

Seconds later the crowd of women were working like busy little ants, cleaning the windows, scrubbing the floors and swiping the cobwebs from the ceiling. Oliver arrived amidst all this and looked surprised but pleased.

'I thought it was going to take us months to get this place ready for opening but at the rate you're all going it will be weeks,' he told the little army of women gratefully. Already, lovely black-and-white tiles were appearing from under the layers of dust and dirt on the floor and as he glanced at Nessie, who was down on her hands and knees scrubbing as if her life depended on it, he had to smile. She was dressed in her very oldest clothes and her hair was tied back into the nape of her neck with a blue ribbon. There was a large smear of dirt across her nose and yet he thought that somehow, she still managed to look so very beautiful.

After several hours, once Nessie had thanked them profusely, the women began to drift away to their homes.

'And I think it's time you went home too now,' Oliver said sternly. 'You look all in. Come on, lock up and I'll give you a lift back.'

Nessie shook her head. 'There's no need for you to do that. I haven't got far to go.'

'Even so, it's getting late and you never know who's about,' Oliver said insistently and she nodded.

When they arrived back at the funeral parlour she looked weary but happy. 'We will make this work, won't we?' she asked as he helped her down from the carriage.

Holding onto her hand for a fraction longer than was necessary, he nodded and once again her heart did a little tattoo in her chest and she wished that the moment could last forever.

'We most certainly will, miss. Now go and get some rest, that's doctor's orders.'

She threw back her head and laughed merrily before tripping away, leaving him standing with a wide smile on his face.

Chapter Twenty-Six

'The mistress called me into the drawin' room to talk to me about a party they're throwin' here in March when Miss Leonora comes home,' Marcie heard Mrs Roe telling one of the grooms as she sat having a morning break a few days after Mrs Dorsey had returned.

'Oh aye, an' what's that in aid of?' the young groom asked.

'It's to celebrate Master George's engagement

to Belinda Lewis. They've not made it official yet, what wi' Miss Leonora still bein' away, but soon as ever she comes home we're goin' to be rushed off us feet. It's to be a right grand affair, by the sounds of it; they're hirin' a band an' everythin'.'

Marcie felt the floor rush up to greet her. She wasn't usually one for having the vapours but this had shocked her to the core.

'Will, grab her quick!' Mrs Roe ordered and the young man managed to catch Marcie just as she slithered off the chair.

'Eliza, get the smellin' salts,' the cook ordered and seconds later the foulest smell was wafted under Marcie's nose, making her sneeze.

'Ugh ... get that away from me.' She pushed the salts away as the room slowly swam back into focus. Mrs Roe was standing beside her, urgently fanning her with a piece of linen but Marcie barely noticed. It had been days since she'd warned George what she would do if he didn't stand by her but this news confirmed that he had no intention of changing his plans to marry Belinda. He'd not been over to the hay loft once since she'd informed him that he was about to become a father. Well fine, she thought angrily, if this is how he wants to play it, so be it! Slightly steadier now, she rose to her feet and yanked off her apron.

'Where is Mrs Dorsey?' she asked Eliza, who was hovering close by.

'Er ... she was in the drawing room when I was polishing in there a while back,' the girl answered.

'Why would you want to know that?' Cook frowned as she watched Marcie roll her sleeves down and fasten her cuffs.

263

'I wish to see her,' Marcie answered.

Mrs Roe looked horrified. 'You can't just go bargin' in on the mistress! If there's anythin' you need to say you must say it through Mrs Bainbridge. You're only a *maid!*'

'I'm quite capable of speaking for myself,' Marcie snapped, heading for the green baize door, then without further ado she slammed through it into the hallway of the main house. Once outside the drawing room she raised her hand to tuck some stray curls behind her ears then she tapped on the door.

'Come in.'

Marcie entered the room to find Mrs Dorsey sitting on the window seat that overlooked the lawns, embroidering. She looked surprised when she saw Marcie and asked, 'Yes? Was there somethin' you wanted?'

Marcie hesitated, then sticking her chin in the air she answered, 'There's something I need to speak to you about. And it's important.'

'Oh, then you'd better go on.' Connie Dorsey lay her embroidery aside and gave Marcie her full attention.

'The thing is, ma'am, I've been seeing your son George for some time now. It was him that told me about the maid's job that was going here.'

Mrs Dorsey frowned as she demanded, 'What do you mean ... *seeing* my son? Of course you must have seen him – he lives here!' There was a note of impatience in her voice now but Marcie would not be deterred.

'What I should have said is, we've been walking out together ... courting ... whatever you want to call it.'

Mrs Dorsey raised an eyebrow. 'I hardly *think* so,' she snapped. 'My son is about to become engaged to Belinda Lewis.'

Marcie shook her head. 'He can't. He's already unofficially engaged to me. He promised that he was going to tell you about us while you were all in London over Christmas but then when he came home he said that he'd had to promise to marry Belinda Lewis because it was expected of him.'

'Utter rubbish!' Mrs Dorsey was annoyed by now. Who did this girl think she was anyway, coming in here saying such ridiculous things? George would never be so silly as to dabble with the maids. He knew which side his bread was buttered and had always known that he and Belinda would wed one day.

'It's *not* rubbish!' Marcie said hotly. 'Just fetch him in here and ask him, if you don't believe me!'

'He's out with his father, as it happens,' Mrs Dorsey answered, her face straight. 'But if it will put an end to all this nonsense come back here at five o'clock this evening.'

'I will,' Marcie said plainly. 'But the other thing you ought to know before I go is that I'm carrying George's child, *your* grandchild, Mrs Dorsey.' And with that Marcie flounced away, leaving Connie Dorsey staring after her open-mouthed.

For the rest of the afternoon, Marcie stayed in her room. She had told Mrs Roe that she was unwell, and after the fainting fit she'd had earlier, the cook had believed her and agreed that she should stay in bed for the rest of the day. Eliza had been up to her twice bringing tea and sandwiches, which she later took away untouched, adding credence to the story that she was ill.

Now, as five o'clock approached, she rose and brushed her hair, studying her reflection in the small, cracked mirror that hung above her chest of drawers. She looked pale but her eyes were steely with determination. She wanted the life that George had promised her and she was prepared to fight for it.

Once downstairs she swept through the kitchen and headed for the green baize door again as the cook watched her bewildered. Mrs Dorsey had sent word that dinner was to be delayed that evening and now here was Marcie waltzing off into the main house as if she owned the place. Something was going on, that was for sure, she told Eliza with a sigh.

Once more Marcie tapped on the door and was told to enter and she was gratified to find Mr and Mrs Dorsey and George all waiting for her.

Mr Dorsey had a face on him like a dark thundercloud as he stood before the fire with his arms behind his back. Mrs Dorsey was standing with her hands folded primly at her waist and George was by the window looking decidedly uncomfortable.

'What's all this nonsense you've been spouting to my wife then, girl?' Mr Dorsey demanded, his moustache quivering with anger.

George was avoiding her eyes, she noticed, but Marcie stood her ground. 'Tell them, George,' she said boldly. 'About us and the promises you made to me!'

'I ... I don't know what you're talking about.'

Marcie reeled, feeling as if someone had slapped her in the face. 'How can you stand there and say that after all the times we've lain together? You told me that you would speak to your parents... That we'd be together.'

'Ah, so *that's* your game, is it?' Johnny Dorsey drew himself up to his full height. 'Wanted to be a lady, did you, and you thought you'd trap my son into making it happen!' Then swinging round to George, he barked, 'Is any of this true?'

George shook his head. 'No ... she's lying.'

Marcie's face crumpled. 'But that's not true, George, for God's sake tell them the truth. I'm carrying your baby ... you know I am!'

As he continued to avoid looking at her and shook his head, tears sprang to her eyes. Connie Dorsey was watching her closely and despite her son's denial, a little measure of doubt crept into her mind.

'I think you'd best leave,' she said surprisingly gently. If she was lying, the man responsible would surely stand by her. She was a very pretty girl, after all. But she was also painfully aware that her son had an eye for a shapely ankle, so could it be that she was telling the truth? The thought of it made her blood run cold.

'I ... I *won't* leave,' Marcie said defiantly. 'This is your grandchild I'm carrying and if George doesn't do right by me I'll shout it from the roof-tops. Belinda Lewis won't be so keen on marrying him *then*, will she?'

'Look, let's calm down,' Johnny Dorsey said,

267

trying to defuse the situation. 'I'm not an unreasonable man so I'll ask you, have you any evidence to prove that George is the baby's father?'

'Such as what?' Marcie was clearly very upset now.

'Perhaps someone who could verify that you have been seeing each other?'

She shook her head, suddenly not so sure of herself. She and George had always gone to great lengths to keep their relationship a secret and it seemed now that was going to backfire on her.

'Hmm.' Johnny Dorsey began to pace up and down. 'It seems that it's your word against his then... But I'll tell you what I'm prepared to do. So long as you keep these malicious little lies to yourself, I'll settle a sum of money to tide you over until after the child is born.'

'Pay me off, you mean?' Marcie flared. 'And then I'm left to bring his baby up while he gets away scot-free? *Never!*'

Johnny Dorsey shook his head. 'Then what *do* you want? You clearly can't go on working here after this, you must see that. In the circumstances, I think I'm being more than generous. I could send you packing with a flea in your ear and without a penny piece. How would you like that, my girl?'

'George, *please* tell them the truth,' Marcie implored, but he simply remained where he was, staring through the window as if she wasn't even in the room.

'You'd best go and pack your things, lass,' Connie Dorsey said then, more gently. She was clearly upset and not at all sure that she believed her son was innocent. 'Stay here tonight and before you go in the morning come and see me.'

Marcie's hands clenched into fists of frustration as she stared at George for what seemed like an eternity. Then, turning on her heel, tears streaming down her cheeks, she stormed from the room, slamming the door behind her so hard that it danced on its hinges.

'Right that's that sorted then. Perhaps we can have dinner now,' Johnny Dorsey said flatly. Connie, meanwhile, was eyeing George suspiciously and when Johnny left the room to give orders to serve supper, she told him in a stern voice, 'We'll talk later, my lad! I'm not so sure that you're as innocent in all this as you're saying.'

'I am so,' George retorted but his voice lacked conviction and as he left the room her eyes followed him suspiciously.

Upstairs, Marcie threw herself onto her bed and sobbed violently. Everything had gone horribly wrong. What would she do now? And where would she go? She shuddered to think of what Reuben would say if she turned up on his and Nessie's doorstep, but what option did she have? It was either go to them or the Union workhouse and she had no intention of going there. She shuddered just thinking of it. It stood in the Bull Ring, a dark forbidding place from the outside. On a few occasions, she had seen the children that lived there being marched to Chilvers Coton Church for the morning service on a Sunday, their eyes dull and without hope. They were all dressed in the same shapeless, grey clothes, the girls' hair shorn so that they were barely distinguishable from the boys. No, she decided, she would rather throw herself on Reuben's mercy than end up in that godforsaken place.

She was still lying there crying when Eliza appeared sometime later. The girl took one look at her and sat on the side of the bed and gave her a hug.

'What's wrong, pet?' she asked gently.

'I ... I'm goin' to have a baby,' Marcie hiccuped. 'An' it's Master George's but he's denyin' it.'

Eliza looked shocked but then suddenly Marcie said excitedly, 'Perhaps you could tell his parents I'm telling the truth. You always wondered where I kept wanderin' off to of an evening, didn't you? Well I was going to see George, see, an' if you told them that...'

'Hold on there!' Eliza held up a hand. 'How do I know you're tellin' the truth? I only know what you told me so if I said any different I'd be lyin', wouldn't I? I want to help you, Marcie, truly I do, but I can't risk losin' me job.'

Marcie's shoulders sagged. She and George had made such a good job of keeping their relationship a secret, it really was her word against his and she knew exactly who his parents would choose to believe.

Chapter Twenty-Seven

That evening Nessie had her first proper introduction to Maria when she came to share a meal with them, and they took to each other instantly. Maria was a pretty girl with curly brown hair and bright blue eyes. She was quite short, but what she lacked in height she more than made up for in personality and as Nessie watched her and Reuben together, she knew that they were just right for each other.

When the meal was finished Maria offered to help with the pots and was more than happy to help Reuben keep an eye on Joseph, so when Oliver once again arrived to pick Nessie up in his carriage, she left with an easy mind. She had told him that she was quite capable of making her own way to the premises but he was nervous about her walking about alone in the darkened streets.

Oliver was such a caring person, but she had accepted that they were too far apart in social standing for there ever to be anything other than friendship between them, but that didn't stop her heart doing a little flutter every time she saw him. If only things could have been different!

As he helped her up into the carriage her heart was beating painfully and her emotions were in turmoil. She couldn't help but wonder what would happen in the future if ever Reuben wanted to marry Maria, which he undoubtedly would.

Then the responsibility for Joseph would rest squarely on her own shoulders, and what about her job? Would Andre still want her living so close to him without the respectability of Reuben there as a chaperone? She was painfully aware that there was gossip already so what would it be like then?

Annoyed with herself, Nessie pushed the thoughts away. Her mother had always been a great one for believing that tomorrow should be faced when it came and now she decided that she would do the same.

'I've got a pile of pots and pans in the back that my mother has donated,' Oliver told her happily, pulling her thoughts back to the present. 'Oh, and you'd best make the most of the ride this evening. From now on we won't be travelling quite so stylishly. I've bought myself a pony and a small barouche that I shall drive about myself from now on. It's much smaller than this one but perfectly suitable for what I'll need it for.'

'I shall look forward to seeing it,' she told him as she settled in her seat. Once again, she had worn her oldest clothes. She had no intention of spoiling her best ones, but as she glanced at his smart jacket and silk waistcoat with a matching cravat, she was suddenly very aware of the difference between them.

They found Molly already there with the oil lamps lit and her sleeves rolled up all ready to start work.

'I reckon we'll have this place ready to open in less than a month at this rate,' Molly said optimistically as they both carried yet more buckets full of dirty water out to the yard. 'Charlie's ready to start limewashin' the walls soon as ever we've got the place clean enough.'

Overhearing her remark, Oliver, who was moving all the tables and chairs into the middle of the room, smiled. Both Molly and Nessie had worked like horses and yet despite the fact that they both looked dead on their feet, neither of them was complaining. He tried to picture Leonora, his spoiled little sister, in their position and could only imagine the tantrums she would have been throwing by now had she had to get her hands dirty. Since going to work for Dr Peek he had seen an entirely different kind of life to the one he was used to. He realised now what an easy life he and his siblings had led. They had had maids to wait on them, private tutors, and when they were old enough, private schools that ensured they received the best education that money could buy. He had never known what it was to be hungry or cold; there had always been good nourishing meals served to them in a cosy nursery with a warm fire roaring up the chimney and a kindly nanny who spoiled them almost as shamelessly as their mother did.

Now, though, he daily visited people who had had to pawn their wedding rings to afford a visit from him. Only that morning, he had pressed a sixpence into the hand of one of his patients whose baby was failing rather than take the money for his fee. He doubted the poor little mite would last the rest of the week and all because the mother was so malnourished she was not producing enough milk to feed him. He had seen children, their small legs bent with rickets and their

273

hair running with lice, clad in clothes that the maids at Haunchwood House would have refused to use for dusters. There was rarely a fire in their homes unless they had managed to find some wood to burn, which meant there was nothing to cook on, so many of them survived on scraps of bread and cheese. And yet, rather than be repulsed by what he saw, it had only made him more determined to help them whenever he could.

In Nessie, he recognised a kindred soul. She too wanted to help wherever she could. After what had happened to her mother, many young women would have left the rest of the family to it and struck out on their own, yet she had taken on the mantel of caring for them all with no thought for herself.

He suddenly realised that he had paused in what he was doing as these thoughts raced through his mind and as he glanced across at Nessie who was pushing a lock of her glorious copper-coloured hair from her forehead, he blushed. Even in her old clothes with sweat and dirt on her face she still managed to look so beautiful. Nessie's beauty shone from within and he wondered what it was about her that drew him to her. He decided it must be her kindness and compassion, for she was nothing at all like the girls he'd had brief romantic liaisons with before. The thought perplexed him but he forced himself to continue what he was doing and almost an hour later they had achieved what they had set out to do that evening.

'There, then!' Molly rubbed her hands together

as she stared about with satisfaction. 'When my Charlie finishes work tomorrow I'll get him round here to start limewashin' the walls.'

'I'll come and help too,' Oliver piped up and Molly and Nessie giggled. His posh clothes were smeared with dirt, as was his face. His hands were filthy too, although he didn't seem overly concerned about it.

'Then I suggest you sort some older togs out to wear,' Molly said light-heartedly. 'Sloshin' lime-wash on the walls can be a dirty business.'

'Don't forget, you'll be roughing it in my little carriage after tonight,' Oliver teased later as Nessie hopped out of the carriage on to the cobbles when he dropped her home.

'Well, seeing as I've only ever been used to Shanks's pony I doubt that will bother me much. And thank you for the lift.'

'It was my pleasure entirely.'

She glanced up at him. The light from the street lamp was turning his hair to silver gold, and she had to resist the urge to wipe a streak of dirt from his cheek. Oh, how she longed to reach out and touch him but instead she bade him a polite goodnight and hurried away up the dark alleyway that led to the back of the funeral parlour, wishing that things could have been different between them.

She was just about to enter the yard when a dark figure appeared and pushed past her with a grunt. Startled, she flattened herself against the wall, watching the shape hurry on down the alley. It wasn't until he emerged into the street and the oil lamp shone on his face that she recognised who it was. It was Snowy White, which could only mean one thing. Reuben must be having dealings with him again! Anger replaced her fear. *Right, it's time me and that brother of mine had a few words,* she decided. Intending to do just that she strode purposefully towards the back door but on entering Reuben had clearly gone to bed. Suddenly very tired, she decided the confrontation could wait till morning.

Chapter Twenty-Eight

The sound of Reuben opening the back door early the next morning brought Nessie starting awake and for a moment she wondered where she was, but then, remembering her confrontation with Snowy White the night before and her determination to speak to her brother, she hurried into the kitchen.

Reuben glanced towards her but before she could say anything, he told her, 'Can't stop now. We've got a really early funeral so I have to get the horses and the hearse ready. We're buryin' that lawyer from Swan Lane an' Andre wants everythin' just right so I'll have me breakfast later. Ta-ra!'

She sighed as the door slammed shut behind him and after glancing at the tin clock on the mantelshelf she was shocked to see that it was almost eight o'clock. After hurriedly filling the kettle she went to check on Joseph but he was still

276

fast asleep. As she was passing Reuben's room, she paused, then without giving herself time to change her mind she opened the door and approached his unmade bed. Slowly she lifted the mattress and gasped as she saw that once again there was a small bundle of bank notes there. Surely Reuben couldn't be stupid enough to try following in their father's footsteps?

Her father had never been the best of providers and she could remember her mother having bitter arguments with him at times when he would suddenly present her with a wedge of money. At other times most of his wages would go over the bar in the pub and he didn't like it at all when his wife had demanded to know where all this money had suddenly come from. Now it looked suspiciously like Reuben might be going the same way. The money beneath his mattress was far more than he had earned in the time he'd been working for Andre and if he was getting involved with Snowy White she was sure that he must be up to no good.

Sighing, she reflected that it hadn't been the best of starts to the new day and with a heavy heart she went to make the tea.

At that moment Marcie was also having a bad time of it. She had bundled her possessions into a bag and after saying a tearful goodbye to Eliza, it was time to go and see the mistress. She had lain awake all night praying that George would have a change of heart and make an honest woman of her and as she tentatively went down the stairs from the servants' quarters, a tiny bit of hope was still alive.

The cook said nothing when she entered the kitchen dressed in the clothes she had arrived in. Word had clearly spread that she was leaving and she merely inclined her head as Marcie passed her heading for the green baize door.

'I didn't think she'd last long,' she commented to Eliza, pausing in her act of rolling pastry for an apple pie. 'Too pretty and too flighty fer her own good, that one is, if yer were to ask me!'

Eliza bit down on her lip. She had told the cook that Marcie would be leaving but she hadn't told her why, although she doubted it would stay a secret for long. Gossip spread like wildfire among the servants.

Marcie, meanwhile, was standing in front of the door that led to the morning room. Raising her hand, she gently tapped on it and almost instantly a voice ordered, 'Come in!' The mistress had clearly been waiting for her.

Connie Dorsey was standing by the long sash-cord window that overlooked the sweeping lawns surrounding the house, but there was no sign of George and Marcie's heart sank. She had come expecting a fight but the mistress seemed perturbed and upset, particularly now that she had seen Marcie again. With her lovely brunette hair and her deep-blue eyes, Connie was again forced to wonder if there was indeed any truth in what the girl was saying. She adored her son but she was also painfully aware of his failings and his weakness for a pretty face.

Crossing to a small armoire she lifted an envelope and held it out to Marcie, saying, 'I hope everything goes well for you, pet.'

Marcie blinked and stared at her without offering to take the money. 'You hope all goes well for me?' she snapped incredulously. 'But how can it after this? I'm carrying your grandchild ... doesn't that mean *anything* to you? How am I supposed to raise it on my own when the money in that envelope has run out? Don't you care that your own flesh and blood will be labelled a *bastard?*'

'That's quite enough of that talk, miss!' Connie had drawn herself up to her full height, but there was a wobble in her voice. 'George still maintains that this child is nothing to do with him.'

'Then he's a *liar!*' Marcie declared passionately. 'And if he thinks I'm just going to walk away without a word he has another think coming!'

Connie sighed. 'Look, just take this and go,' she persuaded. 'There is nothin' to be gained by us standin' here arguing like two fishwives. You'll find there's more than enough in there to see you through till after the baby is born and then I've no doubt some chap will snap you up, a pretty girl like you.'

'But I don't want *some* chap!' Marcie was on the verge of tears. 'George is the child's father. It should be *him* takin' responsibility for his actions!'

'But George is engaged to be married to someone else,' Connie pointed out gently and Marcie tossed her head.

'Yes, Belinda, and we all know why, don't we? It's because his father wants the two families to come together because her father has money. Ask yourself, how would I know that if George hadn't told me?'

Connie had no answer to that and crossing to Marcie she pressed the envelope into her hand. 'I'll talk to him again and if anything changes I'll come and see you,' she promised. 'Oliver tells me that your sister lives at the back of Chevalier's Funeral Parlour in town. Is that where you'll be?'

Marcie nodded, her eyes flashing. 'Yes ... for now. But don't think this is the end of it. I have no intention of watching George marry Belinda and living happily ever after leaving me to raise his baby. If he doesn't do the right thing I shall *personally* make sure that the Lewises are aware of what's going on. Do you think they'll be so keen for their precious girl to marry him then?'

With that she turned on her heel and slammed out of the room leaving Connie feeling shaken. The girl had clearly got spirit and she had no doubt whatsoever that she would do what she was threatening, and what would Johnny say then? Only that morning, before he had left to visit one of his factories with George, he had told her, 'Get rid of the damn girl. Shove a little money her way, that's clearly what she's after, her sort always is, then send her packing!'

Well, she had done what he had requested but she had a horrible feeling they hadn't seen the last of Marcie Carson, not by a long shot.

Back up in her room, Marcie put on the cloak that Nessie had given her for Christmas and put her bonnet on, then lifting her small bundle she took one last glance about the room she had shared with Eliza and made her way down to the kitchen.

Most of the staff were busily going about their duties but Eliza and the cook were there and she tearfully said her goodbyes to them before making for the green baize door.

'Eeh, where do yer think yer goin'?' Eliza asked worriedly.

Marcie stared at her with her nose in the air. 'I intend to leave by the front door,' she informed her plainly and the girl watched in amazement as she let herself into the hallway. Halfway along it, Marcie paused to stare at two beautiful porcelain figures of a shepherd and shepherdess. They were two of the mistress's favourites and were very rare and expensive. She knew because Eliza always panicked when she was asked to dust them in case she broke them. Marcie peered at the Meissen stamp on the bottom of them before untying her bundle and throwing them in among her clothes. They should fetch a pretty penny, she reckoned, should she ever need to sell them. Then looking neither left nor right she marched to the front door and let herself out, leaving the door swinging open behind her. She felt no guilt, only a determination that she would make George suffer for what he had done to her.

It was only when she reached the end of the drive and began to follow the road into town that she slowed her steps and allowed the tears to fall: angry heartbroken tears for the way she had been treated. George had led her to believe that they had a future together but she wasn't done with him yet!

It was mid-morning by the time she turned into Abbey Street. Her stomach was rumbling ominously and she felt sick, but she'd been feeling sick most mornings of late. Through the funeral shop window she could see Nessie in deep discussion with a woman who was clad from head to toe in black. Someone recently bereaved, she supposed, organising the deceased's funeral.

'Why, this is a nice surprise,' Nessie said a little later as she entered the living quarters where Marcie was patiently waiting for her. 'Come into town to do some shopping have...' Her voice trailed away as she saw that Marcie was dressed in her old clothes with a bundle lying at her feet.

'Not exactly.' Marcie squirmed and hurriedly took another gulp of the tea she had just made. 'The thing is ... I walked out.'

'You walked out!' Nessie looked incredulous. 'But I thought you were happy working there?'

'How can anyone be happy washing up after people and peeling vegetables all day?' Marcie spat. 'But that wasn't why I left.' She kept her head down then, avoiding her sister's eyes as she went on. 'The thing is ... someone there, one of the men was ... you know? Making it difficult for me.'

Nessie frowned. Something didn't quite ring true; Marcie was well able to stick up for herself.

'What do you mean ... making things difficult?'

'Just that ... lying in wait for me an' tryin' to take advantage.'

'So why didn't you speak to the mistress about it? From what I've heard Connie Dorsey is a very reasonable woman.'

'Not when the chap I'm on about is her son!' Marcie answered and Nessie was shocked. *Surely* she couldn't mean Oliver.

'Which one?' her voice came out as a squeak.

'George, the youngest.'

Nessie felt relief sweep through her and realised in that instant that she was becoming too fond of Oliver, but now wasn't the time to think about that. For the moment, she must concentrate on Marcie. 'So what do you intend to do?'

Marcie looked at her sheepishly. 'I, er ... I was hopin' you'd let me stay here for a while. Just till I find meself a new job, o' course.'

Nessie frowned. 'But you do realise that it's not up to me? I only work for Andre. I shall have to ask him if he'll allow it.'

Marcie snorted. 'Of course, he'll allow it,' she scoffed. 'You've got him eatin' out o' the palm o' your hand. *Anyone* can see that.'

If only she knew the truth, Nessie thought, but aloud she said, 'I'll have a word with him just as soon as he gets back.' She then turned and went back to what she had been doing with a sick feeling in her gut. Everything had been going so well. Trust Marcie to spoil things. Still, she was her sister at the end of the day, so she would do her best for her just as she always had.

Chapter Twenty-Nine

'Of course your sister must stay for as long as she needs to,' Andre told her generously when he returned just before lunchtime. Nessie had explained to him what had happened and she sighed

283

with relief. She would have hated for him to think that she was taking advantage of his kindness.

Molly appeared then with a wicker basket on her arm. 'I'm just popping to the market to get the food shopping. I've got the list but are you sure there's nothing else you need?'

Nessie flashed her a smile. 'No, thank you, I think that's everything, and don't rush.'

Molly cheerfully went on her way and soon she was walking among the stalls, inspecting the fruit and vegetables and looking for the best buys as she always did. At one stall, she paused to buy some apples and she was just about to pay for them when she became aware of three women huddled together just behind her. She recognised one of them as Lilly Burton. Lilly lived in the next courtyard to Molly and was very well known for being generous with her favours to just about any bloke that was willing to pay for them. Most of her ill-gotten gains went into the gin house and her poor children ran about like wild little street urchins, often in rags with no shoes on their feet. Molly had never had a great deal to do with the woman but now something she was saying made her ears prick up.

'Aye, they reckon the hot-arsed little slut is playin' one against the other,' Lilly said, shaking her head knowingly and setting her double chins dancing. 'She's got that little Frenchman she's workin' for eatin' out o' the palm o' her hand be all accounts, an' *now* she's set her sights on the new young doctor.' She chuckled. 'Can't say as I blame her on that account, mind you! He's a bit of all right, ain't he? But then, so is the Frenchman, so she can't lose, from what I can see of it. Whichever one she hooks will see her right.'

Molly felt her blood begin to boil. It was clear that the women were gossiping about Nessie and she couldn't stand by and allow it. Nessie's kindness had turned her life around and there was nothing she wouldn't have done for her.

'On about Nessie Carson, are you, Lilly?' she asked innocently.

Lilly flushed when she spotted her. 'Oh, er ... yes we were as a matter o' fact but then you work for the Frenchman an' all, don't yer? So you'd know all about what's goin on.'

'Oh, I work for him all right,' Molly agreed as two angry red patches of colour burned in her cheeks. 'And I'd like to know who it is that's spreading these malicious rumours about him and Nessie.'

'Why, it were Seth Grimshaw as told me all about the goin's on. An' he should know. He told me himself that when the family fell on hard times, Nessie used to pay him ... yer know?'

Molly stared at her with contempt. The woman was dressed in a revealing old gown that left nothing to the imagination. The bodice was so tight that her enormous, sagging breasts looked in danger of falling out of it at any minute, and her heavily rouged cheeks stood out in stark contrast to her pale, pock-marked skin.

'*Shame* on you for listening to such rubbish, Lilly Burton!' Molly snapped, her eyes flashing. 'You should know what a malicious man Seth Grimshaw is, after all, it's a well-known fact that you've paid him your rent in kind yourself for

285

years! An' *you* needn't titter, Dora Bell.' Molly wagged a warning finger in Lilly's friend's face. ''Cos *your* husband is a regular visitor to Lilly an' all, especially when he's had his fill in the alehouse of an evenin'! Seth Grimshaw is only spreadin' these lies because Nessie wouldn't lie down for him. Did you know he'd even offered her a cottage if she'd only let him have his wicked way with her? No, I didn't think so goin' by the looks on yer faces.'

Dora Bell's mouth was hanging slackly open now but Molly was only just warming up. 'As for Mr Chevalier, why, he's a gentleman. There's nothin' goin' on between him an' Nessie, I can assure yer. An' as for Dr Dorsey ... he an' Nessie are workin' side by side to open a soup kitchen for the people o' the town who are starvin'. I bet you won't be averse to sendin' your kids there, will yer, Lilly? An' happen it'll be the first square meal the poor little sods will have had fer many a long day cos it's a known fact you don't look after the poor little buggers!'

'Why... How *dare* you!' Lilly spluttered, uncomfortably aware that people were stopping to listen to the altercation now. 'I do *so* look after me kids, don't I, Dora?'

Dora clearly wasn't enjoying herself so much since the revelation about her husband and she stormed off without a word as Lilly stood there with her cheeks flaming. The other woman who had been enjoying the gossip quickly did the same and after a moment, Lilly turned and slunk away into the crowd.

Deeply concerned, Molly promptly made her

286

way back home, her mood for shopping thoroughly ruined. If Seth Grimshaw was telling such malicious lies they would spread like wildfire and Nessie's name would soon be mud!

Reuben was surprised to see Marcie at the kitchen table slicing a loaf when he came home for some lunch. Nessie was standing at the stove stirring a large pan of vegetable broth and he glanced at her before asking Marcie, much as her sister had, 'So what brings you here on a weekday? Not your day off, is it?'

Marcie flushed as she continued with her task. 'No, it ain't. Nessie will tell you what's happened later on. But for now, sit down an' eat. At least while yer in here I don't have to listen to all that hammerin' an' bangin' comin' from the workshop. It's enough to drive you mad!'

'Then I humbly apologise for disturbing you,' Reuben answered sarcastically. 'Me an' Charlie'll have to think of another way to build the coffins wi'out makin' any noise.'

They had almost finished their meal when the bell above the parlour door tinkled and Nessie instantly rose to her feet.

'I'll just go and see who it is and what they want,' she told them as she hurried through to the front of the shop.

'Huh, fancy having to disturb her meal,' Marcie commented as she slathered butter onto another slice of bread.

Reuben gave her a wry grin. 'It's a funeral parlour, Marcie,' he pointed out. 'An' people can call on us in the middle of the night if need be, let alone in the middle of a meal. We're used to it now.'

'Ugh!' She grimaced with distaste. 'I really don't know how you bear it. Being next to all these dead people all the while I mean.'

'As it happens, Nessie never sees a body an' I don't have to very often either. Andre sees to all that side of it,' he informed her coldly. His dish was empty now and scraping his chair back from the table he left the room without so much as giving her another glance. Seconds later the banging and hammering resumed and Marcie sighed. She had an idea she wasn't going to enjoy living here. But then, she consoled herself, it would only be until George came to his senses.

In the shop Nessie found a young woman sobbing pitifully into the arms of a young man. She rightly assumed he was her husband and he confirmed it when he said shakily, 'We lost our baby this morning, miss, an' we wondered if we could arrange his funeral. We ain't got a lot o' money, I'm afraid. The missus ain't been able to work since she gave birth an' I'm an apprentice to the tailor in town so I only earn a small wage as yet. But someone told us that we could pay the bill off monthly. Is that right? We want him buried proper, like. He was our first child, see?'

'Yes, it is right and of course we can help you,' Nessie assured him sympathetically. 'Now, why don't you both take a seat while I go and make you both a nice hot cup of tea and then you can tell me all about him and what sort of funeral you'd like? I'm so very sorry for your loss.' She ushered them to two velvet-covered chairs then hurried away.

When she returned with the tea tray, the woman was still sobbing violently and Nessie's heart went out to her as she reached across and gently patted her hand.

'Me poor lad,' the woman wailed. 'I can't believe I'll never see him again.'

'But you *will*,' Nessie told her gently. 'Just try to imagine that he's gone on before you to a better place.' She pointed at the sky. 'I like to think that up there is an open door that all our loved ones pass through. Once there they are free of pain and suffering and they sit and watch the open door patiently as they wait for us to join them.'

The woman blinked as she thought on her words. 'Do you *really* believe that?'

'Oh yes, I certainly do,' Nessie assured her. 'I've no doubt your little boy will already be up there feeling happy and watching you, enjoying his own little piece of heaven.'

'But how can he be when he's back at home cold and stiff and wrapped in a sheet?' the bereaved mother whimpered.

'Ah, that is only his shell,' Nessie quickly assured her. 'His soul has already flown free.'

The young woman blinked and wiped her nose on the edge of her shawl as Andre, who had overheard the conversation from behind the door of his sitting room, backed away unseen. There was no doubt about it, Nessie had turned his business around with her sympathetic ways and her kindly words. And he quite liked the idea of the open door. Perhaps Jean-Paul was waiting through that door for him? *He truly hoped so.*

That evening Nessie asked Marcie if she would like to go to see the room they were preparing for the soup kitchen but Marcie declined the offer. Nessie was concerned about her. She had barely said more than half a dozen words all day and she seemed to be deeply troubled about something, which led Nessie to believe that there was more to Marcie leaving her job than she had told her. Molly had been unusually quiet too, ever since returning from the town that morning.

Oliver had agreed to come and pick Nessie up in his new cart but she decided that she would leave early and walk to Riversley Road before he arrived. It was only a stone's throw away from the shop and she'd decided that the less time they spent alone together from now on the better. She was becoming far too fond of him for her own good, so as much as it hurt her, she felt that she must distance herself a little, especially now that Marcie had returned home. Oliver was sure to know about the situation and her accusations against George, so it would no doubt affect their relationship anyway.

Molly was already there when she arrived and was busily lime-washing the last wall. 'Looks good, don't it?' Molly said as she paused to stand back and look at her handiwork.

'It certainly does,' Nessie agreed, although privately she thought Molly had probably managed to get more on herself than on the walls. It was in her hair, on her nose and all over her old clothes but Molly didn't seem to mind and the room certainly looked very bright and clean now.

Molly glanced over her shoulder then and remarked, 'On yer own? You usually arrive wi' Dr Dorsey.'

'Oh, I thought I'd come a bit early tonight.' Nessie hastily began to fasten a large apron about her waist but not before Molly had noticed the flush that rose to her cheeks at the mention of him.

Ah, so that's the way the land lies, is it? she thought. Then turning back to the job in hand she continued with what she was doing, sincerely hoping that Nessie wasn't heading for heartache. Oliver was a doctor after all, while Nessie was merely an employee in a funeral parlour. They were from different classes and as nice as they both were, everybody knew that the two didn't mix.

Chapter Thirty

When Oliver drew the horse to a halt outside the funeral parlour he was surprised to find that Nessie wasn't there waiting for him so he knocked on the door.

Reuben answered it and smiled at him. 'If it's Nessie you're after, I'm afraid she left some time ago,' he told him apologetically. 'Said something about wanting to make an early start, I believe.'

'Oh, very well, thanks, Reuben.' Oliver climbed back up on to the seat of the little barouche with a frown on his face. He really didn't like Nessie wandering about at night with a murderer on the loose. He was also disappointed not to get her on her own for a few minutes.

Urging the horse on he set off again, pondering on just how much he looked forward to seeing Nessie nowadays. But now he was concerned that what he had discovered that evening might have already put a distance between them. His mother had told him at dinner that Marcie had left because she had accused George of making her pregnant, which had caused an almighty row among the family.

'If this is true, you should do the right thing and stand by the girl,' Oliver had stated angrily, which had resulted in his brother storming out of the room.

'Why don't you just keep your nose out of things that don't concern you,' his father had ranted. 'I'm well aware that you're seein' far too much o' that sister of hers, an' all. It's bad enough that you chose to go into medicine rather than join me in the businesses without you mixing with trollops like that!'

'Nessie is *not* a trollop,' Oliver had growled, then he too had risen from the table and slammed from the room.

He had got the distinct impression that his mother more than half-believed the girl but his father was adamant that Marcie was a strumpet, and George had flatly denied the union. Now the atmosphere back there was so bad that he was actually grateful to get out of the place.

It was an excuse to be close to Nessie too, and

to him that was never a bad thing. Now he was concerned that if there was any truth in Marcie's accusation, it could well affect how Nessie looked on him. He had no doubt Marcie would be staying with her and wondered how he should approach it. After giving it some thought, he decided it might be best to leave the subject well alone until Nessie broached it.

'Why, you've done marvels,' Oliver told them as he arrived. 'Now what would you like me to do?'

Molly and Nessie nodded a greeting. 'You could fill a couple of buckets of hot water for us,' Molly told him. 'There's some water heating on the range. The next job is giving the floors a final scrub so we can start to set out the tables and chairs. Charlie and Reuben are coming around tomorrow evening to fit some shelves for all the pots and pans and then we can make a list of what else we need. We're bound to have forgotten something.'

Oliver rolled up his sleeves and set off to do as he was asked.

He noticed that Nessie seemed to be unnaturally quiet and he wondered if it was anything that he might have done to upset her or if it was the fact that Marcie had lost her job.

The three worked in companionable silence for a while, but when Molly left early to look after her son, Joe, who had come down with a bad cold, the silence between Nessie and Oliver became awkward.

Finally, Oliver tentatively began to speak, 'I was so sorry to hear that Marcie had left my mother's employment.' He had promised himself that he wouldn't raise the subject until she did but now he felt as if it was lying between them and he wanted to clear the air.

Nessie flushed, embarrassed. 'Don't worry about it. To be honest, I'm surprised Marcie stuck the job as long as she did. She hasn't got the best of records when it comes to holding a job down.'

'Oh.' Oliver was shocked that she hadn't mentioned the baby as the reason for Marcie leaving. Could it be that her younger sister hadn't told her about it yet? If that was the case, he certainly didn't want to be the bearer of bad news, so forcing a cheerful note into his voice he said, 'Shall we get these chairs set out, then? It's going to look grand in here, I reckon.'

Between them they soon had everything in position and they stood back to admire their hard work.

'The sooner we open the better is the way I see it,' Oliver said proudly. 'We're still some way off spring yet and I'm sure that this place will be a real life-saver for some people.'

She smiled, then told him coyly, 'Actually, as I've been going around trying to get sponsors for the soup kitchen, I've also been cadging used clothing for those who really need it, as well as blankets or anything else that the better off no longer need. You'd be surprised what I've got together already. Some of the clothes I've been given are almost new. What do you think of the idea?'

Oliver shook his head and smiled. 'I think you never fail to amaze me. It's a marvellous idea. Some of the patients I visit only have rags to keep them warm so I think they'll come in very handy indeed.'

Their eyes met for a moment and Nessie blushed furiously as she quickly looked away, all of a fluster.

'Er ... I don't think there's anything more you can do tonight so why don't you get off home now?' she suggested hastily.

Oliver nodded and rolled his sleeves down before putting his hat and coat back on. 'Aren't you coming too?' he questioned. 'I was going to give you a lift home.'

'It's all right, I still have a few bits to do,' she answered as she busily began to wipe down the tabletops.

Oliver hesitated for a moment then reluctantly made his way to the door, saying, 'Shall I see you tomorrow?'

She shook her head. 'There's nothing for you to do, really. Charlie and Reuben will be working here tomorrow evening so you can have a well-deserved night off.'

He nodded, slightly crestfallen, and made for the door where he paused to look back at her and said softly, 'Goodnight, Nessie.'

'Goodnight, Oliver.' She kept her eyes focused on what she was doing until she heard the door close behind him and only then did she sag against the table as fresh tears sprang to her eyes. They could never be, she knew that, so why did it pain her so much?

With a determined effort, she pulled herself together and when she was sure that he was gone, she too prepared to leave.

Nessie was approaching the clock tower in the marketplace when she suddenly spotted Reuben. He was talking to someone who stood in the shadow of a shop doorway. She saw Reuben hand them something, just as she had before, then the man, for it certainly looked like a man, hastily took off up Queen's Road in the opposite direction. He was huddled in an old coat with his hat pulled low over his eyes and he was lurching unsteadily from side to side, obviously the worse for drink.

Nessie bit down on her lip and frowned. Could it be that Reuben had been handing over the money he had been hiding under his mattress? And why was he suddenly mixing with these shady characters? He had a good job and prospects now as well as a lovely young lady who clearly adored him. It just didn't make any sense.

When she entered their warm kitchen a short time later she found Reuben standing at the stove warming some milk before he retired to bed.

'Ah, here you are,' he greeted. 'After you left Maria came round to see me, and I just got back from taking her home and Joseph is fast asleep. Marcie's turned in early for a change, an' all. Fancy some warm milk?'

Nessie shook her head as she undid her bonnet and laid it on the table. 'No, thanks.'

'Here's hopin' an early night'll put her in the mood for lookin' for work,' Reuben went on. 'She can't expect to sit back here an' let us keep her, can she?'

'I'm sure she will soon,' Nessie said shortly. She desperately wanted to ask Reuben what he was playing at but thought better of it. Whoever the person was, Reuben clearly didn't want her to know about him. Instead she wished him goodnight but sleep eluded her as she thought of Marcie and Reuben. She was convinced that there was something more to Marcie leaving her post at Haunchwood House than she was telling her, and she was worried about Reuben too. Unfortunately, there was nothing she could do to help either of them until they chose to confide in her so she lay there fretting as the minutes and the hours ticked away.

Chapter Thirty-One

'There's been another murder!' Molly blurted out the second she set foot in the shop the next morning. 'The whole of the marketplace is cordoned off an' there's police everywhere. They reckon she's another one o' the loose women from the whorehouse.'

Nessie caught her breath. She'd had a sleepless night and felt more tired than she had when she'd gone to bed and now this! She felt sick with fear to think that the murderer was still so close.

'I'm sure they'll catch the murderer soon,' she said quietly, trying to assuage Molly's fears. Every time it happened, all the hurt she had felt when her mother had been his victim rushed back tenfold.

'It's a bit too close for comfort for me,' Molly

commented as she tied her apron about her waist before she pottered away to begin her chores.

Andre, Reuben and Charlie had just left to transport a deceased greengrocer to St Nicholas's Church for the burial service when the shop door opened again and a pretty young girl appeared.

'Hello,' she said holding her hand out. 'You must be Nessie. I'm Eliza, Marcie's friend. We worked together at Haunchwood House and Cook has sent me into town to pick up a few things so I thought I'd pop in and see her. If she's in, that is. I hope you don't mind?'

'Of course not, you're most welcome,' Nessie assured her with a friendly smile. 'I'll take you through to our living quarters. Marcie had just got up when I checked on Joseph half an hour ago.'

Minutes later she opened the door to their kitchen to find Marcie curled up in a chair at the side of the fire as Molly cleaned around her. She was still in her dressing robe with her hair loose about her shoulders and looking thoroughly miserable, but she perked up immediately the second she saw Eliza.

'Eliza, what are you doing here?' she asked delightedly. Perhaps she had come with a message from George saying how sorry he was and that he wanted to marry her?

'I can't stay long,' Eliza warned as she pulled off her mittens, 'but I wouldn't say no to a cuppa if there's one going spare. It's enough to freeze the hairs off a brass monkey out there. Cook sent me into town for some bits she needed so I thought I'd stick me nose in an' see how you are.'

She went to hold her hands out to the fire as Marcie turned to Molly and asked, 'Would you mind leavin' the rest o' the cleanin' in here till later, Molly?'

'I suppose so,' Molly muttered, none too pleased. 'But if I do you'll have to watch Joseph till I get back.' She'd already rightly assumed that Marcie didn't even like being in the same room as the child if she could avoid it.

'Of course I will,' Marcie assured her as she ushered her towards the door and when it had closed she turned to Eliza and asked hopefully, 'Has George sent you with a message?'

Eliza looked uncomfortable. 'I'm afraid not. It's as I said, I'm just poppin' into town, but...'

'But *what?*' Marcie demanded, hands on hips. She had the feeling she was about to hear something she wasn't going to like.

'Well, the atmosphere up at the house is so thick yer could cut it wi' a knife since you left, but word has it that George's engagement to Belinda Lewis is still goin' ahead sometime in March. I heard him an' his brother havin' a right old row about it over breakfast this mornin'! Mind you that don't surprise me. Master Oliver is a decent sort, while George is just a cad.'

Marcie's face paled to the colour of putty as she sank down heavily onto the nearest chair.

Eliza stared at her apologetically. 'Sorry to have to be the bearer o' such bad news but I thought you deserved to know,' she said quietly.

They sat in silence for a moment until Marcie frowned and her shock turned to anger. 'Right!

Well, we'll see about that,' she growled. 'I want you to do somethin' for me, Eliza!'

'What's that then?'

'I want you to find the Lewises' address in London for me. It shouldn't be too hard to do. Mr Dorsey is bound to have an address book in his study so when you're cleaning in there you could look for it.'

It was Eliza's turn to look horrified. 'But if I did that an' I got caught lookin' through his personal things, I'd get the sack for sure!'

'So make sure you *don't* get caught then,' Marcie snapped. 'If George can't do the right thing and stand by me after all the promises he made then I'm bloody sure I'm not goin' to stand by an' let him marry somebody else. I'll write to Belinda's parents an' then let's see how they feel about him marryin' their precious girl when they find out I'm carryin' his baby!'

Eliza chewed on her fingernail uncertainly. She did sympathise with Marcie's predicament but all the same she didn't want to lose her job. Connie Dorsey was a good sort and fair with her staff but she knew that there were plenty who weren't. Even so, after a time she sighed. 'All right then, I'll do me best but I ain't promisin' anythin', mind.'

'Thank you.' Marcie hurried across the room to hug Eliza but still her heart was heavy. There could be no happy outcome for her now. George had clearly made his choice, but at least she could spoil that for him. By her reckoning the baby would be due early in August and they were almost into February already, and she wouldn't be able to hide the fact that she was having a child from Reuben and Nessie forever. She had noticed a small difference in her body already, but how would they take the news when they found out? She had no doubt that Reuben would be all for kicking her out on her arse with nowhere but the workhouse to go, but Nessie, well, she was a different kettle of fish entirely. Perhaps she should tell her that George Dorsey had taken advantage of her and evoke her sympathy?

First, though, it might be worth just one more last-ditch effort to talk George around. How to get him alone was the problem. And then it came to her, he was a keen rider and took his stallion for a gallop along the track across Rapper's Hole towards Galley Common most days, regardless of the weather. Deciding that now was as good a time as any to confront him, she hurried away to get washed and changed, leaving Joseph alone on the sofa.

Marcie strode purposely through Stockingford intent on cornering George, even if it meant she had to stand in the copse in Rapper's Hole and wait for him all day. She had gone to especial pains with her appearance: her hair had been brushed till it shone and hung loose about her shoulders just as he had always told her he liked it, and she was wearing her best blue bonnet and the second-hand dress she had bought from the rag stall, which, with a little work was now far superior to anything she had ever owned before. She drew more than a few admiring glances as she walked, but Marcie was oblivious to them. She knew that this would be her very last chance

301

to get George to make an honest woman of her and if she failed the workhouse could well be beckoning.

By the time she reached Rapper's Hole she was breathless and cold but still she moved on until she reached the shelter of the copse, which at least afforded her a little respite from the biting wind. She knew that it must be at least one o'clock by now and if things went to plan George could appear at any minute. He had always liked to take his stallion for a gallop after lunch, unless his father forced him to work that was. As she waited she couldn't help but think of her poor mother, whose body had been found there and she kept glancing about nervously.

The minutes ticked away into hours and Marcie had almost given up hope of catching a glimpse of him. The brightness had gone from the afternoon and she knew that soon it would start to get dark, but still she waited, although her hands and feet were so cold that she could no longer feel them. And then suddenly she heard the sound of hooves pounding the grass and she stepped quickly from behind the trees in time to see George galloping towards her. He saw her almost instantly and even from a distance his mouth was set.

Determined not to be ignored she stood directly in the path of the galloping horse with her hands on her hips and her eyes flashing. As the animal advanced on her, for one awful moment Marcie thought that George was going to mow her down but then, right at the last minute, he reined the horse to a halt just feet away from her.

'Just what the hell are *you* doing here?' he

snarled as he struggled to bring the horse under control.

'What do you *think* I'm doing here? I hardly make a habit of standing out in the freezing cold for pleasure. You know *exactly* why. I've come to try and talk some bloody sense into that thick head of yours!'

'Then you've had a wasted journey,' he snapped. 'Now will you kindly get out of my way and let me get on.'

'No, I bloody will *not,* not till we've talked.' Marcie sprang forward and grabbed hold of the horse's reins and seeing that she wasn't going to be put off, George swung his leg over the saddle and dropped nimbly to the ground.

'Look, Marcie,' he said softly. 'I'm sorry for what's happened if you really are having a child, that is... But at the end of the day I have to do what my father wishes or he'll disown me.'

'So you're telling me that you'll marry Belinda Lewis just to please your family?' Two spots of colour had appeared high in her cheeks and she was having to resist the urge to lash out at him as she suddenly saw him for the spoiled, selfish young man he was.

'That's about the long and the short of it,' he admitted shamelessly. 'But don't worry, I'll make sure that you're all right. I'll drop some money into wherever you're living from time to time so you won't starve.'

'*You bastard!*' She dropped the reins and stepped away from him, and as he swung himself back into the saddle she had one last parting shot. 'Don't think you're going to get away with this. When I've finished, Belinda Lewis will drop you like a ton of hot bricks.'

'I wouldn't go doing anything you might regret, if I were you,' he said threateningly.

But it would take far more than threats from George Dorsey to frighten Marcie. 'We'll see who ends up having regrets,' she said icily as she stepped away from him and just for a second a cold finger ran up and down his spine. But then, gathering his reins, he dug his heels into the horse's sides and galloped away.

Marcie watched for just a moment before turning about to make her way back to the funeral parlour with murder in her heart.

Chapter Thirty-Two

'I reckon that's just about it then,' Molly said with satisfaction as she rubbed her hands together and looked around at the soup kitchen.

It was the first week in March and everyone had worked tirelessly. Now the tables and chairs were set out in an orderly fashion, a counter had been erected where the food could be served from, and a variety of pots, pans, crockery and cutlery were neatly laid out on the shelves behind it.

'I've been thinking,' Nessie said brightly. 'I thought perhaps we could open each evening? It would be hard for me to get away from the funeral parlour in the day. But someone will have to be here to get the food cooked before we open each day, won't they?'

'Don't worry about that, I've got it all in hand.' Molly grinned. 'Some of the ladies from the courtyards and myself are going to do it on a rota. We can't expect you to be here every day, everyone needs a day off. I shall shop for the food each day when I've finished work at the parlour and drop it off and someone will be here ready to cook it.'

Nessie was so relieved. Oliver looked pleased too. It seemed that Molly had thought of everything. She really was worth her weight in gold.

'I had a thought too,' Oliver piped up and both women looked towards him. 'I got to thinking that the sort of people who are going to take advantage of the soup kitchen are highly unlikely to be able to afford doctor's fees, so how about I pop in a couple of times a week to see them for free? I could soon empty another of the smaller rooms where I could mackle up a makeshift surgery. What do you think?'

'I think that would be wonderful!' Molly exclaimed. If only she had been able to afford a doctor her baby might still be alive, but during his illness there had been not a penny spare and she felt guilty about it every single day.

'I think so too,' Nessie chimed in. Over the last few weeks, she had managed to ensure that she and Oliver were never alone together. It hurt deeply and she missed their chats and the laughter they had shared but she knew it was for the best.

'So, how about we make the official opening date this Wednesday?' Molly suggested. 'I can get

305

the volunteers baking the bread tomorrow and get all the food we'll need in. Shall we say six o'clock Wednesday evening?'

'It sounds good to me,' Nessie agreed.

'Right then, if we're all done, can I offer either of you ladies a lift home?' Oliver asked, looking hopefully at Nessie.

The look was not missed by Molly who wondered why Nessie was suddenly holding the poor chap at arm's length. He was clearly very fond of her.

'Er, not for me, thank you. I'll just stay behind for a while and see to the finishing touches, but you get off, Molly. Charlie will think you've got lost. The poor chap has hardly seen anything of you for weeks.'

'Aye, all right, pet.' Molly lifted her shawl and minutes later she left with Oliver, leaving Nessie alone with her thoughts.

Nessie left a little later and she had gone no more than a few steps on her way home when a man stumbling along ahead of her caught her attention. It was too dark to see his face but something about him looked vaguely familiar. And then he passed beneath a gas lamp and the breath caught in her throat. He looked suspiciously like her father, but no, she scolded herself, it couldn't be him. No one had seen or heard a thing of him since the time he had abandoned the family to run off with the pub landlord's wife in Bedworth. She quickened her steps to try and catch up with him but before she was able to he had disappeared down a dark alley and she was too afraid to follow him. Surely if he was back he would have tried to find her? she reasoned. Wrapping her shawl tighter about her she continued on her way, keeping to the light of the sputtering gas lamps as much as she was able to.

You're letting your mind play tricks on you, my girl, she told herself sternly. She prayed that she had been mistaken, but she couldn't be sure.

Marcie was sitting at the side of the fire with a gloomy look on her face when Nessie got home but there was no sign of Reuben.

'Has Reuben taken Maria home?' she asked.

Marcie nodded. 'Yes, they left a while ago.'

'Good, that gives us a chance to have a little chat on our own then, doesn't it? I think it's long overdue. So what's troubling you? And don't say nothing! I know there's *something* on your mind.'

Tears sprang to Marcie's eyes as she lowered her head. It was time to tell Nessie about the baby. She couldn't hide it for much longer so she may as well get it over with.

'The thing is,' she began, running her tongue across her lips nervously. 'I wasn't telling you the *whole* truth about why I left my job.'

Nessie had come to sit in the chair on the other side of the fireplace and was watching her intently.

'You see I er ... well, I fell in love with George, the Dorseys' younger son, and we had a romance. He said he loved me and that we'd be together ... but then ... I found out I was going to have a baby and at the same time I found out that he'd become engaged to a girl from London, the family are friends of the Dorseys.' She was crying now and trying not to look at Nessie's shocked expression. 'I thought that when he knew about the baby he'd marry me but he's dropped me like a sack o' spuds.'

'Oh, *Marcie!* How *could* you be so stupid? It's a well-known fact that men from his walk of life only play with girls like us. They never look on us as marriage material.'

'I know that now, don't I? But I believed him when he said he loved me and now I don't know what I'm going to do. His mother gave me enough money to tide me over until after the baby is born but then...' She spread her hands helplessly. 'I might not even last that long because Reuben will throw me out on me ear when he finds out, won't he?' She was crying even harder now and Nessie couldn't help but feel sorry for her.

'Perhaps I should go and see George's mother?' Nessie mused sensibly. 'And don't worry about Reuben. I'll speak to him when the time is right. Whatever happens, we're not going to see you homeless, although I will have to have a discreet word in Andre's ear to see how he feels about it. It's sure to cause gossip when the word gets out and Andre may be worried about the effect an illegitimate baby could have on his business. You can see that, can't you?'

Marcie nodded miserably as she swiped at her tears with the corner of her shawl. Strangely she felt better now that she'd confided in her sister. It was Nessie who had kept the family together since the death of their mother and she was sure that she'd help her.

'Look, get yourself off to bed and get some rest now,' Nessie said. 'And leave me to have a think about what's best to do. Oh, and when is the baby due?'

'Sometime in August, I think.' Marcie sniffed as she rose from the chair and now Nessie could clearly see her thickening waistline. *Why haven't I noticed it before?* she berated herself. She shuddered to think what Reuben was going to say about it but he would have to be told. Taking a deep breath, she dragged herself out of the chair, rolled up her sleeves and went to tackle the pile of dirty pots in the sink before retiring to bed. As usual, Marcie hadn't bothered to do them.

The next morning, she asked Andre, 'Would you mind very much if I took a couple of hours off this morning? We don't have any funerals booked for today, do we?'

He looked mildly surprised; Nessie never asked for time off. If anything, she did far more hours than she should.

'Of course, take as long as you like. I can handle things here if anyone comes in, although I'm not as good with the clients as you, as you know.' He smiled. 'Going somewhere nice, are you?'

'Not really,' she hedged. 'There's just someone I need to see.'

She was grateful when Andre didn't question her further and slipped away to get ready.

'I'm going to see Mrs Dorsey, so whether you like it or not you're going to have to keep your eye on Joseph for a while,' she told Marcie firmly.

The girl's eyes widened. 'I doubt it'll do much good,' she said, glancing nervously towards Joseph.

'Well, we won't know until I try, will we?'

It was a cool breezy day but Nessie was heartened to see daffodils and primroses just poking out of the earth when she left the town behind. Spring was on its way and it couldn't come quickly enough. It had been a long, cold winter. As she neared Haunchwood House, she began to wonder what sort of reception she might get. What if Mrs Dorsey had her thrown out? Squaring her shoulders, she decided there was only one way to find out, so she marched up to the door and quickly rang the bell.

It was answered almost instantly by the same girl who had called at the parlour to see Marcie a short time ago.

'Hello. It's Eliza, isn't it?' Nessie gave her a friendly smile. 'Could you kindly inform Mrs Dorsey that Miss Nessie Carson wishes to see her, please?'

Eliza looked all of a fluster as she held the door wide. 'You'd best come in an' I'll see if the mistress will see you.' She scuttled away like a frightened rabbit as Nessie looked appreciatively around at the hallway. It was just as beautiful as Marcie had described it. However, she didn't have long to admire it before Eliza was back telling her breathlessly, 'The mistress says she will see you. She's in the drawing room.'

She led Nessie across the hall, tapped on a door then silently disappeared as Nessie stepped into the room.

Mrs Dorsey was standing in front of the fireplace, her back straight and her hands folded primly at her waist.

'Yes, Miss Carson, how may I help you?' she asked stiffly as she eyed the girl up and down. So this was the young woman that Oliver was always talking about, was it? She had to admit that she looked very respectable. It was just a shame that she was related to the maid she had just had to sack.

'I've come to discuss what's to be done about my sister,' Nessie answered calmly, keeping her head high. 'I believe you are aware that your son has left her with child.'

'Ah, now hang on a minute, lass. That's a matter of opinion. George flatly denies that the baby is his but I've still sent her away with enough to tide her over for some time. What more can I do? It's her word against his.'

Nessie suddenly felt deflated. There were many employers who would have cleared Marcie off without a penny and she supposed that the woman was going to stand by her son at the end of the day. Because, like the old saying went, 'blood is thicker than water'.

'B-but this baby will be your grandchild,' she pointed out. She had come expecting an argument at least but the woman was being so reasonable that it was hard to lose her temper with her. In fact, she looked rather upset.

'If she's telling the truth,' Connie Dorsey said and then seeing that Marcie was going to defend her sister she hurried on, 'and I'm not saying that she isn't. But what can I do, lass? I can't *force* my son to marry her, can I?'

'No, I don't suppose you can.' Nessie's shoulders drooped as she turned to go. 'But I'll tell you now, Marcie isn't a bad girl and she wouldn't lie about a thing like this.'

Connie Dorsey lowered her head and turned away. There was clearly no more to be said so Nessie quietly turned and left the room.

Eliza was waiting to let her out and as Nessie stepped outside she hissed, 'Tell Marcie I'll try an' get round to see her next week if I can get what she asked for.'

Nessie had no idea what she was talking about but she nodded anyway.

'Well? Did you see her?' Marcie asked eagerly the second Nessie set foot through the door.

'Yes, for what good it did,' she answered despondently. 'George is still saying the baby isn't his so it looks like you're on your own. Well, as far as they're concerned, that is. I'm not about to turn my back on you, though. As I said last night, it might not be possible for you to stay here. But we'll see what Andre has to say, but I can't really speak to him until we've told Reuben.'

Marcie's face fell but she knew what Nessie was saying was true. There was no way George was going to change his mind now; he had turned his back on her. Without another word she headed upstairs leaving Nessie to worry about what lay ahead. Once again it seemed that the comfortable, stable life they had made for themselves was about to come crashing down around their ears.

Chapter Thirty-Three

'Right, when you're ready you can open the doors.' Molly beamed from her place behind the counter and with a smile Oliver hurried across the room to do as he was asked. Already a straggly line of people was queuing outside and Nessie could have cried with relief. She had been so afraid that all their efforts might have been in vain, but it appeared that word had spread.

Cautiously the people in the queue began to pour into the room and in no time at all she and Molly were busily filling dishes with the tasty vegetable soup they had made and handing out thick slices of freshly baked bread. There were women with sallow faces dressed in little better than rags and hollow-cheeked children whose eyes popped at the sight of the food. Defeated-looking men pushed their families in front of them, grateful to see them getting a good nourishing meal for a change. In no time at all, the first large pot of soup was gone and Molly carried over the second one they had prepared. There was a continuous stream of people right up until seven thirty that evening when at last the queue began to get smaller.

'Phew, I've got a rare old sweat on,' Molly laughed as she wiped her forehead on the back of her sleeve. It was hardly surprising. She had been ladling out soup and standing over the hot pans

313

for almost two hours. Her cheeks were flushed but her eyes were twinkling with pleasure.

'Thanks, missus, that were the best meal I've had in many a long day,' an old, stooped man told them as he returned his bowl to the counter.

Nessie was quick to note that the soles of his down-at-heel boots were flapping giving him no protection at all from the wet weather outside, so she quickly told him, 'Come with me for a moment, would you?'

Looking slightly bemused he followed her across to the large walk-in cupboard on the far side of the room and once inside Nessie quickly began to sort through a pile of boots and shoes that she had neatly stacked in there, all kindly donated by the better-off members of the town.

'Try these on, they look about your size,' she urged, pushing a pair of black leather boots towards him.

Eagerly he kicked off his old ones and slid his feet into them. A huge smile spread across his old wrinkled face. 'Why, I reckon I've died an' gone to heaven,' he declared as he did a little jig. 'It's like walkin' on air. Thank yer most kindly, miss. Yer an' angel, so you are.'

Nessie giggled at his obvious delight. 'You're very welcome,' she assured him and watched happily as he walked away, almost bumping into everything so intent was he on admiring his new footwear.

'Bless 'im, yer just made his day,' Molly praised, and Nessie felt a warm glow inside. At that moment she caught Oliver's eye. He was watching her intently with a tender look on his face but she swiftly looked away. It was bad enough that Marcie was at home nursing a broken heart, there was no way she was going to allow hers to be broken too.

Oliver noticed how Nessie avoided his eyes and sighed. She had still not mentioned Marcie's condition to him but now he could only suppose that this was the reason she was suddenly keeping her distance from him. He couldn't really blame her, given the circumstances, but he loathed what his brother had done, for he had no doubt whatsoever that it was George who had got Marcie with child, despite his denials. However, there wasn't much he could do about it until Nessie chose to discuss it with him.

Two days later, as Molly was mopping the floor in Nessie's kitchen, Marcie noticed her staring at her. Nessie was sitting at the table feeding Joseph and she too noticed that Molly looked perplexed. She knew in an instant that Molly had guessed that Marcie was having a baby and she swallowed. Molly was no fool, she should have known that they wouldn't be able to hide it from her for long.

Flashing a warning glance at Marcie, she said quietly, 'You've guessed, haven't you, Molly?'

Molly didn't argue but merely nodded. 'If you mean about the baby, aye I have. I've seen enough pregnant women in me time to be able to spot one a mile off.'

Marcie scowled as she sat down near the fire. Thankfully the men were all out attending to a funeral so at least Reuben wasn't there to hear her.

315

'So, is the father prepared to stand by you, pet?' Molly asked and when Marcie miserably shook her head, she sighed. 'I see, so what are you goin' to do?'

'I ... I don't know,' Marcie answered in a wobbly voice as Molly came to sit close to her. 'Nessie is going to ask Andre if I can stay here but I know that's not the ideal solution.'

'No, it ain't.' There were enough rumours about Andre and Nessie flying about the town as it was. She dreaded to think what people would say if they were to learn that Nessie had her pregnant sister staying with her too. They'd say the place was a den of vice and that would be the end of Andre's business for sure, and just when it was doing so well an' all!

'I don't suppose you know of anyone who might be able to help me out of this situation, do you?' Marcie asked in a small voice and Molly was horrified.

'Aye, I know a few women who'd butcher you,' she said angrily. 'But you can forget that idea. I've seen women from the courtyards bleed to death after goin' to them.' She chewed on her lip thoughtfully. 'I suppose you could always come an' stay with me till the baby's been born,' she suggested. 'I ain't got a palace, mind you, though I have to say me an' Charlie have got it comfortable since we've worked here, thanks to your sister.' She gave Nessie a grateful smile.

'But we couldn't ask you to do that, Molly,' Nessie objected. 'I know you've got it nice now but you've said yourself there's barely room in your place to swing a cat round, and besides, what would Charlie say?'

Molly shrugged. 'He'll understand if I talk to him. We could always get a little truckle bed knocked up for you in the kitchen. And yes, it'd be tight, admittedly, but we'd manage.'

'But what would he say about...' Marcie tapped her stomach.

'He'd probably say you ain't the first to land yourself in this position an' you certainly won't be the last,' Molly said stoically. 'To tell the truth, I were in the same predicament meself once, but Charlie stood by me an' did the honourable thing. At least this way it'll take the attention away from the funeral parlour.'

'I could pay you,' Marcie told her quickly. 'I have more than enough money to tide me over till the baby's born.'

'And what then?' Molly asked bluntly.

'I haven't thought that far ahead.'

'No, but you do intend to keep the baby, don't you?' Nessie piped up and when her sister didn't immediately answer Nessie looked horrified. 'But *of course*, you'll keep it,' she said. 'It will be a part of you, your own flesh and blood.'

Feeling an argument brewing, Molly quickly stepped in. 'Look, let's just take one day at a time for now, shall we?' she said soothingly.

Marcie pouted and lowered her head. There was no way she could ever see herself wanting to keep this child. But she supposed Molly was right. The birth was still some months away yet so there was plenty of time to decide what she wanted to do.

'I'll speak to Charlie tonight an' then you can

move in as soon as you please,' Molly told them kindly. 'An' hopefully Andre need never find out about it.'

Nessie sincerely hoped that this would be the case.

Shortly after lunchtime up at Haunchwood House, Eliza was instructed to clean the master's office.

'But make sure you don't move anything on his desk, you know how fussy he is about that,' Mrs Bainbridge warned her.

Armed with a mop and bucket and a number of cleaning rags, Eliza set off and once in the room she firmly closed the door and glanced about. This was her opportunity to do as Marcie had asked and find the Lewises' London address, but where was the master's address book likely to be? With her heart in her mouth in case she got caught, she hastily scanned the desk but all that it appeared to hold was a number of papers. She tentatively tried the drawers but to her frustration found them all locked. Then suddenly she spotted a large leather-bound book on a small table by the window and her heart leapt. That must be it! Hurrying over she quickly opened it and sure enough, inside she found lists of names and addresses. Now the biggest problem for Eliza was determining which one was the Lewises'; she had never been very good at reading and writing. She carefully turned the pages until she came to one that she thought might be the right one. L E W I S, she read out painfully slowly. Yes, this must be it! She glanced around for something to copy the address on. She was too afraid to use a sheet of the master's paper from his desk but then she spotted a discarded envelope in the small wicker rubbish basket. That will do, she thought, pouncing on it, then very slowly she began to copy the address, her tongue poking into her cheek with concentration. She was almost done when she heard the door to the office opening and quick as a flash she rammed the envelope into the pocket of her apron and slammed the book shut.

'Just what the *hell* do you think you're doing?' It was George and he was staring at her suspiciously.

'I was er ... just polishin' this table an' book, sir.' Eliza grabbed up a duster and began to dust everything in sight as George narrowed his eyes. Why would she need to open a book to dust it? he wondered. But then with a shrug he told her, 'Very well, just get it done as quickly as you can. I have some work to do for my father.' With that he turned and strode from the room as Eliza gasped with relief.

Phew, that was a close call, she thought, then hurriedly did as he had asked.

It was another couple of days before Eliza had the chance to deliver the address to Marcie when Mrs Bainbridge sent her into town to get some embroidery silks, and she was shocked to find Marcie packing up her few belongings.

'I'm going to move in with Molly until after... Well, you know...' Marcie told her miserably. But when Eliza held the Lewises' address out to her she perked up. The handwriting was atrocious

319

but she could just about read it.

'I nearly got caught red-handed pinchin' that,' Eliza complained. 'An' by Master George, an' all. If he'd clocked on to what I were doin' *I'd* have been out on me ear an' all.'

'I really appreciate it,' Marcie assured her.

Eliza sniffed. 'As it turns out, it might be too late for you to write to 'em anyway,' she confided. 'Mrs Bainbridge informed me that the Lewises are arrivin' a week on Friday an' the engagement party is to be a week on Saturday.'

Marcie's lip curled. 'Is it *really?*' she said cunningly. In that case perhaps she could plan a present the young couple hadn't been expecting. Far better to do it in person than by a letter. The way she saw it, she had nothing to lose now.

Just then, Molly entered the room to ask, 'Are you all fit, pet?' She had just finished her shift and as it was her turn to be in the soup kitchen that evening she was keen to get home and get her chores done and Marcie settled in.

'Yes I am.' Marcie gave Eliza a warm hug. 'Thank you,' she told her. 'I'll keep in touch.'

'Aye, you do that, an' I'd best be on me way now anyway, else the housekeeper will have me guts for garters.' As she left she passed Nessie who was just entering the room.

'Ah, you're all ready for the off then?' she asked Marcie gently.

'Yes, I am but I just wanted to give you these before I go.' Marcie had only just remembered the two porcelain figurines she had stolen from Haunchwood House and now she had come across them in the small bundle she had arrived with she handed them to her sister saying, 'These are a little gift for you.'

'Oh!' Nessie looked astonished as she weighed them in her hands. They were absolutely stunning and far superior to anything she had ever seen before. 'B-but they must have cost a fortune!' she blustered.

Marcie shrugged nonchalantly. 'I told you I was all right for money, didn't I? So just accept them.'

'Thank you, pet, I shall treasure them.' She was tearful as she pulled her sister into a hug. 'Now you be good for Molly,' she warned, as if Marcie was still a little girl. 'And don't come around here for a few days, love. I need to tell Reuben about the baby and he'll probably need a bit of time to cool down. But don't worry, he will, and then we'll decide what we're going to do when the little one is here.' She gently nudged Marcie towards the door and once she was gone she got out her handkerchief and wiped the tears streaming down her cheeks. It felt as if for the last couple of years, the family had lurched from one crisis to another and now she wondered what life had to throw at them next.

Chapter Thirty-Four

'Your sister has gone to live with Molly?' Andre queried the next morning.

'Er, yes ... she has ... for now,' Nessie stammered. 'You see, the thing is ... Marcie is going to have a baby and I didn't feel it was right for her to stay here. There are already rumours floating around about you and me and if it became known that my pregnant sister was also living here, I dread to think what people would make of it.'

'I do not *care* what people say about me,' Andre stated angrily. 'But what of Marcie? Will the father not stand by her?'

Nessie shook her head and smiled at him. He really was a kind man. 'No, I'm afraid he won't and I believe that you don't care about what people say, but think of what effect it could have on the business. We've worked so hard to build it up over the last months. I would feel awful now if you were to lose trade again because of my family. And I haven't told Reuben about the baby yet so I'd be most grateful if you could keep the news to yourself for a while.'

'Of course.' Andre gave a polite little bow and clicked his heels together before handing her a small bundle of notes. 'The money for the food for the soup kitchen,' he informed her. He gave her the same amount as regular as clockwork every week and with that and the money that came in from the sponsors the kitchen was doing remarkably well.

'Just one thing before I go about my business,' Andre said, looking slightly troubled. 'I suggest you tell Reuben about Marcie's baby at the earliest opportunity. As you said, people around here like to gossip and it would be far better for him to hear the news from you than a stranger.'

Seeing the sense in what he said, Nessie nodded, although she dreaded how he would take it. Still, it had to be done so she determined to speak to him that very evening before he went off to see Maria.

As it happened, she never got the chance, for mid-afternoon, Reuben stormed into the shop with a face as dark as a thundercloud.

'What's this I'm hearin', then?' he snapped. 'I just popped out to get some nails an' Fred Blighty, who I used to work with on the railways, stopped me to ask when me sister's baby were due? Why didn't you tell me you were pregnant? Is it Andre's baby?'

Nessie's mouth gaped with shock, 'It's not *me* who's pregnant,' she said indignantly. 'It ... it's Marcie.'

She watched his jaw tighten and his hands ball into fists. *'Marcie!'* He shook his head. 'How could she after...'

'It wasn't all her fault,' Nessie hastened to tell him. 'The man responsible led her to believe that they would be married and then dropped her like a hot brick the second he found out about the baby.'

'Then tell me who it is an' I'll go an' knock some bloody sense into him,' Reuben stormed.

'It wouldn't do any good. It's George Dorsey, you see. And we've already found out that he's about to become engaged to a friend of the family.'

Reuben's shoulders suddenly sagged. *'George Dorsey!* So where is she now?'

'She's gone to stay with Molly and Charlie for a while.'

'So why didn't Charlie tell me? We've been workin' side by side all mornin'.'

'He probably guessed that it would upset you,' Nessie said soothingly and Reuben couldn't argue with that.

'Oh, this will sound great to me future in-laws, won't it?' he groaned and instantly coloured as he realised what he had said.

'In-laws?'

He nodded as he dropped his eyes, his anger gone now. 'Aye, I was goin' to tell you this evenin'. I've asked Maria to marry me an' she's said yes.'

'Why, that's wonderful. You've got yourself a good girl there and I hope you'll be very happy,' Nessie told him. 'When is the big day to be?'

'Ah well, that's somethin' else I was goin' to talk to you about,' he muttered shamefaced. 'The thing is, her dad owns a number o' properties in the town which he rents out and there's one coming empty in Fitton Street in the autumn. It's a grand little house with three bedrooms, three rooms downstairs and a nice little garden, and he's told me an' Maria we can have it as our weddin' present, so we thought we'd get wed in September. I'd still work here o' course... But now this with Marcie...' he finished sadly.

'That needn't alter your plans,' Nessie assured him quickly. 'We'll manage just fine.' Nessie swallowed the lump forming in her throat. 'But you haven't known each other that long and you're both still very young. Are you quite sure this is what you want?'

'I've never been more sure of anythin' in me whole life,' he answered, his eyes softening as he thought of his bride-to-be. 'I knew the minute I clapped eyes on Maria that she were the only girl for me, but now...'

'I've told you, you're not to worry and if this is what you really want I wish you all the luck in the world.' She gave him a gentle kiss on the cheek. At least his forthcoming wedding had softened what he had just heard about Marcie. 'You must invite Maria's parents around so we can discuss the plans for the wedding.'

'Aye, I'll do that,' he agreed, and went back to work leaving his sister reeling with shock. She was pleased for him, of course she was, but now a new problem had presented itself. How could she possibly stay here when Reuben left to live in his new home? At the moment, her brother gave everything an air of respectability but what would people say when they discovered that she and Andre were living under the same roof unchaperoned? Once more she felt the weight of her responsibilities. At the moment she had Reuben to help with Joseph but once he was wed he would start a new life with his wife. Marcie would be no help, she had her own worries at present, which meant that very soon she would have to start looking for somewhere else for her and Joseph to live. And then she would have to find someone to look after him while she came to work. It was all very concerning. With a sigh, she told herself she would manage somehow, she always had before and there was no reason why this time should be any different, but oh, she would miss the way of life she had become accustomed to, and she would miss Andre too, for they had become good friends.

Marcie left the cottage just before six o'clock, dressed in her finest clothes and with her hair washed and curled loosely about her shoulders. It was a relief to get out in the open air, for although both Molly and Charlie had gone out of their way to make her feel at home, they were hopelessly overcrowded. Sometimes Marcie felt as if the walls of the tiny cottage were closing in on her and the little truckle bed that she slept on was so uncomfortable that she often woke up feeling irritable and more tired than when she had gone to bed. There was never any chance of a lie-in, for the bed had to be tidied away to the side of the room when the family came downstairs. The children were noisy too, and never having been a particularly patient person they grated on her nerves.

Marcie knew exactly who was to blame for the predicament she found herself in – George! But tonight, he would get his comeuppance. It was the night of his engagement party and Marcie was determined that Belinda would never wear his ring. She intended to stop his engagement before it even started if it was the last thing she did. She was so lost in thoughts of her revenge that she was surprised when the gates leading to Haunchwood House loomed ahead of her.

Already carriages were driving through them, no doubt the guests for the party, she thought, as she slipped into the grounds and took shelter behind a tree. She skirted the wall until she came to the back of the house where she passed by unnoticed into the laundry room. For a second, she gazed at the mangle, the dolly tub and the coppers and remembered the long, hard hours she had toiled over them. Slowly the light faded and from within the house she could hear the faint sounds of an orchestra tuning their instruments in readiness for the ball. Marcie had never seen the place so busy and could only assume that a lot of people must have been invited. Well, that was fine, the more people there to witness his humiliation, the better, she thought with a nasty little smile. It was true what they said, revenge was sweet!

At last she heard music playing and slipping out of her cloak, she flung it to one side and patted her hair before marching to the kitchen door. It was open and inside was a scene of chaos as waitresses ran in and out with silver trays bearing crystal flutes of champagne. Others were carrying trays and dishes full of food into the dining room and the cook was barking orders at everyone.

'You, girl, get that tray of canapes and carry them among the guests,' she ordered as she swiped the sweat from her brow. The heat in there was almost unbearable and she had been on her feet since five o'clock that morning so her patience was wearing thin. And then she spotted Marcie and her mouth fell open.

'And what are *you* doing here?' she asked incredulously. They had not seen hide nor hair of her since the day she had left. 'You do know there's a party goin' on, don't you? It's hardly the time to come visitin'!'

'I'm not visiting,' Marcie informed her imperiously. 'I'm a guest, if you must know. Mrs Dorsey invited me.'

'Mrs Dorsey invited *you?*' Cook said disbelievingly, but at that moment one of the little maids dropped a silver dish of boiled beetroots that she had been carrying to the dining room and Cook forgot all about Marcie for a second as she turned her wrath on the poor girl, giving Marcie the chance to escape unseen into the hallway.

There, she paused to stare about her in amazement. There were people milling everywhere, the men dressed in fancy waistcoats and the women dressed in silks and satins in all the colours of the rainbow. Until then Marcie had felt that she looked her best but now, looking down at the second-hand dress she had bought from the rag stall, she suddenly felt dowdy. Even so, she stuck her chin in the air and began to move among them as she looked for George. She was quite aware that she was attracting more than a few curious glances but she carried on regardless, intent on what she had come to do.

At the door to the ballroom, she paused. She had never been in there before and was amazed at the sheer size of it. The band was playing a waltz and as the ladies glided by on the arms of their partners they resembled multi-coloured butterflies. The room was enormous and the crystal chandeliers glittered from the myriad candles burning in them. A quick glance about assured her that George wasn't in there, so next she headed for the dining room where she saw the enormous, highly polished mahogany table almost groaning beneath the weight of food on it. There were delicacies there that she had never even seen before but she was too eager to get on with her plan to take much notice, so she quickly moved on to the next room, the day room. She saw Leonora looking radiant in a cream satin gown that showed off her slim figure to perfection but she barely gave her a glance. It wasn't her that she had come to find. The next room was the sitting room. In there were mainly men drinking port, discussing business and smoking fine cigars so again she moved on and in the next room, the drawing room, she was lucky.

The Lewises and the Dorseys were congregated in front of the huge French windows, all smiling and looking extremely elated. Well, I shall soon put paid to that, she thought with some satisfaction, as she glided towards them. George was standing next to Belinda with his arm protectively about her waist and just for a second the sight of him looking so handsome caused a pain in her heart. Belinda looked breathtakingly beautiful in an ivory satin gown with sapphires dangling from her ears and about her throat winking in the light. Her hair was piled high on her head and teased into curls that cascaded into ringlets about her shoulders and for a moment Marcie almost felt sorry for her. Until she saw the huge diamond ring glittering on her finger and then she felt a stab of jealousy in her heart.

Connie Dorsey spotted her first, as she weaved through the throng of guests towards them and her face instantly paled as she smelled trouble. Why else would Marcie have come? But it was too late to do anything about it now, Marcie was almost upon them.

'Hello, George, remember me?' Marcie asked

sweetly as she stopped in front of him. The two families had been deep in conversation but now it stopped abruptly as they all stared at her.

'Who are *you?*' Belinda asked pointedly.

Marcie grinned. 'I'm the one he was going to marry until he discovered I was carrying his *child.*' Marcie stroked the swell of her stomach as Belinda's mother gasped and clutched at her husband's sleeve.

'What is the girl talking about?' she demanded, staring at George, and Marcie had the satisfaction of seeing him squirm like a worm on a fisherman's hook.

Meanwhile, Johnny Dorsey had slammed his drink down and was advancing on Marcie, intent on getting her out of the room.

'Shut up now and get out or I'll have you physically thrown out!' he bellowed.

'Whatever for? For telling the *truth?*' She fluttered her eyelashes innocently and he lunged forward but when he snatched at her arm she threw him off and glared.

'Don't you *dare* lay a finger on me!' she warned with such venom that he took a step back.

'Go on then *tell* her about me,' she said, turning her attention back to George. 'Tell her about all the promises you made while all the time you were visiting *her* in London. Tell her about our secret liaisons in the hay loft and about suggesting to me that we could still be lovers after you'd married her!'

'Is this true, George?' Belinda's eyes were brimming with tears as she turned to him and her father looked so angry that Marcie feared he might burst a blood vessel.

'If it is, by God, you'll not be marrying *my* daughter,' he warned.

'I ... I...' George was so shocked that he seemed to have lost the power of speech but that was answer enough for Belinda's father. He was painfully aware of the silence that had settled on the room and the fact that every pair of eyes was trained on them and he was squirming with humiliation. And to think that he had been willing to accept this cad into his family!

'Give this bloody young whippersnapper his ring back,' Mr Lewis ordered his sobbing daughter who, slipping it off her finger, flung it towards George. Then gathering her and his wife together he said curtly, 'We're going home and I'll not be darkening this doorway again. And if you've any sense, young man, you'll not attempt to darken mine either else I'll have you thrown out on your ear.'

Even the band had stopped playing in the ballroom now as Mr Lewis gathered together what dignity he could and marched his family away.

'Now look what you've done, you little whore! Are you *satisfied?*' Mr Dorsey bellowed, red in the face.

Marcie gave him a serene smile. 'Perfectly, thank you, sir.' And with that she sailed away with her head held high.

Chapter Thirty-Five

It was only when she reached the Cock and Bear bridge that spanned the canal that Marcie allowed her footsteps to slow and then the tears came. Bitter tears for what might have been. Admittedly, she had coveted the life that George could have given her but she had loved him too, which made his rejection all the harder to bear. She was trudging down the hill as if she had the weight of the world on her shoulders when she became aware of footsteps behind her and just for a moment her heart leapt. Perhaps it was George come to try and make amends after realising what a fool he had been!

But when she turned, she saw a dark figure ambling towards her and she knew instantly that this wasn't George. Her heart began to thud painfully as the figure drew nearer and she lifted her skirts ready to run. But there was something vaguely familiar about him. And as he passed beneath the gas lamp, the breath caught in her throat. The man was filthy and unkempt with a beard that straggled beneath his chin and even from this distance she could smell the ripe scent of him, but there could be no doubt about it. His was a face she would never forget. A face she saw in her worst nightmares. *It was her father.*

'Marcie, me little sweetheart, come 'ere an' give yer old dad a nice cuddle now.' He held his arms out to her but she recoiled as if she had been burned and her lip curled with contempt.

'What are *you* doing back here?' she spat. 'Your landlady friend get sick of you, did she? I heard she'd left you and gone back to her old man with her tail between her legs.'

'She was an arsehole,' he said with a drunken grin. 'But now I'm back I need somewhere to stay an' I know me lovely lass won't see me out on the streets, will yer?'

'I wouldn't piss on you in the gutter if you were on fire, let alone give you house room,' Marcie ground out. 'It's all because of you me mam is dead. If you hadn't been such a lousy swine she might still be alive. I suppose you know by now that she was murdered!'

'Aye, I know, an' all I can say is she got what was comin' to her,' he said nastily. 'But now how about givin' yer old dad a few pence to tide him over, eh?'

Marcie had heard enough and couldn't stand there and listen to any more from him. 'I wouldn't give you the snot from the end of my nose. Now get back into the gutter where you crawled from,' she said. 'I don't *ever* want to set eyes on your face again.' And with that she was off. And just when I thought things couldn't get much worse, she thought gloomily as she hurried along.

Back at Haunchwood House the guests were departing just as quickly as they were able to. The party was well and truly over and Johnny Dorsey was in a towering rage.

'You *stupid* young fool!' he berated George.

333

'You've ruined everything now, an' all because you couldn't keep your dick in yer trousers! Why, for two pins I'd cut you out o' me will.' He had hauled George into his office out of earshot of the guests.

'Look, Father, why don't you wait until the morning when you've had chance to calm down,' Oliver suggested, ever the peacemaker, but his words only seemed to incense his father more.

'Fine advice comin' from *you*,' he ranted as he poked his son in the chest. 'When from what I'm hearin' you're gettin' too close for comfort to the trollop's sister. What is it about those girls? Are they bloody *witches* or sommat?'

'Now calm down, Johnny,' a distraught Connie urged. 'You're doin' yourself no good at all gettin' yourself all worked up like this.'

'Pah!' Johnny glared at her, then turning on his heel he barged out of the room, slamming the door so hard behind him that it seemed to dance on its hinges.

'And *you*, young man!' She wagged a stern finger at George. 'I suggest *you* keep well out of your father's way for a few days, if you know what's good for you, and let him calm down.'

'Bloody women,' George muttered as he left the room feeling sorry for himself. Many of his friends from school had bedded maids without all this fuss and palaver. But something was niggling at the back of his mind. How had Marcie known it was his engagement ball this evening? Someone must have told her and he had a damned good idea who it was. *Eliza!* He remembered the way she had started when he found her with his father's address book in the office and the way she had slammed it shut. Had Marcie asked her friend to get the Lewises' address for her so that she could carry out her threat? He certainly wouldn't put it past her. And then perhaps she had decided that rather than write to them she would wait and have the ultimate revenge by turning up at the ball. Well, she'd certainly achieved that, he thought angrily. Marcie had wiped away the future he had planned in an instant, for he knew that there was no way on earth Belinda would ever speak to him again now, her father would make sure of that!

'Damn her to *hell!*' he said furiously as he swiped a fine Dresden figurine from a small table in the hall. It smashed into a thousand pieces and he stepped through them as he stormed off towards the stables. There was only one way to work this mood off and that was to give his horse a good stiff gallop. It didn't matter to him that Prince would be settled in his stable for the night or that it was pitch dark outside, nor that he was totally inadequately dressed for riding. All he knew was that if he didn't get rid of some of the pent-up fury inside him he was in danger of exploding.

The grooms were still busily leading the guests' horses back around to the front of the house and seeing the carriages safely on their way when he entered the stable yard. Word had clearly already spread about what had happened and most of them lowered their heads when they saw him. On a few others' faces he thought he detected a smirk and he had to clench his fists to stop himself tearing into them.

'Bates,' he addressed the young junior groom. 'Get Prince saddled for me! Now!'

The young man looked horrified. 'B-but he's settled, sir.'

'Are you questioning me, boy?' George's eyes were sparking and the young lad quickly shook his head.

'Oh no, sir. I'll fetch him straight away.'

'See that you do!' George snatched up a riding crop then strode across the yard to wait in the laundry room. It was better than standing outside having everyone gawping at him, he supposed. He was going to be a laughing stock now!

The room was in darkness but he had been in there no more than a few minutes when he sensed that he was not alone. Turning, he peered into the darkness and seconds later a figure approached him. It was Eliza, who had just delivered a load of dirty tablecloths for washing the next morning.

George could hardly believe his luck! He had been waiting to question her about her part in this whole sorry mess and now here she was! She clearly knew what had happened because she was staring at him with a guilty expression on her face.

He stepped in front of the door, tapping the crop into his palm as he asked, 'Satisfied now, are you?' His eyes had adjusted to the darkness and he could just make out her face in the light through the window. She looked absolutely terrified. And so she should, he thought.

'I ... I don't know what yer mean, Master George.' There was a tremble in her voice but he ignored it. He *wanted* her to be afraid.

336

'Oh, so it wasn't *you* who told Marcie about my engagement ball tonight?'

'P-perhaps she heard about it in town,' Eliza faltered.

'I rather believe she heard it from you after you took the Lewises' address from my father's book that day I caught you in the office,' he said accusingly.

Eliza flinched. He knew, she could see it in his eyes and now panic set in.

'I ... I thought she was just going to write to 'em,' she babbled. 'I had no idea she was going to *come* here!'

'*You bitch!*' Raising the riding crop George brought it crashing down on her shoulder and she squealed with pain as she sprang further back into the room.

'I ... I'm *sorry,*' she yelped. She was sobbing now but George was in no mood for her apologies. He raised the crop again and this time it whistled past her shoulder and struck her neck beneath the mob cap she was wearing. An angry red weal immediately began to rise on her skin. She screamed again as she made a frantic dash for the door as the blows rained down on her but then her foot caught in the hem of her skirt and she felt herself falling. He watched as her head connected with the deep stone sink and there was a sickening thud and suddenly she was on the floor, blood spreading in a pool about her head and trickling from her nose as she lay quite still.

George gulped. 'Eliza ... get up!' He nudged her still body with the toe of his highly polished boot but she made no movement and in that moment,

337

it came to him that she was dead.

'Is everything all right in there?' A voice from beyond the door made him start. He had killed her. He would have to get away unless he wanted to find himself dangling from a hangman's noose!

Flinging the door wide he saw Prince, ready and saddled across the yard and in seconds he had sprung onto his back and was galloping away as if the devil himself was on his heels. He had no idea where he was going, all he knew was that he must get as far away from there as possible before they found Eliza's body. What had started as a most enjoyable evening had turned into a complete nightmare and one thing was for sure, he would never be able to go home again.

Once back at Molly's house, Marcie found her banking down the fire. The rest of the family had gone to bed and noting the girl's pale face, Molly asked, 'Are you all right, pet? You're as white as a sheet.'

'I ... I just bumped into my father,' Marcie told her shakily.

'Oh!' Molly sat back abruptly on her heels. She'd heard some bad things about the man and could understand why Molly was so upset about him turning up out of the blue again after leaving them as he had.

'Has he changed?' she asked.

Marcie shook her head. Everything that had happened that night was catching up with her now and she was trembling. 'He don't appear to have,' she said miserably. 'He looked like a tramp and smelled something terrible.'

'Well, it might be as well if you warned Nessie that he's back on the scene rather than him turn up on her doorstep and give her a shock,' Molly advised sensibly. 'But for now I should try an' get some rest. Seein' him again has obviously shaken you.'

'It has,' Marcie admitted as she sat down at the side of the fire and wrapped her arms about herself. Far more than you could ever know, she thought, as Molly headed off for bed.

Round at the funeral parlour, Nessie was doing her last-minute chores before going upstairs. She'd not long since returned from the soup kitchen and was looking forward to going to bed. It had been a long day and her feet were aching. When she was satisfied that all was safe in the shop she went back through to the living quarters, passing Andre on the way. He was in a shirt with the collar undone and the sleeves rolled up, and without his formal jacket and cravat he looked completely different.

'Ah.' He smiled at her. 'Forgive my informal attire. I just went through to get my book. I had left it in the office.' He waved it at her. It was one by Charles Dickens. Both of them were avid readers, which was something they had in common, although Nessie didn't find nearly as much time as she would have liked to read.

'There's nothing like a good book to help you get off to sleep.' Nessie smiled. 'My trouble is I always tend to fall asleep after reading the first couple of pages.'

It was then that they both heard a knock on the kitchen door and they frowned as they glanced quizzically at each other. If it was someone who was needing Andre's services they would usually come to the shop door so Nessie had no idea who it could be so late at night.

'I shall stand here while you answer it,' Andre said protectively and with a nod she hurried across the room.

As she inched the door open the light from the lamp spilled out into the yard. 'Yes? May I help you?' she asked the dark form that stood there.

'Yer certainly can, an' yer can start by puttin' the kettle on, I'm fair dyin' fer a decent cuppa!' Nessie gasped as she reeled back into the room and the man followed her, gazing around appreciatively. 'Nice set-up you've got yerself here. Seth Grimshaw said as yer were livin' wi' the undertaker.'

Before she could say a word, Andre stepped forward, his face set. 'Who is this man?'

'I-it's my father,' Nessie answered, wishing that the ground would open up and swallow her. She had never felt so ashamed.

'And do you wish him to be here?'

She shook her head, keeping her eyes fixed on the floor. She couldn't even bring herself to look at him and had hoped that she would never have to see him again.

'In that case, I must ask you to leave, sir.' Andre drew himself up to his full height as the smarmy false smile slid from her father's face.

'Are you really goin' to allow this ponce to chuck me out in the street?' he asked his daughter incredulously.

'Yes, Dad ... I am, and please never come here or try to contact me again. The day you walked out and left us all was the day I decided I no longer had a father and nothing has changed. For all *you* cared we could have ended up in the work-house and we probably would have if it wasn't for the way Mam almost worked herself to death. Now please leave, there's no more to be said!'

Andre took a menacing step forward and Bill Carson scowled. 'Well, at least I know where I stand now, don't I? Huh! You'll be no loss – *none* of yer!' And with that he shuffled back out of the door and Andre slammed it resoundingly behind him.

At that moment Reuben appeared at the bottom of the stairs, disturbed by all the commotion.

'What's going on?' he asked blearily as he knuckled the sleep from his eyes.

'Dad just paid us a visit,' Nessie told him. She expected him to look shocked but instead he lowered his eyes and in that moment, she realised. 'You *knew* he was back in town, didn't you?' she accused.

Reuben remained silent but in her mind she saw him talking to the person in the shadows in town. It had been her father, she was sure of it, and Reuben was handing him something. Could it have been the money that he had tried to hide beneath his mattress?

Nessie was leaning heavily on the back of a chair now, her face as pale as lint, but suddenly remembering Andre was still standing there she managed a grateful smile.

'Thank you, Andre. I'm so glad that you were here.'

'Any time, *mademoiselle*.' Looking between brother and sister and sensing they needed some privacy, he tactfully headed back to his own quarters, leaving them alone.

Chapter Thirty-Six

'Why didn't you tell me he was back?' Nessie asked when Andre had left.

Reuben hung his head and shrugged. 'I suppose I didn't want to upset you.'

'But at least if you'd told me, his turning up here wouldn't have come as such a shock,' she accused. 'And now I may as well tell you something that's been bothering me. I accidentally found some money under your mattress some time ago when I was changing your bed. I saw you talking to Snowy White too, would either of these things have anything to do with our dad?'

Reuben licked his lips. 'Yes,' he admitted. 'Apparently Dad has been doing ... some jobs for Snowy and...'

'Huh! More like robbing for him, you mean,' Nessie interrupted him scathingly. 'Everyone knows what a reputation that man has and if Dad is working for him you can bet he's up to no good! But how have *you* become involved?'

'Snowy White approached me some time ago and told me he had some money for Dad. He

342

asked if I'd pass it on to him; it's as simple as that, I swear I haven't been involved with them other than that!'

'*You fool!*' she scolded him. 'Why didn't you just tell Snowy to get lost? You must have realised the money was probably from ill-gotten gains!'

'I thought if I did that, you know, just pass it on, that Dad wouldn't bother us, but after I'd done it once it was hard to say no... I'm sorry.'

He looked so dejected that Nessie couldn't stay angry with him for long. 'It stops right here,' she warned. 'No more passing on anything, do you hear me? What would Maria say if she knew you were associating with the likes of Snowy White? And why couldn't Snowy just pass the money on to Dad himself anyway?'

'Snowy always covers his back. That's why he's never been caught. I dare say he doesn't like to hang on to large sums of money in case the coppers catch him with it. He'd have to explain where it came from then.'

'Hmm! But no more, *understood?*'

He nodded and disappeared back upstairs, leaving Nessie feeling shaken. Seeing her father again had brought back terrible memories that she would rather forget. They were all working so hard to build new lives for themselves and the last thing she needed was her dad turning up again and spoiling everything for them all. Marcie wasn't going to take the news well either, she mused. Still, at least Andre had sent him on his way and with a bit of luck he wouldn't bother them again.

The next morning Molly arrived at the parlour

long before it was time to open the shop with a very tearful Marcie.

'Whatever is the matter?' Nessie asked, ushering them inside. She was still in her dressing robe with her hair loose about her shoulders.

'Oh, Nessie!' Marcie flung herself into her sister's arms and began to cry.

'That friend of hers, Eliza, is dead,' Molly told her. 'And they reckon that young George Dorsey killed her. He's gone missin' but I think Marcie ought to tell you the rest.'

'How do you know all this?' she asked as she pushed Marcie gently onto a chair and hurried over to fill the kettle.

'The police came to question Marcie a couple of hours ago an' they told us.'

Nessie looked shocked. 'Question *Marcie!* Whatever for? What has Marcie got to do with all this?'

Marcie looked shamefaced and hung her head.

'I ... I went up to the house and caused a bit of a ruckus last night. George was getting engaged you see and I ... I couldn't bear it, so I went up and confronted him in front of everyone, and told them about the baby.'

'Oh, Marcie, *no!* Why ever did you do that?' Nessie groaned.

'Why shouldn't his future in-laws know what sort of a person he is?' Marcie retaliated with a sob. 'Why should *he* be allowed to go off and live happily ever after while I'm left to look after his brat!'

'So what happened?'

'Belinda flung his ring at him and the Lewises left saying they never wanted anything to do with the family again, and then Mr Dorsey threatened to chuck me out so I left.'

'But I still don't understand why Eliza's death has anything to do with you.' Nessie was feeling totally confused.

'It was Eliza who got me the Lewises' address. I was going to write and tell them about the baby but then she told me about the party and I decided to go and tell them all face to face. From what the police said, George must have guessed that Eliza was involved. One of the grooms said he heard someone scream in the laundry room and it must have been her. Then George flew out of there and got on his horse and they found Eliza dead on the floor.' She started to cry again as Nessie tried to take it all in. Poor, poor Eliza, she had been so young with her whole life ahead of her and now it had been snuffed out like a flame. It just didn't bear thinking about.

'So where is George now?' she asked.

Marcie shrugged. 'No one has seen him since he took off on his horse last night... He could be anywhere.'

'Hmm, well there's nothing you can do for now, what's done is done,' Nessie sighed. 'But I suggest in future you think about what consequences your actions might have!'

'Oh, so you're saying all this is *my* fault, are you?' Marcie challenged.

'Of course not, I'm just saying be more careful.'

Marcie pouted as Molly and Nessie exchanged a glance.

'I er ... also ought to tell you that I had a visitor last night,' Nessie said cautiously. 'Dad turned up on the doorstep, but don't worry, Andre was wonderful. He soon cleared him off.' She had expected Marcie to look shocked but the girl merely nodded dully.

'I already know he's back. I was going to come and tell you this morning. I bumped into him last night on my way back from Haunchwood House.'

Strangely, although she hated her father with a passion, him turning up again seemed trivial now compared to the other things that had happened.

'Reuben,' she began tentatively as she ladled his porridge into a bowl later that morning. 'We need to talk about Marcie and George and the baby.'

'So what's she goin' to do when it arrives? We ain't havin' it,' he growled.

'Seeing as the baby is due round about the time you're thinking of getting married I hardly see how this is going to affect you anyway,' Nessie retorted.

'No? And what do you think Maria's family are goin' to think of her?'

'I dare say they'll think she's just another girl who's been rather silly. Maria's family are close-knit, they'll understand.'

'Huh! I'm not so sure.' Reuben shook his head. 'An' I can't help but be disappointed in her. An' now for this to happen on top, all because o' Marcie goin' up there an' causin' trouble...'

'Sadly, that can't be helped now. In fairness, she was just looking for revenge on George because he let her down. She couldn't have known what he would do, could she?'

'I don't suppose so, but what'll happen now? I

mean, will Marcie be in trouble ... with the police?'

'I doubt it, after all she didn't actually physically harm anyone, did she? They have already questioned her first thing about what went on and they're looking for George now.'

'So where do you think he's gone?' Reuben asked.

Nessie shrugged. 'I suppose he could be anywhere, although I dare say he'll try and get on a boat and leave the country.' Nessie sighed, defeated. 'What are we to do, Reuben? It'll be all round the town in no time that she's having a baby.'

Things surely couldn't get any worse for the family, could they?

Soon after, Nessie had to explain everything to Andre, who was shocked and horrified at the turn of events. As they were talking there was a rap on the door of the parlour and when Nessie went to open it she found Oliver standing there.

'I've actually come to call on Andre. We're in need of his professional services,' he told her sadly. 'I dare say you've already heard what's happened up at the house to poor Eliza?'

Nessie nodded and held the door open, allowing him to step inside.

'It is most regrettable what has occurred,' Andre told him solemnly. 'Do you wish me to arrange the funeral for you?'

Oliver nodded. 'Yes, please. I've already spoken to Eliza's family and they expressed a wish that you bring her here to the chapel of rest. They have a number of younger children so it wouldn't really be appropriate to keep her body at home until... Well, until you've got the funeral all arranged. We want her to have the best of everything, the best coffin you can supply, etc. Money is no object; my family will be paying the bill due to the circumstances. It's the least we can do.'

'I shall see that everything is done to your wishes,' Andre assured him, and turning he went back into his living quarters, leaving Nessie and Oliver alone feeling decidedly uncomfortable.

'I er ... apologise for what my sister did last night,' she faltered, feeling that she should say something.

'No, if George *is* the father of her baby, then I can quite understand her being so angry. It was abominable of my brother to think he could just use her like that then get engaged to someone else. I've been wanting to talk to you about the baby but wasn't sure if you even knew about it.'

'Oh, I knew all right, but I was too embarrassed to broach the subject with you,' she admitted. He looked so sad that she wanted to reach out and touch him. But she didn't, of course. What had happened between Marcie and George had put a further wedge between them.

'Have they, er ... said how Eliza died?' she asked tentatively.

Again he nodded. 'Yes, it appeared that she smashed her head on the sink as she fell. But George had clearly been lashing out at her with his riding crop. There were weals on her body.'

'That doesn't mean he deliberately set out to kill her, though, does it?' She longed to ease his pain. 'Perhaps she fell trying to get away from him?'

'However it happened,' Oliver said, 'he will still be tried for murder. The trouble is he's making everything so much worse for himself by keeping away. Why didn't the stupid little devil just go and get help rather than running away?'

'I dare say he panicked. But look, why don't you come through and I'll make you a cup of tea? You don't look as if you've had much sleep.'

In truth he hadn't. He had spent most of the night sitting up with his parents and then this morning the terrible job of informing Eliza's parents of her death had fallen to him. That had been the worst thing he had ever had to do and they had been heartbroken at the loss of their lovely girl. They had also been extremely angry with him too. It was his brother who they believed had caused her death, after all. Even the offer of his family paying for her funeral had done nothing to placate them.

Their eyes locked for just the briefest of moments and once again Oliver had to stifle the urge to put his arms about her and comfort her but then he looked away hastily. If what Marcie was saying was true, then his younger brother had caused not only the death of one young woman but had left another with a child to bring up on her own.

'I won't, if you don't mind,' he said quietly as he turned to the door. 'My mother is in quite a terrible state, as you can imagine, so I need to call into the surgery and get some medication that will calm her down.'

'I quite understand,' Nessie told him as she folded her hands sedately, although her heart ached. 'And please don't worry about your surgery at the soup kitchen for a while. I'm sure you'll have things to attend to.'

He paused to look back at her with a bleak expression on his face that tore at her heart. He opened his mouth to say something, but then seeming to think better of it, he jammed his hat onto his head and left without another word, leaving her to stare helplessly after him.

Chapter Thirty-Seven

Later that morning Andre and Reuben went to fetch Eliza's body from the house and it was duly laid in the small chapel of rest. Marcie was the first to arrive, much to Nessie's surprise, and when she went in to see her friend, she sobbed. Eliza looked so beautiful and peaceful lying there in her satin-lined coffin that Marcie could almost believe that she would wake at any minute and flash her one of the cheeky smiles that she was known for.

'I'm *so* sorry, Eliza,' Marcie sobbed. 'If I'd known what was going to happen I would never have involved you.'

Perhaps my sister does have a heart after all, Nessie thought, as she stole away, leaving her sister to say her last goodbyes to her friend. She had already organised the funeral to take place at

St Paul's Church in Stockingford in three days' time and then Eliza would be interred in the churchyard there.

Later, when darkness fell, Andre went through to the chapel of rest to extinguish the candles and as he came back across the yard Nessie opened the door and asked him, 'Might I have a word?'

'Of course.' He stepped into the room. 'How may I help you?' he asked chivalrously.

'I don't want anything,' she assured him quickly. 'And I know this isn't the ideal time to raise what I have to say, what with everything else that's going on, but I thought you should know...' She took a deep breath. 'Reuben is intending to get married in a few months' time.'

'But that is wonderful, yes?'

'Oh yes, it is,' she agreed hastily. 'But the thing is, it will leave me in rather a difficult situation. He will still continue to work here, of course, but then he and Maria will have a little home of their own.'

He stared at her uncomprehendingly. 'And will this be a problem?'

'It could be. You see, there is already gossip going about that you and I are...' She blushed furiously. 'You know, that we are ... more than employer and employee. Imagine what they would say if they knew that I was staying here without Reuben.'

'Pah! I have told you before, what do I care for tittle-tattle!'

'But it goes deeper than that. What if the talk affected your business? It would be heartbreaking after all our hard work to build it up. And so

351

I think it might be best if I looked around for somewhere else for me and Joseph to live after the wedding. At least that way no one would have anything to gossip about.'

'But you have made this your *home*.' He spread his hands, appalled. 'And I would miss little Joseph ... and you,' he ended sadly. Then, 'Let me think about this, please. There must be a way around it.' He nodded to her briefly and left.

Nessie sighed and rubbed at the dull ache behind her eyes as she wondered why her life always had to be so complicated.

Both Marcie and Nessie attended Eliza's funeral and as they entered the church she saw Oliver sitting at the back. He had come to represent his family as a mark of respect but the congregation studiously avoided him. Nessie supposed she could understand how they felt but she felt sorry for him all the same and longed to sit beside him. He was only trying to do the right thing. As they all filed out behind the coffin after the service, he pressed a weighty envelope into Nessie's hand and asked her, 'Would you see that Eliza's mother gets this, please. It's what Eliza would have earned over the coming years along with a bonus. My mother wanted them to have it. Hopefully it will relieve the family's financial position at least. But I think I should go now. Goodbye, Nessie.'

She stared down at the envelope and gulped deeply, too emotional to speak, and watched helplessly as he strode away with his head bent.

Two weeks later there had been no sign of George

whatsoever, although the police were scouring the countryside for him. Connie Dorsey had very mixed feelings about him being found. Half of her just wanted to know that he was safe. The other half dreaded what would become of him when he was arrested.

Could she have known it, George was now in London. He had stopped in Northampton and sold his horse to a chap outside an inn who recognised good horseflesh when he saw it. Of course, George realised that he had only given him a fraction of what Prince was worth but he was hungry and had to raise some cash somehow. He had then gone into a pawn shop and swapped the fine clothes and boots he was wearing for some work clothes that had seen better days and a small amount of cash which had enabled him to scratch together enough to get the train the rest of the way to London.

Now, with his beard growing by the day and his hair straggling about his collar, he was unrecognisable from the smart young man he had been only a couple of weeks before and looked no different to any of the other down-at-heel chaps who swarmed around the Whitechapel docks each day looking for work. He was scraping together a living unloading the cargo boats that came into the docks, when he was lucky enough to be chosen for work that day, that was. He had soon discovered for that to happen he had to be up at the crack of dawn and waiting in the queue of men who were all desperate for work. He had been used to lying on a feather mattress and rising when he felt like it, not sleeping with tramps and vagabonds beneath the bridges that spanned the River Thames. But hunger had become his master: if he didn't work, he didn't eat, it was as simple as that, and he would walk the streets with his stomach growling for food. On arriving in London all he had left of worth was the fine gold hunter pocket watch and chain his parents had given him for his eighteenth birthday but that had been stolen from his pocket one night as he slept after being befriended by a dirty old beggar who introduced himself as Septimus.

'New 'ere, are yer, lad?' he'd asked.

It was the first kind word George had heard since leaving home and he'd nodded.

'I thought yer were, yer don't sound like yer from round these parts. Have yer got anywhere to sleep tonight?'

George had shaken his head.

'Then yer'd best come along o' me an' share a tin o' tea.' And so George had been introduced to the world beneath the embankment bridge where Septimus had pointed to an old tea chest that could serve as his sleeping place. He had boiled some water over a fire and offered George weak but welcome unsweetened tea while he himself slowly got drunk on a bottle of gin he had stolen from an ale house while the landlord wasn't looking. It wasn't luxurious by any stretch of the imagination but George felt warm inside and not quite so alone when he finally crawled into the crate and quickly slipped into an uneasy sleep.

He had wept with anger and frustration when he had discovered his watch was gone the next morning. All that was left of Septimus was a rank

354

smell of urine and a pile of ashes where the fire had been, but it had taught him a valuable lesson. He had no one to trust now. No one to help him or lean on and he must fend for himself. He had discovered muscles he hadn't known he had and by evening they would be screaming at him. When at last his shift was finished he would be paid a few measly pence then he would stagger off in search of food and a hot drink, usually bought from the street vendors that were dotted all across the city. At one he could buy faggots and peas, at another hot jacket potatoes. Once he had tried jellied eels, which he had quickly vomited back up in the gutter.

Once his stomach was full, he would begin the search for a sleeping place for the night. His favourite places were under the bridges on the embankment where other homeless people lit fires that made him feel a little more comfortable; although since his brush with Septimus he was careful to keep a distance. He had quickly discovered that even if he worked every day he couldn't afford a room in even the cheapest lodging house. But hopefully, he would only have to live like this until he was able to put the next part of his plan into action. Very soon he hoped to sign on a ship as a seaman and travel the world. People had told him that it was hard work but he reasoned that it couldn't be any harder than what he was doing now, and at least aboard a ship he would get regular meals and somewhere to sleep. So he waited, praying that soon he would be able to sail away and leave all his troubles behind.

By the beginning of April, Marcie was unable to hide the fact that she was with child any more. Since word of what had happened up at the house had spread she was a marked woman and she rarely left Molly's home unless she absolutely had to. Reuben was busily planning his wedding and Nessie was still debating what she should do when he left home. She had intended to start looking for alternative accommodation but she always seemed to be so busy that as yet she hadn't found the time. She had seen little of Oliver since Eliza's death apart from when they were both at the soup kitchen and, though she would never dare admit it to anyone, she missed him terribly.

Nessie was surprised when she got back late after another night in the soup kitchen to see a light glowing in the shop, so she went to check and found Andre sitting working on his ledger.

'It's a little late to be doing that, isn't it? Couldn't it have waited until the morning?' she asked with a smile.

He rose from the desk to face her. 'Yes, it could have done but...' He yanked at the stiffly starched collar of his shirt as if it was too tight for him before going on, 'The thing is ... I think I've come up with the solution to both our problems – about you moving out, I mean.'

'Oh?' Nessie raised an inquisitive eyebrow. 'And what would that be then?'

'Well, I admit that I don't want you to go and you have said that you are happy living here ... so ... why don't we ... get married?'

'*What?*' Nessie's eyes were almost popping out of her head.

'Think about it. It is the perfect solution,' he urged, his eyes shining. 'No one could gossip about us if we were man and wife, so I ask you most humbly, will you marry me, Wednesday Carson?'

Chapter Thirty-Eight

Nessie stared at him speechless for a few moments before stammering, 'Is ... is this some sort of a joke?'

'No, no no!' he assured her, grasping her two hands in his and gently shaking them. 'I would be a good husband to you, I swear. We get along well, don't we? And you need never worry about being homeless again.'

'But...'

'Ah, you are thinking of Jean-Paul.' His smile faded a little. 'Of course, it would not be a conventional marriage. We would not ... you know? Sleep together. It would be platonic; two dear friends sharing their lives... Unless of course there is someone you would rather share it with?'

Unbidden, a picture of Oliver's face flashed in front of her eyes, his deep-blue eyes and his thick, fair hair, but she shook her head to rid herself of the image. 'No ... there is no one else. But you must understand, this is a huge step. I shall need time to think about it.'

He nodded and released her hands. 'You must, but please do not dismiss the idea out of hand. I know how dedicated you are to Joseph. Together we could ensure that whatever time he has left is happy and you would have security. You do not find me *too* repugnant, do you?'

'Why, of *course* I don't.' She gave him a tearful smile. His offer had taken her completely by surprise. 'I have a great affection for you and consider you to be a dear friend. But I … I suppose I always dreamed of having children of my own one day.'

His eyes clouded and he looked away from her. 'Perhaps we could adopt?' he suggested.

'Perhaps, but now I must get on and I thank you for the offer.' She gave him one more smile and escaped to her own living quarters where she leaned her knuckles heavily on the table and took a deep breath. Andre had asked her to *marry* him! Were she to go ahead with his plan they would be husband and wife in name only but she had always truly believed that one day a man would come along and sweep her off her feet and they would live happily ever after. A man like Oliver… A man who she would love with all of her heart and soul. She did love Andre but not in the way a woman should love her husband. The sight of him didn't make her heart beat faster, as it did each time she set eyes on Oliver. The touch of his hand didn't make her tingle. But then she knew she was being foolish to ever even hope that she and Oliver could have come together in that way, especially now after what had happened with Marcie. The child her sister was carrying seemed to have driven an even bigger wedge between them.

Joseph disturbed her thoughts when she heard

him whimper and instantly she was at his side, feeling his brow and worrying. If only he could tell her if he was in pain. As she stared down at his sweet little face and stroked his springing curls her heart ached. What if the tumour had started to grow again? The fear of that happening was with her constantly. The door opened then and Reuben breezed into the room.

His smile froze when he saw Nessie hanging over Joseph and he rushed to her side, asking anxiously, 'He's not worse, is he?' He had just walked Maria home and now he felt guilty. 'I haven't been gone for more than ten minutes, honestly. He was fast asleep when I left. He's all right, ain't he?'

'I'm not sure. I don't think so but it's difficult to tell.' Nessie hurried away to return with a damp piece of huckaback that she tenderly mopped his forehead with.

'Should I go and fetch Dr Dorsey?' he asked.

'No, let me keep an eye on him tonight and then if he's no better I'll send for him in the morning.'

'All right, if you're sure,' he said uncertainly.

'I am so now you go and get yourself off to bed and get some sleep. You've an early funeral to attend to in the morning.'

He inclined his head and made for the stairs door with a worried frown, leaving Nessie to watch over the little boy.

Her head was spinning as she tried to concentrate on Joseph. Andre's proposal had knocked her for six but as the minutes ticked away and Joseph drifted off to sleep she began to wonder if it was such a bad idea. Once Reuben was wed and she had a place of her own to keep, the wages she earned now would soon be gobbled up by bills. And then she would have to find someone to care for Joseph while she was at work, someone kind and reliable, and that would cost too, as would his medical bills; she couldn't expect Oliver to keep seeing him for nothing. And what if her father came back on the scene? There would be no one to defend her if she was living alone.

There was also Marcie to worry about. How would she cope when her new baby arrived? Nessie rubbed at her forehead where a headache was forming behind her tired eyes. But oh, she couldn't stop herself from thinking of the babies she had always dreamed of having. If she were to marry Andre that would never come about now, but then she questioned, if she couldn't have Oliver, would it really matter? She knew deep down that she would never love another man as she loved him. Andre would have no expectations in that direction and they did get on, didn't they?

Round and round her thoughts whirled until at last she fell asleep in the chair next to Joseph.

As Nessie slipped into her troubled sleep, George was just boarding *The Mermaid* in the docks at Whitechapel. He had finally got a job as a seaman on a cargo ship and they would sail to China on the tide the very next morning. Having never sailed before his feelings were a mixture of apprehension and fear, but then, he reasoned, nothing could be worse than living as he had been since

360

fleeing from his home. There were a number of other young men boarding the ship, some looked even younger than him and they were immediately ushered down steep, wooden steps to the cramped sleeping quarters below.

'Look lively, you scabby lot,' the steward shouted. 'Drop your gear off and get back up on deck. There's loading to be done.'

George felt as if he were descending into the bowels of hell. The lower they went the worse the smell of stale urine and unwashed bodies became. He found himself in a long narrow cabin with rows of wooden bunk beds three high on either side. There was scarcely room in the middle of them to turn around and as he made for the nearest one he caught sight of a thick black tail disappearing under it.

Sensing his dismay, the young chap behind him chuckled as he threw his belongings on to the bunk above George's. 'Your first voyage, is it, matey?'

He was a tall, lanky young chap with an unmistakable cockney accent but he seemed friendly enough.

George nodded.

'Hmm, I thought as much. Well, as yer can see, it's hardly a hotel, is it? First seaman, are you?'

George nodded again.

'In that case, we'll prob'ly be workin' alongside each other.' The young man began to unpack his few possessions and jam them into the corner of his bunk. Then seeming to remember his manners he stuck his hand out. 'I'm known as Ginger, by the way.'

Glancing at his shock of thick, carroty-coloured hair, George could understand where his name had come from.

'I'm George.'

'Pleased ter meet you.'

'So what sort of jobs are they likely to have us doing?' George asked.

'Huh! As first seamen it'd be easier to tell you what they *won't* have us doin',' Ginger answered wryly. 'We're the lowest o' the low aboard so we get all the shitty jobs. Swabbin' the decks, keepin' watch in the crow's nest, hoistin' the sails. You name it an' we'll probably end up doin' it. This is my second time an' after the first I swore I'd never do it again but the pay's good at the end o' the day so 'ere I am.'

George grimaced as he examined the paper-thin straw mattress on his bunk. There was a thin grey blanket folded on each bed and that didn't smell very good either.

'I shouldn't worry too much about the sleepin' quarters,' Ginger advised. 'Be the time you drop on that bunk of an evenin' you'll be so knackered you'd sleep anywhere.'

'I, er ... thought I saw a rat scuttle under the bed when we first came in,' George said as he stared down at the floor through the gloom.

'Oh aye, you probably did, there's hundreds o' the little buggers on ships like this. An' we'll probably be glad of 'em an' all if we hit any storms an' the food gets ruined. They're right tasty in a stew an' if yer hungry enough you'll eat owt.'

George had to swallow the bile that rose in his

throat at the thought of it but he kept his face straight.

'On the plus side,' Ginger rattled on as he stood back up from doing his unpacking. 'We do get to see places we'd never normally see. We'll head for the Bay o' Biscay when we leave port then on to the Straits o' Gibraltar. We'll sail through the Mediterranean Sea, the Red Sea and the Indian Ocean. Then finally we'll sail the South China Seas afore dockin' in Mawei Port in China. It's some journey.'

'But why do they want us back up on deck this evening if we're not sailing until the morning?' George questioned.

Ginger chuckled. 'We ain't on a cruise ship, matey! They'll have us loadin' the cargo all through the night if I know owt about it. An' don't bovver tryin' to get out of it, we're the lowest rankin' on the ship, remember, so we do as we're told.'

George gulped, suddenly wondering if he had done the right thing. There was no going back now, though, so with a sigh he took one last glance around the dismal sleeping quarters and followed Ginger back up the ladder.

Just as his new friend had predicted they spent the rest of the night loading the boat and by the early hours of the morning George's muscles were screaming. Never in his life had he worked so hard rolling barrels of fresh water and any manner of other things aboard. There were even cows and sheep, which Ginger told him would be slaughtered some way into the voyage to provide food for them all, as well as a number of chickens which would hopefully provide them with fresh eggs. Those that didn't would go the same way as the cattle.

'What happens if we run out of fresh water?' George asked.

'There's barrels put out on deck to catch the rain and everything we take is purely for drinkin'. For washin' and laundry we use sea water.'

George didn't fancy the thought of all that salt on his skin, but then he supposed this was only one of many things he was going to have to get accustomed to. It was like a different world and not for the first time he thought regretfully of the one he had left behind.

The morning after Andre's surprise proposal, the shop door flew open and Marcie appeared in a high state of agitation, two bright spots of colour in her cheeks.

'Me dad just came round to Molly's,' she gushed before Molly or Nessie could get a word in and promptly burst into tears.

Nessie frowned as she hurried from behind her desk to place her arms round her shaking shoulders. 'What did he want?'

'Money,' Marcie sniffed, snatching a handkerchief from the pocket of her skirt and mopping her streaming eyes.

'And did you give him any?'

Marcie nodded miserably. 'Just a bit ... to get rid of him. I was there all on me own an' afraid of what he might do if I didn't.'

'All right, calm down. This won't do the baby any good,' Nessie urged as she led her sister through to the kitchen. Molly had already raced on ahead to put the kettle on. She was a great believer that a good strong cup of sweet tea was the cure for all ills. Nessie meanwhile was wondering why Marcie was so distraught. There had been a time when Marcie had been their father's favourite but that had all seemed to change when she hit her teens and began to go out at every chance she got.

'He didn't threaten you, did he?' she asked and was relieved when Marcie shook her head.

'N-no but who knows what he's capable of. He smells an' he … he frightens me.'

She began to calm down once Molly placed her drink in front of her. 'Sorry,' she muttered, shamefaced. 'But I was too afraid to stay at Molly's on me own.'

Nessie held her close. 'It's all right. But I'm sure he wouldn't hurt you.'

Marcie remained silent as she slowly drained her cup and Nessie and Molly went about their business leaving Marcie with Joseph.

I shall have to have a word to Reuben about him, Nessie thought, as she once again tried to concentrate on the figures in front of her. The last thing she needed was for Marcie to be frightened in her present state.

Chapter Thirty-Nine

When Nessie arrived at the soup kitchen that evening she found Oliver already there and at the sight of him warm colour flooded her cheeks.

'Good evening,' she said, feeling the distance between them.

He inclined his head. He too was feeling ill at ease in her presence now. God alone knew what she must think of him and his family after what George had done to Marcie.

'H-how are things?' he asked cautiously. It was rare that they got a moment alone together anymore.

Nessie shrugged. 'They're all right,' she answered quietly.

Their eyes locked and held until he said softly, 'I'm so sorry about all that's happened, Nessie... I just wish–' But what he wished for remained unsaid for Molly suddenly bustled in and the moment was lost. There was no chance to say any more.

'Phew, that lot soon went,' Molly commented later as she carried yet another empty stew pan to the sink to be washed. 'I reckon the lot that came tonight had hollow legs.'

Nessie smiled and nodded as she flicked a stray lock of damp hair from her forehead. Once again, she had been on her feet since early that morning and now she was longing for bed, but first there was the kitchen to tidy. She and Molly were hard at work when Oliver appeared from his makeshift surgery. He had spent the evening dishing out salves and ointments for minor ailments and lancing boils.

Molly gave him a cheery grin although Nessie kept her head down.

'All done then?'

He nodded.

'I'd best be gettin' off now,' Molly said. 'My little Phoebe didn't seem too well before I left tonight an' though I know my Charlie'll take good care of her I'm keen to be off an' check on her. Can you manage the rest on yer own, pet?'

'Of course,' Nessie assured her and minutes later Nessie and Oliver found themselves alone.

'Is there anything I can do to help?' Oliver asked eventually.

She shook her head. 'No, thanks for offering but I'm just about finished now.'

'Then perhaps I could give you a lift home?'

Another shake of the head. 'It's all right, really. You get off; you must be tired.'

He hovered uncertainly, then with a shrug he bid her goodnight and left. It was then that the silence seemed to close in on her and she lowered her chin to her chest and sniffed back salty tears.

Life is so unfair, she thought bitterly. Her heart ached with the pain of it all.

She left soon after and upon entering the marketplace, she groaned inwardly as she saw the last person in the world she wanted to see coming towards her.

'Why, if it ain't the delightful Miss Carson,'

367

Seth Grimshaw crowed sarcastically as he neared her. 'I hear that brother o' yours will be gettin' wed soon. That should suit you an' yer French fancy man down to the ground. You'll have the place all to yerselves then, won't yer?'

Nessie automatically opened her mouth to tell him that Andre wasn't her fancy man, as he so crudely put it, but then she clamped it shut again and strode purposely on, keeping her eyes averted from him. She would not lower herself to his level and give him the satisfaction of an answer.

'An' by the way, I discovered t'other day why you're so fond o' that brainless little brother o' yours,' he shouted maliciously. 'I happened to bump into one o' yer old neighbours from Bed'orth while I were in the Engine Inn over there an' he informed me that the brat is actually *your* kid. I wonder what yer fancy Frenchman'll think o' that when he finds out, eh? No wonder the kid's a simpleton! Little Miss Carson isn't quite so innocent as she makes out, is she?'

Nessie kept on going with her head held high, even though she was shaking from head to toe. His lewd comments followed her along the road until she finally turned into Stratford Street where her shoulders sagged and her steps slowed. When she finally let herself into the kitchen she was surprised to find Andre sitting at the table reading a newspaper.

'Ah, here you are,' he greeted her warmly. 'Please do not look so alarmed. Reuben's young lady was feeling unwell so he took her home early and I offered to wait in here and keep an ear open for Joseph until you returned.'

368

'Oh ... thank you.' Relief washed over her. She'd had quite enough for one day and all she wanted now was to sink into bed and sleep. She hung her cloak and bonnet neatly on the nail on the back of the door and when she turned it was to find Andre was now standing.

'I will wish you goodnight then, if you have no further need of me?'

'No ... no I don't, but thank you again, Andre. Goodnight.'

He gave one of the stiff little bows she had grown fond of and went back to his own rooms, leaving her alone with her thoughts. Suddenly, she felt as if the safe, comfortable little world she had built since coming to live here was slipping away from her, for Seth Grimshaw was right. Once Reuben and Maria were wed her name would be mud. She could live with that but dare she risk the rumours affecting Andre's business? They had worked so hard to build it up since she had lived there. Perhaps it was worth considering marrying him? There was clearly no future for her with Oliver and if she couldn't have him she didn't want anyone. With a heavy sigh she sank down at the table. She was so tired that she could have just put her head down and gone to sleep but she knew that she mustn't. There were still jobs to do before she went to bed. She had just made some tea and put the cosy on it when Marcie appeared, barging into the room.

'He's been *again!*' she declared, pacing up and down in her agitation. 'Dad ... he wanted more money!'

'I hope you sent him away with a flea in his ear.'

Nessie took the girl's elbow and led her to a kitchen chair where she sank down and started to cry.

'I don't know how much longer I can stand it,' she sobbed. 'He seems to be everywhere I go. That's why I've stopped going out but now he's badgering me at Molly's and it isn't fair on her. Charlie's heard that Snowy White has finally been arrested for burglary. He reckons he'll go to prison for sure this time, which is probably why Dad has no money. Everyone knows he was involved with Snowy. In fact, I reckon he was doing some of the burglaries for him so what will he do now? He'll continue to hound me, won't he?'

Nessie chewed on her lip as she stared into space, trying to think of a solution. 'You'll have to come back here to live,' she said eventually and Marcie gawped at her.

'But what about all the gossip? You said it could affect Andre's business if I stayed here.'

Nessie shrugged. 'I don't see what choice we have anymore. It isn't fair on Molly and Charlie if he keeps harassing you there. I was intending to start looking around for somewhere for me and Joseph to live anyway before Reuben gets married. You'll just have to come with us.'

Marcie looked doubtful but seeing no other way out of her dilemma she nodded. Nessie had always been able to stand up to their father so much better than she had.

'All right,' she sniffed. 'I'll fetch me things back round here tomorrow if that's all right.'

'It is, but in the meantime, you can stay here tonight. Dad might be on the prowl so go and get in with Joseph. I'll sleep on the settee then we'll sort the spare bed out for you in the morning.'

Once she had left the room, Nessie sagged down into the fireside chair and sobbed as she recalled the awful things that Seth Grimshaw had shouted at her. No doubt it would be all around the town again the next day, which would mean yet more gossip to contend with. Why oh why is my life so difficult, she wondered, as she gazed miserably into the banked-down fire.

Chapter Forty

'Come along now, this ain't no place fer a lady to be lyin' at this time o' night.' The young constable who was on night patrol in the town centre nudged the inert figure lying in the shop doorway with the toe of his boot but got no response whatsoever. He sighed, wishing it were time to go off duty. Judging by the gaudy clothes the woman was wearing she was one of Dolly's girls. Dolly owned the notorious whorehouse in town and her girls were often taken to the station for being drunk and disorderly, especially when they'd had a particularly good night with their clients.

'Come along now. You don't want to end up in a cell for the night, do you?' Again there was no response so he bent towards her and gently shook her arm. 'Did you hear me?' He gave her shoulder a slight push and as she rolled onto her back and he saw the blood gushing from a slash in her neck, he recoiled in horror. Feeling shaky, he rooted in his tunic pocket for his whistle, blowing it repeatedly with every ounce of breath he had. The sound pierced the air and then, thanks be to God, he saw another constable striding towards him gripping a man fast by one arm as he dragged him along.

'What's up then, Harry?'

The young man pointed shakily at the woman. 'Sh-she's had her throat cut. Poor bugger!'

'Hmm, an' I just caught this man here, all covered in blood and runnin' the other way as if the hounds o' hell were after him,' the older policeman commented. 'He were grippin' a handful o' money an' all, no doubt her takin's fer the night so I reckon we've got us the murderer here, Harry. How lucky is that? We might just have the murderer we've been after for months! Now, you stay there with her while I get him into a cell – luckily, he's that drunk he ain't put up much of a fight – then I'll be back to see about gettin' the body moved to the morgue.'

The young constable watched the other officer walk away before turning his attention back to the body. The woman's eyes stared sightlessly up at the moon and her mouth was wide open with her tongue hanging out. Her clothes were in disarray and her pockmarked cheeks were heavily rouged. He shuddered. No doubt she had been a fine-looking woman once but cheap gin and the hard life she had led had taken their toll on her. He took his hat off, bowed his head and said a short prayer. This woman and her kind were considered to be the lowest of the low by many of the towns-

372

people but he wondered what circumstances had led her to live the way she did? No matter what they were, he felt that no one should die as she had and he fervently hoped that the other officer was right and they had finally caught their killer. Perhaps then the women of the town might dare to venture out at night alone again without constantly looking over their shoulders.

'Eeh, have yer heard the news?'

Nessie was spooning porridge into Joseph's mouth when Molly rushed into the kitchen early the next morning. Nessie was still in her long, flowing nightgown with her thick copper-coloured hair hanging loosely down her back.

Startled, she glanced up to ask, 'What news?'

'One o' Dolly's girls were murdered last night an' they think they've got the killer. He were runnin' away from the scene o' the crime, apparently, an' he almost ran straight into a copper's arms.' Then suddenly remembering that Nessie's mother had been one of his victims, Molly clamped her mouth shut and flushed with shame. 'Sorry, pet. Me an' me big mouth again, eh? Charlie's always sayin' it'll get me hanged one o' these days.'

'It's all right, Molly. I know you didn't mean any harm,' Nessie assured her as she lifted Joseph. He made little gurgling sounds and stared trustingly up at her from his soft, brown eyes as she carried him to the sofa. 'And I hope it's right that they have caught the killer.'

'Well, we'll know soon enough,' Molly answered as she tickled Joseph under the chin and smiled at him affectionately. 'He's before the magistrates later this mornin'. Oh, an' Marcie tells me she's movin' back in here wi' you?'

Nessie nodded. 'Yes, she is. It isn't fair for my dad to be bringing trouble to your door all the time. It was good of you to take her in but I realise now that people are going to gossip about me and Marcie whatever we do so I'm going to start looking round for somewhere for all of us to live as soon as possible.'

'Andre won't be none too pleased about that,' Molly remarked. 'His business has took off since you and Reuben came here and you practically run it now.'

'But I'll still work here and do what I do now,' Nessie pointed out.

'Even so, it won't be the same,' Molly said kindly before leaving to start her chores.

Nessie stared blankly from the window into the yard. If what Molly said proved to be true and the police had caught the killer, she fervently hoped that they would hang him by the neck until he was dead. Only then would her mother's death and all the killer's other victims' deaths be avenged.

Nessie was dealing with a bereaved client when the men returned just before lunchtime and one glance at Reuben's stony face told her immediately that something was wrong.

Once the distraught woman's funeral arrangements for her husband had been made and she had escorted her to the door, Nessie was about to go and talk to Reuben when Andre entered the front of the shop.

He too looked disturbed and she paused and asked quickly, 'Did the funeral not go to plan?'

Andre removed his tall black silk hat and stared at her gravely. 'It went very well.'

'Then why are you and Reuben looking so glum?' she questioned.

Andre averted his eyes from hers. 'It would be perhaps as well if your brother told you,' he replied.

Worried now, she found Reuben sitting at the kitchen table with his head in his hands and Marcie softly crying near the kitchen sink.

'So what's going on?' Nessie looked from one to the other of them.

'You'd better sit down,' Reuben said quietly, rising to pull a chair out for her. Her stomach began to churn and she had a horrible feeling that she was about to hear something she wouldn't like.

'The thing is...' Reuben licked his lips and yanked at his collar. 'While we were at the funeral this morning we overheard some of the mourners talking outside the church. They were talking about the woman that was killed last night and it seems that they knew the name of the man that's been arrested. It ... it's our dad, Nessie ... *he's* the killer.'

For a second Nessie felt the floor rush up to meet her and she thought that she was going to be sick, but then, pulling herself together with an effort, she responded, 'They must have got it wrong. I mean ... I know Dad was a bit of a rogue ... but he isn't a murderer. It would mean ... it would mean that it was *him* who killed our mam!'

When Reuben nodded she felt the colour drain out of her cheeks and she gripped the edge of the table until her knuckles turned white.

'B-but *why* would he do that?'

Reuben had no time to answer, for Andre appeared in the open doorway at that moment. 'I am so sorry,' he said softly, wishing that he could wipe her pain away. 'This must have come as a great shock to you.'

She nodded numbly before asking, 'So where is Dad now? What will happen to him?'

'It was said that he appeared before the magistrates this morning and was remanded in custody. They have sent him to Winson Green prison in Birmingham until he stands trial.'

'I ... I can't believe it.' Nessie tried to take it in.

'Well *I* do,' Marcie said loudly, making Joseph start. 'The man is pure evil, capable of anything, if you ask me!'

'Marcie, that's *our father* you're talking about,' Nessie cautioned but Marcie's face was set.

'He's a *monster!*' Marcie retorted and with a toss of her head she stamped upstairs, leaving her sister reeling with shock.

'I just can't believe it,' Nessie muttered. 'It's bad enough to think of him killing all those other poor women but our own *mother...*'

Reuben frowned. 'All we can do now is wait and see what happens.'

'*No!* The only way I will ever believe this is if Dad tells me himself. I need to see him; will that be possible?'

It was Andre who answered. 'I will make enquiries and see what I can do. I know some of the magistrates so I may be able to get you a visitor's pass. But are you *quite* sure you want to do this? Prisons are not nice places.'

'I have to,' she said defiantly.

'Very well, then leave it with me.' Andre patted her arm and quietly left the room.

Nessie looked at Reuben. 'Do *you* think it was Dad?'

He shrugged. 'Everything points towards it. They caught him red-handed, covered in blood and running away from the dead woman and worse still...' He paused to stare at her, wondering how she would take the last piece of news. But then he decided that he may as well share it with her. It was only a matter of time before she read it in the newspapers or someone told her. 'I did hear them say that he'd confessed to all the murders. One of the mourners was a policeman and he was at the station when they took him in and questioned him. He was drunk, apparently, so that probably loosened his tongue.'

Nessie stared towards the window with dull eyes. Suddenly she felt so tired of everything. It had been hard enough to come to terms with the loss of their mother but to know that it was their own father who had killed her made it ten times worse. There was Marcie and her forthcoming baby to worry about and Joseph, as well as trying to find somewhere else for them all to live. It all felt just too much to bear and lowering her head she began to sob as Reuben gently stroked her hand.

Two days later Andre discreetly took Nessie to

one side and told her gravely, 'I have arranged a visitor's pass for you to see your father. He will be tried on Thursday and you may visit him in prison on Friday.'

'So soon?' Nessie asked in surprise.

'It seems there is a judge visiting in the next few days, and as he has confessed, there is no reason to wait.'

'I see. Thank you. What do you think will happen in court?'

He took a deep breath. 'I think he will be found guilty of murder.'

'And if he *is* found guilty, he will hang, won't he?' Her voice came out as a squeak as different emotions churned through her.

He nodded, his face solemn. 'I believe you should prepare yourself for that, yes.'

She wrung her hands together as she stared past him. If he was guilty, part of her wanted him to pay for what he had done yet deep down another little part of her couldn't forget that he was her father, albeit he hadn't always been a particularly good one.

'Well, at least we'll know by the time I go and see him,' she said dully and turning about she hurried away to check on Joseph and to hide the tears that were glistening on her lashes.

Chapter Forty-One

On Thursday Reuben had gone out to buy an evening newspaper to find out what the verdict had been in court. One glance at his ashen face told her all she needed to know.

'He's been found guilty,' he told her croakily.

She wasn't surprised. She had prepared herself as Andre had advised.

'He's to be hanged in two weeks' time,' he said, dropping heavily onto a kitchen chair. 'Our own dad ... a bloody *murderer*,' he rasped, his hands balled into fists. 'And to know he killed our *mam...*' his voice trailed away and Nessie laid a gentle arm on his shoulder. Strangely she felt calm, numb almost.

'At least no more women will suffer the same fate at his hands,' she murmured.

As he looked up at her she saw the anger in his eyes. 'Lord only knows what Maria's family will think o' this. Our family must have the worst reputation of any in the town what wi' one thing an' another! I wouldn't be surprised if they didn't make her call the weddin' off!'

'They won't do that,' she soothed. 'They'll understand you're nothing like him.'

He narrowed his eyes. 'You're surely not goin' to see him tomorrow, are yer, now that yer know what he's done?'

She sighed. 'Yes I am. It will be the last time

any of us ever see him so I suppose we owe him that at least.'

'We owe him *nothin'!'* Reuben spat furiously. 'Now I know what he's done, I *hate* him!'

'We've each got to handle this the best way we can,' she pointed out. 'I need to see him one last time to ask him why.' She glanced at the newspaper headlines and the words on the front page jumped out at her:

Nuneaton Man Found Guilty of Multiple Murders.

'I wouldn't be surprised if Andre didn't sack the lot of us after this,' Reuben rambled on. 'First Marcie turns up wi' her belly full an' now this!'

'He won't do that,' Nessie assured him. 'You, for a start, are much too valuable to him.' This was true as, despite his earlier reservations, Reuben was quickly learning the art of embalming as well as all the other jobs he did.

She lifted Joseph and carried him to the table for his meal, although she felt so sick inside that she had completely lost her appetite.

When Marcie returned from a visit to Molly, she was as enraged as Reuben at what their father had done. 'I'm *glad* he's going to get what's coming to him,' she ground out after reading the report in the newspaper.

Nessie was getting ready to go out. It was her night for working in the soup kitchen and although she really didn't feel up to going she didn't want to let anyone down. She knew how much certain locals relied on the place and she didn't want them to go hungry. It was also the night when Oliver would be holding his surgery and although she longed to see him, she wondered how she was going to face him. He must have heard the news by now.

As it was they were so busy that evening that she didn't even get a chance to speak to him until the last hungry customer had left.

'I'm so sorry to hear what's happened to your father, Nessie,' he said softly.

'Why?' She stuck her chin in the air as she blinked back tears. 'He's only going to get what he deserves.'

'Even so, it must be hard for you to know that he killed your own...' He stopped abruptly, realising that he might be talking out of turn. It must surely be hard enough for her to cope with, he thought, without him unintentionally rubbing salt into the wounds.

'Killing my own mother, were you going to say?' She tossed her head. 'Yes, it is hard but nothing will bring her back now, will it? And once he's... Well, once it's all over I have to try and get on with things as best I can. I just hope the fact that Andre has a murderer's daughter living with him doesn't affect his business. He's had enough gossip to deal with since we moved into his premises. I suppose you've heard the latest? Seth Grimshaw has spread it about that Joseph is *my* child but I can assure you he isn't, although I couldn't love him any more if he was.' Her voice faltered then and she took a deep breath, biting her lip.

It was all Oliver could do to stop himself from putting his arms about her to give her comfort but instead he said, 'I never believed he was for an instant and even if he had been I wouldn't have held it against you. Accidents happen, your sister and my brother are a prime example of that.'

'I suppose they are,' she answered with a catch in her voice. 'And look how *that's* turned out. Your mother and father turned Marcie away as if it was all her fault. In fact, they won't even accept that the baby is George's but I'll tell you something, *I* believe her. Marcie may be many things but I happen to know that she genuinely cared about him and why would he have killed Eliza and then run away as he did if there was nothing in what she said?'

'I know.' He felt guilty as he watched her. She had so much to deal with at the moment and he wished there was something he could do to help her but it was as if she had built a wall between them. Perhaps she was afraid of what his parents would say if they discovered he had feelings for her after what had happened with Marcie and George. 'But if it's any consolation I think my mother believes that the child is his.'

'Really?' Nessie was surprised, not that it made much difference what his mother thought. Hadn't she turned her back on Marcie already? As far as Nessie was concerned it was hardly the action of a doting grandmother-to-be. Now she shrugged and realising that the conversation was at an end Oliver sighed and lifted his black bag. 'If there's nothing I can do for you, I'll be off. Or perhaps I could offer you a lift home?'

Ignoring the hopeful note in his voice she shook her head. 'No, thank you, I shall be a while yet.

382

You get off.'

'You were a bit hard on him then, weren't you, gel?' Molly scolded Nessie after the doctor had left. 'It ain't *his* fault his folks acted the way they did, yer know, an' I reckon he's got a soft spot for you.'

'I suppose I was ... but why pretend we could ever be more than friends, Molly? We come from different worlds.'

Molly pursed her lips as she looked at this young woman who she had come to regard as a close friend. Deep down she supposed that Nessie was right, but eeh, the way she saw it, it was a cryin' shame. The two clearly cared about each other but then, as she had learned to her cost, life could be bloody cruel sometimes.

'Are you quite sure you want to do this?' Andre peered at Nessie with concern as they stood on the station platform waiting for the train that would take them to Birmingham. There were dark circles beneath her eyes and her hands were constantly fidgeting but even so she nodded.

'Yes ... I have to. Whatever he's done he's still my father, isn't he? And anyway, I need to know *why* he did what he did, especially to our mam. But thank you, Andre ... for coming with me, I mean. I don't think I would have been brave enough to go on my own when it came down to it.'

He patted her hand, feeling completely at a loss as to what he should say. Words seemed so inadequate when he thought of what she must be going through. She had hardly ventured out of the house since the news of what her father had done had hit the papers and when she had people had called her names and ignored her. It had been the same for Reuben and Marcie too, although they seemed to be handling it far better than Nessie was. They were just angry with him and glad that he was going to get what they considered to be his just deserts, whereas she seemed torn and reluctant to admit that he was really the murderer. Hopefully, after today she would come to terms with it and try to put it all behind her. He heard the train in the distance and took her elbow. 'Here's the train. Are you ready?'

She blinked and nodded as her stomach churned. Riding in a train would be a new experience for her and she wasn't looking forward to that either. As it roared into the station in a hiss of steam and smoke that wafted up to the sky like a fog, she gulped, and when he finally helped her aboard he noted that she was trembling. Ushering her into a carriage he found them seats and then gently taking her hand, he squeezed it. 'It will be all right.' His accent was more pronounced than usual because of his concern and she squeezed his hand back and forced a weak smile, very aware that a plump well-dressed elderly lady sitting opposite was watching them closely. What would she think if she knew where I was going? Nessie wondered, trying to remain calm. She had chosen to dress in a smart navy-blue two-piece costume trimmed with white braid and a matching hat that Andre had bought for her and she looked neat and tidy and every inch a young lady.

Eventually the train set off. Realising how she must be feeling, Andre remained silent and left Nessie to stare unseeingly from the window. She supposed that under other circumstances she might have enjoyed the new experience, but now she was so preoccupied thinking about what she would say to her father that she barely noticed they were moving.

In what seemed like no time at all the train was slowing again as it pulled into Birmingham's New Street station and as Andre courteously handed her down Nessie was shocked at the number of people milling about the station. This place was like another world compared to the sleepy market town they had left behind, but she had no time to do more than glance about her before Andre was ushering her through the crowds to the exit. There were enormous dray horses pulling huge carts laden with barrels which she assumed contained beer, numerous cabs and everywhere she looked there were street vendors standing behind stalls selling everything from faggots and peas to jacket potatoes and flowers.

Andre lifted his hand and within seconds a cab pulled into the kerb and the driver jumped down to open the door for them while his horse stood patiently waiting, seemingly unperturbed at all the noise around him.

'Where to, guv?' The man, who had the most enormous nose that Nessie had ever seen, smiled at her as he doffed his cap.

'Winson Green prison if you please, my man.'

The driver looked momentarily surprised. This pair didn't look at all like the sorts to be prison visiting but then he supposed it was none of his business. A fare was a fare at the end of the day. In no time at all they were seated and the horse pulled out into the busy road and began to clip-clop along. Nessie held her handkerchief to her nose to mask the unpleasant smell in the cab. There was dirty straw across the floor and she dreaded to think what might be lurking in it. The leather swabs they were leaning against were none too clean either but at that moment that was the least of her troubles.

They seemed to travel for a long time but at last the cab left the busier streets behind and they passed rows and rows of identical, soot-clad terraced houses. Smoke belched from many of the chimneys and bare-foot, dirty children played in the gutters. Most of them were terribly underweight and looked as if they hadn't had a good square meal in ages and Nessie wished they lived closer to the soup kitchen. And then suddenly a dark forbidding building surrounded by a high brick wall loomed ahead of them and she knew they had arrived at the prison. A straggle of people, who were also there to visit the inmates, was queuing outside two enormous metal gates and on either side of these were grimy windows covered in metal bars. Just the sight of the place struck terror into Nessie's heart.

When the cab pulled up, Andre helped Nessie down and paid the cabbie, adding a handsome tip before asking, 'Can you wait for us?'

'Hmm, well I could, sir, but it'll cost you.' The man hastily shoved the money into his pocket as if he was afraid that Andre might snatch it back.

'I'm riskin' life an' limb hangin' about these parts as you've probably gathered.'

'Don't worry, I shall make it well worth your while,' Andre assured him, then taking Nessie's elbow he steered her to the back of the queue, aware that they were attracting more than a few curious glances. Many of the people waiting were poorly clad and pitifully thin and as Nessie saw the wooden clogs on the women's feet and the thin, threadbare shawls they clutched about their shoulders she suddenly felt extremely overdressed. More people joined the back of the queue and Andre made sure that he kept his hand over the wallet in his pocket. He was very aware of the pick-pockets that roamed the streets for easy pickings in the city and he didn't intend to be one of their victims.

After what seemed an eternity the huge gates swung open and the queue surged forward. Two large policemen in helmets stood either side of the gates letting in only a handful of people at a time. Nessie peered past them and saw that the people who had entered were in yet another yard with another set of gates where more policemen were checking the visitors' bags.

'You'll go in among the next lot,' Andre whispered, his eyes soft with sympathy. 'And when you come out I shall be here waiting for you. Good luck, *ma cherie.*'

The words had no sooner left his lips than the gates opened once more and Nessie was swept forward with the crowd. She experienced a moment of blind panic as the gates clanged shut behind her and she glanced back to make sure that Andre was still there. She had never felt so terrified in her life and doubted that she ever would again. Andre raised his hand and flashed her a reassuring smile, then, squaring her shoulders, she stuck her chin in the air and opened her bag for inspection.

'Who are you here to see, miss?' the large policeman asked her and after she had answered him, he barked to the man by the second set of gates, 'Let this young lady through, Smith. She's here to see William Carson.'

She stumbled through them on legs that seemed to have developed a life of their own only to find herself in yet another, much larger, court-yard. There were a number of doors leading off it, all of them heavily locked and barred and each one guarded by a policeman. Following the rest of the crowd who seemed to know where they were going, Nessie found herself in yet another queue where people were handing their visitors' passes to a tall policeman. After glancing at hers, the man waved his hand and she found herself in a room where the visitors were waiting for their loved ones to appear.

'Sit anywhere you like, miss.' An older officer seemed to sense how nervous she was and offered a kindly smile as Nessie hastily made for the nearest vacant chair she could find. And then all she could do was wait for her father to appear.

Chapter Forty-Two

When her father made his appearance, hand-cuffed to a guard who looked to be almost twice his size, Nessie barely recognised him. He stood in the doorway then, spotting her, he muttered something in the man's ear and the guard led him towards the table.

Nessie's breath caught in her throat. Was this really the handsome father she remembered? He had lost so much weight he looked almost skeletal and his once gloriously thick hair had thinned so much that she could see his scalp through it. One of his eyes was black and closed and there was a cut on his cheek. Deep down she supposed that she had come to tell him how much she hated him for what he had done but she couldn't stop a pang of pity piercing through her at the sight of him.

He glanced about as he took a seat, still hand-cuffed to the guard, then said, 'Came alone then, did you?'

She nodded. 'Yes, Reuben and Marcie didn't want to come.'

He bowed his head and sighed and just for a second she could have sworn she saw tears on his lashes. 'Can't say as I blame 'em,' he muttered.

A silence stretched between them until she suddenly blurted out, '*Why*, Dad? *Why* did you kill our mam? She loved you so much and she didn't deserve to die like that.' There was a catch in her voice and he caught his breath.

'Cos I'm bad through an' through.' He kept his eyes downcast. 'It's only since I've bin in 'ere an' I ain't been able to get me hands on any opium that I've realised just how bad I am. There ain't nothin' I can say to excuse what I've done but I hope in the future that sometimes you'll be able to remember happier times. The worst thing is that I won't even be able to say sorry to yer mam. She'll be up there.' He thumbed towards the sky. 'An' I'll be down there in 'ell, sure as eggs is eggs, but it ain't no more than I deserve an' I'm ready for it.'

The guard suddenly rattled his handcuffs. 'Condemned men only get ten minutes, Carson,' he reminded him brusquely. 'But you will be allowed a final visit on the day of your execution.'

Tears were pouring down Nessie's cheeks. She had said none of the things she had come to say. There didn't seem to be much point.

'No!' His head snapped up. 'I don't want you to come again,' he told his daughter. 'Just go and try an' think of me kindly now an' again. You look fine an' you're doin' well for yourself so go an' have a good life. An' will you...' He gulped deep in his throat. 'Will you tell Reuben ... an' Marcie ... that I'm sorry? Marcie will know what you mean.'

Too full of emotion to speak she nodded as he rose. He reached out as if he intended to touch her but then seeming to think better of it he sighed and allowed the warder to lead him away without once looking back. Almost instantly the kindly guard who had admitted her was at her side, 'Are you ready to leave, miss?'

She nodded numbly and rising from the hard wooden chair she followed him back through the courtyard and the many locked doors until she found herself outside the prison again where Andre was pacing anxiously up and down.

'Are you all right?' he asked, taking her hands in his, dismayed to see how pale she was.

'Y-yes ... but can we go home now?'

'Of course.'

'Was it ... very bad?' Andre could have bitten his tongue out the second the words had left his lips. What a thoughtless thing to say! Of course it must have been bad, how could it not have been?

She nodded. 'Yes it was ... but strangely not in the way I expected. I went in there prepared to tell him how much I hated him and yet I found myself feeling almost sorry for him. He ... he seems prepared for what's going to happen. In fact, I got the feeling he's welcoming it.'

'Perhaps we could arrange another visit?' he suggested tentatively, but she shook her head as she mopped at her eyes with a crisp white handkerchief he had handed her.

'No, Andre. He doesn't want that, he made it clear. He knows he's done wrong and he's prepared to pay for it now so there's no more to be said.'

'Just as you like.' He was afraid of saying the wrong thing so he just held her hand comfortingly as they headed back towards the station.

Both Marcie and Reuben were waiting for her when she and Andre arrived home and Marcie

391

instantly asked, 'Well, what did the bastard have to say for himself?'

Andre discreetly slipped away, leaving the family to talk.

'Not a lot really.' Nessie removed her bonnet and sank down at the table where she rubbed her brow. She could feel a headache starting behind her eyes. She would always remember this day as one of the worst of her life.

'But didn't he give any explanation as to why he's done the things he's done?'

Nessie shook her head. 'Not really. He seems to have come to terms with the fact that he's going to hang. In fact, I got the impression that he welcomes it and he told me to tell you both ... that he's sorry.'

'*Sorry!*' Marcie snorted in disgust, hands on hips. 'And is *that* supposed to make everything right?'

'Of course not. But at least he's facing up to things.'

'Hmm, well you can forgive him if you like but I hope he rots in *hell*,' Marcie fumed and with that she turned and stamped towards the stairs.

On the day of their father's execution, life went on seemingly as normal. Reuben and Andre had an early funeral to organise and they went about their business as if it was just any other day but Nessie, who was in the shop parlour, kept glancing at the grandfather clock. Not one of them had mentioned what day it was but Nessie knew that, like her, they must be thinking of it.

At a few minutes before ten in the morning she

went to the shop window and peered up at the bright blue sky. On such a glorious May day it was hard to imagine that right at that moment they would be fastening the noose about her father's neck. And then the clock began to strike and she lowered her head. It was done now and somehow the family must try to put all this behind them and get on with their lives.

Chapter Forty-Three

August 1865

On a glorious day towards the middle of August, Maria and Reuben were married and the gloom that had hung over them for weeks was lifted.

As Maria glided down the aisle of the church on her proud father's arm, Nessie was sure she had never seen a more radiant bride. She was wearing a pale-blue dress and matching bonnet with a tiny veil attached to it that matched her sparkling eyes perfectly and she carried a posy of sweet-smelling freesias.

The couple left the church to a hail of rose petals and rice and then, to much laughter, Maria turned her back and tossed her bouquet over her shoulder. Nessie was shocked when it landed squarely in her hands.

'*Eeh!* That means *you'll* be the next,' Molly chortled and Nessie blushed to the roots of her hair. Just for a second a pang of longing shot through her as Oliver's face floated in front of her eyes but then she composed herself again and hastily lost herself in the crowd. There was no point in wishing for things that could never be.

Later, at the wedding breakfast at a local hotel, which Andre had insisted on paying for as his wedding gift to them, the newlyweds had eyes only for each other, which was just as it should be. Even Marcie had made an effort, although now with her baby's birth imminent she waddled rather than walked and raised more than a few disapproving eyebrows. Nessie was still no closer to finding alternative accommodation for herself and Joseph either. She had just been so busy that she hadn't found time to look and now that Reuben would no longer be living with her and Marcie she supposed that the gossips would be having a field day again. But still, I won't let it spoil this special day, she thought.

Once the wedding meal was over the tables were pushed aside and the dancing began. Nessie found herself in Andre's arms as he waltzed her about the room.

'Has anyone told you that you look most becoming today, Miss Carson?' he asked teasingly and Nessie giggled as she was swept away with the moment. Andre was so kind and handsome that he would have been a perfect catch for some woman. Only she knew what his sexual preferences were and she would carry the secret to the grave for she was very fond of him.

The day passed in a whirl of laughter and dancing, but then just before eight o'clock in the evening as she was dancing with Maria's father,

Nessie glanced towards Marcie and saw that she was rubbing her back and had gone very pale. Instantly realising that something was wrong, she excused herself and hurried across to her. 'Are you all right, pet?'

'I ... I don't know.' Marcie's eyes suddenly looked huge in her pretty face. 'I've got this pain in my back an' I...' She lowered her head in shame. 'I think I just wet meself.'

Molly had hurried across to join them and the second the words were out of Marcie's mouth she took control of the situation.

'Nessie, go an' get them to fetch a carriage round to the front doors. We have to get her home. An', Charlie, run for Mrs Felton would you an' tell her she's needed. If I'm not much mistaken there's goin' to be a birth tonight.'

Nessie felt a little shudder run through her. In just the space of a few short weeks their family would have had a death, a marriage and a birth. The circle of life.

Charlie paled and hared away as if the devil himself were snapping at his heels while Nessie hurried away to find a carriage.

Marcie was sweating profusely now, and by the time they got her home Charlie was already back and told them breathlessly, 'Mrs Felton can't come. She's attendin' another birth in one o' the courts an' she reckons she could be hours yet. What do you want me to do?'

Molly's brow creased in a frown for a moment as she thought then she told him. 'Saddle one o' the horses an' ride to Haunchwood House. Tell young Dr Dorsey he's needed. He'll come.'

Nessie paled at the thought of Oliver attending the birth but by now Marcie was doubled over with pains and she knew they had no alternative. Andre had come back with them too and he was a bundle of nerves.

'What can I do?' he asked nervously and Nessie smiled at him. 'You can be in charge of making the tea and supplying us with lots of hot water,' she told him.

'Ah, yes ... this I can do,' he agreed, hurrying away to fill the kettle but he was all fingers and thumbs and she was amused to see that more water splashed onto the floor than went into the kettle.

Meanwhile they were all trying to get Marcie up the stairs to Reuben's old room. It was a lengthy process as the staircase was narrow and steep and every few seconds the poor girl had to stop to take deep breaths. Eventually they managed it and while Molly helped Marcie to get undressed, Nessie laid some towels on the bed, before the two women finally managed to help a groaning Marcie onto it.

'Ouch ... ooh it *hurts*,' Marcie howled as another contraction ripped through her and Molly was concerned.

'Strikes me it ain't going to be long before this little one puts in an appearance,' she whispered to Nessie. 'First babies usually take their time but this one seems in a rush to be born. Her pains are comin' thick an' fast already.'

Nessie frowned. 'But what if it comes before Oliver gets here?' she panicked.

Molly giggled and patted her cheek. 'Bless yer,

396

there's nothin' to fear,' she promised. 'It wouldn't be the first baby I've had to deliver. We women from the courts can't afford doctors an' we often deliver each other's, so if the worst happens I'll deliver it meself.'

A tap came at the door. 'There is hot water outside the door,' Andre shouted, then he was off down the stairs like a shot from a gun. Keeping them supplied with hot water was one thing, but he couldn't imagine having to be present at a birth.

The minutes ticked away and a little while later Nessie let out a sigh of relief when Oliver barged in carrying his large black bag.

'I ... I'm so sorry we've had to bother you of an evening,' Nessie faltered as colour stained her cheeks. 'But Mrs Felton is busy with another delivery and...'

'It's fine,' he assured her as he flung his jacket over the back of a chair and rolled his sleeves up. 'I am a doctor after all. Funnily enough, I delivered another baby this morning. A lovely little girl.' Then hoping to distract Marcie he began to wash his hands and asked, 'What would you like, Marcie?'

She was panting between pains as Molly had advised and she scowled at him. 'I don't care what it is ... I won't want it.'

'Ah, you say that now but you'll feel differently when you set eyes on the little soul,' he soothed. 'Now lie back and relax while I examine you, eh?'

Very gently he pressed his hands around Marcie's bulging stomach, then lifting her nightdress he murmured, 'Hmm, I don't think you're going

397

to be very much longer at all. Just pant between the pains and try not to push until I tell you to.'

'I am *pantin'*, ain't I?' Marcie screeched as another pain took her breath away.

Molly meanwhile was preparing to leave. 'I'll pop back to the reception an' tell Reuben an' Maria what's goin' on,' she offered. 'They looked a bit bewildered when we suddenly all made a beeline for the door.'

'Tell them we'll let them know what she's had just as soon as we can,' Nessie said and Molly scooted away, leaving the mother in the doctor's capable hands.

'Now then, why don't you go down and persuade Andre to make us all a nice cup of tea?' Oliver suggested, noting how pale Nessie looked. 'There's no need for you to be here for the birth if you're squeamish. I'm quite capable.'

'I want her here, ahhhh...'

Oliver grinned as Nessie gulped. 'I ... I'll just go and organise that tea then I'll be back,' she croaked.

True to her word she was back within minutes with a laden tea tray. She poured a cup for Oliver who was timing how far apart the pains were on his gold hunter watch. 'Still eight minutes between each one,' he observed before lifting his cup and saucer. 'Still a way to go but it shouldn't be too long.'

Nessie meantime had taken a seat at the side of the bed and Marcie was holding her hand tight as if her life depended upon it.

The minutes and the hours ticked away and then finally, just after midnight, Oliver told his patient,

'Push now on your next pain as hard as you can.' If what Marcie had said was true it would be his niece or nephew he was delivering but he was trying not to think of that. Earlier on, when Charlie had arrived at the house to fetch him, his mother had overheard who it was that he would be attending and she had flown into a flap as he prepared his bag with all the instruments he might need.

'That could be my grandchild that's about to be born,' she said, much to the annoyance of her husband. 'Perhaps I should come and be present at the birth too?'

'I hardly think that would be very appropriate, Mother,' Oliver had said firmly. 'Particularly when the girl was sent away with a flea in her ear because she told you it was George's child.' He had promptly left, leaving his mother to wring her hands and pace up and down until Johnny Dorsey felt he would explode.

And now the birth was imminent and Oliver shut his mind to everything but delivering the baby safely.

Sweat ran down Marcie's face as she strained to do as she was told and she gripped her sister's hand so tightly that Nessie herself whimpered with pain. When the pain had passed Marcie flopped back against the pillows and Oliver nodded his approval.

'Well done. Now on the next pain do the same again. We're almost there.'

'I can't,' Marcie yelped. 'I'm exhausted.' But all the same as the next pain tore through her she pushed till the veins in her neck stood out like ropes.

'That's it,' Oliver shouted jubilantly. 'I can see the head. One more good push and the baby will be here.'

This seemed to spur Marcie on and with the next pain she leaned slightly forward and pushed with all her might. She felt something warm slither out of her to lie on the towels between her legs and then Nessie was laughing and crying all at the same time.

'Oh, Marcie, you have a beautiful little boy,' she cried as Oliver deftly and expertly cut the umbilical cord. The baby began to wail as Oliver wrapped him in a towel and prepared to hand him to his mother, but she turned her head away and refused to look at him.

'I don't *want* to hold him. Give him to Nessie.'

Oliver and Nessie exchanged a worried glance but Oliver did as Marcie requested, suggesting, 'Why don't you take the little chap down by the fire and get him bathed and dressed? By the time that's done I'm sure his mum will be longing to hold him.'

Nessie found Andre on the stairs waiting for her when she left the room. He had heard the baby cry and his face was glowing as he asked, 'What did she have?'

Nessie lifted the towel from the baby's face for him to peep. 'She had a little boy and he's quite beautiful.' She was sure then that she would never forget the look on Andre's face for as long as she lived and it touched her deeply, for it was a mixture of yearning, delight and envy.

'He is as you say quite beautiful,' he breathed in awe. 'Perhaps if I had not been born as I am I too

400

might have had a child one day.'

Unsure what she should say, Nessie carried the baby down to the kitchen where she bathed him gently and dressed him in the clothes she had prepared in the previous months. Marcie had made no effort whatsoever to prepare for his birth so it had fallen to her to buy the necessary things he would need. The only thing they hadn't got as yet was a cot but she had lined a drawer with a warm blanket in readiness. Once he was clean she and Andre sat together on the sofa admiring him. He had a shock of fair hair that settled about his head like a halo and deep-blue eyes.

'I suppose I should take him back up to his mother and check on Joseph,' Nessie said eventually. Knowing that the wedding might have been too much for him she had left Joseph in the care of one of the women who helped to run the soup kitchen but now he was tucked up in bed and fast asleep. She was hoping that Marcie would show a little more enthusiasm in her baby now. The child was growing restless and no doubt he would need his first feed very soon.

Andre nodded, although his eyes never left the baby's face. He was clearly smitten with him. 'Of course, and I shall make us all another nice strong cup of tea.'

Nessie grinned. He had made so many cups of tea over the course of the night that she felt as if she might drown in it, but she knew that this was his way of making himself feel useful.

'I'm sure Marcie will be ready for one,' she agreed and very carefully she carried the baby back up the steep, narrow stairs.

She found Oliver washing his hands and he smiled as she entered the room. Marcie was lying on her side and he told her, 'All sorted. She's done marvellously. How is the little chap?'

'All nice and clean and ready to meet his mammy,' Nessie said loudly but Marcie made no attempt to turn towards them. Her smile faltered as she glanced towards Oliver but she approached the bed and said brightly, 'Here he is, Marcie. I think he's getting hungry. Why don't I lie him in the drawer and get you washed and changed then you can feed him?'

'Go away, I don't want to see him,' Marcie croaked.

Seeing the concern on Nessie's face, Oliver took control of the situation. 'Let's put him in the drawer by his mother while we go and get a cup of tea, eh?' He could see that the baby was getting hungry and surely Marcie wouldn't ignore him if she was left alone with him? Taking the baby from Nessie he carefully placed him in the drawer then he led her from the room.

Downstairs in the kitchen Nessie paced up and down with a worried look on her face. They could hear the baby crying upstairs but Marcie had clearly made no attempt to lift him.

'Why won't she look at him?' she fretted.

Oliver sighed. 'This happens sometimes but if we leave her alone with him for long enough she's bound to get fed up with him crying and feed him.'

Nessie wasn't so sure. Marcie could be very stubborn when she wanted to be but she supposed Oliver knew what he was doing. He was a doctor after all.

They sipped at the tea that Andre had made for them as the baby's cries grew increasingly louder and then Nessie saw Oliver stifle a yawn.

'How thoughtless of me,' she said. 'You must be worn out. Why don't you get off home now and get some rest? You've done your job and we're very grateful to you but I can handle everything now. But before you go I must pay you for your services.'

'There will be no charge,' he answered quietly as he drained his cup and rose from the table, but her chin came up in that determined way he found so endearing.

'I *shall* pay you,' she insisted and, still in her finery from the wedding, she went to the shelf in a swish of silken skirts and took some money from the tin there which she pressed into his hand.

He sighed but didn't attempt to argue. He knew her well enough by now to know that it would be useless.

'Thank you, I shall call in sometime tomorrow to check on mother and baby but should you need me before then don't hesitate to send for me.' He paused as his eyes found Nessie's as if there was something else he wanted to say but then, clearly thinking better of it, he inclined his head towards Andre and left. They sat on, listening to the baby's cries getting ever more frantic, and each one seemed to pierce her heart. And then suddenly they stopped, as if by magic, and they stared at each other with smiles of relief.

'Hopefully everything will be OK now,' she muttered, praying silently that she was right.

Chapter Forty-Four

After stabling his horse, Oliver made his way wearily to the house. It had been another long day and he was so tired that his eyes felt as if they were full of grit. All he wanted now was to fall into bed and sleep till morning but the second he entered the hallway his mother appeared from the drawing room in her nightwear.

'Well? Has she had the baby?' she demanded. She had clearly been waiting up for him and looked almost as tired as he felt.

He nodded, running his hand through his thick thatch of fair hair. 'Yes. It's a boy.'

'A boy.' She flicked the long plait lying across her shoulder and then asked, 'And is the child all right? Does he look anything like George?'

Oliver had been expecting this question and chose his words carefully as he answered, 'He looks like a new baby, Mother. They all look the same to me.' Although, had he been entirely honest, he could have told her that actually the child did have a look of George about him. They'd heard not a word from him since the day he had run away and all they could do now was pray that he was safe.

'But what colour is his hair ... his eyes?' she persisted like a dog with a bone.

Oliver sighed as he took his coat off and threw it across the coat stand. 'He's blond I think and he has blue eyes but then all babies do, as you know.'

'George was blond when he was born,' she mused as she patted her lip with her forefinger. 'Do you think I should go and see him?'

'I doubt you'd be welcome after the way you sent his mother off in disgrace,' he pointed out and she nodded, knowing that he was right. She had often regretted being so hasty but George had been so insistent that the girl was lying about the baby's parentage. What if Marcie had been telling the truth? If she had been it was her grandson that had been born. How was she to live with herself if she never got to know him?

'Well, we can talk more tomorrow,' she said, seeing that he was almost dropping with fatigue. 'Go and get yourself into bed. I'll bring you a nice cup of hot milk up.'

Oliver willingly did as he was told but when his mother tapped on his door minutes later she found him snoring softly.

They were at breakfast the next morning when Connie tentatively raised the subject again by saying casually, 'Oliver delivered Marcie Dorsey of a baby boy last night.'

Her husband immediately looked up from the devilled kidney he was eating and growled, 'And what has that got to do with us? I hope I never set eyes on her again *or* her brat for as long as I live. Hasn't she done enough damage to this family? If it wasn't for her wild accusations, George would still be here.'

'That's true but what if the baby *is* George's?'

she queried, her lip trembling. 'That would make him our grandson, Johnny, our own flesh and blood, no matter what side of the blanket he was born. And don't look at me like that! You weren't averse to a little slap and tickle afore we were wed, if I remember correctly, so don't go getting all moral on me now. Ask yourself, if Marcie was lying about George being the child's father why did George attack Eliza and then run away?'

Johnny scowled and dropped his knife and fork onto the plate with a clatter. He had suddenly lost his appetite. 'How should *I* know?' he blustered, dragging his chair back from the table. 'Just let it go, woman, can't you? The girl's been paid off and that's the end of it as far as I'm concerned. And now if you don't mind I'm going to work to keep you in the manner you've become accustomed!' And with that he stormed out of the room, his colour heightened and his mouth set in a tight, grim line.

Oliver waited until he heard the front door slam behind him then he asked his mother, 'What are you going to do?'

'I don't know yet,' she breathed. 'The trouble is I can't quite convince myself that Marcie was lying about George being the father, no matter how hard I try. What do you think I should do?'

He shrugged as he too rose to leave. He had a morning surgery to attend. 'That is for you to decide but I shall be calling in to see the new mother and baby today so I'll let you know how they both are this evening. But don't forget, I shall be late back. It's my surgery at the soup kitchen this evening.'

'I'll get Cook to keep something warm for you,' she promised. In actual fact she was very proud of the work that Oliver did for the poor. She could remember a time when she and Johnny couldn't afford to pay doctors' bills. She also had a lot of admiration for Nessie who she knew had planned the opening of the soup kitchen. The girl was now well known and respected about the town for her many fundraising activities, although it was whispered that she was having an affair with her employer, the Frenchman. Connie didn't actually believe that for a moment. She'd never been one for listening to gossip and the girl had seemed very respectable on the one occasion she'd met her.

With a sigh, she rose from her seat and stared sightlessly across the well-kept grounds. A gardener was already hard at work scything the lawn but she hardly noticed him. She had an awful lot of thinking to do. She was still there when Mrs Bainbridge entered the room a few moments later. She had thought that the family had all left but she asked, 'Are you all right, Mrs Dorsey?'

Connie turned to give her a weary smile. 'Yes, I'm fine, thank you, Mary.' She was always more informal with the woman when the rest of the staff weren't about. 'I just have a very difficult decision to make.'

'I see. Is it anything I can help you with?'

'No, but thank you for offering.'

Mrs Bainbridge frowned as her mistress left the room, looking as if she had the weight of the world on her shoulders. But then she hadn't been properly right since all that awful business with Master George and poor young Eliza, which she

407

supposed was understandable. It just went to show, it wasn't only the poor and needy who had things to worry about.

In Marcie's bedroom, Nessie was lifting the baby from his temporary crib. 'I think he's getting hungry,' she said cheerfully, hoping to rouse Marcie from the depression she seemed to have slipped into. Admittedly, the girl had fed the baby each time he had been hungry throughout the night, but she had put him down abruptly as soon as he had finished, leaving Nessie to change his bindings and fuss over him. 'Have you thought of a name yet for him,' Nessie went on.

Marcie shrugged nonchalantly. 'We'll call him George, if you like. It's as good a name as any, I suppose.'

Nessie looked troubled. 'But won't that cause trouble if it gets back to the Dorseys?'

'What if it *does?* George is his father, so why *shouldn't* he be named after him?' Marcie answered despondently. Every time she looked at the baby she saw his father and after George's betrayal she could hardly bear to touch the mite. 'Couldn't we get a wet nurse for him?' she suggested. 'There's always plenty o' women feedin' babies in the courtyards who'd be glad to earn a few pence.'

'Marcie! How could you even suggest it?' Nessie was horrified as she carried the babe to his mother. 'He's *your* baby, you should be happy to feed him.'

'But I'm not,' Marcie stated as she pulled herself up against the pillows and reluctantly took him from her sister. 'I don't want him, I never did, so why should I lie? I want to go away an' make somethin' of me life not be stuck here in the back of an undertaker's with a squallin' brat to look after.'

Nessie was shocked but she clamped her lips firmly together, afraid that if she said anything she might say too much.

The sound of footsteps on the stairs followed by a tap at the door stopped any further conversation and when Oliver appeared, Nessie couldn't help the smile that lit up her face. But then, remembering herself, she quickly straightened her face and told him, 'He's feeding well.'

'So I see.' He glanced towards the bed where the baby was busily suckling and gave Nessie a little wink. It seemed his ploy of leaving the baby alone with his mother had worked, although he was forced to admit she didn't look too happy.

'And how are you feeling?' he asked Marcie.

'How do you *expect* me to feel,' she glared at him. 'I'm stuck with your brother's brat to look after while he's off somewhere probably havin' the time of his life.'

'I doubt that very much. After what happened with Eliza I'd bet he's working his socks off somewhere and trying to keep a low profile.' He waited patiently until the baby had finished feeding, then after giving both mother and baby a quick examination to make sure that all was well he followed Nessie downstairs with a grim face.

'She hasn't exactly taken to motherhood as yet, has she?' he remarked when they entered the kitchen.

Nessie shook her head and he noticed how

tired she looked.

'Not at all. She can hardly bear to look at him, if I'm honest with you, and she says she's going to call him George.'

'I dare say she's entitled to call him whatever she wants,' he answered, but she could see that he looked uncomfortable about it. An awkward silence settled between them, a thousand words unsaid, until he lifted his bag and told her, 'Right, I'd best be off. Both of them appear to be doing well so I won't call on them again unless you're worried about anything.' Before leaving he crossed to Joseph who was in his usual position on the sofa and ruffled his hair.

'And how is this young feller me lad doing today?' Only the week before when he had examined the child he had felt that there had been a slight deterioration in his condition but he hadn't mentioned it to Nessie. He knew she would only worry.

'About the same.'

With a final nod he disappeared out of the door, leaving her feeling empty inside.

Later that morning Maria and Reuben came to visit the new baby, their faces glowing with happiness.

'Fancy having him on the day we got wed, what a lovely end to a happy occasion,' Maria cooed as she leaned over the drawer to admire him. Nessie had taken to keeping him downstairs with her, apart from when he needed feeding, so that Marcie could rest. At least that's what she told the newly-weds. The real reason was because she knew that Marcie didn't want him near her. Somehow, she was having to deal with the customers who came into the shop and watch George as well as Joseph and chase up and downstairs seeing to Marcie's needs and she wondered how long she could keep it up. Even so she plastered a bright smile on her face. Andre had been wonderful too, keen to do whatever he could to help, even if it was only to sit and nurse George.

Once Maria and Reuben had left, Andre said, 'Have you thought any more about what I asked you, Nessie?'

She knew instantly that he was speaking of his proposal and she flushed. It was the first time he had mentioned it but before she could reply he hurried on, 'I only ask because it seems to me you have too much weight on your shoulders, too much responsibility for one so young. If you were my wife I could hire people to help you.'

'Let's not talk about it for now. My mind is too full of other things,' she hedged. 'But thank you. I do appreciate that you're trying to help.'

'I am not being entirely unselfish,' he admitted. 'My mother would be, as you English say, tickled pink if she were to find me a respectable married man when she visits, hopefully at Christmas. My father might even find it in his heart to forgive me if he thinks I have settled down. And you know, you and I get along well. I think we could find contentment together, and of course it would also stop all the gossip.'

Nessie smiled as she lifted George, who was getting hungry again. 'Just give me a little more time to think about it,' she implored and hurried away upstairs to deliver the baby to his mother.

Chapter Forty-Five

One day towards the end of September, Mrs Bainbridge tapped on the drawing room door. 'There are two policemen here to see you, ma'am. May I send them in?'

'Yes, yes, of course.' Flustered, Connie Dorsey rose from the small desk in the window where she had been going over the household accounts and smoothed her skirts. Suddenly her heart was thudding painfully and she had an awful feeling that she was going to hear something she wasn't going to like.

'Good morning, gentlemen, how may I help you?' she asked politely as they entered the room.

They both hastily removed their helmets and glanced uneasily at each other before the larger of the two men said, 'Are you Mrs Dorsey? The mother of George Dorsey?'

Connie gulped. So, this visit was about George then, they must have caught him. She didn't know if she felt happy or sad about it but, remaining outwardly calm, she nodded. 'I am. Won't you both take a seat?'

The young maid who had been busily polishing the parquet floor in the hallway was leaning as far towards the door as she could to try and find out what was going on but all she could make out was a blur of voices and then a sharp cry from the mistress. Mrs Bainbridge appeared at that moment and that put paid to any more eavesdropping. 'Come back and finish this later,' she ordered, stern-faced, and the maid scuttled away as fast as her legs would take her.

An hour later Mrs Bainbridge carried the mistress's tea tray to the drawing room. She had an idea that something was amiss as Mrs Dorsey hadn't left the room since the policemen's visit. It there was something wrong she didn't want to give the young maid anything to gossip about.

After tapping lightly at the door, she entered the room to find Connie sitting staring into space and she was shocked at the sight of her. Her mistress's face was ghastly white and she seemed to have aged ten years.

Slamming the tray down unceremoniously on the nearest table the housekeeper quite forgot her place as she hurried across to her mistress and began to chafe her cold hands.

'Why, lass, whatever is the matter?' she asked, her voice heavy with concern.

For a while Connie didn't respond, then turning to Mrs Bainbridge she told her dully, 'George ... is dead, Mary. That's what the policemen came to tell me.'

Mary Bainbridge gasped and shook her head in denial, 'But he can't be ... they must have made a mistake... He was so young...'

Connie shook her head. 'There's no mistake,' her voice was dull and so low that Mary had to bend close to hear her. 'He ... he caught a ship to work his package to China but cholera broke out aboard when they were just over halfway there. Over half of the crew were lost. George was among them.

He ... he left this letter with the captain and asked him to be sure it was delivered to me when he knew he was dying.' She motioned to a crumpled piece of paper that lay on the chair beside her, and lifting it, Mary Bainbridge began to read,

Dear Mother,

If ever you get to read this letter I will be dead and no doubt feeding the fishes at the bottom of the deep blue sea, just as the crew who have already passed away are. I just wanted to tell you I'm sorry ... for everything. I can't believe I made such a mess of things but I need to try and put some things right. First of all, I believe that the baby Marcie Carson is carrying is mine. I know I denied it but I feel you should know. Secondly, I need you to know that I never intended to kill Eliza, I was rough with her admittedly but I never meant to kill her. I was a coward and a fool to run away as I did – I know that now, too late after the event. Anyway, my life is in God's hands now. If I do survive the cholera that is sweeping through the ship I shall come home and face the music, if I don't survive then the captain has promised that this letter will be delivered to you along with the wages I have earned. Would you pass them on to Marcie for me, they may go a little way towards her seeing that the baby has all it needs.

Finally, I want you to know that I am truly sorry and I love you, Mother. Give my regards to Father, Leonora and Oliver,

Your devoted son,

George xxx

'Oh, *ma'am!*' Mrs Bainbridge's hand flew to her

414

mouth as she finished reading, tears trickling down her cheeks. 'I'm so sorry... Is there anything I can do for you?'

'Yes, perhaps you could get one of the grooms to go and fetch my husband and Oliver, he'll probably be at his morning surgery, but I should let them know what's happened.'

'Of course, straight away.' Mrs Bainbridge lifted her skirts and almost ran from the room as Connie sat on, reliving happier times with her son. In her mind's eye she saw him again in his father's arms shortly after his birth. Johnny had looked so proud. Then she remembered his first tooth and his first tentative steps. So many memories and all so bittersweet, but they were all she had left of him. Bowing her head, she finally let her tears flow and they came so fast and hard that she almost felt as if she were drowning.

Later that afternoon, Oliver called in to the funeral parlour. Nessie looked up in surprise as he entered; he'd said that he wouldn't be calling again unless he was called for. Marcie was up and about again now, still having as little to do with the baby as possible, and she too raised an eyebrow when Oliver told her that it was her he had come to see.

'What would you want to see me for?' she asked in her usual forthright way. 'I haven't sent for you and I'm as fit as a fiddle again.'

'It isn't anything about your health that I've come about,' he told her as Nessie ushered him to a chair. 'It's about a personal matter.'

Marcie scowled. 'And what would that be?'

Oliver ran his finger round the neck of his stiff,

starched collar. It suddenly felt as if it was trying to choke him. 'Well … the thing is… There's no easy way to tell you this but George … George … is dead I'm afraid.'

'*What!*' Marcie sat down heavily, her eyes suddenly looking like saucers in her rapidly paling face.

Oliver hurried on to tell her what had happened and about the letter George had left and by the time he had handed her the money that George had wanted her to have she was openly crying.

'At least he admitted that the baby was his.' Despite his betrayal she had still loved him and she was broken to think that she would never see him again.

Oliver nodded, his face grave. 'Yes, and my mother said to tell you that shortly she'll be in touch to settle a sum of money on you for his upbringing.'

Marcie nodded, then without another word she left the room, leaving Oliver and Nessie to stare at each other, neither of them knowing quite what to say.

Oliver spread his hands helplessly as he looked at Nessie. 'I'm so sorry … for everything,' he told her in a choked voice. Despite the fact that his younger brother had almost driven him to distraction at times he had loved him dearly and he was feeling his loss badly. 'You must hate my family for what George did to Marcie.'

She shook her head, her eyes full of tears. 'No, I don't. If anything, your family must hate mine. Let's face it, we don't have a lot to be proud of, do we? Our father was a murderer, I have a younger sister who has just had a baby out of wedlock, everyone believes that Joseph is mine after the malicious gossip that Seth Grimshaw is spreading about and there are also those that believe that Andre and I are living together as man and wife.'

'But none of that is your fault and I want you to know...' He looked embarrassed. 'That I have nothing but admiration for you ... and I care for you ... deeply. Look at all you've done since you came to work for Andre. Since I had the idea of opening the soup kitchen you've worked tirelessly to make a success of it despite everything else you have to do and I...'

'Please ... don't say any more,' she implored, her face full of sorrow. 'I admire you too but I think both of us know that anything more than friendship between us would be frowned upon by everyone. We come from different worlds and we have to accept that. Look at how your mother and father reacted to the news when Marcie told them she was carrying George's baby. They would never accept me, so it's best if we just stay friends.'

'But...'

'No, Oliver.' Her voice had a firm edge to it now. 'Go and meet a nice girl from your own class. Make your family proud. And do offer them my condolences about George. No matter what he did, he was their son and they will miss him.'

He slowly stood up and moved towards the door where he paused to tell her, 'I'll always be here for you if you need me, Nessie. And I shall still continue to call to monitor Joseph's progress.'

When he was gone, Nessie lay her head on her arm on the table and sobbed. But at least they had both acknowledged that nothing could ever come of their feelings now. It was done.

One evening early in October Nessie returned from the soup kitchen to find George screaming his little head off and Marcie sobbing at the table.

'Marcie, what's going on here?' she scolded, hurrying across to the crib to lift the baby and rock him. 'This little chap is crying for his feed, why haven't you seen to him?'

'I can't,' Marcie whimpered. 'I've *tried* to love him, really I have, but every time I look at him I see his father and I can't bear it.'

Nessie hardened her heart. 'That's all well and good but he can't live on fresh air, can he? And he didn't ask to be born. Pull yourself together and feed him now, this instant! I do just about everything else for you but I can't do that.'

Marcie sniffed as she reluctantly lifted the baby from her arms and unfastened her blouse. She nodded towards an envelope on the table, saying, 'Oliver called in earlier to give me that.'

'Oh, what is it?' Nessie was worn out and if truth be told all she wanted was her bed.

'It's a hundred pounds ... from Mrs Dorsey.'

Nessie's eyes stretched wide. 'A *hundred* pounds!'

Marcie pouted. 'I don't know why you should sound so surprised. That's got to keep George until he's old enough to work.'

'It's still an awful lot of money,' her sister pointed out. 'You'll be able to find somewhere for you both to live in comfort now without having to worry about going out to work and leaving him.'

'Actually...' Marcie gulped. 'I was thinking of sending it back and asking her to take George to live with her.'

'You were *what?*' Nessie was horrified. 'But how could you even *think* of doing that? That baby is a part of you.'

Suddenly calm, Marcie shook her head. 'But he isn't, not any more than Joseph is,' she said dully, addressing a subject that they had never spoken about. 'I can remember the night I told you and Mam that I was having him and the trouble it caused when she told our dad. When Mam said she'd pass the baby off as her own when it arrived, can you remember how angry Dad was? It wasn't long after that he left us all. Didn't you ever wonder why? And didn't you ever wonder why I would never tell you who Joseph's father was?'

Nessie was staring at her bewildered, but now that she had started, Marcie wasn't going to stop. She had carried her deep, dark secret for too long and now she wanted to share it.

'I didn't tell you because ... it was *our dad* who fathered Joseph... He raped me,' she confided dully.

Chapter Forty-Six

Nessie's bottom connected with the hard wooden chair seat with a dull thud as she stared in horror at her sister. She didn't want to believe a word she was saying yet suddenly it was as if the pieces of a

419

jigsaw were falling into place. The way her father had wanted Marcie out of the house the second he knew she was carrying a child. The way Marcie suddenly couldn't be in the same room as him. It had seemed strange at the time because Marcie had always been his favourite. Until she had hit her teens, that was, and had suddenly started to go out and then her father had been enraged. He had never minded Reuben or herself having friends yet he had wanted Marcie at home with him.

'Is ... is this true?' she croaked, but somehow before Marcie said a word she knew by the look on the younger woman's face that it was.

'Yes ... I *swear* it,' Marcie answered in a small voice as tears ran down her pale cheeks and plopped onto George's fair hair as he fed. 'It started when I was quite little.' She visibly shuddered as the memories she had tried so hard to lock away flooded back. 'Whenever we were alone in the cottage together he would lift me onto his knee and stroke me. At first, I liked it. He told me I was his special girl. Then he started to undo his trousers and he would make me stroke ... his thing. I didn't like that but he said if I told anyone he would just say I was lying. Next, he started to stroke me when I was undressed while he... Well, anyway, when I was about ten he came into my room one night while you were all out. I'd been in bed poorly with a cold and that was the first time he ... he *raped* me. I remember crying and telling him I was going to tell Mam, it hurt so much. But he said if I did she would send me away for being wicked. He also said that this was what all dads did to their girls and after that

420

it happened regularly.'

'Oh, Marcie, you *should* have told someone,' Nessie gasped.

Marcie shrugged. 'What would have been the point? Mam always thought the world of him. She'd never have believed me. I was shocked that she stuck to her word and tried to pass Joseph off as hers. The problem was the close neighbours knew the truth and Dad felt that she'd sided with me rather than him. That's why he left, I suppose; he thought that if she'd sent me away he could have tried to pretend none of it had happened. I believe that's why he killed her. He couldn't stand the thought of the truth coming out.'

Nessie was shaking now and felt as if she was trapped in a terrible nightmare. That must have been why her dad had said what he had when she visited the prison, *'Marcie will know what I mean.'*

'So now you know why I've never bonded with Joseph,' Marcie went on. 'How could I after the way he was conceived? And now this one.' Her breath caught in her throat as she stared down at the baby in her arms. 'George never raped me, of course. In fact, I loved him, that's why every time I look at this child I remember how he betrayed me. I don't think I shall ever be able to love him as he deserves to be loved.'

Silence stretched between them until Nessie said brokenly, 'Why don't you go up to bed now, Marcie? I need some time to think. I just can't seem to take it all in.'

'But you *do* believe me?' Marcie looked concerned.

Her sister nodded miserably. 'Of course I do,

421

and I'm so sorry you had to go through all that.'

Marcie rose and placed the baby, who was gurgling contentedly, into the drawer, then lifting it she made for the stairs saying, 'We'll talk some more tomorrow if you like, when you've had time to take everything in.'

Nessie nodded numbly. Eventually she went to bed but even though she was worn out, sleep evaded her as the things Marcie had told her went round and round in her head. She tossed and turned in a tangle of sheets until finally exhaustion claimed her as the first fingers of dawn were streaking the sky.

George's screams woke Nessie the next morning and with a little start she saw that it was daylight and realised that she must have overslept. Dragging on her night robe she padded down to the kitchen. It was deserted, Marcie must still be upstairs with the baby, she thought.

She spooned some warm tea and porridge into Joseph. He hadn't seemed too well for the last few days and she'd been keeping a close eye on him. It was nothing that she could put her finger on, he just seemed even more lethargic than usual. Then after settling him under a warm blanket on the sofa she hurried upstairs as George's howls became louder.

She rapped on Marcie's door and called, 'Marcie! Wake up, George needs a feed.' There was no reply so with an annoyed sigh she moved on to her own room. If Marcie hadn't done it by the time she was dressed she'd go in and give her a shake.

George's cries were deafening now and Nessie wondered how Marcie was managing to sleep through it. 'Marcie, will you please see to that baby, or do I have to come in there?'

Still no reply, so with a muttered curse she flung the door open and crossed to the drawer that George slept in which was placed at the foot of Marcie's single truckle bed. The room was in darkness, the curtains still tightly drawn, so after scooping George into her arms she crossed to them and yanked them open furiously. Turning to the bed, she prepared to let loose a torrent of abuse but stopped abruptly when she saw that it was empty.

'Marcie.' A sick feeling was forming in the pit of her stomach as she slowly went to the wardrobe and swung the door open. It was empty and she knew straight away that Marcie was gone for good. For a moment she just stood there feeling as if someone had tipped ice water down her spine, but then George's lusty cries brought her sharply back to the present and rushing downstairs she flung the back door open and shouted, 'Reuben, I need you!'

Both he and Andre were there in a second. They could never remember seeing her in such a tizzy before.

'What is it? Is it Joseph?' Reuben could see how distressed his sister was.

'No... It's Marcie ... she's *gone!*'

'What do you mean she's *gone?*' Reuben looked bewildered as she unceremoniously dumped the howling baby into his arms.

'I'll explain everything but for now just hold

him will you while I warm some milk up? I'll have to feed him with a pap bag for now.'

Rueben began to rock the baby up and down to try and soothe him but George was having none of it and if anything, his cries became even louder, upsetting Joseph who started to whimper too. Andre meanwhile stood to one side looking concerned. He sensed that something was seriously amiss.

At last the milk was ready and when Nessie hastily took him from Reuben and began to drip milk into his open mouth his cries stopped as if by magic.

'Phew that's better!' Reuben mopped his sweating brow with a handkerchief. 'Now, what's this you say about Marcie being gone?'

'Just what I said,' she said dully. 'And after what she confided in me last night I'm not surprised.'

'Huh! She's probably got another beau snooping around,' he snorted with disgust. He had never forgiven Marcie for getting pregnant with Joseph and leaving his mother and Nessie to bring him up.

'Please don't judge her until I share with you what she told me last night,' his sister implored him. 'Perhaps then you'll have a little sympathy for her.'

'I doubt it,' Reuben growled, crossing his arms stubbornly.

'Perhaps it is better if I leave,' Andre said uncertainly, but she shook her head wearily.

'No, stay, Andre. You know everything that's happened to our family so you may as well know the rest.'

424

Slowly she began to tell them what Marcie had confided to her the night before. For a moment Reuben looked at her in disbelief but gradually as she went on his face crumpled and he was devastated.

'My God, and I've been so horrible to her,' he muttered. 'Fancy her trying to keep something so awful to herself all this time. Why didn't she tell us sooner?'

'I don't suppose she knew how to. Or perhaps she was just afraid that we wouldn't believe her. I think she only told me now because George let her down so badly. I think she really loved him.'

'And you're quite sure she's gone and taken everything?' Reuben asked.

Nessie nodded as she swirled the tea leaves in her cup.

'Right, I'll go up and have a look round,' Reuben decided, heading purposefully towards the stairs. 'There might be something up there that will give us a clue as to where she's gone. We have to find her and bring her home.'

They heard him seconds later rummaging about upstairs in Marcie's room and reaching across the table, Andre stroked her hand. 'Try not to worry, my dear. She cannot have gone far. As for George, I'm sure Molly will know someone in the courtyards who can act as a wet nurse for him.'

Before she could answer they heard Reuben's footsteps pounding down the stairs again and they both glanced towards him.

'I've found this,' he cried triumphantly. 'It had slipped off the chest of drawers onto the floor.

She left you a note.' He thrust it towards Nessie. It was a piece of paper with her name written on it, so turning it over she began to read.

Dear Nessie,

I'm so sorry for goin off an leavin you in the lurch like this but I just cant stay round ere any more. Theres too may memries. Let George go to the Dorseys. I'm sure he'll have a good life an he'll be so much better off without me. I hope you an reuben will forgive me an understand why I need to have a fresh start sumwhere new where nobody knows me. Don't worry about me, I've got plenty o money as you know an I'm goin to make sumthin of meself. One day I'll be back in touch I promise.

Lots of luv to you all
Marcie xxx

'She never was much good at spelling,' Nessie sniffed as she swiped a tear from the end of her nose.

'But what about George? Are you going to let the Dorseys have him?' Reuben questioned. 'And where's all this money she's on about come from?'

'Mrs Dorsey sent her a hundred pounds to make sure that she and George could live comfortably, I suppose she's taken that,' Nessie explained.

'At least we know she won't starve then. But what do we say to the Dorseys about the money?'

Nessie hadn't thought about that. 'We won't tell them she's gone,' she said eventually. 'I'll look after George.'

Reuben scowled. 'But you're *already* lookin' after Joseph an' he's a full-time job on his own,'

426

he pointed out worriedly, angry that yet more responsibility should fall on his sister's shoulders.

'I'll get by. Molly will lend a hand,' she answered stubbornly. George might be only a few weeks old but she loved him already and couldn't bear the thought of letting him go.

'Look, we'll talk more later but for now we'd better get on else that poor chap in the chapel o' rest is goin' to be late for his own funeral. Once it's over I'll go round to the station an' see if anyone can remember if she got on a train.'

He hurriedly left the room with Andre at his heels and as she sat there, she began to wonder how she was going to manage. How would she find somewhere for herself and *two* little ones to live now? And who would look after them both while she was at work if she did?

Joseph began to whimper then. From the way his hand kept rising she suspected his head was hurting but he was unable to tell her. Thankfully Oliver was due in to see them later that morning. She would mention her concerns to him she decided.

When Molly arrived, Nessie told her that Marcie had gone. There was no point in trying to hide it. Everyone would soon know anyway but she did refrain from telling her about Joseph's true parentage and she completely trusted that Reuben and Andre would do the same.

Molly immediately shot off to see a young woman she knew from the courts who was nursing a baby only a few weeks older than George and within minutes she was back to tell Nessie, 'Young Alice Pickering has agreed to feed George through the day, though you'll have to manage with a pap bag through the night if he wakes. You need have no worries, Alice is a nice young lass an' clean as the courtyards will allow her to be. Give the little soul to me. You look shattered so I'll get Alice to keep him for a few hours while you do whatever you need to. Then this afternoon I'll keep an eye on Joseph an' you're to go out for a couple of hours. I can't remember the last time you had a bit of time to yourself.'

Nessie raised an eyebrow and gave a tired smile. 'And just where am I supposed to go?'

'I don't know.' Molly scratched her head then with a bright smile she suggested, 'You could go an' see that nice Mrs Hewitt, that old neighbour o' yours that calls in for a cuppa from time to time.'

'And what if Marcie comes back and I'm not here?'

'Then I dare say she still would be when you got back.'

'I suppose I could,' Nessie admitted. The thought of getting away from everything for just a short time was suddenly very appealing.

Chapter Forty-Seven

'It's probably nothing to worry about; we all have our off days,' Oliver told her later that morning after he had examined Joseph. But deep inside he was concerned. He felt that the swelling on Jos-

428

eph's head was growing once more and wondered if he should speak to his friend in London again to see if there was anything more that could be done.

'But it's not just today that he's been unsettled. He's been like this for a few days now,' Nessie told him worriedly and when he didn't reply she went on quietly, 'There's nothing more you can do for him, is there?'

He hesitated for just a fraction of a second but he had never lied to her before and couldn't bring himself to start now.

'I don't think so, but I will speak to my colleague in London again if you'd like me to.'

She shook her head as she held back tears. 'I think we both know there'd be no point, don't we? But could you tell me what to expect if he... When anything happens.'

'Hopefully when the time comes he'll just go to sleep.' Oliver had to stop himself from taking her in his arms. He knew how much she doted on the little boy. In fact, he'd become very fond of him himself in the time he'd been caring for him.

'And he won't be in any pain?'

'Hopefully not.' Oliver folded his stethoscope and placed it back in his bag. He then handed her a small phial full of clear liquid. 'Just give him a few drops of this in a drink when you think he might be uncomfortable.'

'More laudanum?'

'Yes, I promise it's safe when used properly.'

'Thank you.' She dropped it into her pocket, keen for him to be gone now. She had purposely not told him about Marcie leaving but she knew that he was bound to find out sooner or later, as would his mother, and then she'd have a visit from her no doubt.

'Right, I'll be off but you know where I am if you need me. Shall I see you at the soup kitchen this evening?'

'No!' She shook her head. 'I, er ... have a few things to do this evening so Molly's going to go in my place. Truthfully, the women are running it so successfully that they don't really need me there now. They're more than capable.'

'Thanks to you.' His face softened. She really didn't seem to have any notion of just how much all the things she had done had improved the local people's lives.

She managed a weak smile as he bade her goodbye, longing to feel his comforting arms around her.

Later that afternoon, Reuben returned from making enquiries at the station. 'The chap in the ticket office said someone matching Marcie's description bought a ticket to London early this morning,' Reuben confirmed. He was suffering all manner of guilty feelings now as he thought back to how he had treated Marcie when he had found out that she was having Joseph. Marcie had tried to hide her pregnancy, but his mother had noticed when she became too large to hide it any longer. And then all hell had broken loose. His father had demanded that she be kicked out onto the streets for bringing shame on them but her mother had been determined to stand by her. Soon after that, their father had left them and deep down Reuben had always blamed Marcie for that. But it was too late to put that right now and, somehow, he was going to have to live with himself.

'*London!*' Nessie looked horrified. 'But how will we find her there? London is a big place. It's full of pickpockets and whores from what I've heard of it. What if anything happens to her?'

Reuben ran his fingers through his hair distractedly. 'She'll be all right,' he soothed, although he didn't entirely believe it. 'She's got money and not *all* areas of London are bad. Marcie's got a good head on her shoulders. And hopefully she'll come home eventually. It's no good us trying to find her. It would be like looking for a needle in a haystack. It's a big place and she could be anywhere.'

Glancing about he asked, 'Where's George?'

Nessie explained about the wet nurse Molly had found who was willing to feed him through the day then went on to tell him her concerns about Joseph.

'All you can do is what you're doing now, give him lots of love,' he sighed. 'I wonder now if the reason he's always been a bit slow has anything to do with the fact that our dad fathered him?' he asked carefully.

'I doubt very much if the tumour would be anything to do with that. That's something that could happen to anyone, but you could be right about him always being a little behind other children his age,' she admitted. 'We'll never know now. We just have to make him as comfortable and happy as we can for whatever time he has

431

left, poor little mite.' Tears gathered in her eyes again and Reuben did his best to console her. He knew how much she loved the child and dreaded to think how it would affect her when the worst happened.

Molly appeared then with a smile on her face. 'George is as snug as a bug in a rug wi' a nice full belly tucked in the crib wi' Alice's little 'un. So you get yourself ready now an' go an' have a bit o' time to yourself. It's a grand day an' a bit o' fresh air will do you the world o' good. Joseph will be fine here wi' me, won't you, me little chap?' She tickled him under the chin.

Nessie left the house soon after. It was, as Molly had said, a beautiful clear day if a little chilly. The leaves were just beginning to start to flutter from the trees and as Nessie left the town behind her she began to feel slightly better. She hadn't realised how much she'd missed the open fields and the countryside since moving into the town. After a time, she removed her bonnet and took the pins from her hair enjoying the feel of the wind on her face. As she approached the cluster of cottages where she had lived with her family she saw Mrs Hewitt outside her back door feeding a sheet through the mangle.

The old woman beamed at the sight of her. 'Why, blow me down wi' a feather, this is a nice surprise,' she said, straightening. 'I were just about to go in an' get meself a nice warm drink. It's getting chilly out these days. Come on in, it'll be warmer inside.'

As Nessie followed her she saw a cluster of children playing in the dust outside her old home

432

and she hastily looked away. There was no point in thinking about the past. What was done was done and it was time to think of the future. But it was what the future held that was troubling her now.

Once inside Mrs Hewitt's little cottage the old woman swiped a fat tabby cat from the seat at the side of the fireplace and hurried away to make some tea.

Then, placing two cups on the table in front of Nessie, she asked, 'So, to what do I owe the honour of this visit then? An' don't say nothin' cos I can see by yer face that somethin's troublin' you, lass.'

Nessie stared into her drink as the tears that never seemed to be far away flooded down her cheeks again. 'Marcie has gone,' she sobbed. 'She couldn't take to her baby so I'm left with him and Joseph to look after as well as work and I can't stay at Andre's for much longer, especially now that Marcie has gone and I'm left there on my own with him. The gossips are loving this already, so goodness only knows what they'll say now, so I also have to find us somewhere else to live.'

'Is there no alternative?' Mrs Hewitt could be very sensible.

'Well...' Nessie faltered. 'Andre has asked me to marry him.'

'I see, so what's the problem? He's a kind, fine-lookin' man from what I've seen of him. A catch for any girl.' When Nessie didn't answer, Mrs Hewitt nodded. 'Is it because yer don't love him that yer hesitatin'?'

Nessie nodded miserably as the older woman

took a long swig of her drink. 'Could it be that you 'ave feelin's fer someone else?'

Another nod was her answer.

'An' is this someone else someone yer can't have?' She saw by the girl's face that she had hit on the truth and she sighed before saying wisely, 'Sometimes we don't allus get what we want in this life, pet. Perhaps yer should consider Andre's offer? He's a good man an' you an' the little 'uns would have a good life wi' him an' want fer nowt. Just think on it, eh? Yer do *like* him, don't yer?'

'Oh yes,' Nessie answered quickly. 'Andre is lovely and we get on very well.' She didn't, of course, tell Mrs Hewitt of Andre's sexual preferences.

'Well, there yer are then!' Mrs Hewitt lifted her swollen feet onto a stool and took another long swig of her drink. 'There's many a lass married a man she had no feelin's for an' ended up lovin' him. Love can creep up on yer when yer least expect it. Just think on it, eh?'

They went on to talk of other things then and when Nessie left she was in a thoughtful mood.

When she got home she found Andre rocking Joseph on his knee and she was surprised to see a fine wooden crib standing to one side of the kitchen.

'I bought it for George,' he explained, following her gaze. 'He is getting too big for the drawer now and I did not like to think of him being uncomfortable.'

Once again, she was deeply touched at his kindness so taking a deep breath, she said, 'Andre ... does the offer you made me ... of being your wife still stand?'

He looked mildly surprised. 'But of course.'

'Then...' She licked her dry lips and rushed on before she could change her mind. 'In that case I would be proud to accept it.'

And it was done and now she knew that there could be no going back.

Chapter Forty-Eight

The look of pure joy on Andre's face made her feel ashamed, for it was clear he was thrilled with her decision. Laying Joseph gently back down on the sofa he hurried across to take her hands gently in his. 'You do understand that this would not be a conventional marriage? I mean there would be no children and we would not...'

'I know exactly what you mean,' she answered hastily. 'And I accept that.'

'Good, then please wait there for just a moment.' He disappeared back into his own living quarters only to return minutes later with a small velvet box. When he sprang the lid and revealed the contents, Nessie gasped. It was a ring but a ring the likes of which she had never seen before. Nestling into a gold band was a fine ruby surrounded by ice-white diamonds that caught and reflected the late afternoon sunshine pouring through the window, sending rainbow prisms all across the walls. 'This has been in my family for many generations,' he explained. 'And because my parents were never gifted with a daughter it was given to me many years ago for my wife.' He chuckled then. 'Needless to say, at the time my parents did not know that I was... Well, let us just say that I never imagined it would be worn so I shall be delighted to see it on your finger.'

'Oh no, Andre. I can't accept it. It's far too grand,' Nessie objected, curling her fingers into a small fist.

He laughed as he gently uncurled them. 'Nonsense. As my wife you shall have many jewels and fine clothes, the best that money can buy, which is no more than you deserve,' he insisted and before she could protest further he slipped the ring onto her finger and told her tenderly, 'We may not be entering a conventional marriage, Nessie, but I want you to know that I *do* love you, as much as I would be able to love any woman. You are the kindest, most thoughtful person I have ever known, after Jean-Paul of course, and I have a feeling that we are going to be very content together.'

She nodded numbly as images of Oliver's face floated in front of her eyes but she firmly pushed them away. She had agreed to marry Andre now and had every intention of being the very best wife she could be to him. Molly walked in then with a mop and bucket in her hand and at the sight of the two of them her mouth dropped in amazement.

'So ... what's goin' on 'ere then?'

'Nessie has just done me the very great honour of agreeing to be my wife,' Andre told her with a flashing smile.

Molly looked mildly surprised for a moment but then hurrying over to them both she placed her arms about them.

'Why, that's bloody *wonderful* news. It's about time somethin' nice happened around 'ere! Congratulations. When is the big day to be?'

She noticed that Nessie looked a little stunned and it was Andre that answered.

'We haven't got as far as planning that yet. But I would like it to be before Christmas when my mother is visiting.'

'Hmm, well that don't give us much time to plan everythin',' Molly said.

'Oh, we won't need much time. I only want a very quiet wedding,' Nessie said hastily. 'The smaller the better, in fact, with just you and Charlie and Maria and Reuben present.'

Andre looked somewhat surprised, although he didn't argue. 'Are you quite sure?' he questioned and when she nodded he smiled.

'Then so it shall be,' he agreed as Molly enviously admired the sparkling ring on Nessie's finger. 'How about the first week in November then? There is no point in delaying. And it will be nice to arrange a wedding instead of a funeral!'

Nessie nodded again then left with Molly to fetch George home from the babysitter.

Once they were alone Molly peeped at her curiously before asking cautiously, 'Are yer quite sure about this? What I mean is, an' it's no business o' mine, o' course, but I had an' inklin' you had feelin's for young Dr Dorsey.'

Nessie managed a weak smile although inside she was crying. 'I'm *quite* sure, Molly. It's the best solution all round. It will be security for me and the children and Andre needs someone to look after him. He isn't always in the best of health, as you know, and his heart condition isn't likely to improve.'

Molly looked doubtful but held her tongue. Nessie had turned her and Charlie's lives around with her kindness and there was nothing that Molly wouldn't have done for her but she didn't feel able to interfere. She just prayed that Nessie wasn't making the biggest mistake of her life.

The following week Connie Dorsey was sitting in the drawing room thinking about George. Since the news of his death, her grief had not lessened. If anything, she felt even worse than she had on the day the policemen had come to visit. The door was slightly ajar, and as the sound of voices stirred her out of her thoughts, she realised two of the maids were talking about Marcie. She perked up, suddenly interested.

'Aye, she cleared off to London early one mornin' be all accounts,' one of them said. 'So now it's down to her sister to look after the baby an' she *already* looks after her little brother. Mind you, I dare say now she's marryin' that rich undertaker it won't be a problem. He'll probably hire a nanny to care for 'em.'

The news startled Connie out of her maudlin thoughts and set her mind racing and over dinner that night, she asked Oliver, 'Is it true what I'm hearing? That George's mother has run away?'

'I did hear a whisper in the surgery,' he admitted. 'But I don't know how true it is. I haven't

438

seen Nessie this week.'

'She's probably too busy making plans for the wedding,' Connie remarked, her mind fixed firmly on her grandson.

Oliver's head snapped up. 'What do you mean? *Whose* wedding?'

'Marcie's sister's, the one that opened the soup kitchen with you. Nessie. She's marrying the Frenchman she works for apparently, and rather hastily by all accounts! But enough about that. If Marcie has left, who will look after George?'

Her husband glared at her across the table then so Connie didn't notice the colour drain from Oliver's face. He felt as if someone had thumped him in the stomach and it took all his willpower to remain quiet.

'Now don't you start interfering in that direction,' Johnny Dorsey warned, wagging his fork at her. 'We've paid the girl off and that's an end to it, as far as I'm concerned.'

Connie straightened in her seat and laid her knife and fork down. 'That is our *grandson* we're talking about, Johnny, in case you've forgotten,' she told him, her face set.

Johnny groaned. 'Oh, for *goodness* sake, woman, *don't* start that again. I'm sure this Nessie will be more than capable of looking after him if his mother has disappeared off the scene.'

'That isn't the point.' Connie had no intention of not being heard this time. Every other time she had tried to talk about the baby he had changed the subject or left the room but this time she was determined. 'I'm going to see him,' she informed her husband firmly.

Johnny slammed the table with his fist. 'Over my bloody dead body!' he declared.

Connie rose from the table her eyes never leaving his face. 'I'm sure that can be arranged,' she quipped and turning she sailed from the room leaving him open-mouthed.

Oliver left minutes later and paced up and down his room. His mother must have it wrong, he reasoned. Nessie and Andre getting wed? He was one of the very few who knew about Andre's former partner, Jean-Paul. Why would Andre suddenly want to marry a woman? *His* woman, a little voice said. Well, there was only one way to find out, he would call into the funeral parlour tomorrow after surgery. With his mind made up he prepared for bed but it was a long time before he was able to fall asleep, as thoughts of Nessie married to Andre whirled around his head, making him feel sick with jealousy.

When Oliver arrived at the funeral parlour the next day, he found a young woman nursing George and he quickly averted his eyes. Before he could speak, Nessie appeared from the stairs. She looked mildly surprised to see him.

'Oh ... hello, Oliver. It's not your day to visit Joseph, is it?'

Slightly embarrassed he shook his head. 'No ... no, it isn't but seeing as I was passing I thought I'd just pop in and take a look at him. How has he been?'

The young woman rose discreetly, fastening her blouse as she handed George back to his aunt. 'There yer go, missus. He should be fine fer a while now. I'll pop back to feed him again in four hours, shall I?'

Nessie smiled at her. 'That would be fine, thank you, Alice.'

The girl scuttled away and it was then that Oliver noticed the ruby ring sparkling on Nessie's finger. It was so beautiful that it would have been difficult to miss it. Leaning over Joseph he cleared his throat and asked, 'How has he been?'

'Oh, much the same.' She lay George in his crib and came to join him, feeling awkward.

Once Oliver had finished his examination he turned to face her and asked quietly, 'Is it true that Marcie has left home?'

'Yes.' Nessie studiously avoided his eyes.

'And is it also true that you are now betrothed to Andre?' His voice was no more than a whisper, his eyes fastened on her face, but before she could answer him Andre swept in beaming with a wide smile.

'Hello, Oliver. Come to check up on the little chap, have you? How do you find him?' He took his place at Nessie's side and gave her an affectionate peck on the cheek.

'No worse,' Oliver answered as his heart sank.

'Good, good, and have you heard our news? Nessie and I are going to be married, the first week in November.'

'Then congratulations are in order. I hope you'll both be very happy.' Suddenly Oliver just wanted to be gone. He felt as if his heart was being torn in two and he didn't know how long he could keep up the pretence of being happy for them when all he wanted to do was ask her *why?* Her

441

and her damned silly ideas about class. Surely she knew how much he loved her. But it was too late now, soon she would be another man's wife.

'Right, I'd best get on.' He headed for the door as fast as his feet would take him and Nessie experienced a moment of such despair that it was all she could do to stop herself from running after him. Yet she knew she had done the right thing. His family would never have allowed him to marry her. And so she turned to her fiancé and forcing a smile she said, 'I'd better get on. I have to visit St Nicholas's Church to organise a funeral with the vicar there. Molly is going to keep an eye on Joseph.'

'Very well, and on your way back you must call in at the dressmaker and choose the material for your wedding gown. Even if you don't want a big wedding, I insist you have a new outfit.'

'All right,' she agreed reluctantly, then hurrying to the door she lifted her cloak and bonnet and hurried on her way.

On her way back from the church Nessie visited the dressmaker as Andre had requested and looked through the bolts of material. She knew that she should have felt excited to be choosing the material for her wedding gown yet as the dressmaker suggested various fabrics she felt nothing. Eventually she settled on a soft-green satin that the woman assured her would be perfect for her colouring and the occasion. Finally, once she had been measured and discussed patterns, she set off back to the funeral parlour feeling weary.

'How has he been?' she asked as she stepped through the kitchen door and then stopped abruptly when she saw Oliver's mother sitting on the sofa with George in her arms. She was staring down at George as if he was the most precious child in the world. A ripple of unease coursed up her spine.

'M-Mrs Dorsey. What can I do for you?' she asked when she managed to find her voice.

Molly was standing by the sink wringing her hands and she instantly babbled, 'I'm sorry, I asked her to come back later when you were home but she insisted on waitin' and then George woke up and...'

'It's all right, Molly,' Nessie assured her, then remembering her manners she asked, 'Have you offered our visitor a drink?'

Molly shook her head, so going towards the sink to fill the kettle, Nessie told her, 'You can get off now, if you like, Molly.'

Molly looked uncertain but when Nessie gave her a reassuring smile she nodded. 'All right. But if you need anything yer know where I am.' She hurried away and when Nessie had placed the kettle on the range to boil she turned back to Mrs Dorsey and asked again, 'So what can I do for you?'

Connie was slightly taken aback at her forthrightness, but she couldn't help feeling a certain admiration for her. She seemed very sensible and down-to-earth for one so young with so many responsibilities weighing on her shoulders.

'Actually, I think it's more a case of what I can do for you,' she responded. 'You see, I heard that your sister had left leaving you with another child to look after so I've come to take him off your hands.'

'Take him off my hands! He isn't a *parcel* to be passed about you know,' Nessie answered heatedly. It was all she could do to stop herself from rushing over and snatching George from the woman's arms but she forced herself to remain calm. 'I assure you, George is receiving the very best of care, so thank you for the offer but he'll be staying here with me.'

'I don't *think* so.' Connie Dorsey gave her a cold stare. 'I'm his grandmother and he belongs with me.'

'And I'm his aunt and I say he stays here!'

Connie bit her lip. She had hoped that the situation could be handled without resorting to unpleasantness but now she saw that she had no choice but to make a threat.

'Did your sister leave the money I settled on her for George's upbringing?' she asked suddenly.

The question took Nessie by surprise. 'Well ... no,' she faltered.

'And did she ever tell you where she got the Meissen figurines on your mantelpiece from?' She had spotted them the second she came through the door.

'Th-they were a gift from her,' Nessie croaked.

'Hmm, a gift straight from *my* house. She stole them from my home on the day she was dismissed.'

'I ... I didn't know.' Nessie's eyes were wide with fear now. How could Marcie have been so stupid as to steal something so valuable?

444

'I'm sure you didn't but the thing is, if I were to report that she'd gone off with my hundred pounds and stolen the figurines there would be police everywhere looking for her. She would never be able to return to her home town again without finding herself in an awful lot of trouble. You wouldn't want that for her now, would you?'

Nessie stood so still that she might have been turned to stone and Connie suddenly felt sorry for her. 'Why don't you let me take my grandson and give him the sort of upbringing he deserves?' Her voice had softened now. 'We can forget about the money and the figurines then. And I promise you that he will be loved. He's all I have left of his father now, don't you see?'

'What if I were to raise the hundred pounds? And you are welcome to take the figurines back. I don't want them!' Nessie declared.

Connie shook her head. 'That's no real solution, is it? She would still be guilty of theft on two counts and that is a punishable offence.'

Nessie felt torn between the devil and the deep blue sea as she stared back at the woman. Her heart ached at the thought of letting Marcie's baby go, for she still hoped that her sister would come home one day to claim him, but how could she if Mrs Dorsey carried out her threat?

'Would I be able to see him sometimes,' her voice was heavy with tears now.

'Of course,' Connie told her gently.

Nessie's shoulders sagged. 'When would you want to take him?'

'I could come back in the carriage for him later today.'

Nessie squeezed her eyes tight shut for a second then slowly she nodded. Deep down she knew that, for Marcie's sake, she really had no choice.

Chapter Forty-Nine

Not long after Connie Dorsey had left, the door to Nessie's kitchen burst open and Andre came in smiling broadly. 'I have just been to see the vicar at Chilvers Coton Church to set the date for our wedding and he has agreed...' He stopped talking abruptly as he saw Nessie sitting with George in her arms on the sofa sobbing bitterly. 'Wh-what's wrong?' he asked tentatively, his voice loaded with concern.

'It ... it's George,' she croaked. 'His grandmother came to see me a short while ago and he's going to live with her now.'

Andre looked shocked. 'But *why?*' He knew how much Nessie doted on the child.

'She has said that she will set the police on to finding Marcie if I don't let her have him. She went off with the Dorseys' money, you see, and those figurines on the mantelshelf... Marcie stole them from their home on the day she was dismissed. I just can't risk her being found and sent to prison.'

Andre looked shocked for a moment but then he said, 'Then that can be sorted. *I* shall give them their hundred pounds back and you can

446

return the figures.'

She shook her head miserably. 'I already offered to try and raise the money and told her that I didn't want the figurines but she's adamant she wants George. And she *is* his grandmother after all. If it were to go in front of the magistrate they would probably say that he was better off with her anyway. They're a very powerful family in the town and very well respected, despite what their younger son has done. It's useless. I just have to let him go.'

Andre's heart went out to her but he didn't argue because deep down he sensed that she was right.

The carriage drew up later that afternoon and minutes after Connie Dorsey appeared at Nessie's door. Strangely, she appeared to show no pleasure in what she was about to do and was almost sympathetic when she saw Nessie's reddened eyes.

The girl had packed all his clothes neatly into a valise along with the china ornaments. 'You're welcome to keep those,' Connie told her but Nessie shook her head.

'I don't want them now that I know they were stolen,' she told her quietly as she wrapped a shawl about George. Funnily enough, now that the time had come for him to go she didn't want to prolong it. It would only make things worse.

'I've had a wet nurse coming in to feed him during the day,' she told the woman but Connie stopped her from going any further.

'It's all right, lass. I've got all that in hand,' she assured her. 'The nursery is all ready for him and everything is sorted. In fact you can come back with us to see if it will put your mind at rest.'

Nessie shook her head. 'Thank you but no. Perhaps I could come in a couple of days when he's had time to settle in?' She knew that she wouldn't be able to bear to leave him there if she went with him today.

'Of course.' Connie approached her and gently took the sleeping baby from her arms, thinking how much he looked like his father. As he nestled against her breast, Nessie saw the love in the woman's eyes and it gave her comfort. She had no doubt at all George would be loved, which was something to cling onto.

Connie nodded to the coachman standing at the door and gestured towards George's possessions. 'Would you mind putting those in the carriage?'

'Yes, ma'am.' He lifted the bag and disappeared with it. In truth, Connie could have told Nessie that there was no need to send the clothes. He had a wardrobe waiting back at Haunchwood House fit for a little prince but she didn't want to make the girl feel worse. After all, none of this was her fault.

'Right, we'd best be off and get him settled.' She too was eager for this part to be over with. She could almost feel Nessie's pain coming off her in waves. 'And we'll see you in a couple of days, shall we?'

Nessie nodded numbly as Connie headed for the door, feeling as if her heart was being ripped out of her chest. And then they were gone and as Nessie listened to the clash of the horse's hooves as the carriage rattled away on the cobbles, fresh tears rained down her pale cheeks.

A couple of days later, Andre suggested, 'Why don't you let me drive you to Haunchwood House today? It's time you went to see how George is settling in. You will not be happy until you do.'

She nodded, knowing he was right yet dreading it all the same. It was going to be so hard.

'All right, shall we go this afternoon? I have a client coming in this morning to organise their husband's funeral.'

'Very well.' He smiled and left her to prepare for the meeting.

Later that afternoon, as they arrived at Haunchwood House, Nessie's stomach was in a knot.

'It might be best if I wait in the carriage for you,' Andre suggested tactfully and she nodded appreciatively. She had dressed carefully and twisted her hair into a neat pleat on the back of her head and when a young maid answered the door she told her, 'I am here to see Mrs Dorsey. Would you mind telling her Miss Carson is here, please?'

The maid's eyes stretched wide as she realised who Nessie was. She must be Marcie's sister, the one who had been looking after Master George before the mistress brought him home.

'O' course, miss,' she answered. 'Would yer step inside? I'll tell the mistress yer here.'

Nessie stepped into the large hallway and once the maid had scurried away she glanced around. It was a very beautiful home for a child to be brought up in, she was forced to admit, and she tried to find some comfort in that.

The maid returned shortly and said, 'The mistress will see you now, miss. She's in the morning room.' She led Nessie along the hall and stopped to tap on a door before opening it. 'Go on in, miss.'

Nessie entered the room and the first thing she saw was Connie Dorsey sitting on a large sofa with George fast asleep on her lap.

'Ah, Miss Carson,' she greeted her. 'I was hoping you'd call soon. Would you like to hold George while I order us some tea? He's just been fed and he's all full up and content and has dropped off to sleep, I'm afraid, but there's time for you to give him a cuddle before the nanny comes to take him back to the nursery.'

Her greeting was so friendly that Nessie was at a loss as to what to say so she merely took George from her arms and feasted her eyes on his face. He did indeed look very well and contented, she had to admit, and Mrs Dorsey did seem to be genuinely fond of him.

The woman pulled a long, silken bell pull at the side of the fireplace and once the same little maid who had admitted Nessie appeared, she ordered a tray of tea before turning back to her guest.

'He's settling beautifully,' she assured her kindly and Nessie nodded. She could see that she was telling the truth. His clothes were exquisite, far better than any she had ever been able to supply him with.

'We've employed a nanny and a wet nurse for him,' the woman went on, keen to put her mind at rest. 'Although, I have to admit he doesn't spend an awful lot of time up in the nursery. I like to bath and change him myself. Perhaps you would like to meet them and see the nursery?'

'N-no, it's all right,' Nessie told her. Somehow, she knew that the woman was telling the truth. 'I ... I just wanted to see for myself that he wasn't fretting.'

'As you can see,' Connie Dorsey replied, 'he appears to be well.' Then not wishing to hurt Nessie's feelings she hurried on, 'Although, I'm sure he's missed you in his own little way.'

Nessie shook her head. Thankfully he wasn't really old enough to miss her and she was glad of that for his sake.

The tea arrived then and Connie hastily began to strain it into two fine bone china cups and saucers. Thankfully she knew that Nessie could have no idea of the trouble George's coming had caused between herself and her husband. She and Johnny had rowed bitterly on the night he had arrived home from one of his businesses to find George there.

'Why the *hell* have you brought that bastard into our house?' he had roared.

'Because he's *our* bastard, that's why, and he's staying so get used to the idea!' she had roared back, equally angry.

'But what are people going to say?'

Connie had snorted and tossed her head and in that moment Johnny knew he had lost the argument. She could be as stubborn as an old mule when she set her mind to something. 'Since when have we ever cared what people say about us, eh? He's George's son, even if he was born the wrong side of the blanket and he's going to be brought up with us where he belongs, so get used to the idea!'

And funnily enough, he appeared to be doing just that. Only the night before she had caught him in the hallway talking to the child as the nanny took him up to the nursery while they had their meal, and now she had every hope that in no time at all he would dote on the little chap as much as she did. Johnny's bark had always been worse than his bite so now she was prepared to sit back and let nature take its course. After all, who could resist such a beautiful baby for long?

She handed Nessie her tea but she could see that the girl was keen to be gone. 'It's very kind of you but now that I've seen him, I really ought to be on my way,' Nessie told her politely.

'Are you sure? You're very welcome to stay for a while, lass.'

'No, I … thank you.' Nessie quickly handed him back and headed for the door.

She was almost there when Connie told her, 'Do come again as soon as you like. You're his auntie and I want you to stay a part of his life.'

The two women stared at each other for a long moment and despite everything, Nessie some-how knew that they were going to get along. 'I will and thank you.'

'That was a quick visit,' Andre said, surprised when Nessie got into the carriage. 'Was the baby all right?'

'Very much so,' she admitted, keeping her eyes straight ahead. 'I think Mrs Dorsey loves him already.'

'Then that's good, yes?'

She nodded. 'Yes, Andre, it's very good.'

Noting the conflicted look on her face, Andre said no more and they continued their journey in silence.

Chapter Fifty

Nessie and Andre were married at Chilvers Coton Church in the first week in November. As she had requested, it was a very quiet affair with only herself and Andre, Reuben and Maria and Molly and Charlie present. Nessie looked stunning in the green gown Andre had insisted she should have and as she walked down the aisle carrying a posy of small white roses, Reuben, who was giving her away, whispered, 'You look beautiful, sis.'

She peeped up at him and smiled, but as she took her place at Andre's side she couldn't help thinking of Oliver and she had to blink back the tears. His mother had informed her the week before on one of her visits to George that Oliver had gone to take up a medical practice in London and she missed him every single day. At least now they wouldn't have to constantly see each other and think of what might have been. And so, with the weak sun shining down on them through the stained-glass windows, she and Andre solemnly made their vows to each other, and Nessie pushed all thoughts of Oliver aside and silently promised herself that she would be the best wife to Andre that she could possibly be.

After the service, Andre took them to a hotel in the town where he had booked a delicious wedding breakfast. The mood was light as Andre stood after the meal and announced proudly, 'I wish to propose a toast to my new wife.' They all raised their glasses, smiling and wishing them well. Nessie smiled back, determined that she would make the best of this marriage, if only for Andre's sake. After all his kindness, it was the least he deserved.

Once they arrived back at the funeral parlour, two of the soup kitchen volunteers who had stayed behind to look after Joseph rushed forward to greet them and shake their hands.

'How does it feel being Mrs Chevalier?' they teased with a wicked twinkle in their eyes.

'I'll tell you when I get used to it,' she answered, blushing.

Andre had another single bed moved into his room in his living quarters and it had been agreed that Molly and Charlie would now live in Nessie's old rooms. They were so much nicer than the cottage they lived in in the courtyards and Molly was thrilled.

'I'll keep Joseph in here wi' us fer tonight,' she told Nessie with a saucy wink and it was all Nessie could do not to laugh aloud. If only they knew the truth. Even so as bedtime approached she felt strangely nervous. She was painfully aware that the marriage was not going to be a conventional one but just what would Andre expect of her?

She need not have worried. Andre undressed behind a screen in the corner of the room, emerging in a long nightshirt and once he had climbed into his bed she discreetly did the same. As she was passing him to get to her own bed he caught her hand and told her softly, 'You do know that I love and treasure you, don't you, Nessie? As much as I am able to love a woman, I mean. You have given me respectability and I promise you that from this day forward I shall honour you and do all in my power to make you happy.'

Looking down on his dear face she realised that she had come to love him too. Not in the way that she loved Oliver, admittedly, but as she was discovering, there were all different kinds of love.

'And I love you too and I promise that I will be the very best wife to you that I can possibly be.' She hopped into bed and they held hands across the gap that divided them until they finally fell asleep.

Word of their marriage soon spread about the town and suddenly Nessie was treated with a newfound respect. She was no longer the penniless girl from a tumbledown cottage and the daughter of a murderer, but the wife of a prosperous businessman and she used the fact to her advantage. Now the doors to the more salubrious homes were open to her and invites to afternoon tea or coffee mornings arrived on an almost daily basis. Nessie attended them whenever work permitted, keen to get the wealthier members of society involved in the soup kitchen and her other charitable schemes.

Personally, as she confided to Andre, she found many of the women she visited were terrible snobs but even so they were keen to outdo their neighbours and help, and in no time at all they were donating money so that many of the children whose parents could not afford the penny a day to send them to school were now able to attend. All in all, things were going well and despite their rather unorthodox marriage, Nessie was content and as each day passed, her affection for her husband grew.

There were still times when she thought of Oliver but each time he popped into her head she firmly pushed thoughts of him away. She was still busy helping Andre to run the business, which was thriving. She visited George, who was also thriving in his grandmother's care, on a weekly basis, as well as continuing to care for Joseph, and do her charity work. All of this left her very little time to herself. Some days, when she tumbled into bed, she was so tired that Andre was concerned she was doing too much. But the distractions helped to ease the pain of losing Oliver.

Almost before she knew it Christmas was racing towards them. The shop windows in the town were decorated with holly, ivy and Christmas baubles and there was a hint of snow in the air, and Nessie couldn't help feeling nervous as she thought of the visit they were expecting from Andre's mother.

'But what if she doesn't like me?' she fretted to Andre as they sat together in front of a roaring fire one cold, frosty December evening.

Andre chuckled. '*Ma cherie*, my *maman* would like you even if you had two heads,' he assured her. 'You have made an honest man of me. In her latest letter she says that even papa can bear to have my name mentioned again now. No, you need have no fears on that score. She will love you as I do.'

And so Nessie made the guest room as comfortable as it could be and eventually, two weeks before Christmas, they went together to meet his mother from the train.

'Are you sure I look all right?' she questioned nervously as they stood on the platform waiting for the train to arrive. She was wearing the new burgundy velvet dress and cloak that Andre had bought her and she looked every inch the lady.

'You look perfect.' He squeezed her hand affectionately just as they heard the sound of the train approaching and she sighed. It was too late to do anything about it now, even if she didn't.

Within minutes the train drew to a halt in a hiss of steam and the guard began to pace alongside it, throwing the carriage doors open.

'There she is!' Andre pointed to a woman who was stepping down onto the platform two carriages away and before she knew it, Nessie was being hauled along beside him.

'*Maman!*' The woman turned and at first sight of her Nessie was shocked. She was tall and slim and although she was no longer in her first flush of youth she was still remarkably attractive: her skin was unlined apart from a few tiny ones around her eyes and she had high cheekbones. Nessie imagined that she must have been quite beautiful when she was younger. She was elegantly dressed in a hat trimmed with tall feathers that fluttered becomingly at the least movement of her head and a travelling costume in a rich royal-blue colour made of fine wool that matched the colour of her eyes.

'Andre!' She opened her arms and he walked into them. Then suddenly remembering his manners he turned to Nessie and drawing her forward he told her, 'This is my wife, Nessie, *Maman*.'

The woman smiled and held out her hand. 'It is a pleasure to meet you at last.' The woman's smile was genuine and Nessie began to relax a little. Perhaps the visit would go well after all.

'It's lovely to meet you too,' she responded, and while Andre went to fetch a porter to collect his mother's luggage, Nessie was left to guide the woman from the station to the waiting carriage.

Once they were seated inside the woman clasped Nessie's hands in hers. 'I have *so* looked forward to this,' she told her with a happy smile. 'I am sure we will get along well.'

Nessie returned the smile.

'And I believe from what Andre has told me in his letters, you have your little brother living with you too, yes?'

Nessie nodded. She and Andre had discussed what they should tell her about Joseph's true parentage and had decided that there was no need for her to know the shocking truth.

'Joseph, isn't it? And the poor little soul is not well?'

'That's right, the doctors think that he has a brain tumour.' Nessie was finding her very easy to talk to but there was no time for any more chat, for Andre arrived then with a porter loaded down with luggage. The woman had come for a week but Nessie was sure that she had brought clothes for at least a month if the number of boxes and trunks were anything to go by. Once everything was loaded they set off for home and Nessie observed her mother-in-law from the corner of her eye as the woman chatted away to her son in French. She could only assume that Andre took after his father, for apart from the colour of his eyes he looked nothing like his mother.

The woman suddenly seemed to remember herself and turning to Nessie she apologised, 'I am so sorry! I forget my manners. I must speak in English while I am here.'

'It's quite all right,' Nessie assured her, smiling warmly. But even so, she continued the journey chatting happily in English to her son as Nessie listened.

When they arrived outside the funeral parlour, Andre's mother looked at the building approvingly. 'I detect a woman's touch,' she said as she stared at the velvet drapes in the window and the freshly cut holly in the vase.

Nessie smiled modestly and, leaving Andre to lift down his mother's luggage from the carriage, the two women went inside. 'My dear, I should have said that while I am here you must call me Jewel, it is my name and you may not feel comfortable enough to call me *Maman* just yet.'

What a curious but beautiful name, Nessie thought, as she showed Jewel to the room she had prepared for her.

She soon found that her mother-in-law was

remarkably easy to get along with and she took to Joseph instantly, billing and cooing over him at every opportunity, although when she first met him her eyes filled with tears of sympathy.

'Ah, he is destined to be an angel child,' she said gravely. 'He will not stay long on this earth.' Then she explained, 'I am of gypsy origin and I have the gift. Did Andre not tell you?'

Surprised, Nessie shook her head.

'Yes.' The woman gave a trill of laughter. 'My Pierre's parents were not at all impressed when they met me. I was very young, as you are, and my husband-to-be was much older. They thought I was far beneath him but we have had many happy years together. Our only regret was that we were not able to have more children. There was only Andre which was why his father was so upset when we discovered that he was...' Her voice trailed away and her face became serious as she asked, 'You knew about Jean-Paul, yes?'

Nessie nodded uncomfortably.

'Ah, his papa knew then that he would never present us with grandchildren.'

Nessie blushed, but this woman was no fool and, her voice soft, she said, 'And there is still no chance of that, is there?'

When Nessie dropped her eyes, she shrugged. 'Ah well, at least you have given him the cloak of respectability and he does seem to care for you most sincerely. As much as he can care for a member of our gender, that is. Am I right?'

Nessie wondered if she should lie but Jewel seemed so perceptive that she sensed she would know. She had the feeling that she could see right into her soul.

'He says he does. And I ... I do care for him.'

'Of course you do. That is plain to see ... but your heart and soul belongs to another. Am I right?' She patted her hand then. 'Do not bother to reply. But rest assured, one day your dreams will come true and you will find happiness.'

As Nessie's mouth gaped she turned her attention back to Joseph and the strange conversation was at an end.

The week passed all too quickly for Nessie and when they finally stood on the platform to wave Jewel away on the train, her eyes were full of tears.

'Come again soon, it's been so lovely to have you,' she told her mother-in-law as they hugged.

'It might be a long time before I can make such a long journey again,' Jewel told her sadly. 'Pierre is many years older than me and not in the best of health so I do not like to leave him for too long. But thank you for being so kind to my son. You have turned his business and his life around and one day you will be rewarded.'

There was no more time for chat then, for the guard was ushering everyone aboard and after one last kiss the woman climbed into the carriage and pulled the window down.

'Take care of my son, Nessie,' she called as the train chugged into life and drew away and they all waved until it was just a spot in the distance.

'That wasn't so bad, was it?' Andre said, smiling.

'I loved having her stay,' she answered truthfully. 'But why didn't you tell me she used to be a gypsy?'

'I suppose I never think about it.' He grinned. 'And what difference does it make? If two people love each other it shouldn't matter what walk of life they come from.'

Just for a second a picture of Oliver flashed in front of her eyes. If *only* it were so, she thought, but then she plastered on a smile and took her husband's arm. She had made her choice and she would stand by it.

Chapter Fifty-One

January 1866

'So, did you have a good Christmas and New Year, pet?' Connie Dorsey asked as she and Nessie sat on the hearthrug in front of the fire in her drawing room. 'And how did you get on with your mother-in-law?'

'In answer to your first question we had a very nice Christmas, thank you. Maria and Reuben, and Molly and Charlie and their children all came for dinner. I cooked a goose with all the trimmings and it was wonderful to see everyone enjoying themselves, especially the children. We bought each of them a little gift that I put beneath the Christmas tree and they were so thrilled with them. Did I tell you Maria was having a baby, by the way? And as for the second question, my mother-in-law was lovely! I don't mind admitting I was rather worried about how we'd get on but I was sorry to see her go.'

George, who was five months old now and as fat as butter, was propped up by cushions and happily throwing about some brightly painted wooden bricks. Nessie was shocked at how much he seemed to have grown in just three weeks. Normally she tried to visit every week but what with the Christmas holidays, her mother-in-law's visit and one thing and another this was the first chance she'd had since before Christmas.

The awkwardness between herself and Connie had disappeared completely and now they got on well. So much so, in fact, that Connie actually looked forward to her visits. Nessie had also been heartened to hear about how George's grand-father had softened towards him, despite not initially wanting the baby there. George now had him wrapped around his little finger and it was more than obvious that Connie, in fact the whole household, doted on him. He only had to whim-per and someone would rush forward to soothe him and she was forced to accept that this was perhaps the best place for him to be brought up after all. She could never have devoted all the time that Connie did to him.

Connie had ordered coffee for them so when the door opened Nessie glanced up, expecting to see the maid, and when she saw Oliver standing there with a tray in his hands she felt the colour drain from her face.

'I thought I'd play maid and make myself useful,' he said, his eyes tight on Nessie and then an awkward silence settled on the room, save for baby George's gurgles of glee as he tried to eat one of his wooden bricks.

Picking up on the tension immediately, Connie told him, 'Well, come and put the tray down then! It'll be stone cold if you stand there for much longer.' The look that she had seen pass between Oliver and Nessie when they had first set eyes on each other only confirmed her suspicions. Her son loved Nessie and judging by the young woman's reaction to his appearance, his love was returned. But why then, she wondered, had she married Mr Chevalier? Perhaps that was the reason Oliver had suddenly decided he wanted to go and work in London? It was all fitting together now and she thought it was a crying shame.

'Did I mention that Oliver was home for a few days?' she asked casually to break the uncomfortable silence.

'No, you didn't. How are you, Oliver?' Nessie asked politely, desperately trying to disguise her surprise and sheer joy at seeing him again.

'Very well, and yourself?'

'I'm well... How is your practice in London going?'

He could have told her that he hated it there, had only gone because he couldn't stand to see her married to another man. He missed the small market town he had been brought up in, and the soup kitchen, but most of all he missed *her*. Instead he merely said, 'Oh, it's going well, thank you.'

'Good.'

'Right, I'm just going to go and check with

Cook how lunch is coming along,' Connie said. 'You will join us, won't you, Nessie?'

'Er, thank you but I should be getting back. We have a funeral scheduled for this afternoon,' Nessie replied quickly.

'Oh, what a shame. But never mind, perhaps next time.' Connie left and Nessie tried to focus on George, painfully aware that Oliver's eyes were on her.

'And how is Joseph?' he asked after a time. 'And Andre, of course.'

Since Oliver had left, Andre had arranged for the new doctor to visit Joseph each week.

'Andre is well but Joseph' – she hesitated – 'is not doing so well these last few weeks. The doctor who attends him now thinks that perhaps the tumour is growing again.'

'I'm so sorry to hear it,' Oliver answered, although secretly he was surprised that the little chap had lasted as long as he had. He was quite sure that it was all thanks to her loving care. They talked of the soup kitchen then and the other charitable works she was involved with, pointedly avoiding anything personal, and they were both relieved when Connie returned.

Nessie left soon after, glad to make her escape, and as she made her way home her heart felt like lead. Seeing Oliver again had awakened all the feelings she had tried to bury but by the time she got home she managed to plaster a smile to her face and she kissed Andre's cheek affectionately.

'How was he?' He had always encouraged her to visit George, which was one of the kind things she loved about him. There were so many things, but their marriage was a façade and sometimes she grieved for the children she would never have. Even so, what was done was done and she was determined to make the best of it.

The sound of Joseph whimpering in the next room woke Nessie early one morning in mid-February.

Swinging her legs over the edge of the bed she dragged her dressing robe on and tiptoed from the room, hoping not to disturb Andre, but he was already awake and he arrived in Joseph's room looking concerned shortly after she did.

'Should I send for the doctor?' he asked worriedly as Nessie bent over the child.

'Yes ... I think so.' Nessie was trying hard not to panic. 'He's very hot and I think he's in pain.'

Andre rushed away to throw his clothes on and was clattering down the stairs in seconds. Charlie hadn't yet arrived so he would go for the doctor himself.

Luckily old Dr Peek was just sitting down to his breakfast when Andre arrived and he hurried back with him, then shooed both Nessie and Andre from the room while he examined the child. When he joined them on the narrow landing shortly after his face was grave.

'I fear you should prepare yourselves for the worst,' he told them solemnly and Nessie's fist flew to her mouth. 'I recommend you up his dose of laudanum to ease the pain, there is little more we can do. I shall call in again after I have finished my rounds.'

She nodded numbly. She had always known

that this would happen one day and had thought she had prepared herself for it but now that the time had come the thought of losing the dear child was unbearable.

The doctor called twice more that day and Nessie stayed close to Joseph's side, talking soothingly to him, holding his hand and mopping his fevered brow but as evening closed in he didn't even seem to be aware that she was there and she knew he was slipping away.

'You go to bed and get your rest,' she urged Andre. 'There is no point in us both sitting up.'

Reuben had been there for most of the evening too, anxious about the little boy, but she had sent him home to Maria, insisting that she could manage.

Andre reluctantly did as he was told, sensing that she wanted some time alone with Joseph but he tossed and turned for most of the night, finding it hard to sleep.

The first fingers of dawn were painting the sky with a palette of purples and pinks when Joseph suddenly opened his eyes and turned his head to look at Nessie. For the first time in a long while he appeared to be focusing on her.

'Hello, sweetheart,' she said, swallowing the lump in her throat. 'Would you like a little drink?'

He gave her the sweetest smile. A smile that would live in her heart forever and she turned to lift the glass of water she had placed on the small table at the side of the bed. But when she turned back she saw that his eyes were closed and she knew that he had slipped away.

'No... No... No... Oh, *Joseph!*' Tears ran down

her cheeks as she stared at him. She felt as if her heart was breaking in two but then she thought of what she had told Molly when she lost her child. He is up there waiting for you beyond the open door. Hopefully Joseph would be there waiting too now, whole and able to do all the things that little boys his age should be able to do. Even so, her sense of loss was overpowering and Andre found her there clinging to his tiny body and sobbing broken-heartedly a short time later.

'I am so sorry.' He saw at a glance that Joseph was gone and he too was deeply upset. He dealt with dead bodies almost every day of his life, it was his job, but it was very different when one of those bodies was someone he cared about personally. 'He shall have the best funeral this town has ever seen,' he promised his grieving wife, but his words gave her little joy. Some time ago she had agreed to marry him to give Marcie, her new baby, and Joseph a secure home and now they were all gone. From now on it would be just her and Andre.

'W-would you get word to Reuben about what has happened please?' she asked tremulously. 'He will want to come to say his goodbyes.'

'Of course.'

True to his word, a few days later Joseph was laid to rest in a small white coffin that Andre had ordered especially from London. The glass-sided hearse that took him to the church was full of pure white lilies and no expense was spared. But nothing could ease Nessie's pain and as the tiny coffin was lowered into the ground she felt as if a part of her heart was being buried with him.

Chapter Fifty-Two

November 1869

'Happy anniversary, *ma cherie*. I cannot believe that we have been married for four years.' As Andre took a small velvet box from his pocket and made to rise from his chair to give it to her, she pressed him back into the seat.

'Oh, thank you, Andre. But don't get up, please.' She took the box from him and when she sprang the lid she found a glittering diamond brooch in the shape of a leaf twinkling up at her.

'Oh, darling, it's beautiful,' she gasped. She had many such trinkets now, although she didn't often wear them, for Andre spoiled her shamelessly. 'So that's where you got Charlie to take you in such secrecy the other day,' she scolded but there was a twinkle in her eye.

He shrugged. 'You deserve it. I only wish I could take you out somewhere nice. It is so boring having to sit here,' he grumbled.

'Well, boring or not, the doctor said you were to have complete rest and I shall see that you do,' she told him firmly as she tucked the rug across his knees; since he'd become ill, Andre tended to feel the cold more keenly. As her hand brushed his leg she had to stifle a little cry of distress as she felt his bones. He had lost so much weight that his clothes hung from his frame no matter how many tasty tit-bits she tempted him with. But it was his face that had changed the most. It was gaunt and his lips always had a frightening blue tinge to them.

The doctor called in weekly, just as he once had for Joseph, but there was little he could do apart from advise Andre to rest. His heart condition had worsened dramatically over the last few months, to the point that he could no longer actively take a part in the business. Thankfully that wasn't a problem as Charlie and Reuben had everything running like clockwork. To cope with their rising trade, they now also owned another parlour in the borough of Weddington which was run by Dick Villiers, a friend of Charlie's from the courtyards who was very dependable and capable. And so now Nessie found herself frequently running between the two businesses and dealing with the financial side of things and with that and her charitable works, she barely had a minute to herself. Not that she ever complained. She liked to be busy.

The year before she had purchased a run-down house just outside of town from Seth Grimshaw of all people, and after having it renovated, she had employed a teacher and set up her own little free school. When it had first opened she had feared that no one would ever use it but as word had spread the children had begun to attend and now it was full to capacity. Andre was more than happy to fund it, with two businesses doing well he could afford to and he knew how much pleasure it gave his wife.

He watched her now as she flitted across to the

highly polished mahogany sideboard that took up one wall of their drawing room to return with a parcel for him.

'And this is my anniversary present to you,' she told him, watching with pleasure as he carefully unwrapped it. It was a beautiful book of poems with a fine-tooled leather cover. He sighed with pleasure as he flipped through the pages.

'It is beautiful,' he breathed, then sighed regretfully. 'Once I dreamed of travelling the world but that is not going to happen now, is it?'

She forced a smile. 'How do you know that? I'm hoping your health will improve when the weather gets warmer. We could perhaps take a little holiday then? Somewhere in this country for now. Reuben and Dick can manage without us for a few days.'

'We shall see,' he replied but deep down he feared it would never happen. He was gasping for breath if he took more than a few steps now, although he always tried to put on a brave face for Nessie. He knew how much she worried about him.

'Anyway, I must be off to the shop at Weddington,' she told him as she patted her hair into place in the mirror above the fireplace. 'I promised Dick I would prepare some bills for him today but if you need anything while I'm gone just shout. Molly will be about and I shouldn't be too long. You sit and relax and have a read of your book while I'm gone.'

Long after she had left, he sat staring thoughtfully at the door. She had been a good wife to him and he had never regretted marrying her for a minute, although he still missed Jean-Paul, who had been the love of his life. His life might have been very different had Jean-Paul lived but it hadn't been meant to be. Strangely, the thought of dying didn't frighten him now, for he hoped that when his time came they would be reunited. With a sigh he turned his attention to the book to while away the hours.

'This came for you along wi' all the other letters,' Molly informed Nessie later that morning when she arrived back from Weddington. 'It's got a London postmark. Who do yer reckon it could be from?'

Nessie took it from her, her heart pounding. Oliver and Marcie were both in London but Nessie was almost afraid to hope that it might be from either of them. She ripped open the envelope and her heart leapt.

'It's from Marcie,' she cried. She had longed for her sister to write to her for such a long while that she couldn't wait to read it.

She gave a cry of delight as soon as she saw the signature at the bottom. Although she noticed that there was no return address even so she was thrilled to hear from her and her eyes began to greedily scan the page as she read aloud:

Dear Nessie,

I hope this letter finds you well, as I am. I'm sorry it's taken me so long to write but I've been very busy. I'm writing now to tell you that I'm about to be married and also about what has happened to me since I came to London.

I'm sorry for the way I ran away leaving you to care for George and Joseph, I hope you'll forgive me but I needed to get away from everything that had happened. I hope you'll understand. It was very hard when I first arrived here, as within hours of arriving I was robbed – every single penny of the hundred pounds was stolen and I didn't even have enough money to catch the train home. Luckily a woman who worked at a theatre took pity on me when she saw me crying and walking the streets and gave me a home. I then joined the dancers at the theatre where she worked and eventually I became a singer in the music halls.

Last year I met my future husband. I don't know that you'd approve of him. He's much older than me and a widower but he treats me like a queen and I know he'll look after me. He's very rich so I'll never have to worry about earning a living again and once I move into his lovely town house I'll have servants to wait on me. He paid for me to have elocution lessons and for a teacher to help me improve my reading and writing as I'm sure you will have noticed. It sounds selfish, I know, but you more than anyone know that I've always been that way inclined and I am fond of him in my own way. Anyway, I just wanted to let you know that I am all right. Perhaps one day we will meet again but until then know that I think of you all often. Give my love to Reuben and Maria,

Much love
Marcie xx

'Well I never,' Molly muttered, amazed. 'Sounds like she's dropped on her feet. What do you make of that?'

Nessie stared down at the letter in her hand.

473

She had married Andre for security for herself and the children, so how could she condemn Marcie for doing the same thing now? She was clearly doing what she thought was in her best interests. And her handwriting had certainly improved while she had been away.

'I'm just grateful to know that she's safe,' Nessie answered eventually, then she rushed off to show Andre the letter.

When she was visiting George the following week, Connie said casually, 'Oliver's coming home for a couple of days next week … and he's bringing a young lady with him for us to meet.' She watched closely for Nessie's reaction.

Nessie felt the colour drain from her face but she managed to smile as she answered, 'How lovely. He must be keen on her if he's bringing her here to meet you all.'

'Aye.' Connie nodded. 'I reckon they've been walking out together on and off for a while now. Sylvia her name is. Her father owns a tea import company an' he's quite rich, from what I can gather.'

'Then I wish them both every happiness,' Nessie forced herself to say, while inside she was crying. But then I'm just being selfish, she scolded herself. She had made her decision when she had agreed to marry Andre, so it was only right and proper that Oliver should find happiness elsewhere. The thought of him in another woman's arms still hurt terribly though, and for the rest of the visit it was all she could do to concentrate on what Connie was saying.

'I, er ... I won't come next week,' she told Connie as she was leaving. 'You'll be busy entertaining Oliver and his young lady.'

'All right, pet. If you think it's for the best.' Connie wasn't fooled for a minute, but there was nothing to be done about it, so all she could do was hope that her son would find happiness elsewhere.

On the way home, Nessie called in to see Mrs Hewitt whose cheerful chatter could usually put her in a happy mood but today even that didn't work. Mrs Hewitt happily bragged about her beloved Zillah, who had recently brought a bagful of clothes that the lady she worked for had given her. 'I shall be able to cut 'em down an' make some lovely skirts an' blouses out of 'em,' she chuckled gleefully, but half of what she said went in one ear and out of the other and Nessie was glad when she could leave.

As Nessie approached the funeral parlour a short while later she was surprised to see Dr Peek's carriage outside and she hurried her steps.

'What's wrong?' she asked Molly as she burst through the door.

'It's Andre. He had a funny turn a while ago so I got Charlie to run fer the doctor. I hope I did right?'

'Of course.' Nessie hurried into their drawing room to find the doctor just closing his bag.

'Is he all right?' Nessie asked, trying hard to keep the panic from her voice. Andre was leaning back in the chair with his eyes closed. His face was ashen and his lips even bluer than usual and he looked absolutely dreadful.

'Perhaps I could have a word outside?'

She nodded and hastily followed Dr Peek out into the parlour where he shook his head gravely. 'I fear he has had a seizure of some sort and his heart rate is very erratic.'

'B-but he will recover?'

The doctor shrugged. 'It's hard to tell. All you can do is keep him as quiet as possible and make sure he takes the pills I have left with him.'

Guilt washed through her like icy water. She had spent the afternoon thinking of Oliver when her husband needed her!

The second the doctor had left after promising to return the next day, she shot back to Andre's side and took his hand.

'I don't know, I can't leave you alone for a minute,' she teased but when he opened his eyes to look at her he saw that she was fighting to hold back tears.

'I think,' he said quietly, 'that it is almost my time.'

'Don't *say* that!' The tears were flowing now as she kissed his hand. 'You'll get better. You *have* to.'

He smiled. Suddenly he was so tired that he just wanted to sleep. 'You have been the best of wives,' he told her softly as his eyes fluttered shut. Nessie quickly tucked a blanket around him and for the rest of the afternoon she stayed close to his side watching him rest.

Reuben was reluctant to leave her at the end of the working day but she waved his worries aside saying, 'You get off home to Maria. If I need anyone Charlie and Molly are only next door and I'm quite capable of looking after my own husband.'

After he left Nessie settled down next to Andre. He'd been asleep for hours but she knew that sleep was a good cure for all ills so she was reluctant to wake him. Eventually she slept too, waking in the early hours with a crick in her neck and feeling cold.

Andre was still fast asleep so she tiptoed to the kitchen to make them both a cup of hot milk. She decided she would try to get him upstairs to bed where he would be more comfortable when he'd drunk it.

'Come on, sleepy head,' she said cheerfully some minutes later when she returned with their drinks. The light from the oil lamp was shining on his face and he looked so peaceful that it seemed a shame to wake him.

'Andre.' She shook his arm gently and as his head lolled to the side the terrible truth hit her like a blow. He had slipped away peacefully in his sleep.

'Oh, *Andre.*' Dropping to her knees she flung her arms about him and held him tight as she sobbed bitterly. She was still there an hour later when Molly appeared in her long nightgown with a shawl tight about her shoulders.

For some reason she had found it hard to sleep and she had felt the need to check on her friend. With a sinking heart, she realised why.

'Come away, pet,' she crooned, placing her arm about Nessie's shaking shoulders. 'There's no more you can do for him now. He's gone to a better place, God rest his soul.'

The church was packed to capacity for Andre's funeral and Nessie was touched to see how many people had attended. Throughout the service she sat as if in a daze, twisting the ruby and diamond ring round and round her finger as she thought back to the day he had given it to her. She had written to his parents immediately following his death telling them the bad news, but she had no way of even knowing if they had received the letter as yet, so the funeral had had to go ahead without them there. She hoped that his mother would forgive her. She knew how much Jewel had loved him.

When the service was over they made their way to the churchyard and Nessie stood numbly as the coffin was lowered into the ground. The words the vicar was reciting went over her head. She felt as if she was locked away in a little world where nothing and no one could touch her. She hoped the feeling would last, for in this little world, the all-enveloping pain she had felt when she realised he had gone could not touch her. She was vaguely aware that Reuben had his arm tightly about her waist, almost as if he feared she might slip into the grave with her husband. And she was also dimly aware that Connie Dorsey was there ... and Oliver. At any other time this would have given her pleasure but not today. Today her thoughts were centred solely on the kind man who had turned her life around and saved her and her family from the workhouse. At last it was over and the mourners began to move away, leaving the gravediggers, who were standing with their shovels ready in the shadow of the church.

She glanced up at the sky as Reuben led her towards the lychgate. It seemed wrong that anyone should be buried on such a beautiful day with the winter sun shining so brightly, she thought miserably. And then there was the wake to be got through. Molly had organised it at the same hotel where she and Andre had had their wedding breakfast. She sat there as people came to her in a constant stream to offer their condolences and at last, when Reuben could see that she'd had enough, he ordered the carriage to be brought to the door and took her home. Even then the dreadful day wasn't over, for she had to sit and listen to Andre's solicitor read the will.

There were only Reuben, Molly and Charlie present as he slowly began and Nessie was pleased to hear that Andre had remembered each of them with a goodly sum of money.

'And finally, to my wife, Nessie Chevalier, who has been a loyal and loving companion, I leave both of my businesses, any monies in the bank and all my worldly possessions with all my love and thanks to her.'

Reuben beamed. 'You're rich, gel,' he crowed and she could hardly take it in. Even in death, it seemed that Andre had wanted her to be secure. That realisation caused the dam to break and her tears finally came in great sobs that shook her body and Reuben placed his arms comfortingly about her.

'Wh-what shall I do without him?' she queried tremulously and Reuben lifted her chin and stared into her eyes.

'You'll do exactly what he would have wanted. You'll grieve for him then you'll make the best of your life, otherwise you'll be letting him down.'

She nodded, knowing that he was right. But oh, it was going to be very hard.

Christmas came and went and despite many invitations Nessie chose to spend it alone as a mark of respect. It was a sad time for her as she grieved for her husband, but slowly she began to recover and two months after Andre's death she handed the new business in Weddington over to Reuben, whose eyes almost popped out of his head when she gave him the deeds.

'I want to,' she insisted. 'Both the businesses are thriving and I want you to have it.'

'Are you *quite* sure?' Reuben was shocked but she merely nodded. 'Yes, I have far more than I need with just this business here,' she assured him and he was humbly grateful.

Slowly, she was beginning to return to her old self although she still missed Andre every single day and the long, lonely nights seemed never-ending. She had resumed her visits to George and they went a long way to cheering her up too. He was such a lovely little boy, clearly adored by the whole household from his grandparents right down to the cook who was forever baking him little treats.

'You'll have him as fat as a little pig,' Connie would scold but Nessie noticed with a smile that she never took the treats off him.

The following month she resumed working at the soup kitchen and she found that keeping busy helped enormously. While she was busy she didn't have time to think of anything else and slowly the hurt lessened and she was able to smile when she thought of all the kind things that Andre had done.

Then one day in late October the shop door opened and Nessie turned expecting to find a customer standing there, only to find herself face to face with her sister.

'Marcie!' She covered the distance between them in seconds, laughing and crying all at once. Marcie looked absolutely beautiful, like she had just stepped from the pages of a fashion magazine. She was dressed in a scarlet velvet gown trimmed with black braid that nipped in at the waist with a tiny peplum and then flowed into a full skirt and she was carrying a matching fur muff. The most elaborate bonnet that Nessie had ever seen decorated with feathers and flowers was perched at a jaunty angle on her head and she looked so stunning that she almost took Nessie's breath away.

'I heard what happened ... to Andre,' Marcie told her. 'Or rather, James, my husband, did. I didn't even know that you'd married him until James told me. He knows one of the businessmen who owns a ribbon factory in town and he told James about Andre's passing last week while he was visiting London. I have to admit that I was surprised to hear you'd married him. I always thought you and Oliver Dorsey were sweet on each other. Anyway, I came as quickly as I could. I'm so sorry ... for everything.'

'It's all right. But how long are you here for?'

'Just tonight, I'm afraid,' Marcie apologised. 'James and I are having a dinner party for some of his business colleagues and their wives tomorrow so I have to catch the first train back to London in the morning.'

'Ah well, it's better than nothing.' Nessie smiled properly for the first time since Andre had passed away. She had wondered if she would ever see her sister again so now she was grateful for even one night together.

Nessie hastily sent a message to Reuben and Maria inviting them to dinner. Maria, though, decided to stay home with their little one, tactfully allowing the siblings to have some time alone together, and the three of them spent the evening telling each other of all that had happened to them during their time apart.

After Reuben had left, Nessie and Marcie curled up on the sofa together. 'And what about that loathsome Seth Grimshaw?' Marcie asked.

Nessie giggled. 'You'll never believe it but he's *married!* A widow got her hooks into him and he thought he was on to a good thing because she had her own house. But it seems the second he put a ring on her finger she turned into a shrew. From what I've heard, Seth Grimshaw is well and truly under the thumb now and daren't say boo to a goose.'

Marcie almost choked she laughed so long. 'Good, it's no more than he deserves.' And then her face became suddenly serious as she asked, 'But what about you? What are you planning on doing with the rest of your life?'

Nessie blinked. 'Why, I'll be running the business of course.'

Marcie frowned. 'But, Nessie ... you're still a young woman. Far too young to just settle for running a business. Was I wrong about you having feelings for Dr Dorsey?'

'Not exactly,' Nessie admitted. 'But we were too far apart in class. He came from a wealthy family and then there was what happened between you and George. They would never have accepted me.'

'But you're a wealthy young woman in your own right now,' Marcie pointed out. 'Is there no chance?'

Nessie shook her head. 'No, he's walking out with a young lady from London now. Sylvia Beckett-Brown I believe her name is.'

'How sad,' Marcie commented but then brightening, she added, 'But you never know, things have a habit of coming right in the end. Look at me, for instance; I openly admit I married James for money but now...' she blushed prettily. 'Well, he's so kind to me I've come to love him and I couldn't be happier.'

'I'm glad.' Nessie squeezed her hand. At least she wouldn't have to worry about Marcie anymore. She was the picture of health and glowing with happiness. Reuben and Maria were happy together too and looking forward to the birth of their second baby, which was another blessing, so she supposed that she had a lot to be thankful for.

Their parting the next morning was tearful. Reuben drove them to the station in the carriage and once he had deposited her bags in the guard's van, Marcie pressed a piece of paper into Nessie's hand.

'It's my address and when you're not too busy, I insist you come to see us,' she told her sister. 'And you and Maria too, Reuben.' Marcie and Reuben had made their peace the evening before. 'From now on I want us to be a family again.' She gave each of them a last kiss and boarded the train. Brother and sister had waited until the train pulled out of the station before heading home in high spirits.

Chapter Fifty-Three

Christmas 1870

As Christmas approached Nessie began to feel sad again. It would be her second without Andre and although she had had numerous invites from Reuben, Molly and various people, she had turned them all down, politely saying that she preferred to spend it quietly alone.

When she visited Connie on Christmas Eve, loaded down with presents, however, it soon became clear that the woman had other ideas.

'I shall be sending the carriage for you at eleven o'clock sharp tomorrow morning,' she told her in a voice that brooked no argument. 'And don't try to refuse, my girl. I won't take no for an answer!'

Nessie felt as if she had no choice in the matter, although secretly she did think how nice it would be to spend Christmas with George.

That night she was restless and when she finally did manage to rest, her sleep was full of dreams. Andre was there standing at the foot of the bed, holding Jean-Paul's hand with a wide smile on his face. She awoke in a tangle of damp sheets, for the dream had been so vivid that she wasn't even sure if it *had* been a dream. It was as if Andre had been trying to tell her something – but what? She looked around the room, half expecting to see him there and when he wasn't she felt a pang of sadness. But it was time to start getting ready so she fell out of bed and started to wash.

As she was washing the ruby ring caught the weak light pouring through the window and she smiled thoughtfully. Strangely, now seemed the right time to remove it. Perhaps Andre had been trying to tell her that he was happy and it was time for her to move on? Slowly, she took off the ring as well as her thin gold wedding band and placed them in the drawer of her dressing table. She had written to ask Jewel if she wished her to return the ruby ring following Andre's death but the dear woman had insisted that she should keep it. Although she knew that she would never wear it again, she also knew that she would never part with it.

Next, she crossed to her wardrobe and ignoring the black gowns that she had worn since losing Andre, she chose a pretty plum-coloured gown with a matching cape that Andre had bought for her just before his death and she had never worn.

Right on time the coach arrived and looking elegant in her new gown, Nessie set off for Haunchwood House. It was nice to wear something bright again, although it felt strange after wearing black for so long.

When she arrived, she was taken aback to find Oliver there, playing with a train set with George in the drawing room. She was even more surprised to see that his young lady wasn't with him, but then she supposed she had probably chosen to spend Christmas with her family, although now she came to think of it, Connie hadn't mentioned her for some time. Leonora wasn't there either as she had decided to stay in London with her aunt for Christmas. 'Though I think it has more to do with a certain young man she's become fond of,' Connie confided to Nessie with a grin when Nessie commented on her absence.

Dinner was a happy affair with much laughter and merriment. Nessie ate so much at Connie's insistence that she was sure she would burst but she enjoyed every mouthful. There was a huge goose served with home-made stuffing and such a selection of winter vegetables that she didn't know which to choose first and that was without the crispy roast potatoes. This was followed by a flaming Christmas pudding that had little George clapping his hands with glee but finally Connie said, 'Right, I'm going to take this little chap up for a little lie-down. Why don't you and Oliver take a turn around the garden and walk some of your dinner off? It'll blow the cobwebs away.'

Nessie felt deeply embarrassed at the idea but Oliver seemed all for it, so while Mr Dorsey retired to his study for a glass of port and a cigar she collected her cloak and they wandered out into the garden. They were surprised to see that it had started to snow during dinner and already the grass had a fine coating, giving the night an almost magical quality.

'How lovely,' Nessie said as Oliver took her elbow and led her towards a summer house at the other side of the rose garden where they could sit and watch the flakes gently fluttering down.

For a time, they were silent as they watched a little robin digging in the snow. It was so peaceful that Nessie could almost believe that they were the last two people left in the world.

'So how have you been?' Oliver asked eventually and she shrugged.

'Very well, I like to keep busy... And yourself? I was surprised to find your young lady hadn't come with you.'

'My young lady? Oh, you must mean Sylvia.' He chuckled. 'That was over a while ago. We'd seen each other on and off occasionally for a couple of years but let's just say she was keener than I was. She was a lovely girl but the minute I suggested she come home to meet my parents last year, I regretted it. She quite rightly took the invitation as a statement of intent, and I realised then that I couldn't marry her or any other girl, so I had to retract the invitation. I felt very guilty, but it wouldn't have been fair to bring her home when there is only one woman I have ever wanted to marry.'

When Nessie blinked with surprise he took her hand and asked gently, 'Can't you guess why?'

She shook her head.

'Then let's just say that I could never love anyone but the girl I've had my sights on for some long time.'

Seeing her blush, he took her arms and turned her to face him. 'You must know that I've loved you since the very first moment I set eyes on you. I have remained silent since Andre's death as a mark of respect for him. But now there's nothing to stand in our way. I mean, I know that you're still in mourning for Andre, but the *official* mourning period is over so I wondered... Well, is there *any* hope for me?'

She lowered her eyes.

'How could there be?' she questioned gently. 'I might be free again now but we are still miles apart in class. What would your family say?'

He threw back his head and laughed. 'Oh, not *that* again. In case you hadn't noticed you are now a very wealthy young woman. And even if you weren't, my mother thinks the *world* of you. She'd be thrilled to welcome you into the family. So what do you say?' His head moved forward and as his soft lips came down on hers, Nessie shivered. She felt as if every nerve in her body was tingling and when they finally broke apart she gazed up at him with bright eyes. 'In that case... Yes ... there's every hope,' she told him breathlessly. 'Because I love you too. I always have.'

He took her in his arms then and just for a fleeting moment she could have sworn she saw Andre across his shoulder. He was standing on the lawn in the snow, smiling broadly, but when she blinked and looked back he was gone. It was as if he was giving her a sign that this was right, so gazing up at the man she loved – the man she had always loved – she gave him her full attention, glowing from head to toe despite the coldness of the day.

Epilogue

July 1873

'Come along, Mrs Dorsey, I think I heard some of our guests arriving,' Oliver teased as he straightened his silk cravat, bought especially for the occasion, in the cheval mirror.

'I'm coming,' Nessie answered as she slipped the delicate silk christening robe over her baby son's head. He gurgled up at her from his position on the bed and Nessie felt a tidal wave of love sweep through her. When she had walked down the church aisle to marry Oliver two and a half years previously she had thought that things could never get any better, but her tiny son had made her happiness complete and never a day went by when she didn't thank God for him.

'There, what do you think?' she said when she had fastened the last button on the back of his robe and held him up for inspection. It was a wonderful concoction of satin and lace.

'Perfect, just like his mother,' Oliver assured her, coming to place his arms around them. They were both admiring him when a tap came to the door and Ginny, their young maid, told them, 'The carriage is at the door ready to take you to the church, ma'am.'

Nessie giggled, she still wasn't used to being addressed as ma'am, or to having a maid, if it came to that, but Oliver had been adamant on that point when she had found out that she was expecting a baby. They also employed a cook and a groom who looked after the horse and the stables at the back of their grand house in Swan Lane but Nessie had put her foot down when Oliver had suggested they should employ a nanny and pointed out indignantly that she intended to care for their first child herself.

'You must at least have a maid to help in the house now or you'll make yourself ill,' he had insisted and although Nessie still found it strange, she was quite glad he had now. Ginny was a little treasure, as was the elderly cook and the groom and they felt like one big happy family.

'Right, are we all ready?' Oliver glanced at Nessie admiringly. She was wearing a new gown in a lovely shade of blue and her copper-coloured hair had been fastened into a neat chignon.

'I'm ready.' She hoisted her six-month-old son onto her hip and, side by side, they made their way down the sweeping staircase to meet their guests.

Oliver's parents were waiting in the hallway, keen to get a glimpse of their latest grandson in the christening robe that George, their first grandson, had once worn. George meanwhile, a sturdy eight-year-old now, was charging around the hallway pretending to be a horse.

'Eeh!' Connie Dorsey's eyes filled with tears at the sight of the baby. 'Why, he looks like a little angel.' She absolutely adored her grandson, as did Oliver's father, Johnny, and they were both frequent visitors to the house. 'But come along now, we don't want his lordship to be late for his own christening, do we?'

Ginny waved as they all set off for Chilvers Coton Church, Nessie and Oliver in their carriage with the Dorseys following behind in theirs.

When they arrived a short time later they found the church packed and everyone smiled as Nessie proudly carried the child to the font at the end of the aisle where the Reverend Lockett was waiting for them with a broad smile on his face.

Marcie was there, looking every inch the lady, with her husband, James. They had come all the way from London. Molly and Charlie were there too and Molly gave Nessie a little smile as she passed her. They now managed the business in Abbey Street and lived happily with their children in the rooms where Nessie and Andre had once lived. Molly looked radiant and it was hard for Nessie to remember her as she had been when they had first met. She had been so poor and downtrodden back then but now she was a beautiful, confident woman. Maria and Reuben were there too and would be standing as godparents.

Leonora was also there with her new fiancé and the rest of the congregation was made up of people who Nessie had helped through her charitable works, which still took up a lot of her time.

If only my mam were here it would be just perfect, Nessie thought as the reverend began the service

491

but then she forced herself to concentrate on what was being said and very soon the vicar took the baby from her arms and began the solemn job of welcoming him into the church.

'I christen you Joseph Oliver Dorsey,' he said as he made the sign of the cross on the baby's forehead and Nessie felt as if she would burst with pride. There had never been any question about what his name would be, for from the second he had come into the world he had been the double of the darling child she had once cherished. He had the same colour hair and eyes and the same sweet nature and Oliver had been only too happy to go along with her choice of name.

Tears welled in her eyes as she glanced towards the congregation and it was then that she saw them and her heart missed a beat. She blinked, thinking it must be a trick of the light but when she looked back they were still there. Her mother was standing at the back of the church holding Joseph tightly in her arms with a broad smile on her face. Shock coursed through her as she looked towards Oliver who seemed oblivious to their presence and this time when she looked back they had gone. Even so, she felt a sense of peace as she once again turned her attention to the service.

Everyone congregated outside when it was over and the warm July sunshine shone down on them as the birds in the tall yew trees surrounding the churchyard seemed to squawk their approval.

'Back to ours and let the party begin,' Oliver told everyone. 'Please say you'll all come. Our cook has been baking solid for days and we have enough to feed an army back there!'

Everyone was happy to oblige and while they were trotting back to Swan Lane, Oliver took a tiny box from his pocket. He flipped it open and Nessie found herself staring down at a fine sapphire and diamond ring that reflected all the colours of the rainbow as it shone through the carriage window.

'My mother wanted you to have this,' he told her solemnly. 'I've been saving it for today. It's been in our family for years and hopefully one day we'll have a daughter for you to pass it on to.'

'Why, it's *beautiful*,' Nessie sighed. 'And that rather brings me to the present I have for you.'

When he raised an eyebrow she grinned. 'I wasn't going to mention it just yet as I haven't had it confirmed... But the thing is in about another seven months' time you might just get your daughter.'

His jaw dropped and he gazed at her in amazement. 'What? You mean you're...'

She giggled and nodded and then gasped as he caught her and Joseph to him.

'Why, that's wonderful!' He became solemn then and his face softened as he said quietly, 'Have I told you lately how *very* much I love you, Mrs Dorsey?'

'Not since this morning,' she answered demurely. 'But you can tell me again.'

As his lips found hers a picture of her mother and Joseph standing in the church flashed in front of her eyes and she smiled. It really had turned out to be the most perfect day.

Acknowledgements

A huge thank you to my wonderful team at Bonnier for making our days of the week series into a *Sunday Times* Bestseller. Thank you, Eli, Sarah, Kate, Tara and everyone else in the team who has worked so hard and shown such love and support. Also thanks to my brilliant agent, Sheila Crowley, not forgetting Abbie and my lovely copy editor Gillian Holmes. I am blessed to have you all behind me xxx

My Dear Friends,

I can't believe that Christmas is almost here again, where does the time go? It doesn't seem like the blink of an eye since I was writing to you all last year! It's been a very up and down year for me beginning with yet another bereavement, in January. A dear boy who was very precious to us sadly passed away and left our whole family devastated and so I am dedicating this book to him. Strangely enough it is titled *The Blessed Child*, which is just what he was. He was just eighteen years old and was the sweetest, most innocent person I have ever had the privilege to know. His passing has left a huge gap in our lives and we can only hope now that the angels love him as much as we did and that he can now run and talk and do all the things that he was never able to do on earth. Sadly life goes on for those left behind and we are now just beginning to be able to talk of the many happy times we shared without busting into tears.

As always this year we pinched as much time as we could at our holiday home at the coast during the summer, but as usual nowhere near as much as we would have liked to. I'm happy to report that the rest of the family are all well and following our sad bereavement early in the year we then had a happy family event when our new granddaughter, Poppy, was christened in our local village church in February. It was a very happy occasion and Poppy was a little star and looked absolutely lovely (not that I'm biased of course!) although it snowed, which didn't go too well with all the outfits myself and the guests had bought to wear! I don't recommend high heels in the snow.

During the course of the year I have visited libraries and done talks here and there, always one of my favourite pastimes as I get to actually meet some of my lovely readers instead of being locked away in my office with all my imaginary characters! And now once again we're at the time where we're frenziedly shopping for Christmas. Ours will be spent with the family as usual and then it will be time to hit the sales and for a quiet New Year in with my dogs. We never like to go out on New Year's Eve because there are usually fireworks going off and the dogs are frightened of them so we usually spend the night all tucked up in bed with them, munching chocolate and watching telly!

And it's also time for the release of this book, *The Blessed Child*, number four in my 'Days of the Week' collection, which I loved writing. In this one we follow the fortunes of Nessie and I hope you enjoy it. I'm delighted to report that the last book, *A Mother's Grace*, which came out in the spring, spent four weeks in *The Sunday Times* bestsellers lists and also that I have now finished the next one, out next spring which is yet to be titled. Do join the Memory Lane community at www.MemoryLane.club to be the first in the know.

Again I really loved writing this one. Because it is about Thursday's child, who according to the rhyme 'has far to go' and I have taken us all on a trip on the *Titanic*. Now I am busily writing the one for next Christmas so, as the saying goes, 'there's no peace for the wicked!'

All that remains now is for me to wish you all, my very dear readers, a very Merry Christmas and a very Happy New Year. I hope it will be a good one for all of you and thank you all for your continued support. Here's to a very special 2019!

Much love,

Rosie
xx

Roast goose
with home-made sausagemeat stuffing

This mouth-watering dish makes an exciting and traditional alternative to the usual Christmas dinner just like the recipe that was passed down to Nessie from her mother.

You will need:

For the stuffing:
25g butter
1 large onion, very finely chopped
1 garlic clove, crushed
100g soft white breadcrumbs
1kg pork sausagemeat
3 tbsp finely chopped sage
1 egg, beaten
Salt and pepper to season
For the goose:
5kg fresh goose
2 tbsp sunflower oil
Salt for seasoning

Method:
1. Pre-heat the oven to 220°C (200°C fan oven), gas mark 7.

2. For the stuffing gently fry the onion for 10 minutes in a small knob of butter. Once soft and translucent (but not browned) place the onions in a bowl to cool.

3. When the onion has cooled, stir in the garlic and breadcrumbs with 75ml of water and use your hands to work in the sausagemeat and sage. Season well before stirring in the egg.

4. Remove any excess fat from the cavity of the goose, as well as the neck and giblets, which you can save for gravy. To ensure crispy skin after cooking, pour boiling water over the goose to make the skin tight and pat it dry with kitchen roll.

5. Prick the skin all over, particularly under the wings, with a fork to release the fat but make sure not to pierce the flesh. Fill the cavity with the sausagemeat stuffing and secure with skewers.

6. Sit the goose on a wire rack in a deep roasting tin, which will collect all of the fat that is released without allowing it to touch the goose.

7. Roast the goose for roughly 3.5 hours, or a calculated time using 20 minutes per 500g. After the first hour, make sure to drain off the excess fat and baste the goose, and repeat this every half an hour or so. If the fat looks in danger of over-spilling, drain it away with a turkey baster.

8. To check if the goose is done, pierce the thickest part of the thigh with a knife and make sure the juices run clear.

9. Once cooked, remove the goose from the oven. Cover with tinfoil and allow it to rest for 20 minutes before carving.

10. Enjoy!

The publishers hope that this book has given you enjoyable reading. Large Print Books are especially designed to be as easy to see and hold as possible. If you wish a catalogue please ask at your local library or write directly to:

Magna Large Print Books
Cawood House,
Asquith Industrial Estate,
Gargrave,
Nr Skipton, North Yorkshire.
BD23 3SE

This Large Print Book for the partially sighted, who cannot read normal print, is published under the auspices of

THE ULVERSCROFT FOUNDATION